MAGIC SPELLS

G·K
Hall
&Co.

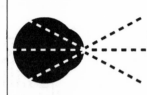

This Large Print Book carries the
Seal of Approval of N.A.V.H.

MAGIC SPELLS

Christy Yorke

G.K. Hall & Co. • Thorndike, Maine

Published in 2000 by arrangement with Bantam Books, an imprint of The Bantam Dell Publishing Group, a division of Random House, Inc.

G.K. Hall Large Print Core Series.

The text of this Large Print edition is unabridged.
Other aspects of the book may vary from the original edition.

Set in 16 pt. Plantin.

Printed in the United States on permanent paper.

Library of Congress Cataloging-in-Publication Data

Yorke, Christy.
    Magic spells / Christy Yorke.
      p. cm.
    ISBN 0-7838-9028-1 (lg. print : hc : alk. paper)
    1. Mothers and sons — Fiction. 2. Mute persons — Fiction.
  3. Vermont — Fiction. 4. Magic — Fiction. 5. Large type
books. I. Title.
PS3575.O634 M34 2000
813'.54—dc21
                                                 00-029579

For Claire,
who proves magic exists

☆

☆

☆

Prologue

Although there had been four murders in three years in the town of Pendleton, Vermont, no one called it a trend. A man no one liked anyway was poisoned by his wife, a New Yorker admiring Vermont's renowned autumn leaves was nabbed by a hunter's bullet, and two years ago, two vacationing college seniors were bludgeoned to death by a serial killer whose trail led west to California. All of these, needless to say, were tragedies that happened to other people. On Indian summer nights, the people in Pendleton left on their front porch lights not to scare away murderers, but to distract the moths that multiplied by the billions while they slipped through unlit back doors.

Even Graham Payton, who had had an unlucky life, did not believe anything truly bad could happen in Vermont. He was walking fast on a warm September night for two other reasons: to slice through the beams of five yellow porch lights without hitting a bug, and to get as far away from his brother as possible.

He walked four blocks, all the way to Francis McGinnis's rundown colonial, with its rotted ivy and plyboard downstairs windows, before the stink of marijuana and beer retreated. A light was on in an upstairs bedroom, a heavy velvet curtain pulled to the side, but he couldn't see the old man. Francis McGinnis rarely came out and when he did he never smiled. When his wife had died giving birth to their daughter, he'd vowed he couldn't live without her. To anyone with the guts to question his subsequent fifty-year survival, he had replied, "My body betrayed me."

Bodies betrayed. Graham knew it was true. At least it was true of his brother Ned's body, wrapped at this moment around Carol Atkinson's exquisite tan limbs. Lust superseded logic and, in Ned's case, honor. It wouldn't even have occurred to him, as he stroked Carol Atkinson's thigh, that with a pregnant fiancée and his wedding the following Saturday, this was something he shouldn't do.

The light went off in Francis McGinnis's bedroom and Graham wondered if the old man was staring at him now, if he'd stared at all the kids over the years who'd thrown stones at his windows. If, like Graham, he simply expected bad things to happen to him.

Graham turned away from the house. One block over was the Common, which had not had a single dandelion in the bluegrass for ten years, thanks to Vince Ludlow's vigilance. Vince's son Tyler mowed the grass every Friday night for free, because his father said he had to and because by Friday night Vince Ludlow was so plastered, Tyler would have used any excuse to get out of the house.

At the Common's center was a bronze statue of Ethan Allen still tinted red after its annual defacing by the high school seniors. Graham's parents' house had been built in 1794 and faced the park. As a child, Graham had been too shy and too smart to have many friends. Good location was the only thing going for him.

Pendleton had two bars, but only one market, where oranges in the summertime ran one dollar apiece. The Eat 'Em Up served chicken-fried steak and hamburgers; if anyone wanted a taco or fancy shoes, he drove to Rutland. It took Graham just half an hour to walk the town's perimeter. He could have kept circling, gone round and round until he spun a web around the people he loved and bent them to his will, but he was one of those people who underestimated his own power. He took a deep breath and walked toward home.

He lived in a 1974 aluminum-sided tract house that made his mother cry. She'd taken one look at the maroon carpeting and green canvas drapes and crossed herself. She had offered him free room and board while he went to medical school; she even offered to pay the rent on the garage apartment of a nice colonial. Graham had been amazed at how good it had felt to tell her no, like he'd gotten a little bit drunk and lost his caution.

Anyone could look at him, he realized, and get the wrong impression. A stranger could pass by his house tonight, hear his brother's rock band, recognize the makings of a wild bachelor party, and imagine him carefree and happy. He'd think Graham had been the one who'd booked the entertainment, Carol and Hannah Atkinson, the notoriously easy, deep-throated twins, then figure he planned to sample them himself, that he was too young and horny to believe in love.

Anyone might think, listening to him toast his brother's happiness, that he harbored no grudges. No one would ever guess the truth, that he wished he'd never had a brother or, shy of that, never introduced his best friend, Jane, to Ned. He had two problems: One, he loved a woman who looked at him only as somebody's brother and two, he often overestimated a person's strength. He had thought Jane immune to Ned. He had thought her different. He had thought, with eyes as clear and blue as hers, that she'd see right through Ned.

Graham had met Jane on the Common when they were both five. She'd had a dying robin cupped in her hands and tears streaming down her cheeks. In his dreams, even as the two of them got older and he could have pictured her in a bikini or recalled the time he caught a glimpse of breast, he still remembered her in that blue polka-dot dress, her black hair

10

clinging to her wet cheeks, her eyes pleading with him.

"Its wing is crushed," she had said.

He had sat down beside her. He didn't say a word, but when her hands began to tremble, he took the robin from her and held it gingerly. He held it until it died of starvation or fright, and then the two of them got a shovel out of Graham's garage and buried the bird in front of Ethan Allen's statue.

She was someone special, that was what he'd always told her. Her father left when she was three, and she never once asked where he'd gone. She taught herself to tie her own shoelaces. When she learned to drive, she could very well have loaded up the sick animals her mother doted on and dumped them on the side of some highway, but instead she sneaked away to read in the dusty attic her mother had long ago forgotten about. She heard her mother's softest voice through wallboards and wafer-thin plaster.

She never bought a stick of gum in her life; instead she used her allowance to buy novels by the armload and flea-killing detergent. She once spent two full days in the woods, eating peanut butter sandwiches and waiting for her mother to come looking for her. When she finally came out on her own, she looked Graham straight in the eye and said solitude was the only thing she could count on.

Despite all that, when she was only seven she

11

fell in love with Ned, like everybody else. All of a sudden her eyes had glazed over and turned passive, like a deer who saw the barrel of a gun and still stood there. She'd disappointed the hell out of Graham. She'd forgotten she'd seen twenty falling stars by the time she was five, that magic ran alongside blood in her veins so that sometimes she didn't bleed when cut, that she could have had anything or anyone she asked for.

She remembered the magic later, when she was so far gone she refused to trust her future to fate. On her sixteenth birthday, Jane said, "My grandmother taught me a spell to make a man fall in love with me. I'm going to use it on Ned."

"Jane, don't," Graham had said. He had wanted to say more. He'd wanted to tell her that Ned was no good, that he smiled at everyone that way, that he thought love was something owed him. He wanted to tell her she'd been looking at the wrong Payton all these years. He hated football; he only learned to play so he could tackle her. He wanted to tell her every ball he'd ever thrown had meant he loved her, but even to his own ears, this sounded ridiculous.

"I have to," Jane said. "He's just the kind of man women love."

"You're not just any woman."

"In this case I am."

Graham did not believe her spell would work.

Even though he had been witness to a number of Jane's bloodless cuts, his life had not been good enough for him to believe in magic. Still, he had to admit that when Esther Gregory, Jane's grandmother, looked at a man funny, he choked on an apple seed within twenty-four hours. Twice, Larry Myerson had gagged so badly somebody called an ambulance, and now he shivered at the sight of a jar of apple sauce. Five years ago, the entire male population of Pendleton had breathed a sigh of relief when Esther moved to Middlebury. Now the Middlebury men left daisies on Esther's doorstep as offerings, and a disproportionate number of them wore hats low over their eyes, so she couldn't get a good look at them.

He also had to admit that when Jane cast her grandmother's spell, Ned fell in love. Ned's kind of love. Jane's grandmother hadn't given her enough power to make it the kind of love women want. Ned did love Jane, but he loved pleasure too. The kind girls like Carol and Hannah Atkinson gave with their fingertips and tongues. When Graham had opened the door on Ned and Carol half an hour ago, Ned had simply looked over Carol's bare shoulder and smiled sheepishly, like a boy with blue lips who swore he hadn't eaten the blueberry pie.

Graham walked up the juniper-lined path to his porch. The aluminum siding was quivering while the band, minus Ned, played something very bad they'd written themselves. He hoped his neighbors would get fed up with the racket and call the police. Then his father, Pendleton's sheriff, would come to check it out, word would leak out that Ned was in bed with Carol, and Jane would dump him. Graham wished for too much, that was what Jane had always told him. "God's sick of you," she often said.

He saw motion along the side of the house and turned to find Ned, hair rumpled, his shirt half buttoned, stumbling toward him. In the darkness, Graham almost believed Ned was nothing, just a drunk rock star wanna-be, a small-town gangster. But when Ned stepped beneath the lemon yellow porch light, Graham saw the truth; even when drunk, Ned's eyes were electric. That's why women like Jane fell in love with him, why Carol Atkinson had crawled into his bed, why he'd never gone anywhere without a dozen friends trailing along behind him. You had the idea that if you got close enough to Ned, it might sting a little, but you'd add ten years to your life.

"You finished?" Graham asked.

Ned ran his hands through his hair. He had gotten the luxurious blond hair their mother, Vivian, had as a child. It was thick, long, and shaggy, and Graham had seen women and babies reach out to touch it while passing Ned on the street. Ned was tall and thin, a runner who avoided the track, a man who couldn't stand anything that ended up where it had started. He ran to the garage where his band

14

practiced, to his part-time job at the record shop, to his assignations with Jane. He'd been spotted on the other side of Middletown Springs, a flash of dazzling smile, a whiff of intoxicating cologne, running just for the hell of it, to see how far he could go.

"Come on, Graham," Ned said, putting his arm around Graham's shoulders. "What was I supposed to do? Refuse?"

He laughed, and Graham wondered, not for the first time, if his brother had been born without a conscience. As a child, Ned had laughed while stealing candy and BBs from Jim's Mercantile. When he was caught spray-painting his name on the elementary school roof, their mother merely gave him a can of white paint and told the principal, "Boys will be boys." Even Jane, whenever Ned called her by some other girl's name, said, "Ned is Ned," as if he was handsome enough to get away with anything.

Graham jerked out of his brother's embrace. What he wished was that he'd chosen a medical school out of state. He wished he'd been born first, so Ned's football feats would be compared to his academic achievements, not the other way around. He wished he had the guts to punch his brother in the nose and then to say, when his father asked him why, that boys will be boys.

"I won't let you hurt Jane," Graham said.

"What she doesn't know won't hurt her."

15

"She's pregnant, for God's sake. You're ruining her life."

Ned's smile faded. Jane had told Graham of her pregnancy even before she told Ned. In late April, on a night so still it tricked the wood owls into sleeping, she had tapped on Graham's bedroom window three times. He hadn't come awake right away, because in his dream the sound was the stroke of her fingers across his cheek, and his skin warmed from the contact. Then Jane slid open his window and tossed the first birch leaf of the season at his head.

"The moon is red," she said, when he finally came awake. "It's the kind children are conceived under."

Graham stood up and walked to the window. The moon was full and not merely tinted red, but bright as blood.

"I already feel different," Jane went on. "Like part of me has turned into Ned."

"You should have waited until you were married," Graham said, but even he understood that some children were destiny.

"Oh Graham." Jane laughed. "You are so *good.*"

Now, Ned leaned against one of the sinking porch columns and said, "Look, I can understand your concern. She's your friend. But I'm the one marrying her. This is between her and me."

"No, it's not. You'll never tell her. You'll

16

marry her and screw around because you think you're entitled to some extra pleasure. One day she'll find out and hate you, but she'll hate me even more for not warning her."

Ned stalked along the porch. He kicked one of the loose railings and stopped only long enough to watch the two-by-four fly. Each step he took sounded like a word Graham would never say. *I hate you, Ned. I hate you. Hate you.*

"You won't tell her," Ned said, turning and staring at him.

Graham shrugged. Ned was probably right. He hadn't told Jane anything of consequence for years. Since she and Ned had gotten engaged, he hadn't started up a conversation or given her more than a three-word answer to any question, for fear of letting something slip. It was all too possible that he'd start out talking about his plans to set up practice here in Pendleton, and then, right in the middle of explaining his billing policy, tell her he loved her instead.

Those three words were attached to a thousand others; they'd grown intricate, suffocating webs through his vocabulary in the years he'd been pretending to be just her friend. He'd had plenty of schooling, but over the years he'd learned only two things for certain: One, no matter how hard he wished it, Jane would never love him back and two, he was less than a man for not telling her how he felt anyway.

"I don't know what I'll say," he said finally. "I

only know she's an idiot to marry you."

Ned cocked his head. He was like his golden retriever that way. Neither of them seemed quite capable of understanding the human language.

"You don't like me very much, do you?"

Graham stepped back. He glimpsed his reflection in the single-pane window. He was shorter than Ned, softer, with lackluster, dirty blond hair. He looked like a medical student and Ned looked like a rock star, and that had been the curse of Graham's life.

"I have to like you," he said. "You're my brother."

Ned laughed and slapped him on the back. "See? You can be funny when you want to. Why don't you try more often?"

"I am who I am."

"Right. You and Dad, with all that seriousness. You're always looking at the sky, waiting for bombs to drop."

"We take our lives seriously," Graham said.

"Exactly. Why?"

Graham shook his head and walked away. He heard Ned calling him back, but he put his head down and ran the way Ned himself did, full speed and heedless of obstacles. He didn't see the garbage heap the raccoons had made from the ingredients of David Brentwood's trash can until he tripped over a Mountain Dew can. He reached out to break his fall and landed hard on his right arm.

For a long time, he just lay in the street amid newspapers and non-recyclable plastic, labeling the bones he might have broken — carpus, ulna, radius, humerus. When something was painful to look at, like Jane's slim hand on Ned's hip, that was how Graham stood it, by naming bones. Fibula, tibia, patella, femur. Sometimes he had to go through the entire human skeletal system before he could pretend to smile.

He got up, twisted his arm to make sure nothing was broken, then headed to Jane's. Along the way he passed his girlfriend's house, and he crept behind the silverberry hedge. He saw the flickering blue light of the television in the family room and the lamp shining through the lace curtain in Ginny's bedroom. He was supposed to call her tonight. She wanted to go on a picnic tomorrow, hike to Mt. Carmel in the Green Mountains before the weather turned cold. She wanted to take off her shoes and dance beneath the sun. It was a wonderful thing to want to do and Ginny was a wonderful woman. Graham obviously had a problem with wonderful because, in his dreams, he danced on that mountain not with Ginny, but with Jane.

He crept past Ginny's house, then raced down the rest of the block toward Jane's. She lived alone, in an apartment above the Atkinson's garage. She liked Carol Atkinson, that was the irony. She was always telling Graham that the girl was misunderstood, that she was just social.

Graham walked up the stairs and knocked on Jane's door. She opened it immediately.

"Oh," she said, then replaced that thirsty smile with the one he knew well, the tame grin you gave a friend. "I thought maybe Ned got tired of all that carousing."

That's when Graham knew she had no idea who she was marrying. No one, except him, had any idea who Ned was. Everyone in town thought Ned was a playful kid in men's clothing, that it was ambitious, not indulgent, to want to be a rock star. Ned flirted with all the town widows, rescued kittens from slippery trees, and had so few responsibilities, he could spend whole afternoons playing chess with the lonely old men in the park. He was so adorable, people forgot he was twenty-six years old and didn't have a real job, that he'd stolen from every store in town and never been arrested because he was the sheriff's son, that he was one of those boys who would never amount to anything. He smiled so widely and genuinely, half the men in town forgot their daughters had lost their virginity to him.

"Walk with me," Graham said.

"Is everything all right?"

Graham looked into her eyes. They were deep blue, the color of the Vermont sky on a cold autumn morning, and they lived inside his mind. Ginny's eyes were green, and they were lovely, but in dreams he scratched them out and colored them blue.

"Jane," Graham said and Jane stepped away. Her black hair was pulled back loosely in a ponytail. Only her bangs dusted the skin on her forehead. He looked down at her stomach, just beginning to protrude at five months, and felt sick. Ned's child. It would be a boy, he had no doubt, because Ned always got what he wanted. Graham reached out his hand, then stopped just before he reached the bulge. The child already burned with Ned's kind of heat; even from a distance, Graham's fingertips grew warm and began to itch.

Jane's grandmother had been known to make predictions, but Graham bet on losing horses and wore shorts on rainy days. Still, as his hand hung in the air by Jane's stomach, he pictured himself tossing a football to a boy with Ned's gray eyes. He drew his hand away as if he'd been bitten; he was only prepared to hate Ned's child.

They went down the stairs and followed the trail that wound through the birch woods behind the house. The air hummed with insects; the white wings of moths got tangled in their hair and tickled Graham's ears. Jane walked calmly beside him, then slid her hand into his. She did that all the time, she considered him her best friend. She had no idea it killed him.

"Tell me," she said.

21

The words, in his dreams, came like this: *Jane, I love you. I always have. Ned's no good. He'll never be a rock star. He can't give you the kind of life you deserve. But I can. I can.*

In reality, he let go of her hand because he couldn't think straight, not while he was touching her. Jane studied his face in the starlight. He imagined every emotion he'd ever felt was there, easy to read, but she only looked confused.

"Did Ned do something?" she asked.

Graham stepped back. It would be so easy. He only had to tell the truth, rat on his brother, and perhaps then he'd have a chance of getting what he wanted. It would be so easy, only he was the good son, the one who had sat by his mother's bedside for three days after she had her hysterectomy, even when she called out for Ned, the one who went to medical school so he could help people, the one who had kept Ginny Slocum as his girl all these years even though he'd stopped loving her the moment he said he did.

It would be so easy, except he'd overheard Ned's marriage proposal to Jane.

"Do you love me enough to marry me, even though I'll probably end up hurting you?" Ned had said.

It was so honest and lacking, Graham was certain Jane would finally come to her senses and walk away. Instead, like someone he didn't know at all, with a voice so breathless he

22

couldn't find a single familiar strain in it, she had said, "I have to. I can't dream of anyone but you."

Graham had known then that he could try every spell in the universe and still not make her love him instead. No matter how powerful Jane swore magic was, some men, like him, were untouched by it.

Now, Graham stood in speckled starlight, mute, but somehow Jane read his face anyway. She slipped to her knees and Graham decided that, among other things, she was too thin for Ned. His carelessness could crush her.

Graham crouched down and took her in his arms. "Never mind," he said, but she shook her head.

"Carol," she said, and some treacherous part of him nodded. "She said it would be a harmless striptease. She told me not to worry."

Graham said nothing, but he was thinking that when a girl like Carol Atkinson told you not to worry, you got out the thick rope and tied her to a chair.

He rested his head against Jane's as she cried. She had a scent all her own, of some kind of herb, maybe mint or poppy seed, and something so sweet it curled the hairs on the back of his neck when he stood this close to her.

"Ned doesn't think," he said at last.

"He doesn't think about me, you mean."

She cried for only a minute, then pulled out of his embrace. She wiped her tears and stared up at the cameo of white limbs and midnight sky.

"I've loved him since I was a child," she said. "I never asked him for anything, except his loyalty."

The thing was, Graham knew Ned was loyal. He was loyal with his heart, if not with his body. He would kill for Jane, for his family, even for Graham. He'd once hunted down a stray Rottweiler who had attacked his golden retriever. He hadn't stopped until he'd come back with a shiny black pelt.

Graham could have told this story, he could have defended his brother, but instead he held Jane's hand and marveled at how white her skin was.

"He forgot me once," she said, "when the band played in Boston. He left me in the audience when they went out to celebrate. He didn't come back for two hours, not until he had to pay for drinks and realized I had his wallet."

"Jane," Graham said.

"He warns me, you know. He thinks that makes everything all right. If he tells me he's bad, then it won't matter as much when he is. He's told me a hundred times he won't be a very good husband, that I'll have to do all the work with this baby because he's not the kind of guy who changes diapers. He tells me he loves me, but he loves his music too, and his friends, and beer, and partying.

He loves everything."

"You're special," Graham said. "You're . . ."

"I wish I'd never met him." Jane lowered her head and stared him straight in the eye. "I wish he were dead. That's the only way I'll ever be free of him."

Cruel words actually stung; hours later Graham would find dozens of tiny red marks on his forearms. He pulled away; he could already feel the beginnings of a rash.

They started back half an hour later. When they reached Sheep Creek, a slimy green trickle this time of year, Jane paused. She stroked her hand along the flaking trunk of a paper birch and jumped when Graham's shadow crossed her face.

"It's just the starlight," he said.

She nodded, but when the trees thinned out and the Atkinsons' pit bull started barking and wouldn't let up, she slipped her hand back into his. Her palm was sweaty.

"What is it?" he asked.

"I don't know. Something bad."

The woods stopped suddenly in the Atkinsons' backyard. There were no more birch trees until Hagerman's Woods, on the other side of Pendleton Hill. The Pendleton family had made their money first in granite, then in concrete. Fifty years ago, when the unruly birches started uprooting nice concrete sidewalks, the last Pendleton to live in this town, Thomas Pendleton, hired a dozen ex-cons to come in while people were sleeping and rip each one out by its roots. In their stead, they planted sugar maples every fifty feet, smack-dab in the middle of people's lawns.

Graham and Jane walked out of the Atkinsons' backyard and around to the street. For a moment, the light dazed them. An ambulance stood idling, its red light whirling in silence. A dozen gawkers, all people Graham had known forever, nudged one another when they noticed him and Jane.

Graham tried to run, but Jane held him back. She stared right at the ambulance, but no light was reflected in her eyes, as if she were shutting down, not seeing what she couldn't stand to see.

"Jane, come on," he said, but she didn't budge. He tried to pull her along, but she'd made herself heavy as stone.

"I'll check it out," he said finally. He left her and ran toward the throng of his neighbors, who let him pass. As soon as he reached the ambulance, he saw it clearly, his brother's car, smashed head-on into a tree.

Graham braced himself against the ambulance. They'd already extracted Ned's body, a blanket covering everything but a thatch of golden hair. No one was talking. Someone touched his shoulder, but he shrugged it off.

He told himself later that the hush of the crowd unnerved him. It was shock that made him giddy, that made the first feeling that sank into his heart one of relief.

From a few blocks away, Graham heard the shrill siren of his father's police car. It took William Payton just two minutes to cross town and pull up beside the body. He got out of the car and surveyed the scene, his gaze faltering when it reached his dead son. Graham had never seen his father cry or shiver or give away anything. At that double murder two years ago, when he'd discovered the bodies mutilated beyond recognition, William Payton hadn't even blinked.

His father lifted his gaze from the body and looked at Graham. Mothers see what they need to see in their children; fathers see the truth. William Payton saw a flash of joy in his son's eyes. He walked over to the bushes and threw up.

One

Seven Years Later

Six-year-old Alex Payton had never laughed out loud, and he wasn't about to start now. His mother pulled up in front of tiny Pendleton Elementary, where a circle of Kentucky bluegrass gave way to a border of marigolds dyed blue and gold, the school colors. A group of brightly clothed boys kicked a soccer ball around the small courtyard and high-fived each other when they scored goals through the door of Mr. Hiawatha's sixth-grade classroom.

"It's Mrs. Hazelton's first year," Jane said. "She's really enthusiastic. I spoke to her about everything. I just know you'll love it here."

Alex stared at her. His mother was beautiful — black hair, eyes bluer than the bluest sky — but she was a bad liar. She looked everywhere but at him and clenched her hands so tightly he was sure she could bend steel. Last week, when she'd been packing up the last of their things for the move to his grandmother's house in Pendleton, he'd actually seen her break a broomstick in half with her bare hands.

Since they'd moved back to her hometown three days ago, her lying had only gotten worse. She'd told him she was happy to be back, that this was a new start for him, but she had permanent half-moon indentations on her palms. The truth was, she was getting nervous. He could feel it, even taste it in the air around her. When wind bounced off her, it reeked of mint and perspiration.

Alex opened the door and got out. Before he was halfway to the wrought-iron gate, his mother had leaned over to the passenger side and stuck her head out the window.

"Alex," she said, and Alex turned around. She hesitated, and in that hesitation he knew she waited for him to ask her what, to say something. He looked at a fat caterpillar crawling toward his shoe. He already knew the color of disappointment; it turned his mother's blue eyes black.

"It's only a semester," Jane went on when he said nothing. "Think of this as a fresh start, a chance to make new friends."

Alex nodded. What else could he do? He was six years old and had no choice in anything. His mother picked out his sheets — Batman and Robin, even though he wanted race cars — and made the final decision between Nikes and Reeboks. He didn't even get to part his own hair; if he combed it to the right, his mother licked her fingers and halved it down the middle. Whenever she piled peas on his plate without asking, he glared at her; he didn't care how old he was, he ought to get a vote on something.

It was worse when someone died. In fact, it had screwed up his entire life. He'd lived his whole life in Middlebury in his great-grandmother's house, and if he wasn't exactly happy there, at least he'd known what kind of misery to expect. Then last month his grandmother, Salvation, had not only died, but left her house to his mother.

"I'm just going to sell it," Jane had said to Alex's great-grandmother, Esther, after they'd read the one-page will.

"You won't be able to get a dime for the place the way it is," Esther had said. "You know how your mother lived. All those animals. It'll need a good six months' airing just to get out the smell of urine."

Then Esther had turned that steady gaze of hers on him, and he'd known he was done for. "They practically ran you out of kindergarten," she'd said. "Don't tell me you don't want to move. I wouldn't believe it for a minute."

Alex had looked at his mother, but Jane just shook her head. "Alex and I need a pool."

"If you'd stepped foot in Pendleton in all these years, Janie," Esther said, "you'd have known the high school put one in three years ago."

"But Pendleton . . ."

"It's just a town," Esther told her. "It can't haunt you."

Alex's great-grandmother had been wrong. His mother did look haunted. Ever since they'd moved into his grandmother's house, Jane had woken with dark circles beneath her eyes. He had hardly known his grandmother, Salvation. They had never gone to her house and she had visited them only on holidays, and then always with two or three of her dogs, usually the ones in diapers. She had looked like the kind of woman who could haunt a town. Tall, with wild black hair streaked with gray, and a voice hoarse from too many cigarettes.

With a vote, Alex could have saved his mother from a haunting. In fact, he would have swooped her out of Vermont entirely. Right now, they'd be on a cruise ship to an island no one had ever heard of, they'd be conjuring up new lives. They'd be where the air was so sweet and wet, it slid down the back of the throat like ice.

Instead, he was walking across the bright green grass of a school so clean he didn't want to breathe on it. He put his hand on the arm his mother rested on the car window. The crows flying overhead suddenly stopped their screeching and Jane looked up. She frowned, but when she turned back to him she'd replaced it with a smile.

"Have a good day," she said.

Alex nodded, though he thought it was highly unlikely.

As soon as his mother turned the corner, Alex squared his shoulders. He walked fast and straight, causing girls in his path to leap out of his way. He was tall for his age, which had always been a help; the boys boasting that they'd never gotten up before eleven all summer long took one look at him and did not even risk a hello.

He reached the first-grade classroom, decorated with the alphabet and glossy posters of the planets, and looked over the students. He picked out two boys who might be trouble; they were already flinging sharpened pencils at the back of some girl's head. He took a seat in the rear and flung his legs out in front of him, so the other kids would have to take a wide path to get around him.

He tensed when the bell rang, and one of the boys he'd been watching took the seat beside him. The boy was a redhead, with more freckles than skin. He picked up the lid of the desk, then slammed it shut and smiled. Alex smiled back at him, because sometimes he could fake it. Sometimes he could go for hours before they realized there was something wrong with him.

Mrs. Hazelton raced through the door. She was his mother's age, he figured, but she dressed older, in a blue polyester dress with a bow at the collar. She was so plump and pudding-like, the thin silver band of her watch disappeared in the folds of her wrist. She wrote her name on the board in perfect block letters, then underlined it three times. Within fifteen minutes, there were two dark stains on the blouse beneath her fleshy arms.

The boy beside him nudged Alex with his elbow. "You could swim in those armpits," he said, smiling.

Alex nodded, but he curled his legs up beneath him.

The boy jabbed him again. "You new here? You move into one of those new houses out past Hagerman's Woods?"

Alex pressed his hands flat on his desk. He pressed until his fingers got white and tingly, while Mrs. Hazelton went on about reading groups and the physical fitness tests they'd have to take, though she couldn't see how any girl could be expected to do a chin-up.

"Hey," the boy said, louder this time, so that the two girls sitting in front of them turned their heads and told them to shush. "Hey, you hear me? You deaf?"

Alex stared straight ahead. Mrs. Hazelton was looking their way now, so the boy had stopped jabbing him. He had even, Alex thought, leaned slightly away. That's always what happened. Alex's silence leeched through his skin and fouled the air around him, and nobody with any brains wanted to get too close.

He'd gone to sixty speech and hearing specialists by the time he was six. He'd had cameras rammed down his throat and been asked, with his mother sitting right beside him, if he'd been abused into silence. A year ago, he'd stood outside an ear and throat specialist's office and listened to his mother ask yet another doctor if there was a chance she'd poisoned her own son.

"Could something other than nutrients have flowed through that umbilical cord?"

"I don't understand," the doctor had said.

"I'm asking if guilt can get through."

The doctor had laughed, but Alex was sensitive to things other people weren't — like the uneasiness that bit off the end of a chuckle. "Miss Gregory, don't be silly."

"Believe me," his mother had said, "I'm not."

If Alex could have talked, he would have told them all what had happened. A monster lived in his throat, a fire-breathing dragon. It was so mean and hot, every word he tried to speak was burnt to a crisp. Sometimes his throat got so dry, he gagged on toast and crackers. If he looked real hard in the mirror, he could see wisps of hot, stale steam escaping from the corners of his mouth. He could see smoke spewing out of his ears.

And the dragon was getting stronger. Now even his cries got singed. Though everyone had been impressed last year when he'd broken his arm and not called out, the truth was that even his pain had been incinerated by the dragon in his throat.

Mrs. Hazelton finally excused them for recess. The red-headed boy leapt out of his chair and set his legs apart.

"You got a problem with me?" he said.

Alex stood up slowly and balled his hands into fists. He had learned to fight early, though his mother didn't know this and had seen only a fraction of his scars. She'd never seen the pale pink indentation beneath his belly button, where Michael Dean, who'd flunked fifth grade four years in a row, had punched him hard. Or the brown bruise on the back of his thigh he'd gotten from the boot of Corey Phelps, who was six two and two hundred pounds by the time he hit sixth grade.

Only the meanest boys in Middlebury had come near him, and then only in packs, because he knew where to kick and that if he hit a spot just below the earlobe, a two-hundred-pound bully would sit down and cry. He would have liked to be good at math or skiing, but it turned out he had an aptitude for boxing. He figured he'd saved his own life a dozen times already.

This boy just stared at him. He took a step forward, then one of the girls who had shushed them, the one with long blond hair drawn back in two braids, came up beside him.

"You gonna play soccer, Billy?" she asked.

Billy stared at him a moment longer, then finally shrugged. "Whatever." He jabbed Alex in the chest. "What do I need with you?"

He shoved Alex going past. Alex took a step forward, then decided not to land a punch between the boy's shoulder blades, one that would have sent him facedown on Mrs. Hazelton's newly scrubbed floor. The girl chewed on one of her braids.

"You want to play?" she asked.

Alex shut his eyes for a moment and imagined himself standing on a vast expanse of ice, the wind so cold it could freeze a dragon in his tracks. He opened his mouth, but when he turned to the girl, nothing but steam came out.

She must not have noticed, because she took a step forward. "Can't you talk?"

Mrs. Hazelton had chosen that awful moment to come up beside him. She laid a moist hand on his shoulder.

"Linda, Alex hasn't spoken since he was born. I'd really appreciate it if you could watch out for him. Make sure the other kids understand and don't pick on him."

She smiled down at Alex and he turned red. He stood as straight as he could; he imagined himself a soldier, a hero, a man no one messed with. At his last school, he'd been called a mute, an imbecile, an idiot, a retard. When the summer afternoons had been especially torrid and the teenagers bored and broke, they'd thrown stones at his window and called him a stupid mute, at least until he'd slipped quietly into their midst and taken them down one by one with precise karate chops to the neck.

It was only kindness that rattled him. Gentle hands on his shoulder seemed to sink him three feet into the ground.

He shrugged off the teacher's hand and forced himself to meet Linda's gaze. He was surprised to find she was not looking at him with pity at all, but with her brows knitted together, as if he were a bright piece of trash in the woods, something she hadn't come across before.

He stepped back. He didn't want to be different; he wanted to be so like the other kids, they mistook him for their brother. He wanted to fade to brown and blend into the trunks of trees.

He turned his back on them and walked outside. He walked right past the soccer game and the girls playing hopscotch with juniper cuttings as markers. He stomped over scrubbed red cobblestones and around the corner of Principal Dreyfuss's office, where the shouts were muffled and a crack willow took the edge off the morning sun. He leaned against the red brick wall and listened to his own breathing.

He could survive because he knew one thing for certain: The silence was not part of him. He just knew it, the way some people know the moment they fall in love — with absolute certainty and no facts to back it up. He knew that no matter how comfortable the dragon had made himself in his throat, Alex wasn't learning to fight for nothing. One day, when he was strong enough, he was going to kick the awful thing out.

It took only a week and a half for the women of Middlebury to track down Esther Gregory in Pendleton. For years, Esther had had a clientele of more than a hundred — women, mostly, who arrived on her doorstep asking for cures for bruises and heartache. Jane was scrubbing thirty years of yellow grit off the windowpanes when Patricia Snyder, who'd come to Esther for help with everything from ulcers to un-planned pregnancies, knocked on the door.

"Hiccups," Patricia said, pointing to her throat as it spasmed. "It's been going on for two days now."

"Grandma!" Jane called, then walked right past her grandmother when Esther stomped out of a back bedroom in her long skirt and army boots. Esther smelled of something burning and Jane checked the white hair coiled on her head for signs of smoke. No doubt she'd been setting willow root on fire again, which she swore would keep lost souls from roosting in a house.

"I'll leave you two alone," Jane said. "I'm going to the attic."

She had lived with this sort of thing for seven years, and for seven years she had loved her grandmother enough not to say what she really felt — that aspirin and a good cry would have cured these women just as well as herbs and what Esther called magic. The only real magic Esther had was that these women believed in her. They knew she would hold their hands and not say a word, no matter how long it took them to pour out their sob stories. Jane had seen rashes disappear before Esther even rubbed them with salves of tea-tree oil and echinacea. Women started healing the second they walked through Esther's door.

Jane did not have time for magic spells; every waking moment since they'd arrived had been devoted to trying to salvage her mother's house. She walked down the hall and glanced at her new bedroom, the one her mother had slept in for twenty years. Sal's twenty-year-old bed sagged on the left and was still brand new on the right. These last few nights, Jane had tried to sleep on the good side, but some time around three every morning, she always woke up abruptly, curled into the imprint of her mother's lonely life.

Salvation had died a month ago, on a hot August morning, when she stepped out her front door, took three steps onto her dead lawn, and was broadsided by a teenager on a motorcycle who hadn't yet mastered the art of the turn. Jane had arranged the funeral, picked the plot beneath the sycamore tree in Pendleton Cemetery, and then did not show up for the ceremony. She hadn't cared what anyone thought. She hadn't shown up for Ned's funeral either, and she could imagine what her old neighbors in Pendleton had thought about that.

Sal had scared the daylights out of everyone but animals. Grown men had ducked when they'd seen her walking the streets with her steel loppers, though she never used those on anything except the chains that kept dogs trapped in indifferent men's yards. No child other than Jane had said a word to Sal in all the years Jane lived at home, as if she might turn on them and bite. Yet squirrels crawled right into Sal's lap. Birds ate sunflower seeds from the palm of her hand. The night Dan Carey, her husband, punched her in the nose and she beat him off with a fire poker, she followed the sound of pitiful crying to the woods and picked up her first stray bulldog. From then on, she haunted the pound and back roads, and never had less than half a dozen cancer-ridden dogs and incontinent cats sleeping in her bed. She had often looked at Jane in confusion, as if she couldn't quite believe she'd had a daughter and not a German shepherd.

Sal had often said that animals were the only creatures she could rely on, the only ones worth loving. To prove it, after the divorce she cut up all of Dan Carey's sweaters and turned them into dog boots. She took back her maiden name and changed Jane's name as well. She threw every item Dan Carey had ever touched into a heap in the backyard and set a torch to it. All these dramatics, as far as Jane could tell, were for nothing. She could have taken a torch to her heart, too, but it would not have done any good. She still cried out Dan's name in her dreams. Years after Dan left, whenever she looked in the mirror, Jane knew she still saw an unhappily married woman.

Jane walked past the bedroom to the second bathroom at the end of the hall and flipped on the light. Behind the bug-filled light fixture, the corners of a three-by-three trapdoor had been obscured by dust. One of the brass hinges had fallen off, and the handle, still molded by the shape of a little girl's fingers, hung by a single, wobbly screw.

She glanced over her shoulder, as she always had, then quickly pulled on the handle. After an initial resistance, the trapdoor finally gave way and a three-step ladder fell halfway to the floor. When she was seven, she had easily swung herself up onto the lowest rung and scampered up into the attic. At thirty, she thought she might have lost the knack for climbing. She tentatively hoisted a foot up, but once her shoe struck metal, it all came back to her. Suddenly, her bones felt light as paper; she rose up with hardly any effort at all.

She poked her head through an elaborate system of spiderwebs and immediately felt light-headed. The dust in the attic was so old and dense, it had eaten up most of the oxygen.

41

There was a strong smell of animal, mice probably, and in the dim light she could make out droppings and shredded paper all over the plywood floor.

On the south side of the attic, there was one slatted square window beneath the eave. It was no more than a foot across, strictly for ventilation, and it was almost completely blocked by leaves. What little light got through was gray, and speckled with floating dust. Beneath the window, amazingly, there was still her favorite pillow, most of its stuffing now lost to mice, and a stack of novels all dog-eared and soft from long-ago handling.

Jane stepped out into the attic. All week long, she had been thinking how much she hated this house. Every corner was another monster, this one the place her mother had hunched over some dying animal, that one with the window she had looked out of onto other people's better lives. She had not forgotten the afternoons she and Graham had sneaked up here to whisper and read; she had only forgotten how good they had been. How even dim light, if it fell at just the right angle, could warm a body all the way through. How clear and pure rain on a tin roof sounded, like a melody only children could compose.

She stepped forward and nearly slipped on a magazine. She bent down and picked it up. The dust was a quarter-inch thick, so moldy things had begun growing in it. She turned her head away and brushed it off. When she finally reached paper, she saw the magazine was *Maritime*. On the cover was a photo of a schooner anchored off a white sand beach in Bora Bora. She ran her hand over it and a moist, decayed edge came off in her fingers; she remembered Graham bringing this magazine one afternoon, then poring over the details of things to do in the South Pacific.

"Sea kayaking, shopping, native dances at the cultural center," he had said. "It's the most beautiful place on earth. Says so right here."

He was nine years old and absolutely certain he was going to be a fishing boat captain, though Vermont was landlocked and he'd never seen the sea, never been on more than the paddle boats at Lagoon, the amusement park outside Boston.

"You'll sail all the way from here?" she'd asked, smiling at him from across the room, where she was reading *Jane Eyre* for the fourth time. She knew it by heart, but that didn't stop her from getting a chill up her spine each time the mad Mrs. Rochester was discovered, and it became obvious as anything that Rochester had loved that other Jane all along.

"Sure. Through the Panama Canal, straight across the doldrums."

"What if you get seasick?"

He looked at her like she was crazy. "I'll build my house right on this beach," he said, "but I'll never sleep in it. Only on the sea, or in

43

a hammock I'll hang between two palm trees. You can have a hammock, too. And a maid to do everything. We won't eat anything that isn't sweet. I swear to you, not another lima bean or bite of salad for as long as we live."

Jane set down *Jane Eyre* to come sit beside him. He had his own cubbyhole in the corner, where he stashed his travel magazines, Hershey's with almonds, and paper and pencils for those times when Sal was in the house. The miracle was that Jane's mother had never known about the attic. Jane would tell her they were going out to play, then she and Graham would sneak through the back door, into the bathroom, and up into the attic before Sal had finished changing a dog's diaper. When Sal was below, they passed notes — "Did you hear George Beckett broke up with Mary Lou?" and "Are you reading that *again?*" They sat right over Sal's unsuspecting head and rolled their eyes when they heard her crooning over some incontinent cat in a soft voice no one in Pendleton would believe her capable of.

"You'll come with me, won't you?" Graham had asked, after she laid her chin on his shoulder to study the glossy pictures.

Jane had thought of Ned, who hadn't yet noticed that she was alive. "Of course. Ned too. If he hasn't kissed me by then, I'll make him walk the plank."

Jane clutched the magazine in her hands. Graham had been the only person she had allowed in the attic. Ned would have stepped one foot in there and told her he couldn't breathe. He would have said, "Come on. Let's *do* something." He would have kicked aside books and Graham's bathymetrical charts to get back down where there was enough space to run.

Jane looked around. In her memories, the attic had seemed smaller, but now she realized an adult could stand upright nearly to the corners. She was on a tight budget; there was no way she'd have enough money to remodel this space. Still, she couldn't help wondering what she would see if she cut a skylight right through the rafters. For all she knew, she and Graham had been nesting in the branches of maple trees, or even farther up, riding the wakes of clouds.

She was considering these possibilities when she heard the scream. She raced to the trapdoor and eased herself down. She jumped to the bathroom floor, then ran to the dining room. Patricia Snyder was standing at the mirror, holding her hand over her mouth. She was still hiccuping, but now, in addition to that, a lock of her black hair had turned white as chalk. Esther was staring down at the potion still bubbling in a pot on the sink.

"Well," Esther said, "*that's* never happened before."

Patricia raised her hand to her hair, then whirled around at Esther. "What were you" — hiccup — "trying to do to me?"

Esther said nothing, but she picked up the handle of the pot and dumped the ingredients into the sink. Jane walked over to Patricia.

"A little Clairol will fix that right up," she whispered. "And when you get home, put a knife in a cup of water and stare up at the blade while you drink. That's not magic, it's just the way you cure a bad case of hiccups."

After Patricia left, Jane knew better than to talk to her grandmother. It was no secret that Esther's magic had begun to misfire. In addition to this fiasco, one of Esther's ointments had given a neighbor a horrid case of hives and, a few months ago, a woman who had asked for a simple laxative had ended up shedding forty pounds, dyeing her hair red, and running off to join the circus in New Jersey.

Jane walked into the living room and picked the rag out of the bucket of vinegar and water she'd left by the window. For three days now, she'd been trying to scrub the yellow grime off the panes. Before that, she'd filled a thirty-pound garbage can with dog hair vacuumed off the hardwood floors.

She scrubbed hard, releasing the trapped stink of thousands of her mother's cigarettes. She had stood at this window often as a child, watching Regina Appleby drive the carpool with such single-minded focus, she had never noticed lit joints or how often the teenagers in the backseat flipped off her neighbors. When Mrs. Appleby had pulled her wood-paneled station wagon into her driveway, Jane had imagined herself getting out of the car with her and marching right into her house as one of her children. She'd eaten oatmeal raisin cookies and chased them with ice-cold milk.

She had watched Nancy and Robert O'Brien come home every week from the doctor, paler but still childless. She had held their hands and become the daughter they'd always wanted. She'd kept her room as neat as the rest of their house and never given them a reason to worry.

She must have said something because Esther came up behind her and put a hand on her shoulder. "Sal did her best with you," she said.

"That was her best? When I had my first period, you know what she did? She made me watch a greyhound be put to sleep and told me it could be a lot worse."

Esther laughed as Jane slammed the rag against the soiled pane. "Oh, Janie, that was just your mother's way. She didn't know how to deal with you, with all that drama you had. You used to cry for old, lonely women and throw tantrums over the color of your shoes. You used to do a lot of things."

She started coughing and Jane dropped the rag to help her to the kitchen. Esther grabbed a vile-looking concoction out of the refrigerator — tea spiked with wild cherry bark and pulverized marigold petals — and drank it down.

Then she stood over the sink and coughed even harder.

Jane gently patted Esther's back, until she coughed up a chunk of blood-streaked phlegm. Esther used to stand an inch or more above Jane's head, but lately she'd been shrinking. She now came only to the tops of Jane's eyes.

"I'm fine," Esther said. "Stop looking at me like that."

"Whatever you say," Jane said, though she checked her grandmother's forehead for fever before Esther could argue.

"You know," Esther said, "I had a dream last night. About Ned."

Jane dropped her hand. She turned back toward the living room, but the smell of cigarettes and vinegar there was stifling. She headed for the back door.

"I'm going to find that old Schwinn for Alex," she said. She'd found, in the last few years, that she could nearly shut down her breathing. On humid summer nights she could go so still, dew puddled on her shoulders.

"I felt him," Esther said, oblivious. "I heard him, somehow. He was speaking with Alex's voice."

Jane stopped and whirled around. "Don't. Ned is dead. I should know."

"I'm just talking, Jane," she said. "This place —"

"Is temporary," Jane finished for her. "We're here so Alex can have a fresh start, but that doesn't mean we're staying. I'm going to use the Paytons' money to fix up this place, and then we're moving on."

She had expected Ned's parents to take an interest in their grandson, but instead they had decided to just leave her money. Six years ago, when they had sold their house on the Common and moved to Florida, they'd given her the proceeds from the sale to help raise Alex. "We can't bear it," Ned's mother, Vivian, had said to her. Jane had stared at her enviously, because she had a choice.

"And something else," Esther said. "Have you noticed the grass?"

Sal's lawn had been dead for as long as Jane could remember, but when Jane had stepped outside the morning after they moved in, she'd noticed bright green tufts in tracks from the driveway to the door. Since then, the new shoots had grown two inches tall.

"I must have spilled some fertilizer when we moved in."

"They're footprints, Janie," Esther said.

Jane opened the door. "I'm not listening," she said over her shoulder. She didn't believe in magic, but nevertheless, she felt something prickle across her skin like a spider. Her skin crawled in a foreshadowing of trouble and something else. Something that surprised her. Something like yearning.

A car had not fit in Sal Gregory's garage for

twenty years. Moldy boxes, power tools and giant Santas were stacked ten feet high. Broken skis, an old guitar with the strings cut out, and bags and bags of moth-eaten baby clothes pressed down on the already sagging rafters. The only way through the debris was by walking sideways down claustrophobic alleys Sal had carved. It took Jane over an hour to find her old Schwinn bicycle behind two vinyl lawn chairs and a cracked plastic swimming pool with faded purple fish on the bottom.

She took the bike into the overgrown back-yard. It was coated in dust and twenty-year-old grime; by the time she scrubbed down to metal, she saw it had faded from dark green to cloudy gray. There were indentations in the torn rubber handlebars from her fingers; her sweat, all those years ago, had dripped down and rusted the spokes.

She took the pink flags off the handlebars and the Barbie stickers off the seat. She wheeled the bike out front, where Alex was sit-ting in the lowest branch of the maple tree, his arm slung over a knotted limb. He had sat there every afternoon after class for the week and a half they'd been in Pendleton, silencing the birds who roosted in the branches beside him.

"It needs some air in the tires," Jane said, shielding her eyes and looking up. "But other-wise it's in pretty good shape. You could take it down to Nate's service station. He's got a pump in the back, as I recall."

Alex just stared. He was going to get better here; she had already decided that. She didn't think it was possible that he could get any worse. Silence, believe it or not, had degrees; in the last year, he had grown so quiet old wood no longer creaked beneath his feet. She could not hear him swallow. The only time Jane hadn't noticed his muteness was during their twice-weekly swims. She had taken him to the pool at the university in Middlebury since he was a baby; he was so good now, he could swim the length and back in one breath. He could dive, eyes wide open, to the bottom of the deep end to retrieve the goggles and fins of petrified four-year-olds.

She'd checked out Pendleton High's pool yesterday. There was open swimming from three to seven every afternoon. If Alex only smiled while doing the backstroke, she would take him to the pool every day. She would feed him his meals underwater.

"Come on, Alex," she said. "Hop down and try it out."

Alex climbed slowly down the tree. He walked around the bicycle and rolled his eyes at the girl's frame.

"It's the best I can do," Jane said. "Take it or leave it."

He shrugged, but he also hopped on. He rode past the eight houses on this side of Sycamore Lane and back again, hitting the brakes at each driveway and checking behind him for the quality of his skid. By the time he reached Jane's side, he was smiling. That smile, as always, turned her heart over.

At one time, when Alex was two and she was just beginning to panic about his lack of speech, she had thought she could love words into him. She loved him with such ferocity, sometimes she ran to another room sobbing, just trying to get away from all that feeling. She, more than anyone, knew what a risk it was to pour all your love into one body. Tragedy, when it came, had only one place to strike.

All that love had done nothing. In almost seven years, Alex had not said a word. Jane had taken him to every doctor on the East Coast, but she knew they would not find anything. She knew what had happened: Alex had gotten her life by mistake. He had nightmares while her dreams were black as space. He felt guilty over something he didn't even know about.

Alex was riding off down Sycamore Lane. "Don't go too far," Jane yelled. "Don't go on the highway!"

He had already turned the corner. Jane looked down at her clenched fists. She wondered when the day would come when she wouldn't imagine all the horrific things that could happen to him when he was out of her sight. She wondered when he would stop squeezing her heart, or when she would cure him the way a mother should, with a snap of her fingers, just like that.

Esther Gregory could see in pure darkness, but the last of the gray starlight streaming through the kitchen window lit a path anyway. Quietly, she unlocked her apothecary chest; she didn't want Jane waking up and trying to talk her out of it. Jane, in these last seven years, had grown too cautious for her own good.

Inside the chest, Esther kept her most lethal supplies: the pulverized tips of a hundred stinging nettles, liquefied wormwood, and a thirty-eight caliber revolver used only once, to scare away seven hooded teenagers who were spray-painting a pentagram on her garage door. She took out a dozen stinging nettles, all the wormwood she owned, and a bottle of vinegar.

She massaged her chest, though this did nothing. The pain had gone deeper these last few months, down to muscle and bone. She repinned a loose strand of the hair she had never cut around her head. Everything else about her had sagged, clogged or broke over the years, but her hair had not lost its luster. By the time she was fifteen, it had grown to her waist and, by thirty-five, it was pure white. Every morning, she rolled it into incredible contortions on the top of her head.

Beneath a man's work shirt and wool skirt, she wore her dead husband's army boots. Thirty-one years earlier, Walt Gregory's single-engine plane had gone down somewhere in the Rockies; to date, nothing had been found but a single black strip of fuselage and three of Walt's gold-capped teeth. People thought she wore the boots as a tribute to Walt Gregory, but actually, they were the only shoes wide enough for her feet.

Esther looked in the mirror, then blinked. A square of dusty purple light shined through the window behind her, exactly where her right earlobe should have been. Most women would consider this a trick of the light, or a by-product of too many sleepless nights, but Esther knew a sign when she saw one. She knew, once a person reached a certain age, time left on earth became not only finite, but visible; like smoke from an extinguished candle, one could actually watch it fade. Even as she thought this, the morning light turned pink and shined through a section of her right cheek.

She cooked the potion while the sky turned from pink to sleepy blue, while her neighbors woke up angry and sped off to work without saying goodbye, while every baby on the street yelled simultaneously for milk. She did this by rote — she could whip up a poultice in two minutes flat and stick a needle in a baby without him feeling a thing — but not without an inkling of dread. She had found her magic on a strong wind on the edge of a mountaintop no one else had ever stepped foot on. She had thought it the kind of thing that never harms or dies. But now, she knew, she was getting dangerous.

She couldn't cure the simplest illnesses. All her herbal teas ended up tasting like gasoline and, if held too close to a flame, ignited. To her family, she was probably the most menacing of all. Seven years ago, when Jane had arrived on her doorstep tear-stained and stiff with guilt, Esther had brewed a love potion. Twenty-five crushed white rose petals, two tablespoons of blackened honey, and a splash of sweet plum wine. For a few months it had seemed to ease Jane's suffering; at the very least, she had stopped standing for hours in the backyard, facing south, in the direction of the last memory she had of Ned. But then Jane had a painless labor — always an ominous sign — and Alex slid out from between her legs without making a single whimper. When Esther caught him, he simply stared back up at her, his thumb in his mouth.

Six and a half silent years later, Esther was taking her chances with another potion. She knew only one thing, and that left her with little choice how to act. She looked out the window while stirring, trying to read the future. Before her magic had begun to fade, she'd easily read fortunes in clouds. She'd predicted eight pregnancies, three divorces, and that the butcher's wife would leave him to become a Las Vegas showgirl. When Jane was eight, and a bit over-confident, she had wanted to know when she would marry Ned Payton. Esther had stared at a storm cloud and then patted Jane's hand.

"Think of men as bandages," she'd said. "Handy when you break something, but really, how often does that happen?"

This morning, unfortunately, the clouds looked only like clouds, as if the future were up for grabs, which she knew for a fact it was not.

Once the potion had been boiled down, she poured it into one of Sal's beloved Bugs Bunny juice glasses and took it out onto the front porch. The September air was hot and saturated, too thick for deep breathing. She padded across the grass, to the white Grandiflora hydrangea beneath Alex's window.

She knew no spell to elicit words, so she merely poured the potion over the hydrangea, then stepped back as the liquid sizzled into the dirt. A sickening odor, much like the stink of all those deer carcasses Walt had brought home and expected her to turn into steaks, rose up out of the usually sweet-smelling petals, and Esther knew she'd gone wrong again. The petals should have gotten sweeter, risen up on a bed of warm air to Alex's window, and tickled awake his voice. Magic ought to live forever in a woman who knew nothing else; at the very least, she ought to be able to cure those who meant most to her.

Instead, the shrub oozed its putrid fragrance and a sudden strong wind carried the stink up over the house. Esther studied the wind, then lost its trajectory; it swirled first north, then south, then died altogether.

She looked back at the hydrangea. Where the potion had spilt on the clustered petals, they'd turned a sickly yellow. The grass blades beneath them were burnt black.

She dropped the juice glass when she felt eyes on her. She turned and caught a man hurrying across his immaculate lawn next door, then disappearing inside his house. She stiffened, until she realized it was only old Robert O'Brien, who had lived next door to Salvation forever, who had lost his wife to cancer and had since poured all his devotion into roses.

Esther kicked the juice glass as she walked back inside. She headed toward the fireplace and stared at the portrait of the sea she'd hung over the mantel as soon as they had moved in. Fifty years ago, Walt Gregory, her husband, had commissioned a portrait of himself and hung it proudly over their mantel. Eighteen years after that, when he was gone so often he did not notice the change, Esther began to paint over the top of him. She covered first his hair with blue oils, then his chin and cheeks, then at last his eyes with a froth of white foam. Sometimes, when she was very tired, she imagined eyes peeking out at her from beneath the waves.

She stared hard now, but saw only waves. She was disappointed. She had never missed her husband, but sometimes she missed his cynicism. She would have liked him to peek through the foam and tell her she was crazy for

57

thinking that magic could work at all, let alone do harm.

The stranger came on a Monday, two weeks after Jane had arrived in town. He went first into Jim's Mercantile, where the new clerk, sixteen-year-old Sandy Aberdeen, fell immediately into a fit of girlish giggles. When the man put a twenty-dollar bill into her palm, she later told her friends, when his tan fingers grazed her skin, she shook so badly the whole counter swayed. He had to operate the cash register for her, which he did with a smile and a wink.

Next, he gassed up his '69 yellow Mustang at Nate's Service Station, and ended up showing the new mechanic, Sandy Aberdeen's brother Peter, a thing or two about classic engines. After ten minutes, head mechanic David Sidler and even old Nate himself were lured out by all that glittering metal. When Mark Sharkey, the sheriff, drove by five minutes later, he noticed Nate had bought the stranger a root beer and put his arm around him as he hadn't done to anyone but the son he'd lost to prostate cancer. Later, Peter Aberdeen told his sister Sandy that Nate had offered the stranger a lifetime of free oil changes.

Next, the stranger went to Jensen Realty, to see about renting a house. Marilyn Ludlow, who was the top agent in the area and immune to charm, got sweaty palms the second he leaned against her desk and told her she was the prettiest thing he'd come across all day. She excused herself to go to the bathroom and instead called Marjorie Dumas, her best friend, and told her things were finally, thank God, starting to liven up in this stupid town.

Marilyn showed the stranger a dozen obviously overpriced or oversized houses, just for the chance to sit beside him in her car. His muscles strained against his jeans and the scent of him — woody, deep, and dark — saturated her usually banana-scented Saab. He took her in stride; in fact, by the fourth house priced way out of his range, he put his hand on the small of her back, and Marilyn got the shivers like she hadn't gotten in years.

The thirteenth house was the one she'd had in mind for him all along. It was a tiny two-bedroom on the end of Sycamore Lane. Not the slums by any means, but at best what could be called the "affordable" side of town. The stranger walked in, took a quick look at the bedrooms, then told her he'd take it. After they signed the lease papers, he gave her a kiss on the cheek, which she swore, despite the obvious melodrama, she wouldn't wash for weeks.

Marjorie Dumas lived only two doors down from the stranger's house and was at his door within an hour, a dozen freshly baked chocolate mint cookies in hand. Marjorie's husband had been dead for ten years, and she hadn't thought about sex once in that time, but when the stranger ran a hand through his shoulder-length hair, she immediately started imagining the things that hand could do to her. She prayed so hard for youth and whatever kind of beauty he desired, she dropped the cookies all over his floor.

By the time Marjorie got to Jane's house an hour later, where Jane was kneeling beside her mother's ancient Perfume Delight rosebush, her face was red and splotchy with longing.

"We've got a new neighbor," Marjorie said breathlessly.

Jane had deadheaded the already faded flowers, and was deciding whether or not to rip the remainder of the plant from the ground.

"Oh?" she said, looking up briefly, then returning her gaze to the plant.

"Right across from you. The corner house? Used to belong to Matthew and Caroline Irving, until Matthew decided, at fifty, mind you, that he'd been gay all along. Now that was a scandal, let me tell you. Caroline Irving has never lived that down."

"Someone new, you said?" Jane asked, and decided the bush had to go. It was old and had churned out only half a dozen roses, all of those a sad, tired pink. She scratched at the hard soil with her fingers, then opted for the shovel and began digging toward the roots.

"Yes, right. I heard from Marilyn, and then I just had to go over there. You cannot be too careful with neighbors, especially renters. But let me tell you . . ."

She giggled, and Jane sat back on her heels. She had never heard Marjorie reach a note that high in her life. The middle-aged woman fanned herself with her hand, but even so, the sweat stood out in beads on her forehead.

"Marjorie!" Jane said, smiling.

"Oh, you aren't going to believe him, Jane," she said. "His name is Devon Zeke. Hair like a rock star's and eyes gray enough to make you weep."

Jane had just reached a root and she gripped her hand around it. She yanked and twisted, but it wouldn't budge.

"The girls will all be after him," Marjorie went on. "I'd say he's twenty-five, twenty-six. A little young for you, but believe me, that won't matter when you see him. I might even start wearing mascara again and . . . My goodness, what is that smell?"

It came upon Jane suddenly, the stench of a nasty death, of an animal rotting in the sunshine, attracting flies. She wrinkled her nose and tried to locate the source, but it seemed to be coming from all around her.

"Probably that damn Harry Waterson's septic system backed up again," Marjorie went on. "I've told him again and again to hook up to the city sewer system, but no, he calls himself an individualist. My, that's strong this time. There's probably something trapped in the tank, poor thing."

Jane looked across the street. A man had

come out of the house and was walking toward his yellow Mustang. He opened the door, reached into the backseat, and took out a guitar in a slick black case. He was turning to go back inside when he suddenly looked their way.

Jane rose quickly to her feet. The man was tall, over six feet, with long, light brown hair. He wore blue jeans rolled at the cuff, and a white T-shirt. Jane took a step toward him before she wondered what she was doing.

Marjorie was still talking. "There he is. Didn't I say he was gorgeous? Let me tell you, Marilyn Ludlow is already plotting to leave her husband."

The man waved, then slung his guitar over his shoulder and walked back inside. Jane ran her hands down her arms, where all the hairs were standing on end.

"Devon Zeke," Marilyn was saying. "Remember that name."

She laughed, and hurried off to Rachel Simpson's house to tell the news. Jane looked again at the rosebush, unearthed but still lodged tightly in the ground. Her chest ached, and she massaged a hand over it. She ought to finish her digging, but instead she dropped the shovel and headed for the kitchen. She felt a sudden yearning for something sweet, a chocolate cake even, the likes of which she hadn't had in years.

Two

Graham Payton listened to the lungs of his last patient of the day, forty-year-old Josie Aberdeen. She took short, shallow breaths, but not because of any fluid buildup. She'd been breathing like that for the last seven months, since her husband left her for a younger woman in California.

"How long have you had this cold?" he asked.

"Weeks now," Josie said, smoothing down her latest haircut, a blunt wedge with the tips frosted blond. "I just keep getting infected. You know how it is when you see so many people."

Josie ran Josie's Hair Styling, though Graham himself went to a barber in Rutland — Josie had a thing for sideburns and gel. She might have taken offense if Graham hadn't been so willing to schedule her after hours. He was also the only doctor in Pendleton, which didn't leave Josie or anyone else much choice. Yesterday, he had delivered Paula Weston's boy, diagnosed two cases of chicken pox, and spent the better part of the afternoon trying to talk ninety-six-year-old Thomas Ezra out of liposuction treatment on his thighs.

He looked in Josie's throat and ears and finally diagnosed a sinus infection. He wrote out a prescription. "Antibiotics," he said. "Take them twice a day for ten days and this should clear right up."

"I hear those don't work anymore."

"They'll work."

"How much will it cost?"

"Ask for generic," he said. "That'll save you a fair amount."

Josie scrunched the prescription into her pocket. She tapped his bare cheek where she would have left a sideburn. "Can you believe Jane's back after all this time? Have you seen her yet?"

She stared right at him, but Graham was busy writing a diagnosis on her insurance form. She was the fortieth patient in the last week to have asked him that question, and he always gave the same answer.

"Not yet," he said. "Ginny and I have been busy."

"She's got a boy now," Josie said. "Marjorie says there's something odd about him."

"Yes, I heard."

After she left, Graham ripped the paper off the examining table, then went into his office and changed into sweatpants and a T-shirt. He had let his receptionist go home an hour earlier, so he locked up himself. Outside, the sun had already dipped behind Blackbird Peak, but the unusual September heat lingered, curling the white paint on the windowsills.

He hopped on the bike he'd started riding regularly a couple years ago, to keep in shape. It was nothing fancy, just a dependable ten-speed he'd picked up at Michael's Bicycle Shop. Randy Weaver, sweeping the stoop outside Jim's Mercantile, waved to him as he rode past and would be in tomorrow, for antidepressants. Marilyn Ludlow was just coming out of her office, high heels spiking the concrete. Her husband Vince had a bad liver from too many vodka tonics. Her youngest boy, Scott, had sneaked into Graham's office a week ago, a suspicious-looking rash under his shorts. He had hardly breathed until Graham gave him some sample packets of cortisone so he wouldn't have to go to the local drugstore. Now, Graham waved at Marilyn, but he didn't stop to chat. When he'd taken on secrets, he'd given up small talk. At first, he had felt privileged to know the medical secrets of nearly everyone in town, but now all that knowledge weighed him down. It made him leave footprints deeper than anyone else's in town.

He rode every night, usually out along Highway 7 where the maples were still green, though autumn would begin officially next week. The bike tours and fall-foliage bus trips were already in full swing. A group of irate senior citizens, up from Florida, had already picketed the governor's office, until he promised to return their vacation money if the leaves did not turn this week.

They were not going to turn, not in this heat. After less than an hour, Graham's legs felt heavy and sweat rolled down his back. He passed a gang of twelve-year-olds who had dumped their bikes along the road and were wading in an irrigation ditch. He turned around and headed toward home.

He lived on the nicest street in Pendleton, Welton Place. He and his wife, Ginny, had bought the place two years ago, when their combined salaries made it possible for them to choose nearly any house they wanted. This one was colonial style: four bedrooms, three baths, a huge backyard for the children they had envisioned. When they first bought it, they spent weekends tilling in compost, watching *This Old House*, and then putting up wallpaper themselves. For a while, Ginny took to stenciling and left little pink hearts around the bathroom mirrors. Then when she couldn't get pregnant, she began working late nights and Saturdays, and for months now had not gone near the upstairs bathroom, where the pink hearts stopped abruptly two feet above the sink.

Ginny's Volvo was not in the driveway when he rode up. She almost always worked later than he did, though no one in town believed this. She did not look more than sixteen, and certainly not like a CPA. She was only five foot two, and still battling baby fat. Ginny left for work in Rutland so early, not even the young mothers with babies saw her in her gabardine suits, her curly, clay-colored hair pulled back in a bun. It had taken her only four years to get her degree and CPA license, but the teachers in Pendleton still thought her straight A's some kind of fluke. The clerk at Jim's Mercantile always counted her change twice.

She had left him some store-bought lasagna in the refrigerator, but Graham had lost his appetite. He showered and dressed, then got into his car. He drove past the flower shop, but did not pick up a bouquet. He had sent a dozen white carnations to Ginny's office once, early on in their marriage, but they had shriveled in two days. He ought to have kept it up, he knew, but he was busy, she was busy; it just seemed a waste of vegetation. For anniversaries and birthdays, he bought her practical gifts, like the food processor he'd gotten her on their two-year anniversary last year.

He drove past the florist's and into Rutland, where Ginny worked in a modern glass building. He parked between a Land Rover and one of the new super-safe Volvos. He took the elevator to the third floor and surprised Ginny's secretary.

"Mr. Payton," Maddie said, glancing back at Ginny's closed door. "She didn't tell me she was expecting you."

"She's not," Graham said.

He had come to Ginny's office three times in three years, twice for Christmas parties and once to pick her up after her car battery went out. When Ginny brought work home, she did it in their home office, with the door locked. "I'm not hiding anything," she told him once. "It's just mine. I want it to be just mine."

"Why don't you go on in?" Maddie said. "I'm sure she'll be thrilled to see you."

Graham nodded. He walked to the door and knocked. Ginny said, "Come in," in a voice totally unlike her.

He opened the door. Ginny was behind her desk, custom-made an inch shorter than most, so she would appear taller to her clients. The walls were painted dark green and covered with built-in bookshelves. Thick, textured shades blocked the view. Ginny's hair was slicked back; she had a pencil tucked over each ear while she studied the stack of papers in front of her. She didn't even look up.

"Maddie, I need you to run the Fredericks file down to Greg. He —" She looked up and stopped. For a moment, she seemed unsure what to do, and Graham realized he didn't have the slightest idea what she did here. When they finally met up in bed late at night, they were usually too tired to do anything but make love, or talk about the basics — how old the milk in the refrigerator was, who was supposed to empty the dishwasher in the morning. Sometimes they made love and discussed car maintenance at the same time. In the last two weeks, they had made love only once, and they hadn't talked at all. There had been an ominous hush to those minutes before they fell asleep, when all they could do was listen to each other's breathing.

"How nice," Ginny said at last, sliding the pencils off her ears and stepping out from behind the desk. She walked over to him, her high heels sinking into the lush green carpet. She kissed him lightly on the cheek.

"I just thought . . ." He trailed off. He hadn't thought anything through, to tell the truth. He'd only known if he'd kept on riding, he was eventually going to end up on Sycamore Lane. When he'd first heard Jane was back in town, he'd imagined he and Ginny would go over together, bring a casserole, drink a bottle of wine, and talk about their high school days. He had thought everything would be different. Instead, Ginny hadn't once mentioned Jane's name, and every night that omission got louder, until they had to turn on the television, to drown it out.

"I want to take you to dinner," he said.

Ginny glanced down at her cluttered desk. "That's lovely, Graham. Just let me get my purse." She pulled a small handbag out of her bottom drawer, then slipped an arm around his waist. "Really, Graham, this is so nice."

Graham looked down at her hand on his waist and was surprised to find a freckle on her knuckle he'd never noticed before. She had painted her fingernails red, which she never did at home. He figured she must spend an hour in the bathroom here before heading home each night, taking off nail polish and combing the grease from her hair.

"What do you do here?" he asked abruptly.

Ginny let go of him and started toward the elevator. "Don't be ridiculous, Graham. I work."

They went to a Chinese restaurant downtown, and the second Graham smelled the sweet and sour vegetables and lo mein, he couldn't eat a thing. Ginny took a few bites of noodles before she noticed he wasn't eating and set down her chopsticks.

"This is about Jane, right?" she said, pushing away her plate.

Graham did not look at her. Outside the frosted window, business men and women hurried past, ties loosened, their faces drawn and tired.

"Are you having an affair with her?" Ginny went on.

It was so ridiculous, Graham laughed. As if Jane had ever, could ever, love him that way. As if wishes came true.

"She's been back only a couple weeks," Graham said, then realized that was the wrong answer. "I haven't even seen her."

He reached across the table and took her hand. "Ginny . . ."

"You still love her," Ginny said, sliding her hand out from under his.

"Ginny, I married you."

He and Ginny had dated since high school. Up until then, he had called her Jenny; he kept forgetting he knew her. It had taken him ten years to propose to her, though he'd known all along she was the right woman for him, that he just wasn't special enough to attract her kind of devotion twice.

He'd held out for one simple reason: He wasn't certain real love was like a cool hand on the forehead that helps bring down a fever. He was afraid he'd get married and discover, too late, that love was the fever itself.

He held out even after Ned died, and Jane left without a word, and his world went black. Even after he found himself unable to name the bones of the human body, or to take a single note in any of his lectures. Even after he started cutting class and driving to Middlebury, where he stopped at the end of Jane's street, relieved, actually, that he'd finally reached a line he couldn't cross.

Seven years ago, he learned how to lie — everyone in town thought the circles beneath his eyes meant he was grieving for Ned. Obviously, they never looked closely at his chest, which rose and fell in deep, luxurious breaths, as if Ned, while he'd been alive, had been taking more than his fair share of oxygen. They weren't in his bedroom that day he took everything Jane had ever given him, the gold watch and compass and first-edition copy of *Treasure*

Island, and threw them all in a garbage bag. They were not there that morning he sat on the curb and watched Earl Dannon, the garbageman, toss it into the Dumpster, where it was crushed between milk cartons and eggshells.

He told the truth only once, in the single letter he sent to Jane two months after Ned's death. He wrote:

I wanted you to know, I wished the same thing a hundred times. Thousands, maybe. You loved Ned. I hated him. If I could have wished him dead, I'd have done it.

Graham

Jane did not reply and, after six months, he realized she was not coming back. Ned's child would have been born by then, and somehow the thought of that infant, of Ned living on, shot a hole through what he'd thought was impenetrable devotion. He felt, ridiculously, betrayed by Jane. After a year, he wasn't sure if her hair had been jet black or dark brown. After two years, he forgot the sound of her voice. After three, he figured if love was a fever, he was lucky not to have it. He started paying attention to Ginny again, who, for reasons he would never understand, was still paying attention to him.

He didn't deserve her. Just as Ned had not deserved Jane. Graham did not deserve Ginny, but after a while he realized he wanted her, he wanted to be loved by someone constant and loyal.

"Marriage has nothing to do with it," Ginny said now. "You've loved her forever. I've always known that. I've been in the woods, you know. I've seen the carvings."

Graham stared at her. "That was a long time ago."

"Maybe. But now she's back. I think I have a right to know what you're going to do."

Graham sat back, surprised by her directness. He and Ginny and Jane had all gone to school together, but from sixteen on, Ginny had not once said Jane's name, she had taken care never to stand too close to her. Beside Jane, whatever beauty Ginny had, disappeared. In another town, Ginny might have been popular; people would have noticed how smart she was. But in Pendleton, she was just fat little Ginny.

"I'm not going to do anything," Graham said. "I came here to have dinner with you. Can't we just enjoy ourselves? Please?"

Ginny turned away. The right side of her mouth twitched, and then she stilled it. "This is not Pendleton. I don't want . . . I can't have Jane here too. It would be too much."

Her voice broke, but then she smiled, and Graham didn't know what to believe. How was he supposed to know if he'd hurt her if she never told him? Ginny was always staring at him, then walking off in sulks, as if she'd expected him to read her mind.

"Forget about Jane," Graham said, though even to his own ears the words sounded flat and ridiculous. "Let's eat, and then let's drive somewhere and make love."

Ginny looked at him, unsure whether or not to take him seriously, just as he was unsure whether or not he was serious. He wanted to tell her he loved her, to ease the uncertainty in her eyes with kisses. He knew he at least ought to move to the chair beside her and tell her everything would be all right. Instead, for a host of old reasons, he just sat there, letting the doubt hang between them as thick as the sickly smell of cold lo mein. When the waitress came by, he asked for the check.

They did go for a drive, which surprised Ginny. She had thought Graham was only kidding, just saying something to say it, to *sound* right. But instead of taking her back to her car, he drove east on Highway 4 toward the hills.

What the fall-foliage tourists didn't know was that autumn was just a breath away, plunging down from the north, leaving a spectacle of color in its wake. Things changed so fast in the fall, it was only natural that a woman would try to re-create herself as well. Every year, when the leaves turned gold, Ginny got over her fear of flying and booked solo trips to the West Indies and Tibet, places she'd only dreamed about. When the maple leaves turned so vibrantly scarlet it hurt her eyes to look at them, she was no longer afraid of saying what she felt, even if it meant losing someone in the process.

Every year, before the weather got really cold, she hiked to the top of Mt. Carmel and danced barefoot in the lush grass, though Graham did not know this. Once, she had asked him to come with her, but the night before they were supposed to go, Ned died. She had put off her trip for a week, and then went alone. In a way, she was glad she had never brought him. Mt. Carmel was the one place on the planet that was hers alone. For a single afternoon, she was a different woman, the kind who hiked mountains by herself, who danced just for the hell of it, who was sure she was happy.

The rest of the year, Ginny was not certain of anything, except of her love for Graham. She loved him, but love was not happiness; sometimes they were even mutually exclusive. For a while, after Jane's engagement to Ned, Ginny had held out hope that Graham would finally set his sights on her instead. Even when that didn't happen, she didn't give up. What else could she do? She was born to love Graham; it was in her genes, a passion chromosome that spelled out his name.

Then Ned died, and Jane went off, and Ginny thought her time had finally come. Instead, Graham went into mourning — not for Ned, she knew — but for Jane. She nearly gave up then. She began dating Phillip Richter, who would take over his father's hardware store someday. She forced herself to imagine a life with him, even when those images caused a pale pink rash to erupt all over her skin.

Then Graham just came out of it. He began taking her to parties. After he finished medical school, he proposed.

Graham looked her in the eye when he said his wedding vows, but later that night, in the honeymoon suite at Boston's Ritz Carlton, he slipped inside her and said Jane's name without even noticing he'd done it. Ginny had not paused; she pretended she hadn't heard. The worst thing would have been to hear him apologize, to make excuses she couldn't believe. To feign love. She knew from then on he would be careful. He would never make the mistake again. If she didn't listen to his sighs, he would seem a perfect husband.

Graham drove them up Sherburne Pass, then as dusk turned the woods gray, he suddenly pulled off the highway onto a bumpy dirt logging road. He drove in a mile, past pines and golden poplars, then cut the engine. For a long time, he just sat there, his hands still on the wheel. Ginny stared straight ahead; she watched a robin land on the hood, then leave a scratch taking off again. The truth was, being alone with Graham still made her weak and silly. Being within touching distance, and not touching him, made her want to cry.

"Ginny," Graham said, a mixture of longing and confusion in his voice. Usually, at times like these, Ginny would fall right into his arms. For years now, like any smart woman, she'd known that if she wanted to be happy, she could not infer too much from a man's tone. She had to take him at his word.

Today, she hesitated before following him into the backseat. She didn't touch him back when he slipped his fingers up beneath her blouse. When he kissed her, she opened her eyes and imagined what they must look like through the car window, a strangely desperate tangle of bodies, clenched fists slicing the air, clinging to something that wasn't even there.

Usually, when they made love, Ginny did not know what time it was. But tonight, the glow of her watch said it was eight-thirty. She whispered his name, but over that she heard what she knew Graham had been hearing for years. Not the murmur of a lover's breath, not the beating of a heart, but everything else: birds squawking over pinecones, the drone of a low-flying plane, the clicking of the engine as it cooled. The wind scattering leaves and dirt, so that when they finally emerged from the car, nothing would be as it was.

When they got home, Graham immediately turned on the television. Ginny kissed him goodnight and went upstairs, and he knew if someone had taken that moment to look in his living room window, they would have sworn his marriage was a good one. He and Ginny argued in whispers and always made up before falling asleep. Ginny cooked, he cleaned, they deposited their earnings in a joint savings account. Their neighbors thought them a perfect couple. They were considered good luck at weddings; and teenagers, in the heat of passion, often showed up on their doorstep, asking how to make it last.

He flipped off the television and walked upstairs. Ginny was already in her cotton nightgown, curled on her side of the bed. He got in beside her and kissed her cheek. While he waited for her breathing to slow, he reminded himself how lucky he was. As he quietly got out of bed again, he told himself any decent man would be thrilled to have his life. Even as he took his car keys off the kitchen table and walked out the front door without looking back, he was telling himself he shouldn't be asking for anything more than what he already had.

It took him just five minutes to drive across town to Sycamore Lane, where Sal Gregory's old house stood on the corner. Not enough time to think things through, or to come to his senses and go home. Not enough time for luck, either, as it turned out, because when he slowed in front of the house, he spotted Jane sitting on the front porch swing, staring back at him.

He had no choice then but to park the car and think up excuses about being in the neighborhood. He walked up the path and ducked his head when he stepped beneath the porch light, so she wouldn't see what was still in his eyes after all this time.

He was about to speak when she did. "Graham," she said softly, and Graham lifted his head and forgot about excuses. His memory had been cruel, squaring off her jaw, coloring her eyes a duller blue. He had remembered her ugly, so it was a shock when she sat before him, once more the most beautiful thing he'd ever seen.

"I was on my way to . . ." He let the lie drop. It didn't seem worthy, when he was standing that close to her, when her hands in her lap were white as stars.

Jane looked past him to Marjorie Dumas's house down the street. "She still knows how to get the word out."

"It's been a long time," he said. "Were you going to call?"

Jane stopped the swing with her feet and looked at him again. He had thought losing Ned would steal the color from her eyes, but they were still the clearest blue. Her hair was black as oil, tucked behind her ears.

"I've been so busy, getting Alex into school, trying to get the place fixed up. The house is a disaster. You know how my mom was. Oblivious to everything but her animals."

"I can't believe you're back."

"Believe me, I'd rather be anywhere but here."

Graham walked to the swing and sat down beside her. He left enough distance between them so he wouldn't be tempted to touch her. "Why'd you come back?"

She shrugged. "Because Mom left the house to me. Because the money your parents left me won't last forever. Because of Alex. Have you also heard that my son doesn't speak?"

"For how long?" he asked.

"Forever."

"Have you checked his larynx? His epiglottis? His hearing? Maybe there's some psychological —"

Jane held out her hand, and Graham looked at the spot where Ned's engagement ring used to rest. The skin was tanned over. Seven years was a long time, but suddenly he couldn't remember any of it. Not a single thing he'd done, not a word he'd said to Ginny.

"We've checked everything. My grandmother had a dream that Ned was speaking with Alex's voice. That he's holding it hostage or something."

She laughed, but her voice was shaky, and after a while she began to cry. Softly, with no tears, her body trembling so much the swing began to rock. Graham looked back at the dark house, then down the deserted street, then he lost all caution and put his arm around her.

"Graham," she said, tucking her face into his shirt.

It didn't take more than a second for him to realize that just what he'd feared was true: Love was the fever itself. A marriage can be a good one and still be a mistake.

"I'm sorry," she said, wiping her dry eyes.

"Don't be sorry. Why don't you bring him by my office? Maybe there's something the other doctors overlooked."

Jane shrugged and Graham pulled away. "I'm a good doctor, Jane," he said.

Jane touched his arm. "I always knew you would be. It's just that Alex has been through every test imaginable. It's impossible to find something that isn't there."

"At least let me try."

She still hadn't removed her hand from his arm and Graham's skin grew warm. "I went into the attic," she said.

She didn't seem to notice her fingers stroking his arm. "It's a mess," she went on. "Mice everywhere. But I can't get it out of my head. With a skylight or two, some hardwood floors, it would be a beautiful room."

"It was always a beautiful room."

"I found one of your magazines. *Maritime.* You were going to sail to Bora Bora. Do you remember?"

"Hammocks for beds," he said, smiling. "Nothing but candy bars for breakfast. We were going to sail through the Panama Canal and build our huts side by side."

They smiled at each other, then she finally pulled her hand away. "We should have done it."

She pushed off and the swing glided gently up and back. In the light of the street lamp, hundreds of moths danced. Through that tiny window in the attic, Graham knew, there would be a yellow stamp of light, just wide enough for two children to read by, if they sat close enough.

"Did you get my letter all those years ago?" he asked.

She tucked her hand on her lap. "Yes. I couldn't write back. You *know*, Graham. You were there that night. You understand, don't you, how hard it is to see you even now?"

He didn't understand at all. Seeing her was the easiest thing in the world. It was like breathing; it was what kept him alive.

"We were in it together, Jane," he said. "We always will be."

"You didn't wish him dead. I did. And now Alex doesn't speak."

"Are you saying one has anything to do with the other? That's ridiculous. Ned died because he drove drunk, and Alex doesn't speak because of some medical reason. You can't blame yourself."

"You talk like a man without kids yet," she said. "I blame myself for everything. For every cut Alex has gotten, every bad dream, every single silent moment. I blame myself for not fixing war and poverty before he was born."

It all came back then, the admiration of her passion, the yearning to touch her, the way, when he looked at her, there was no other light for miles. It was far too easy to torture himself; all he had to do was close his eyes to imagine his life differently, to pretend she had fallen in love with him instead.

He stood up and ran a hand through his hair.

"You should go," Jane said, as if sensing his thoughts. "Ginny will be wondering where you are."

His legs were heavy, but he made them move down the path toward his car.

"Graham," Jane called after him, and he stopped without turning around. "I'm glad you finally married Ginny. I hope you're happy."

The sincerity in her voice nearly crippled him, but somehow he found his legs. He walked to the car, then turned around. "I am," he said, then he went one step further, dropped the acid into the cut. "She and I would like to come over, bring a casserole. I'd like to meet Alex. What about next Sunday?"

Jane smiled at him. "That would be nice."

Tuesday afternoon after school, Jane and Alex walked the quarter mile from Pendleton Elementary to Pendleton High. This was the first cool day they'd had, and the air smelled of cider, from a press thirty miles north.

They headed into the gymnasium, where the indoor pool was seventy degrees, cool to the touch and heavily chlorinated. The Pendleton High swim team shaved their heads and bodies, but after the Mommy and Me classes that ran all summer long, every toddler and young mother in town sported green hair. The air reeked of bleach, which was the scent Jane always dreamed of when her dreams were good.

They had their swimsuits on under their clothes, and Alex stripped to his shorts in seconds. Jane took off her jeans and sweater and boots and eased herself down the steps into the shallow end. Alex ran to the diving board and bounced until he was four feet off the ground. He checked that she was watching, then did a perfect jackknife dive into the deep end.

He didn't come up forever. At first, she had panicked at his ability to hold his breath. Half a dozen times, she'd swum down to the drainpipe, only to find him clinging to it and smiling, for some reason exultant that his brain needed so little oxygen to survive. When his lungs finally ran out, he blasted toward the surface and took huge gulps of air.

Now, Jane just sat on the steps, fighting off the chill. She tried to look calm, but she couldn't help swirling the water. When Alex finally surfaced like a slick dolphin, looking at her through silent, intelligent eyes, she hid her sigh of relief with a smile.

She watched him swim back and forth, hugging the bottom, his stomach getting raw from contact. That was how she felt, raw, as if she were down to bone and this town had a sharp edge she kept getting snagged on. Just yesterday, she'd seen Ned's shadow dodging traffic on Main Street. She couldn't look at Jim's Mercantile without craving sparkling apple juice, which she had drunk every afternoon, waiting for Ned to get off work at the record store and come for her. She couldn't even walk across the Common without feeling slightly sick to her stomach; they'd made love on the grass, swung on the low branches of the maple trees; they had owned the park, except for Ethan Allen's statue, which in her mind would always belong to her and Graham.

She felt raw from wondering what was going to happen now. She had bought a 1979 Cabernet and a white lace tablecloth to set out when Graham and Ginny came over Sunday night, but she knew even the fanciest things would not make up for what she'd done. For nearly seven years, she had denied Alex a part of his family, Ned's part. She would have given him anything, yet she had talked herself into believing that meeting Graham would only make Alex miss someone he'd never known.

Now, though, when Alex swam past her grinning, when she would have let him swim forever if he would only ask her if he could, she knew the truth. She was afraid to let him look his uncle in the face. Graham had been witness to the worst of her, those lovesick days, when she'd literally grown thin and sick from love. She was afraid the things he'd seen — things a friend could pity but a son would scorn — had stuck like pictures on his eyes. Images of her rocking back and forth on their front porch till late in the night, even after it was obvious Ned wasn't going to show, her kneeling there in the woods, wishing spite as hard as she could. Or maybe, even worse, Alex would look at Graham and see Ned, and then they'd realize they'd been fooling themselves, that the grieving hadn't even begun.

Alex swam to her side and splashed her. She laughed and splashed him back. No matter what, she told herself, he deserved to have family. He deserved to know where he'd gotten his eyes. He deserved to know what he might sound like when he finally spoke.

"I'll race you," she said.

They both took off, in the strokes she had taught him three years ago — right stroke, left stroke, breathe. She had a longer stride, but sometime in the last year he had learned to kick so ferociously, he now swam past her easily. He had a body length on her by one lap, a quarter pool length by the time he reached the shallow end again.

"This isn't even fair anymore," she said, standing up and breathing hard. He splashed her, then dove underwater. He picked up lost rings and goggles. He never once closed his eyes.

Jane sat back on the step and watched him. There was a group of teenage boys in the corner of the deep end, and when their splashing got too loud, she too slipped underwater. The chlorine burned her eyes, but she kept them open. She watched Alex push off the side and swim a full lap underwater. He swam around her once, then took her hand as they rose to the surface together, breaking through to a world of crying babies and a teenage boy telling another to go to hell.

"Your uncle Graham's coming to dinner Sunday," she said. "And his wife. Your aunt Ginny."

Alex stopped splashing. He cupped the water, then let it fall between his fingers.

"Your uncle and I were best friends," she said. Alex looked up suddenly, his stare eating her up, as if she could never give him enough information. "He wanted to be a boat captain," she went on, "then one weekend the seventh-grade class took a field trip to Manhattan, and half an hour across the harbor, he got sick as a dog."

Alex smiled. Of course, he thought this funny. He had not been there after Graham had finished throwing up, looking worse than green, looking like a boy who was going to have to re-think everything and start all over again.

"So they're coming," Jane said, "him and

Ginny." She wondered why she was rattling on, and why, when Alex finally turned away and took off across the pool again, she was so nervous and so curious about what Ginny would think of her.

Three

The next afternoon, after school, Alex hopped on his bike once again. He had not even wanted the bike when his mother had given it to him a week ago — it was a ratty, girly old thing — but once he was on it, something came over him. A need for speed, a daring he couldn't come close to when he was standing on the ground. When he found a hill steep enough and shot down fast as a torpedo, a freak of nature occurred. The wind rushed through the gap between his two front teeth and, when he hit twenty miles an hour, it turned into a whistle, the sound of *Whish, whish.*

He was already halfway down the street when his mother came out on the front porch and called after him. Reluctantly, he turned the bike around and headed back.

"We'll go to the pool in an hour," Jane said. "And remember, don't go out of town."

Alex nodded and whizzed away. He went straight to Nate's service station and the old, feeble pump at the back. He had to fill the tires every day; he'd patched half a dozen leaks, but every rock and pothole punctured another one.

The pump was frustratingly slow; he tapped his foot against the black asphalt while waiting. He looked up; the heat had finally broken this morning and in its wake, the sky was a soft denim blue. The kind of sky that drew boys in, that made them ride for hours.

When the pump finally filled the tires, he hopped back on the bike. On fresh wheels, he nearly sailed out of the station. He checked for cars, remembered his mother's command to stay in town, then set off straight out of it in the direction of Pendleton Hill, where he'd been longing to go for a week.

As soon as he started pedaling up the hill, he knew he'd underestimated how tough it would be. He couldn't see the top; it was a steep, twisting grade, probably one of the largest elevation gains in western Vermont. His legs burned after ten minutes, but he would not get off the bike and push. Not when he slowed to a crawl and a jogger passed him, not even when a man with long brown hair, on the most incredible mountain bike Alex had ever seen, zoomed past him with a smile and a thumbs up.

He made his legs turn even when they were on fire. He didn't look at the white, square houses on either side of him, with their Smith and Hawken porch swings and specimen trees. He lowered his head and stared at the brown glass from shattered beer bottles. He counted cracks in the asphalt. He had no idea how much time passed, and he didn't care. As he neared the top of the hill, he welcomed the burning in his legs. He welcomed any fire, as long as it wasn't in his throat.

He pushed himself beyond what he'd thought he could do; he pushed himself all the way to the crest. Then he fell off the bike, onto the cool grass of someone's lawn, and closed his eyes in weary delight.

A minute later, a shadow passed over him and he opened his eyes. The man who'd passed him on the mountain bike was staring down at him and smiling. Alex sat up quickly and scooted back.

"Excellent ride," the man said. "Not many can make that hill."

He smiled again, and had the whitest teeth Alex had ever seen. White as fresh paper, as if they'd never been stained by anything. The man had pulled his long hair back in a ponytail and wore black cycling shorts and a neon green, body-hugging cycling top. He'd had on wraparound sport sunglasses while he rode, but now they were pushed back on his head.

"I'm Devon," the man said, offering his hand. Alex hesitated only a moment, then gripped the man's hand. It was large and warm and it hoisted him to his feet as if he were nothing but air.

"This is a KHS Montana Comp," Devon said, gesturing to his bike. "Ever seen one?"

Alex shook his head, and the man led him over to the bike. "It's a racer. It's got heat-treated tubing. Awesome no-tread tires, so you can pull some serious G's around the bends. I'm lining up sponsors. Gonna enter next month's off-road race in New York. I'm gonna be famous someday."

He laughed, and Alex smiled. The wind up here swirled in circles. A page from the comic section twirled in a mini-tornado.

"You want to get on?" Devon asked.

Without waiting for an answer, Devon lifted Alex onto the bike. His toes didn't reach the pedals. Devon held the handlebars and rode him around in circles.

"You'll ride one of these one day," Devon said. "I could see that when you were coming up the mountain. You've got the knack. You've got something, kid."

As Devon rode him around, Alex realized the man hadn't asked his name. He hadn't seemed to notice that Alex had not said a word. And for the first time in a long time, Alex's throat did not burn in the midst of conversation, he was somehow passing for normal.

"There's a dirt path through Hagerman's Woods," Devon said. "Your bike could take it. Then we'll come back and scream down this hill together. You up for it?"

Alex jumped off Devon's bike and ran over to his own.

The man laughed. "Excellent. It'll be nice to have some company for once."

They rode to Hagerman's Woods, where

Devon led them to a single track through the thick stands of birch and pine. The man did not seem to slow down for him, like most people did, assuming his silence had also made him weak. Alex rode so hard, mosquitoes couldn't catch him, and he never fell more than a turn or two behind. His bike was not made for dirt; his tires skidded on every rock and twig and the chance of falling thrilled him. Every bump and jolt bruised him, and every bruise felt wonderful.

They came out of the woods near Middletown Springs, then hooked up with Highway 140 that circled back toward Pendleton. Devon said nothing while he rode, and the *whish, whish* through Alex's lips got louder. Occasionally, Devon looked over at him and smiled.

They took the cutoff to Pendleton Hill and by the time they reached the crest, the sun was setting and the air thick with moths. They stopped and got off their bikes. The hill looked steeper in the oncoming darkness, and more deadly, which Alex thought was wonderful. He glanced over at Devon and smiled.

"There's nothing like going straight down," the man said. "Nothing cute or fancy. Just you against the road." He took off his helmet and tossed it to Alex. "Next time, you get your own."

Alex slipped it on. It was far too large and Devon helped him tighten the buckle so it wouldn't slip down over his eyes.

"All right then," Devon said. "Bombs away."

Alex took off first, and the wind was like a blast in his face. He expected more speed out of the chute, then all of a sudden there was a dip in the road and he took off flying. He rode like he never had before, straight down, fast as a rocket, keeping his hands away from the brakes, so he wouldn't be tempted to slow down. He knew any rock or slight irregularity in the pavement could kill him. He knew anyone who took that moment to look out their living room window would stare at him in horror. He knew his mother would die if she knew what he was doing, and all of those facts made the wind on his face feel cleaner and colder. His blood rose to the surface of his skin and burned his face deep red.

He heard the whizzing of Devon's bike beside him, but he didn't dare look away from the road. He held onto the handlebars so tightly his fingers went numb. Halfway down, when his tiny bike was picking up speeds of forty miles an hour, he opened his mouth and the *whish, whish* came out as a scream of pure joy.

Jane paced the living room floor, from the hallway to the window and back again. Esther sat on the couch, watching her.

"He wouldn't miss our swim," Jane said.

"He'll be fine. This is normal. This is what you say you want."

Jane stopped at the window and watched the

94

streetlights turn on automatically. The pool had closed an hour ago; their swimsuits and towels were in a bag by the front door.

"Don't be ridiculous," she said. "What I want is to never worry. To be sure he'll always be happy and healthy."

Esther laughed. "Oh Janie. You want what even God can't have."

Jane walked outside, where the moths were vying for the heat of the porch light, the fall air snapping at the ends of their wings. She sat down on the swing. She pushed herself up and back, then hopped off. She looked down the street, but saw no signs of Alex. The dark had a quiet danger; it seemed too much for a little boy to stand.

As she was turning to walk back in the house, she heard a man's shout and the whirring of bikes. She whirled around and saw them, two of them, turning the corner and speeding fast as cars down Sycamore Lane. As they flew beneath the street lamp, Jane recognized her son's face. His eyes were wide, his mouth set in tight concentration, and he looked as happy as she'd ever seen him. She reached out, as if relief were in the air in front of her, and tucked it over her chest.

They turned into the driveway and Alex immediately hopped off his bike. He took off a helmet she'd never seen before and tossed it on the mottled grass. The man on the bike beside him laughed.

"What a ride, hey sport?" he said.

The two of them only had eyes for each other, and Jane dropped her hand and stomped toward them. She reached Alex, touched the top of his head, and for a moment her worry and anger faded. He was safe, he was happy. He had so few pleasures in his life, she should not ruin this. Then she looked at the man, who she recognized as the stranger who'd moved into the house across the street. He was smiling so innocently, she realized he had no idea the things a mother could imagine, when left alone long enough.

"What do you think you're doing?" she asked.

The man sat back on his bicycle and looked at her. Even in the darkness, she could make out the gray of his eyes. She removed her hand from Alex's head and tucked it over her chest.

The man got off his bike and leaned it against the maple tree. "I was riding," he said quietly. "I was glad for some company. Your son's terrific. You should have seen him coming down Pendleton Hill."

"You went down that hill?" Jane asked, turning to Alex. "We were supposed to go swimming. Didn't you hear me when I told you to stay in town? You could have killed yourself."

Alex looked at his shoes, tears piling up at the corners of his eyes. She wrapped her arms around herself to keep from shaking him. She didn't understand anything that courted speed and danger. She didn't know what a mother was supposed to do with a son's tears.

"I was crazy with worry, Alex," she said. "Don't do that again. All right? Promise?"

Alex nodded slowly. Sometimes she envied her neighbors with their tough, obnoxious children, children they could yell at, kids so full of themselves they looked their parents right in the eye and said nothing they could say would ever touch them.

"Were you careful at least?" she asked, sighing.

Alex blinked back his tears and nodded more forcefully. He picked up the helmet and handed it to the man. He smiled a smile Jane had never seen in her life. Unselfconscious and pure — the kind given strangers who had never demanded a thing.

"I'll get you your own helmet," the man said. "Safety first, right, Mom?"

Esther appeared on the front porch, her hands on her hips. "Come on in, Alex," she said. Alex glanced at the man once more as he was pulling off his gloves.

"Go on," the man said. "We can ride again tomorrow."

Alex smiled delightedly, then ran past Esther into the house. Jane turned back to the man.

"Did you ask his name?"

"It's Alex," he said.

"Did you ask him anything? While you were

trying to kill him, did you notice he doesn't speak?"

The man stared at her. "I only noticed he could ride."

"Who are you?"

"Devon Zeke. I would think you'd already know that from Marjorie."

Jane looked over his shoulder at the Perfume Delight rosebush directly beneath the street lamp. It was still unearthed, its roots exposed, but where she had deadheaded the faded flowers, a single vibrantly pink one stood in their stead. It was well past the growing season, yet it had budded and bloomed, opening its petals as wide as a baseball. The pink was nearly neon, the color of hard candy.

She took a step toward it, then stopped. She felt the spiders again, crawling down her arms to her fingertips. She wiped her hands down her hips.

"Alex is special," she said at last.

"I know that."

"No. I mean he can't speak. You've got to tread lightly."

"Why? What does talking have to do with biking?"

Jane stomped her foot. "He's my son. I think I know what's best."

"Maybe. Or maybe you're too close to see clearly."

"Excuse me?" Jane said. "Are you telling me how to raise my son?"

Devon shrugged and she started for the house. "He's not to go up that hill again," she said over her shoulder, but he was suddenly right beside her, reaching his hand out toward her grandmother, who was still standing on the porch.

"Where are my manners?" he said. "I'm Devon Zeke. You must be Esther Gregory. Magician extraordinaire, according to Marjorie."

He held out his hand, but Esther ignored it. She squinted at him.

"Where is it you're from?" she asked.

He drew back his hand. "Here and there. Last known residence, Laughlin, New York. I was there for a race. Played a few gigs."

"Gigs," Esther said, then turned to Jane. "I'm going inside."

Jane started in after her, but Devon grabbed her wrist. "Jane Gregory," he said. He must have gotten her name from Marjorie, but still it surprised her, the familiarity with which he said it. He ran his thumb over her knuckles, then slid it between the gaps of her fingers.

She was shocked at how good it felt, but she still pulled her hand away. She'd learned a few things in seven years. How to live without being touched, for one. How to spot trouble.

"Okay," Devon said. "I should never, ever take him up Pendleton Hill again. I got it."

He was doing his best to look earnest, but she could see the smile tickling the corners of his mouth.

"I'm going," she said, but she just stood there.

"Maybe you and Alex could come over some time," he said. "I'll barbecue. I do that pretty well."

Jane stared at him. "Are you serious?"

"I'll play music. You like music, don't you, Jane?"

"No."

"Come on. Just a neighborly dinner."

Jane shook her head. She pushed open the screen door, then looked back at him. "Don't you see?" she said. "I was worried to death. I didn't know where he was. If anything were to happen to him . . ."

Devon said nothing and, in the twilight, she could not make out his features. But she saw what she thought was a gap between his feet and the floor, which meant he was light on his feet, and things like strong winds and repercussions probably passed right through him.

"I watched out for him," he said finally. "Let him live a little. He'll be all right."

She stepped into the house.

"How about Saturday night?" he asked.

She didn't turn around, because a smile was pulled from her despite her best intentions. "You're crazy."

"Sunday then."

"I've got plans."

"Well, I'm nothing if not patient. The following week then."

She closed the screen door behind her and looked at him through the mesh. "Don't bet on it," she said, but she knew he already had.

Ginny and Graham arrived at six o'clock on Sunday, Ginny toting a casserole dish of vegetarian lasagna and Graham a bottle of zinfandel.

"Wow, Ginny, you look great," Jane said. She gave Ginny a hug and Ginny kissed the air beside her cheek. Ginny still had eyes the color of lemon grass, but she was thinner than Jane remembered, and better dressed. She wore a Liz Claiborne wool suit. Jane ran her hands down her jeans, then smiled at her.

"This is so nice," she said.

Ginny put the lasagna in the oven, then looked around. Jane could see her taking in the peeling wallpaper, the scratched floors, every miserable piece of Sal's furniture. Though she agreed with the disgust on Ginny's face, she still had a desire to block Ginny's view, to protect what was left of her mother's wretched existence.

"I've got a lot of work to do," she said.

"You could take out a wall here," Ginny said, walking to the divider between the kitchen and living room. "It would open up this entire space, bring some light in."

"That might be beyond my budget."

"Call Bob Wylie," Ginny went on. "He's a retired contractor who can't quite retire. He'll give you a fair rate."

"Actually, I was thinking about remodeling the attic."

Graham looked at her, then uncorked the wine.

"Why on earth would you want to do that?" Ginny said. "You'll never recoup your investment. Nothing personal, Jane, but take a look out your front window. You'd be overbuilding if you added a second story."

Graham busied himself opening every cupboard, searching for wineglasses.

"Above the sink," Jane told him, then turned back to Ginny. "So you think it's a waste of time, then," she said.

"Well, not a waste. But certainly not smart business."

Jane nodded, because that sealed it. There were already a hundred reasons to remodel the attic and now she'd just added another: to prove Ginny wrong.

"Where's Alex?" Graham asked. He clinked the wineglasses together and both Jane and Ginny looked over at him. Jane reached out to touch his arm, then noticed Ginny's gaze on her and dropped it.

"In the backyard," she said. "Come on."

Her throat tightened as she led them out back, where Alex sat beside Esther on the picnic table, his hands in his lap. By the time she reached him, she couldn't have said a word even if she'd known what to say. Graham touched her shoulder as he stepped around her and knelt down in front of his nephew.

"You, sir," he said, "must be Alex. I'm your uncle, Graham."

He held out his hand and Jane watched as Alex slowly reached out and shook it. His eyes never left Graham's face. He studied each feature carefully, though he'd never seen a picture of Ned and had no idea Graham's eyes were wider set, his nose smaller, his lips a quieter shade of pink. He did not let go of Graham's hand.

"This is my wife, Ginny," Graham went on. Ginny smiled at him, then sneaked him a Tootsie Roll from her pocket. Alex smiled. Ginny had wanted three kids, as Jane recalled. Two girls and a boy, all with names starting with J.

"You throw a football?" Graham asked. "I see you've got a good set of muscles in those arms." He gripped Alex's upper arms, and Alex flexed for him.

"He's never played," Jane said.

"Well then, it'll be my pleasure to teach you. I was never a star running back like your dad, Alex, but I played a little in my day."

Jane watched Alex go still, then slip his hand into his back pocket the way Graham did. She went inside for the wine. By the time she came out, Graham was leaning over to kiss Esther.

"You have no idea how much I've missed

you," Graham was saying. "I've had this stomach pain . . ."

"Don't suck up to me, doctor," Esther said, but she was smiling. "I know damn well you never believed in my potions."

"Now, Esther."

"Virginia," Esther said, "I haven't seen you for ten years. You look lovely."

Ginny gave her a kiss, too, then slipped her arm around her husband's waist. Jane's gaze followed Ginny's fingers as they slid into the creases above Graham's belt, as if she'd touched him so much, she'd made them herself. Graham poured the wine and handed the first glass to his wife. He put one hand on Alex's shoulder, and Jane stared straight into the setting sun beyond Blackbird Peak.

She had a sudden desire to see the inside of their house, the curtains Ginny had picked out, the fabric of her sofa. She wanted to climb the trellis outside their bedroom window and peer in, discover the kind of room her best friend slept in, if he had covered his walls with paintings of the sea or settled for landscapes. She suddenly wanted to know if, after a nightmare, he got a stiff drink or curled into the warmth of his wife's back.

Jane sat down to drink her wine. Autumn was at their backs, a deep blue sky along the horizon and a loud wind blowing down Blackbird Peak. The backyard, though, was hot and still. Esther lit a candle, then stared triumphantly at

Jane when the flame did not even dance. Since nothing else was working, she was taking credit for trapping summer in their backyard.

"Just so happens, Alex," Graham said, "I've got a football in my car."

Alex jumped up, and the two of them raced around the side of the house. Ginny stood up too. She paced between the maple trees.

"It must be very hard," she said quietly. "Being back."

Jane sipped her wine. "I'm fine."

"But all the memories," she said, and turned to look right at her. "Of Ned."

If Jane were to stand up, she knew Ginny would come only to her shoulders. But there was no doubt about it; Ginny was standing on tiptoes, ready to fight.

"I haven't forgotten who I was engaged to," Jane said, "if that's what you're saying."

Graham and Alex came back, Graham tossing the football in the air. "All right, Alex," Graham said. "Go long."

Alex ran around the table toward the maple tree in the back. Graham threw a perfect spiral that landed square in Alex's chest. The force knocked Alex to the ground, but before Jane could get up, Alex had gotten to his feet, retrieved the ball, and tossed a wobbly pass back.

"Hook right," Graham said, and threw another, then another, and by the sixth pass, Alex was catching them, curling the ball into the crook of his arm. Ned might have been the star varsity running back, but Graham had been the quarterback of the junior varsity team. He had led them to a state championship in his senior year.

He called out patterns Alex could not possibly have known, yet the boy broke right and left, dodging imaginary blockers. And it struck Jane, as it hadn't for nearly seven years, since she'd first seen Ned's eyes staring up at her from her son's face, that Alex was Ned's child. Alex could do what Ned had done. He would grow up and become a star running back, as Ned had, and all the girls would fall in love with him. He would be the kind of man who broke a million hearts, including hers.

Jane set down her wine and stood up. "I'd like to play," she said. "How about you, Ginny?"

Ginny lifted one of her high heels. "Not in these shoes."

Graham smiled and sailed an easy toss in Jane's direction.

"You can do better than that," she said. Then she beamed the ball back at him.

It caught him in the stomach, and he fell down dramatically and gasped. Jane laughed and, when she looked over, Alex was laughing too. To normal ears, he made no sound, but Jane had tuned her hearing to his frequency alone and heard the hum in his throat. She forced herself not to react, not to ruin it. Graham got back up.

"You asked for it," he said. He pretended to rocket the ball at her, but after it left his hand, Jane knew he'd taken most of the force out of it. Still, the football came at her fast, and she had not caught a ball in years. She went to her right to catch it, and was snared by the memory of a star running back telling her to close her fingers around the webbing and bring it in to her chest.

Alex sat beside Graham during dinner and ate exactly what he ate, which even included zucchini. Jane drank most of the wine. By eight o'clock, the candle had burned down, Blackbird Peak had retreated into the black sky, and they were all shivering. They went inside and Ginny grabbed her purse off the couch.

"Wait," Jane said, the wine making her giggly. "You've got to see the attic first."

She walked to the bathroom and reached for the handle. She missed it a foot to the right. "Silly girl," Graham said softly, reaching around behind her and pulling down the trapdoor himself.

She was drunk, but not drunk enough not to make it up the ladder easily, or to find the flashlight she'd left up there the night before. After Esther and Alex had gone to bed, she'd brought up a new pillow and read the conclusion of *Jane Eyre* once more, the part she was always waiting for that began: *Reader, I married him.*

She flipped on the light and waited for

Graham and Ginny to come up after her. After some discussion below, only Graham did. Jane listened to Ginny's and Esther's muted voices through the floorboards.

"The heels," Graham said.

Jane nodded and ignored the heat in her chest, in exactly the same way she was going to ignore the desire to turn off the light, to stand in the dark with Graham and see what would happen. She was going to stand here, light on, and remember very clearly the night, after Ned had proposed, when she'd said to Graham, "Why don't you propose to Ginny? Come on, Graham, what's taking you so long?"

She might even have to turn the light into her eyes, until she was as blind as she'd been back then, seeing only what she'd always seen, a holder of robins, a boat captain, somebody else's true love.

"It's just like I remember," Graham whispered, stepping out onto the plywood floorboards. He bent down, then started tracing lines through the dust. "Remember?" he asked, looking up at her.

She crouched down next to him, so close his wine-laced breath was on her cheek. She made an X in the upper left square he drew.

"I wanted to live here," he said so softly no one below would be able to make out the words. He put an O in the middle square.

"This place saved me." She drew an X on the bottom.

He blocked her on the left, then looked around. "It really could be beautiful. I'd love to see how high up we really were."

Jane looked right at him. Her breath hurt going down, and when she heard Ginny pacing back and forth down below, she figured she deserved that. Finally, Ginny came to the trapdoor and called up. "Are you two through?"

Quickly, Jane made another X, and Graham an O, and then she finished the top line of X's and put a line through it.

"You always won," he said.

"You always let me."

They stared at each other a moment, then Jane stood up and walked to the ladder. She climbed down to the bathroom, where Ginny was waiting. When Graham came down behind her, Ginny pulled a cobweb from his hair.

"We need to go," she said.

"Just let me find Alex and say goodbye." Graham glanced once more at Jane before leaving.

Jane was closing the trapdoor when she felt Ginny step up behind her.

"Don't do this," Ginny said.

Jane secured the door before turning around. "Don't do what?"

Ginny grabbed Jane's sleeve and tugged hard. "I'm asking you to leave him alone. I'm saying it nice."

"Ginny, Graham's just my friend. You know that."

"I know what I know," Ginny said. "Leave him alone, Jane. He'd love me if you'd just give him a chance."

"You don't know what you're talking about," she said, but when they heard Graham's laughter coming from Alex's bedroom, Jane realized she probably did.

A few minutes later, Graham came out and she walked them to the door. "Thanks for coming," she said, and realized the effects of the wine had worn off abruptly. She was completely sober as she watched them walk hand in hand to their car.

She waited until they'd driven away before stepping out onto the speckled lawn. Autumn had swept in while they were inside, coating windshields with a light layer of frost and killing all the moths in one fell swoop. In the light of the street lamp, a steady stream of lifeless wings floated to the ground.

She didn't once look down at the grass. She didn't care if her feet matched the size-six imprints of green perfectly. Her grandmother could tell her she was leaking some kind of magic all she wanted, but Jane knew what she felt like; right now she felt magicless to the bone.

She walked to the end of the drive and looked at the Perfume Delight rose. Two more flowers had bloomed, more vibrant than the first. She felt a sudden urge to run, then told herself she was being ridiculous. She stepped up to the bush. She leaned over one of the blossoms, breathed in the fragrance, then staggered back. It smelled nothing like a rose, but of something deeper, darker, almost woody. Without thinking, she stared across the street.

Last night, when she'd gone to the attic, she had heard Devon Zeke's music. She had known the guitar strains came from him as surely as if he'd been in the room with her — every note had pierced skin and stained her blood a deeper red. When the music had stopped abruptly, in the middle of a love song, she had started trembling.

Just like the man, something about the rose seemed dangerous, although the truth was, when she looked closely, she saw it had no thorns at all.

Brenda Carlton had never done an impulsive thing in her life, but when she looked out her window one early October morning and saw fog so thick no one would recognize her in it, she tiptoed into the kitchen and took the scissors out of the junk drawer. Just in case her husband or daughter woke up early and found her gone, she left a note.

Don't worry, she wrote. *Everything's going to be fine.*

She had no reason to think so. She was thirty-eight years old, twenty pounds overweight, and her husband, Daniel, just to make things simpler, had taken to calling her

"Mom." She was a homemaker, a job she'd been proud of until this year, when her daughter Linda learned to braid her own hair and spell four-syllable words. Recently, Brenda hadn't imagined she was growing useless; she'd had no doubt about it.

Yet this morning, when she stepped out onto her front porch and was enveloped by the scent that had smothered the town the last few days, a scent as moist and rich as virgin earth, she suddenly remembered every kiss Daniel had ever given her. She couldn't help thinking that, just a few years ago, when she'd still had the nerve to put on satin negligees, her husband hadn't been able to take his hands off her.

She crept down Olive Street, then followed the scent two blocks, to Sycamore Lane. She had no idea what was happening, except that all the women in town had pink roses on their tables and had stopped watching soap operas. In the early afternoons, before their children came home, they all gathered at Jim's Alibi to drink those new amber ales. There had been a run on hair dye and massage oil at Taylor Drugs, and there was a rumor no husband had gotten to work on time in three days. The scent of that rosebush was driving people crazy, that's what Brenda thought. Wonderful crazy, the kind of crazy people felt only when they were eighteen or in love.

Since everyone seemed to be feeling it, it wasn't much of a surprise when Brenda turned the corner of Sycamore Lane and a figure emerged through the fog. Karen Wright was already at Jane's house, standing over the rose-bush, pruners in hand.

"I can't seem to stop crying these days," Karen said, wiping tears from her face. "Buck says it's the chain-saw racket and all the downed trees, but the truth is, I just keep imagining my whole life differently."

She knelt down and ran her hand over the roses, then snipped off the biggest one. "You know, I wanted to be a dancer," she went on, laughing uneasily. "Can you imagine that, with these hips?"

She ran her hands down her hips, which Brenda Carlton thought were actually exactly the size dancers' hips should be. Karen's husband was Buck Wright, a wealthy lawyer twenty-five years her senior who had three kids by a previous marriage, kids who openly admitted to anyone who asked that they hated their father's guts. Everyone in town heard what Buck said to Karen right after their wedding ceremony, that if she got pregnant, he'd leave her on the spot. Everyone knew Karen spent her afternoons out at Pendleton Pond, standing guard over the toddlers who had a tendency to wade in too far. Karen had saved four three-year-olds already, and four young mothers she couldn't bear to look in the eye were forever in her debt.

"Well, why not?" Brenda said. "Why not just

go to New York, or wherever it is a dancer goes, and see what happens?"

Karen clutched a neon pink rose to her chest and didn't seem to realize she was already standing on tiptoes.

Brenda bent down to the bush. She had never believed in hauntings, but then she'd never had a scent like this turning up everywhere — in her newly washed socks, in the beef stew she'd let simmer on the stove for eight hours. She had never spent so much time wondering what had possessed her to cut off all her hair, and just how expensive it would be to take her husband to a fancy hotel in Hawaii, alone.

She picked a tightly formed rose on the bottom, the edges of its petals frosted white. She snipped it off, then slipped the blossom in her jacket pocket, right next to her heart. Daniel hadn't French-kissed her for seven years, since Linda was born, but somehow she knew that if she waited until Linda went to bed one night and slipped into the new white negligee she'd bought at Miller's, he wouldn't even notice how much weight she'd gained. If she went to Taylor Drugs along with every other woman in town and stocked up on beeswax candles and Merlot, Daniel would stop playing golf every Saturday and tell her it was good to have her back.

The fog lifted just after dawn, in time for Esther Gregory to step out on her front porch and see two women scurrying down the street, pink petals streaming from their pockets. They clutched scissors to their chests and talked in voices so high-pitched, they sounded like girls. She looked at the rosebush, but it was so full of blossoms, the theft, like all the others, had done no damage at all.

She stepped off the porch. She had known what was happening long before the women of Pendleton started skulking around Jane's rosebush. Magic, like rain, had a scent all its own, and from the moment they set foot in Pendleton, Esther had smelled it on Jane. Jane herself would not believe it — she said it was only a wayward ocean breeze, a confused lilac blooming late and too sweetly. She said the dead grass that was reborn beneath her feet was some quirk of nature.

Esther stomped on the lawn, right atop Jane's green, size-six imprints. Why couldn't she have this kind of power? She, at least, would put it to some use. She'd make all the right people fall in love, she'd catch stars and stick them on the ceilings above babies' cribs, so they'd never wake up crying. She'd stop the seasons right now, when it was just beginning to get cold, when the leaves were scarlet and every time you took a deep breath, you couldn't help thinking you were the luckiest person alive.

She looked up, trying to spot the sun, but it no longer hit the roof of Rachel Simpson's house at nine-thirty, and it never cleared the top branches of the maple tree at all. It was getting colder every year, that's what Esther had decided. By November, not even three layers of Walt's shirts and a roaring fire would get her warm.

She spotted the newspaper in the driveway and headed toward it. As she was bending down, a weathered hand beat her to it.

She stepped back to find old Robert O'Brien, who lived next door, stooped before her. He held the paper with one hand and, with the other, reached around to the small of his back and hoisted himself up.

"You're not doing me any favors if you have a heart attack on my property," she said.

He smiled and handed her the paper. Esther could still remember when Salvation had come home from high school sulking, because she'd gotten Mr. O'Brien for chemistry. He had not been the hardest teacher at Pendleton High, only the most enthusiastic. None of his colleagues could understand his devotion to the periodic table, his whoops of joy when his volcano of half an ounce of ammonium dichromate spewed gray-green ash all over the room. His students carved obscenities into their desks during his animated lectures and thought his love of learning ludicrous.

Salvation had gotten a C, as Esther recalled, and then gratefully moved on to biology, where Mrs. McCarthy was nearing retirement and lectured straight from a book. Robert O'Brien had never yelled at a single one of his students until he lost his wife to lung cancer when she was only fifty. Then when sixteen-year-old Caleb Dreke came in late for the twenty-seventh day in a row, Robert threw a Bunsen burner at his head, walked out the door, and never came back. Since retiring, he had done nothing more scientific than put high-nitrogen fertilizer on his roses, as if it were science, not cigarettes, that had burned him.

Now, he handed the newspaper to Esther, smiling. He still had a full head of hair, all of it now a shiny gray. He had the nicest house on the block, with the nicest roses until Jane had touched the Perfume Delight.

"It's so nice to have you back, Esther," Robert said. "I never could understand why you moved to Middlebury."

"It was time to leave my daughter to her life," Esther said, tucking the paper beneath her arm.

"You'll be staying here now though."

"Only until Jane sells the house. I've still got my place in Middlebury."

Robert eyed the strange lawn, but said nothing. Esther knew he paid Tyler Ludlow five dollars a week to mow and fertilize his perfect patch of green. She'd seen him, after Tyler had gone, appraising the boy's work while folding the business section of the newspaper six times, making sixty-four perfect squares.

"I didn't get a chance to tell you at the funeral how sorry I was about Salvation," he said.

117

"I was here that day. I saw that boy coming a mile away. It was just dumb luck that he lost control right here."

Esther looked away. She'd gone to bed for a week after Salvation's death, and had planned to die there. She was not a melodramatic woman; it simply went against all laws of nature for a daughter to die before her mother. Then Jane had come into her room and told her Georgia Quail, somebody else's daughter, was in the kitchen vowing to kill herself over some boy who didn't deserve it. Esther had sighed deeply, then finally rolled out of bed. She had pushed past Jane to get to her apothecary chest, where she kept her balsam root and skunk oil which, when boiled down and held to a young girl's nose, was a surefire cure for foolishness.

"I'm sorry," Robert went on now. "I shouldn't have brought that up."

Esther looked at her neighbor. "I have to get back inside."

Robert tucked a hand up beneath his arm, but did not walk away. "Esther, I was wondering . . . If you're not busy, there's a fall garden show in Rutland today. I thought . . ."

Esther stared at him until he blushed. She had never been asked out in her life, not even by Walt. "I'm seventy-five years old, Mr. O'Brien."

Robert looked at her, his cheeks still red. His smile was so warm, Esther's hand fluttered around her chest.

"And still beautiful, Mrs. Gregory," he said.

Esther shook her head and started back toward the house. "I've got to be here for Alex," she said over her shoulder. "Jane's out looking for a new job. She was making seven-fifty an hour at the florist shop in Middlebury, but I told her she'd never get close to that anywhere here."

"It'll only be a couple hours. You'll be back long before Alex gets home. I'll pick you up at eleven."

Esther turned around, but Robert was already past the lilac hedge, out of earshot. She forced her hand away from her chest. She couldn't help wondering what her life might have been like if Walt had asked her to a garden show, if he'd taken the time to court her. She wondered what a little effort on his part might have done.

She'd met Walter Gregory when she was seventeen and he twenty-nine. It was at a small airfield outside Burlington, Vermont, where a hundred people were watching the first taxiing of the infamous all-wood Pon-du-liel. Suddenly, a slim black plane streaked out of the northern sky like a vulture. It headed straight for the Pon-du-liel and its terrified pilot, who stopped his taxiing, punched a hole through the cockpit window, and leapt to the ground. An opportune thing, it turned out, as the Pon-du-liel, or Flying Flea, quickly became known for killing most of its pilots in uncontrollable dives.

Just as the vulture seemed ready to crash, the pilot pulled up, leaving behind him a thick crust of black smoke and terror. While everyone around her was coughing and crying, Esther caught a glimpse of the pilot's face — black eyes and sunken cheeks, vulture-like too.

The reckless pilot landed ten minutes later, with a perfect touchdown. He climbed out of his plane, dressed all in black. Nobody went near him except for Esther, who had shimmied out of her mother's clutches.

"Bet you think you're something," she said.

He gave her one glance, then walked away. She was wearing her best dress, she knew for a fact she could not look any better, and his quick dismissal made her cheeks burn. Her hair was black then, and already fell to her waist. The boys in her senior class would rather run their hands through it than over her small breasts.

The vulture raised the hood over his engine and peered inside. He stood six foot three or better and was thin as a pole. Esther heard her mother calling her, but for some reason she would never understand, and would later regret, she walked the other way, toward the man's plane.

"What were you trying to prove?" she asked.

The man stood up from the engine and peered right at her. Esther, who had not known about magic then, didn't realize she was getting her first glimpse of it. Magic was a stranger looking in her eyes and her feeling like she'd known him all her life. Magic was knowing the man she would marry before he'd said a single word to her.

"Nothing," he said at last. "I wasn't proving anything. It was just something to do."

Esther's mother's voice became frantic. Someone was threatening to call the police. Esther ignored them. She took her future in her hands and molded it. She put a hand on the stranger's arm.

"Meet me at Bailey Park," she whispered. "At ten-thirty tonight."

Then she turned and ran. She ran right past her mother, and the waiting car, and off the airfield. She ran four miles without stopping, until she was breathless and aching and couldn't stand the thought of feeling any other way. She ran to her house and up to her room, where she locked her door and threw herself on the bed. She wrapped her arms around her pillow, closed her eyes, and cried at the inadequacies of memory, which could not conjure up a true enough picture of him.

He was forty-five minutes late that night, but Esther didn't mind. By the time he arrived she was furious, and she knew when she was furious she was beautiful. The man took one look at her and fell in love as far as he could, which turned out to be not very far at all.

"You're a little girl," he said, but his voice was soft. "What would I do with a little girl?"

Esther did not dare say the many things she wanted him to do, the things she'd thought of all afternoon, things she had found disgusting when the boys in her senior class suggested them. She did not tell him just the thought of his hand on her bare back sent her into hysteria. She simply marched up to him and jabbed a finger at his chest.

"Let me tell you something, whoever you are. No one shows up late to see me. And no one scares me, either. You could aim your plane at my heart, ram it straight through, and I'd never even flinch."

He threw back his head and laughed and Esther knew, if she had any sense, she would walk away before she did anything irreparable. But she hesitated, and looked up at the brittle stars for a moment, and by then it was too late. He had a hand on her shoulder.

"I'm Walter Gregory," he said. "Bush pilot."

"Esther Malden. Your future wife."

They left that night. Esther didn't call her mother for two days, until the police had combed the woods for her remains. She didn't call until her mother had no real say in anything, because Esther and Walter had just been married by a justice of the peace in Atlantic City.

She expected her mother to be furious, but all she said was, "Oh, Esther. I wish you'd thought this through."

But Esther had known then, as she knew now, that no one fell in love while they were thinking. Love happened on the fly, often when you were too young to handle it, or too old and crotchety to tell him it had been years since you'd met anyone so sweet.

Four

The day after Jane got the job at Mementos, the gift shop on Main Street, she asked over semi-retired builder Bob Wylie and led him into the attic.

"So see," she said, walking across the plywood floor, "I'd like to take out that trapdoor and add a real staircase. I'll need two skylights. One here, and one on the south side. Full insulation in the walls and subfloor. And hardwood floors. Knotty pine."

"Well, sure," Wylie said. "I could do that. Take me about a month, if the snows don't come early. We're talking seven, maybe eight thousand."

Jane stared at him. She had been afraid of what she would dream of in Pendleton, but it had turned out she dreamed only of this attic. In her dreams, the walls and floor were painted white and radiated their own light. The ceiling was glass and beyond it the sky never clouded over or turned to night. In every dream, Alex sat in the corner reading *Jane Eyre*, reciting each line out loud.

"Are you sure?" she asked. "Isn't there a way

to go a little cheaper?"

He shrugged and walked around the attic, his heavy boots testing the floor with each step. He looked back at her, sizing her up. "You could do some of the work yourself. Home Depot's got flooring that's already laminated. You could probably handle that. But the skylight? All that insulation and wallboards? I'm not so sure."

"I thought I could get two of those manufactured skylights. You know, the ones that come with everything."

"Everything but know-how," Wylie said. "You know how to cut a rough opening? Put in flashing? Sealant?"

Jane put her hands on her hips. "I can handle a saw."

"Sure, lady. And I could probably handle a tube of lipstick, but that doesn't mean I'm putting any on."

Jane stared at him, then started laughing. "All right. Tell me what I can do."

"Realistically, if you're willing to work day and night, you could lay floors, roll out insulation, tape the walls, paint. You're not strong enough to put up wallboards, and frankly, I wouldn't feel comfortable sending you up on the roof to cut out holes for the skylights, whether you can handle a saw or not."

Jane walked to the small window on the side. She had cleaned the leaves out of the slats, but still the light streaming in was paltry. She could block it with a single hand.

"From you then," she said, "I'll need two skylight installations, wallboards, a little wiring, and a real staircase. How much?"

Wylie stomped over to the small trapdoor and peered down. "You're gonna lose that second bathroom adding stairs."

"I don't care."

He was silent for a moment, figuring. "Three thousand," he said. "And that's giving you materials at cost, because I like you."

Jane turned around. "I'll take it."

He shrugged. "It's up to you. Me, I'd just fix up the downstairs and sell. You know this neighborhood. You're gonna overbuild if you add another story."

"So I've heard."

"And if the snows come early and hard, like they're supposed to, we're never gonna get those skylights in."

"So you'll start tomorrow."

"A couple days after. I've got a job to finish in Rutland."

Jane picked up one of the old pencils Graham had left there to mark where each skylight would go. Then she followed Wylie down the ladder and walked him out.

Downstairs, she had stripped four walls of yellowed wallpaper, and filled two Dumpsters with the old plywood cabinets she'd taken out of the one bathroom worth saving. She was going to replace them with solid oak, then put in tile and a pedestal sink. She had nine thousand dollars left in savings and she might not get to everything, but the things she did remodel were going to be perfect.

Esther walked into the living room after Wylie had left. "You're really going to fix up the attic?" she asked. She eased herself onto the couch.

"Don't say it."

"I'm not saying anything. You can be a fool if you want to."

"It'll be beautiful."

"Of course it will. I'm sure the people who buy the house will appreciate that."

Jane walked past her to the window. Alex and Devon were riding up and down the street, Devon showing her son how to do wheelies. They rode every afternoon; Alex had gotten tan and his hair was always windblown. She had taken him to the pool only once this week; every other day, he had been too busy riding.

"What do you think of him?" she asked Esther.

"Devon? Do you really want to know?"

By the tone in Esther's voice, Jane knew she didn't, but Esther just went on. "I think a man should have something better to do than spend all afternoon doing wheelies with a six-year-old. I think certain women should steer clear of men who look that good. Certain women are the kind who get stuck without even knowing it. They go on living in the same moment forever."

Jane stared at her grandmother. "No, really," she said. "Don't hold back. Tell me what you feel."

Esther laughed. "Work on the attic, Janie. Dig your hands into something more substantial than that man."

"You sound just like Mom did about Ned," Jane said. "She used to wipe down his seat after every visit."

Esther just stared at her, and Jane turned to the window again, for one more look. When the sun hit Devon on the back, he was no more than a flash of gold light. When he rode fast enough, he was just a blur, and she wasn't certain she was really seeing him at all.

When Devon Zeke came into Mementos, the only gift shop in Pendleton, Rachel Simpson, who worked mornings with Jane, dropped a five-pound crystal paperweight on her foot. It shattered, splaying glass shards everywhere, and when she bent to pick up the largest piece, she cut the palm of her hand.

"Oh God," Rachel said, as the blood dripped from her palm to the new beige carpeting Bill Burgis, the owner, had installed just two weeks earlier. "Oh shit."

Devon walked over to her and crouched down, and that's how Jane found them, Devon cradling Rachel's tiny wounded hand in his own.

"You got a Band-Aid?" he asked with a smile.

Jane walked quickly to the supply room. She searched the cupboards for bandages, but found nothing but paper towels and tissue paper and Styrofoam coffee cups. She wetted a few paper towels, then went back out front.

By then, Devon had led Rachel to a chair near the door and was still cradling her hand. The bleeding had stopped, so Jane used the paper towels to clean up the bloodstain on the carpet.

". . . so clumsy," Rachel was saying in her bird voice. Up until this moment, Jane had not found that voice irritating. Up until the moment Devon put his arm around her, she had liked her just fine.

"Rachel, if you're all right," Jane said, "you could help me clean up this crystal."

"Oh, I don't know, Jane. I'm still a little woozy."

Devon pulled her close and Jane bent to pick up the largest shards. She was sweating for no reason at all. She tossed the glass into the trash can, then went into the back, where it felt ten degrees cooler. She splashed water on her face, then grabbed the vacuum cleaner. By the time she hauled it out, Rachel was gone and Devon stood beside the cash register.

"I sent her home," he said. "She'd gotten blood on her shirt."

Jane vacuumed up the remainder of the glass, then took the vacuum back to the storeroom. When she finally came back out, Devon was helping himself to the seventy-five-cent pumpkin marshmallows on the counter.

She snatched one out of his hand and moved back behind the counter. When he just stared at her, smiling, she busied herself arranging the $1.99 fountain pens in a cup on the counter.

"Was there something you wanted?" she asked.

The door to the shop opened, then Devon's hand was suddenly around the pens, stopping her tinkering. "Actually, Jane, I've come to romance you. Believe me, you've never experienced anything like it."

She would have laughed out loud, if he hadn't dropped the pens in favor of her hand, and if she hadn't looked up to find Graham standing there.

"Hello," Graham said. He put his hand on the counter, then pulled it back. He turned to Devon. "I don't believe we've met."

"Devon Zeke." He squeezed Jane's fingers, then offered Graham his hand. He was taller than Graham, thinner, but when they shook, their hands were indistinguishable, both the same size, with the same gold hairs below the knuckles.

"The mountain biker, right?" Graham said. "I'm Graham Payton."

"Graham's the town doctor," Jane said. "You'll need him when you break something."

Devon laughed, dropped his hand, and turned back to Jane. "So, what do you say? A little dinner and dancing?"

Both men were watching her, so Jane walked out from behind the counter to straighten the glow-in-the-dark skeletons she'd set out yesterday. She hoped they couldn't see her arms, where all the hairs were standing on end. She could say no all she wanted, but the truth was, a man like Devon wanting her was lovely; it was like sun on bare skin.

"No," she said, without turning around. Graham jingled the key rings on the counter.

"Why not? I'm not a villain, you know," Devon said.

"I know," Jane said softly, though in fact she thought he might be. What else would explain the way he'd taken to standing on his front porch every morning when she came out for work, looking so good she had trouble getting the key in the ignition? Or the fact that, every night before she went to sleep, she couldn't help looking out her front window, just to see if he was there?

"Think about it then," Devon said. "Don't say no. Just think about it."

He turned back to Graham. "Nice meeting you," he said. He whistled as he walked out of the store.

Jane glanced at Graham, then quickly turned away from the heat of his stare. What she needed was a good, long walk. She needed to stop all this wanting; it was driving her crazy. She felt on the verge of all kinds of foolishness;

she felt capable of doing or saying anything, including asking Graham why he wasn't the one saying these things when he was looking at her like that.

"Well," Graham said at last, "so that's Devon."

He walked past her to the card aisle, leaving a trail of sweet aftershave and spicy tension in his wake. He stared at the sentimental cards, then picked one out without even reading what it said.

"I'll get this for Ginny," he said, walking back to the counter and laying it down.

Jane rang up the purchase and decided right then that, whether she believed in her grandmother's magic or not, she was going to try it. She had to do something; she was not about to start falling for the wrong man all over again, especially when there were two of them in this town. She was going to do something drastic, because as far as she could tell, love was a dead-end road. Either she crashed along the way or reached the end, stuck where a man could do what he wanted to her, trapped on a cul-de-sac, loving him. Even when love was good it was awful, it stung going down, it made her someone different, usually weaker, someone she didn't really want to be.

"Two-fifty," she said to Graham. He held out a five-dollar bill, but when she went to take it, he just held on. She looked up, but by the time she blinked, he had dropped it. He didn't even wait for change. He just picked up the card and walked out.

That same night, after Alex and Esther went to bed, Jane sneaked into Esther's apothecary chest. There were a hundred tiny drawers inside, each housing crushed leaves and vials of colorful liquids. None were marked, but Jane had picked up a few things these last seven years. She'd seen, for instance, how cherry bark soothed a cough and Ching Wan Hong, a mix of Chinese herbs, speeded recovery from burns.

She wasn't as clear on what to use to stop yearning, but she took a chance on witch hazel, fennel and wormwood. She crushed the leaves and seeds together, then steeped it in a tea. When it had cooled, she drank it down like a nasty shot of tequila, but half an hour later, she was still looking across the street and wanting something, though she wasn't exactly sure what.

When she started wondering what a kiss from a man like Devon would feel like, she got desperate and took out her grandmother's dead nettle leaves. She'd seen Esther do the same once, after she was robbed. She'd set fire to the leaves and blown the smoke into the cracks of the front door, to seal out unwanted intruders. Jane could only hope it would do the same for wanted ones.

She found the matches in a drawer and went to the front door. She felt stupid sitting on the floor, torching leaves. When she set the rug on fire, she knew she was in way over her head. Still, she blew the smoke toward the cracks, but the front door had warped and expanded over the years and the fumes came right back at her. She coughed and blew out the leaves. When she turned around, Alex was standing behind her.

"It's all right," she said, standing up and stomping out a tiny ember still glowing in the rug. "Don't pay any attention to me."

She led him back to his room and tucked him in. She tried to sit on the edge of the bed, but there was a hard lump beneath her. She reached under the covers and found a purple helmet, with two new biking gloves stuffed inside.

"Did he give you these?" she asked.

Alex nodded and grabbed them from her. She squelched the desire to snatch them back. Every time he went outside, he leaned so far toward Devon's house, he was practically already there. Every afternoon, he took a little longer to look at her when she spoke, as if she was becoming more and more dim.

"Tomorrow, we're going swimming, all right? No biking. No Devon."

She kissed his forehead, then walked out. By then, Devon had started playing his guitar, and on a still night like this one, the serenade penetrated every corner of her house. She threw open the front door and stomped out on the porch. Devon was sitting on his own porch stoop, stroking the strings.

"Good evening," he said, his voice a tickle, carrying easily across the street.

"Could you keep it down?" she asked. "You're driving me crazy."

He laughed and set the guitar aside. "Whatever you say, Jane. I'm at your command."

After meeting Devon Zeke, Graham did not change a thing. He went to work just like always, but all the babies cried when they saw him. Usually calm mothers got jittery and bombarded him with questions about SIDS and the rare side effects of immunizations. His most level-headed patient, Eleanor Stiger, came in complaining of chronic fatigue syndrome, then yanked her arm away from his grasp, as if he was the root of her suffering. Even Graham's perennially optimistic receptionist, Beth Shultz, said he was giving off some kind of bad energy, that every night for a week she'd gone home and cried for an hour.

By Wednesday, all but three of his appointments had canceled, and he took the afternoon off. First, he merely walked the clean streets of Pendleton, smiling at Josie Aberdeen through the window of her hair salon and stopping to hear what her kids were going to be for Halloween. When Randy Weaver headed over, he forced himself to debate the merits of the Farmer's Almanac prediction of heavy snows this winter. He caught a glance of himself in the sparkling glass of Michael's Bicycle Shop and was surprised by how unchanged he looked. He had not fallen apart, or lost any of his hair, or taken to screaming. Yet inside he felt he'd come undone. He imagined his veins and muscles had all unraveled. He was holding himself together by thin skin and sheer will alone.

He left the main streets of Pendleton and headed out toward the country. The maple leaves were finally outlined in red; a thin layer of them coated the streets and made running perilous. A group of tourists had poured out of their vans and were gawking even at this slight display of color, as if back home in California, everything was painted in black and white.

He turned away from them and headed south. He reached the Pendleton covered bridge before two o'clock, just as the sky turned ominous. The electric lantern hung at the entrance blinked on, but the interior of the bridge was damp and dark and, for some people, full of memory. Still, it was starting to rain, so Graham stepped in.

His footsteps echoed on the rotted floor-boards. Water dripped from one of the over-head pine boards while his breath flew up around him. He always took Highway 133 around town rather than drive this shorter route to 140. He had not walked this bridge for years, not since before Ned died, when he'd still had a faint hope of someday getting what he wanted. Everyone in town had come here at least once in their youth, to carve what they were certain would be lifelong devotions into the wallboards — devotions that were later often crossed out, or painted over, or occasionally pried out with crowbars. Pendleton's teens still came to make out in the center of the bridge, over the hole in the pine floorboards, so they could see the Poultney River streaming by beneath their lovers' breasts.

Years ago, when it was obvious Jane was falling for Ned, Graham had made a deal with God. As long as Jane did not carve her name alongside Ned's in the wood, Graham would still have a chance of winning her. As long as her love was only an idea, a hope, it would not be entirely real, and he might be able to talk her out of it.

He came monthly for two years. When he found *Matt and Sue 4-ever* and *Fuck U, Shithead,* but nothing about Jane and Ned, he grew bolder. He took to the woods, found a grove of birch trees, and into the heart of each carved *Graham loves Jane.* He even dared to skip a month at the bridge, after he and Ginny started going steady, then the next month came right from making love with Ginny, thinking it didn't matter what he found, that he was over that stupid crush anyway.

What he found were two lovers in the middle of the bridge, lying above the hole. He heard their breathing, the smack of their lips when they came apart momentarily for breath, then the deep, throaty *mmmm*'s as they kissed again. He heard the sticky slidings of their legs as they curled them around each other.

It was the hottest night in ten years, the Poultney River sending up shoots of steam, but that was not why Graham was sweating. He stood at the entrance and nearly turned around. He could just go home; he didn't have to know a thing. But something made him stand there. At sixteen years old, his whole life ahead of him, he had already had enough.

A car came around the bend, then entered the rickety planks of the old bridge. (There was a bet amongst the townspeople when the bridge would collapse and who would be on it when it did. The most popular date was December 31, 1999, with then eighty-nine-year-old Francis McGinnis driving across, still crying over his dead wife.) It took only a moment for the head-lights to illuminate the bodies curled together along the wall. They were plain as day, Ned and Jane, his long blond hair falling protectively over her bare breasts.

The car sped past and Ned burst out laughing. Many years later, Graham would wonder why he didn't just turn around and go home then. Why he had to go and make things worse.

He stomped across the bridge and right up to the lovers. He grabbed his brother by the hair and yanked him off her. "Get up," he said.

Ned leapt to his feet. No one in Pendleton would fight him, they loved him so much, so he often stole into Rutland or Middlebury, just to make some biker or pool shark mad. He was instantly on tiptoes, buck naked and ready to go.

"Jesus, Graham," he said, when he made him out. "You idiot."

He ran his hands through his hair and laughed. Jane was pulling Ned's T-shirt on. The heat from her body attracted fireflies, and by the time she stood up, they were swirling around her hair.

Graham pushed past his brother and grabbed Jane's wrist. "You want this guy? You really want him?"

For a moment, she said nothing. For a moment, he almost thought he had her. But then she looked at Ned, and Ned smiled; he even threw back his head and laughed.

"Of course she does," Ned said. "What the hell do you think we're doing here?"

"Graham?" Jane said. "Are you all right?" She touched his cheek, but he jerked away. He was a thousand degrees and ready to explode, that's what he was. He was thinking of murdering his brother, because even in the darkness, he could make out burn marks all over Jane's neck from Ned's kisses.

"I'm great," he said. "I'm fine."

He turned away while Ned got dressed, then

the three of them walked out of the bridge, into the starlight.

"Let's run," Ned said, then took off before they could answer. He ran around the turn and was lost in the trees.

"You're in love with an asshole," Graham said. "That's all I'm gonna say."

"Don't hate me," she said. "I couldn't bear it."

Then she took off running too, and Graham just let her go. He realized then there were going to be two parts to his life — when he'd had hope and after he lost it. That moment when Jane ran off after Ned was the dividing line. Three months later, when he found her devotion carved right above the spot where she had lain with Ned, it was anticlimactic. *Jane Gregory will love Ned Payton forever.* As if he didn't already know.

Now, Graham walked to the center of the bridge and stared at that carving again. On the opposite side of the bridge, carved just as deliberately, was this:

Ginny loves Graham. 1984

Ginny loved him enough to carve her name beside his. Jane loved Ned enough to carve hers. Graham had etched his name beside Jane's in a dozen birch trees. Ginny loved Graham, Graham loved Jane, Jane loved Ned, Ned was dead. It was like an awful song, like something Ned would have written.

Alex wanted to be haunted. He closed his

eyes at night and prayed for the sound of clanking chains. He wished a dead man's moans into his dreams. When he jumped out of bed every morning, he was not only disappointed, he was disgusted with the entire supernatural world — no furniture had changed positions, no pictures had turned upside down. Contrary to what he'd seen on TV, ghosts seemingly had no power at all.

He woke up wanting something so badly he tasted it. Even after downing a bowl of Frosted Flakes and brushing his teeth with the awful baking soda toothpaste his mother insisted on buying, the taste was still there, stale and gritty, like seawater. At first, he assumed it was just speech that he wanted, but the more he studied his uncle Graham for signs of familiarity, the more he rode with Devon, the more Alex realized what he really wanted was his father.

It was not only a stupid thing to want, it was unfair to his mother. Jane had given him everything, she cried into her pillow over him, but the truth was, sometimes he just got sick of the smell of her perfume. He wished someone would play in the mud with him and not gasp every time he climbed a tree. He couldn't help himself — he missed someone he'd never even known.

Jane, though, seemed to think that what he missed was friends, since he hadn't brought anyone home in over a month of school. What she didn't know was that most of the kids at

Pendleton Elementary were afraid of him; Billy Weinstock picked fights with him every morning, and three times those insults had degenerated into fistfights, of which Alex was up two to one. They took their scuffles behind the school, where Principal Dreyfuss couldn't stop them, and punched until they couldn't hold up their arms anymore. Billy had knocked the wind out of him once, but Alex had given him a bloody nose and knocked him out. When Billy had come to, he'd narrowed his eyes at Alex and said, "Next time, loser, I'm gonna fuckin' kill you."

So when Alex got off the bus after school one Thursday afternoon, and Billy Weinstock, along with two other boys from his class, was sitting on the couch in his living room, he froze. His mom walked out of the kitchen she was slowly demolishing — she'd already ripped out cabinets, light fixtures, and the old cast-iron stove.

"See, honey?" Jane said, smiling. "I invited some of your friends over to play. Why don't we all go on out back? I'll rake up the leaves and you guys can jump in."

Alex shoved his hands in his pockets. Billy had probably been dragged here kicking and screaming and that meant, Monday morning, he was going to go ballistic. It was going to be two to two, no doubt about it, and if he wasn't careful, this time there would be scars his mother could see. He'd give her yet another reason to cry into her pillow, to think she'd given birth to the ultimate loser.

"I'll get lemonade," Jane said. She smiled at Alex going by, but behind her, her hands were twisted into knots. Alex still stood at the doorway as Billy got up.

"You know what I heard, muteboy?" he said. "Your mom's a witch. Your great-grandma's a vampire. So what are you? The mummy?"

He stuck his arms out straight and the other boys laughed. Alex was dead for sure, especially when his mom came back in not only with lemonade, but with Twinkies no one under five ate anymore.

"You want me to get out the Lego's?" Jane asked. Alex dropped his backpack and walked right past her. He went into his room and locked the door. He didn't care if she killed him. If she grounded him for life, he'd consider himself lucky. It would give him time to bone up on his karate, to perfect a jump kick that would break Billy Weinstock's jaw, so he couldn't pick another fight for a long, long time.

All Jane did, though, was call the boys' mothers to come get them and wait an hour to knock on Alex's door. When he let her in, her hands were in fists, but she only wrapped her arms around him. "I just wanted to help," she said. "You'd rather I stayed out of it, right?"

He nodded. Jane sat down on his bed and

smoothed out his Batman and Robin comforter. "I wish that boy was right. I wish I was a
witch. I'd put a hex on him."

Later that night, he heard his mother digging around in Esther's apothecary chest, probably trying to find the ingredients for a good
hexing. He walked to his bedroom window,
knowing it would do no good. She and his
great-grandmother might have streaks of magic
in them, but for whatever reason, they'd never
been able to cure him.

His bedroom faced the street, where the fog
hugged the street lamps and every house on the
block was dark, except for Devon's. His was full
of yellow light and humming with rock music.
His front door quivered; one of the railings on
the rickety porch popped out and landed on
the frosted grass.

A woman Alex recognized as one of the wait-
resses at the Eat 'Em Up stumbled out Devon's
door, wearing only one of Devon's T-shirts.
This was the fourth night in a row the temperature had dipped below freezing, but all the
woman did was stretch her arms above her
head, then laugh when a strong hand pulled her
back inside.

Alex walked out of his bedroom. He opened
the hall closet and began searching through his
grandmother's boxes. They smelled of wet
cardboard and vinegar, and when he ripped off
the chalky masking tape, pale, dazed moths
flew right at him.

He tossed aside the first things he found —
dusty candlesticks, a homemade ceramic ash-
tray, dozens of bottles of long-expired cat medicine. He found a carton of Christmas decora-
tions his mother had made — newspaper
snowflakes with "Jane" written in wobbly script
on the back. Finally, in the largest box at the
back, beneath smelly blankets and pottery with
no apparent use, he found what he was looking
for: a large photo album and a stack of un-
sorted photos.

He went through the loose photos first.
There were pictures of a man he assumed to be
his grandfather, wearing cutoff jeans and no
shirt, his hands on his hips, a cigarette between
his thin lips. Black-and-white photos of his
grandmother in her youth, leaning against
funny cars, making faces at the camera, thin
and happy, like a stranger.

He set the photos aside and opened the
album. The first picture was of a baby, with
"Jane, September 1967" written in bold letters
beneath it. He turned the pages of his mother's
life. There were pictures of her father holding
her, his arm slung around her pudgy baby
stomach, but then, after two pages of empty,
yellowed squares, Dan Carey disappeared.
From then on, the photographs jumped not
months but years. There was one of Jane eating
chocolate cake on her tenth birthday, holding a
hand over her braces on her thirteenth, and
then with her hands on her hips, her gaze away

from the camera, on the day of her high school graduation.

Alex turned the final page and finally found what he was looking for. A photo of his mother and the man he instinctively knew to be his father sitting together on a stained blue sofa. His father's hair was the same color as his own, golden blond, his eyes the same dark gray. His arm was draped casually around Jane's shoulder, while her arm was fastened securely around his waist. He was leaning toward her and must have just whispered something funny because Jane's head was tossed back, her mouth wide open in a laugh. Alex touched the corners of her mouth; he had never seen her laugh like that in all his life.

He heard footsteps and turned to find his mother behind him, her robe clutched to her chin. He started to close the album, but she knelt down and put her hand on the page.

"Your father," she said quietly, with a voice so hoarse she still sounded half asleep. "Edward Payton. Everyone called him Ned."

Alex looked back at the photo. He ran his hand over it. He imagined he touched skin and bone. Jane stared over his shoulder. She reached out as if to stroke the photo, then suddenly closed the book. She tossed it back in the box.

"You should go to bed," she said. "You've got school tomorrow."

Alex's throat swelled, and when he opened

his mouth he saw steam coming out. He snapped it shut quickly, but his mother had not noticed. She just stared down at the closed book. He started back for his room, then halted when the rock music from across the street stopped abruptly and a guitar started up in its stead. The notes were played so slowly, Alex stood on tiptoes, anticipating each one.

"He plays beautifully," Jane said. "He always did."

Alex was a little scared, though he had no way of telling anyone, and probably wouldn't have admitted it if he had. He was scared, but it was his mother's hand that was trembling as she laid it on his shoulder. He jumped out from under it and hurried back to his room.

Jane brought Alex to Graham's office after school. She sat on a black vinyl chair in the corner of the examining room, her hands in fists as they'd been sixty times before. She'd been staring down at speckled linoleum for the last twenty minutes, while Graham poked and squeezed her son. Now, he shined a light into Alex's right ear.

"Perfect," Graham said, smiling at Alex. "The best-looking inner ear I've ever seen."

Alex smiled and Graham winked at Jane. She finally loosened her hands. With all the other doctors, she had imagined they'd find some sign of neglect on her son — an unwashed ear-lobe, caked blood from an old scab. She had imagined they would discover all her sins just by looking at the color of Alex's eyes.

But Graham was Graham. He had never commented on her bad haircuts or the way she had snubbed all of Ned's ex-girlfriends. She knew, if he found her sins on Alex, he would just keep them to himself.

"Open wide," Graham said, and stooped down to look at Alex's throat. Alex no longer gagged on tongue depressors. He didn't even flinch when tubes were inserted down his throat. Graham touched his cheek as he pulled away.

"Well, sport," he said, "why don't you go on out to Beth? She's got some Hershey bars in her bottom drawer, but don't tell her I told you. Your mom and I are just going to have a little chat."

Alex walked down the hall, and Jane followed Graham into his office. It was not well-lit, as if it had been just an afterthought. It was filled to the rim with patients' charts and reference books. Alex's thick file, which Jane had dropped off yesterday, sat on the top of his cluttered desk.

"I looked over everything last night," Graham said, picking up the file as Jane sat down. "I hoped I'd stumble across something the other doctors overlooked, but they've been very thorough. You've been thorough, Jane."

Jane leaned her head back and took a deep breath. "I didn't expect anything different."

Graham walked around his desk and sat

down. "Well, I did. I want to solve this for you. I'd do anything to solve this for you."

He was looking right at her, but she wasn't stupid. She stared over his left shoulder, at a smear on the wall. She had started out wanting only a fresh start for Alex, but now she wanted extra floor space, more sunlight, and working magic. With time, there was no telling where she would end up, but she was damn sure it wouldn't be wanting a man who slept beside someone else each night.

"I'm not giving up," Graham went on. "I can run a battery of tests. I'll have to send you two to Boston for a few of them, but I think it's worth a shot. There's a doctor there, Thomas Swirling. He's a specialist in —"

"Graham," Jane said, but then she stopped. She suddenly remembered that day she'd sat beneath Ethan Allen's statue with a dying robin in her hands. When she'd faltered, Graham had taken over. She'd been alone so long, she'd forgotten what a relief it was to let someone else hope for her. "Thank you," she said.

"Don't thank me until I actually do something."

"You already have."

And then she chanced it. She looked at him. By then, though, he was gathering together the papers of the file. She pushed back her chair and headed toward the door.

"So are you going?" he asked.

She grabbed the doorknob and did not turn

around. "Going where?" she asked, though she knew.

"Out with him. With Devon."

She breathed deeply, because the office was small and getting smaller, and she could hear Graham's own breathing, rising and falling sharply.

"I don't know," she said. "Maybe." She turned around and he was just sitting there, the file in his hands, staring at her.

"I'm only going to say this once," he said. "He's another asshole, Jane."

"You don't even know him."

"Oh yes I do."

The silence lingered, then Jane sighed. "If that's the argument, it's no good. I've had experience with assholes. I know all the lines."

Whatever he might have said was stopped by the telephone. Graham jerked, then picked it up.

"Hi, Scott . . . What? . . . Well, come on in then. I've got more samples."

Jane turned away and opened the door. She could feel him watching her, so she squared her shoulders and walked out. She found Alex on the floor beside Beth's desk, on his sixth Hershey bar. Two teenage girls sat waiting for their appointments.

She looked around the waiting room, filled with pictures of the babies Graham had delivered. She reached down and took Alex's hand.

"Come on, chocolate face," she said. "I'm tired. Let's go home."

Five

The Monday before Halloween, Graham heard about the renovation on Jane's attic from Kate Henderson, the cousin of Rhonda Wylie, Bob Wylie's wife. Kate was forty-seven, on her fourth marriage to a fourth struggling poet, and understood about ripping things apart so you could start fresh.

"She's gutting it," Kate said, while Graham gently turned the ankle she'd sprained. He wrapped it tightly, and prescribed 800 milligrams of ibuprofen.

"That's the only way to do it," Kate went on. "Take down everything. Strip the place clean. Then you can see what you've got to work with. Sometimes, frankly, you haven't got anything."

Graham walked to the small window without answering. He pressed his hands firmly on the sill, as if that would keep him there. He felt like a man denied bread. He could eat sweet fruits and vegetables, succulent meats, any kind of candy he desired, but after a while, the only thing he craved was bread. It became all he thought of. Brown crust that crackled in his mouth, chewy sourdough, the darkest pumpernickel he could find. His mouth watered at the smell of warm yeast, and pretty soon everything else he ate tasted like dirt.

He was a little scared, too, because something was happening to him. These last few weeks, he'd gone back in time instead of forward; his hair had started growing like crazy. One morning, he was going to wake up ten years younger and reckless; he'd wake up the kind of man who ate exactly what he wanted, who was willing to risk everything.

After his last appointment at three, he went home and took out his old scrapbook, the one with postcards of exotic places he'd planned to sail to, before he'd found out he was prone to seasickness. He removed one of Fiji, where he had planned to dock for a year or more, until he was brown as a coconut hull, until Jane, who would be there with him, would be so used to the sight of him, she couldn't think of living any other way.

He stuck the postcard in his pocket and stepped out into cool October sunshine. The sky was deep blue, a color usually found only in children's books. It was the kind of sky that made people wish they could live in one moment forever. Unfortunately, that moment was ruined when Devon Zeke cycled past in a blur of black Lycra, sending up dust. He wore a helmet, but his long brown hair sailed out beneath it. When he spotted Graham, he lifted his arm and shouted something indistinguishable, but probably slang.

Graham had hated very few people on sight. His first-year anatomy teacher, who gave pop quizzes halfway through a dull lecture, and Aaron Doheny, the meanest boy in his seventh-grade class, who had taken pleasure in holding people's kittens for ransom and pulverizing any boy with the nerve to look him in the eye. And, of course, Ned.

Add Devon Zeke to the list. Handsome, athletic Devon Zeke; the kind of man who made reservations before asking a woman out. Graham had heard from Beth who'd heard from her boyfriend, a waiter at a small French restaurant in Wallingford, that Devon had made reservations for two for Friday night. He just assumed Jane would change her mind about dating him and, unfortunately, so did Graham.

A dozen people saw him while he walked to Jane's, and that was the way Graham wanted it. He was going to prove to Ginny and to himself that there was nothing wrong with his friendship with Jane. He was going to prove he could handle it. But of course, as soon as Jane opened the door and smiled at him, he knew he could not.

She led him up the new staircase Bob Wylie had already roughed out in plywood. "We lost the bathroom," Jane said. "But who cares? It was awful. Wylie's going to cut all the treads and risers for me. All I've got to do is glue and screw them in. And look, Graham. The sky-lights."

He emerged in the attic, where Bob Wylie had already cut out a rough opening for one skylight and was sawing the second one straight through the old tin roof. Through the hole in the ceiling, Graham could see a single branch of scarlet maple leaves, and beyond that a sky the color of Fiji water.

"Amazing," he said.

"I know it. I'm going to use up all my savings, but I can't help it. It's going to be so beautiful."

"What can I do to help?"

She looked at him, then quickly turned away. "Nothing. I've got it covered."

"Jane, I want to. It's all right."

She said nothing, and over the screeching saw, luckily, she could not hear the pounding of his heart. She couldn't make out the lie in his short breath.

"Well," she said, "Wylie's going to do all the flashing work on the skylights. But I'm going to add molding on the inside. And then there are the floors. I've got to insulate, then put down the floorboards. The lumberyard already delivered the wood."

The wood and rolls of insulation were in the corner. Graham headed that way, but then Bob Wylie suddenly stopped sawing. "Look out below," he shouted, then dropped a chunk of ceiling through to the floor. He peered down through the new hole.

"Hello, doctor," he said. "Thought I might find you here. Rhonda wanted me to give you this." He reached into his pocket, then dropped down a check for Rhonda's last mammogram.

Graham didn't look at Jane as he stooped over to get the check. He wondered when everyone in town had figured out he loved her. If it had been obvious from the start, or something more subtle, like the wild ivy no one had noticed until it smothered the south wall of the mayor's office. He had the idea they just took it for granted, him loving Jane; it was one of those things that defined the town, like the statue of Ethan Allen, and Francis McGinnis's sorrow, and the birch trees in the woods.

"All right, Jane," Wylie said. "I should have the exterior work done by tonight, and I'll rough in the glass, if it doesn't rain. You can start on your molding after I've sealed it, although I told you —"

"I know. I'm just wasting my money with these extras."

"Well," Wylie said, standing up on the roof, "you are."

"Let's start on the floor then," Graham said. "We'll need to pull up this plywood, then lay out the insulation. Have you got a crowbar?"

Jane pretended to look at him, but he could see her gaze landing on something over his left shoulder. "I don't want to do anything that would —"

"You're not. I'm going to be your friend, Jane. I'm entitled to that, at least."

And then she looked at him. She looked at him with something in her eyes he'd never seen before, something that almost made him take a step toward her before Bob Wylie dropped one of the skylights into the hole, startling him. He took a deep breath, but all she did was walk past him and grab the crowbar.

He stayed at Jane's for three hours, ripping up plywood. He still expected to beat Ginny home, but when he walked in she was there, breading pork chops. When he came up behind her and kissed her shoulder, she stiffened. She did not say a single word, and he realized he did not have to tell her he'd been at Jane's, because someone in town, obviously, already had.

They ate dinner in silence. A neighbor knocked on the door while Graham was trying to slice through an overcooked pork chop. Ginny got up slowly, her smile in place by the time she reached the door. She chatted gaily for ten minutes, then gave the woman the two eggs she'd come to borrow. When she finally came back to the table, her lips were pressed so tightly together, her skin cracked in the folds.

After dinner, Graham did the dishes and got in his pajamas. He usually went downstairs to read, but tonight he just got into bed. He knew it was only a matter of time before Ginny came to him.

She surprised him by waiting half an hour to

come upstairs. When she finally walked into the bedroom and found his book set aside, his gaze right on her, she tapped her small foot on the floor.

"So here we are," she said. "Again."

Graham ought to have refuted her, but he couldn't. He just tossed back the blanket and sat on the edge of the bed. The other day, he'd let Josie Aberdeen cut his suddenly luscious hair, but she had just dropped her scissors and run her fingers through it instead. His neighbors had told him how good he looked lately, but when he looked in the mirror, he cringed. He hadn't been able to stop himself from going to Jane's today, and he knew he wouldn't be able to stop himself tomorrow or the next day, either. A downside to getting younger every day was that he kept forgetting about consequences. He chafed against his wool suits and hectic work schedule and the notion that things might not turn out as he planned.

Ginny opened her mouth, then closed it again. She had no idea her mountains of unasked questions were electrically charged; it was that and not the wind that made sparks fly from their fingers whenever they touched. Her unquenched curiosity made her hair stand on end, and her frizzes had gotten worse, so that now not even gel could hold them in place.

His unsaid answers were her polar opposites. *No, I don't know why I love her. I'd give anything, anything, to love you instead.*

She came and sat beside him and, where they touched, there was a faint pulse of steady electricity. Graham reached for her and they both jerked from the shock.

"I'll tell you something," Ginny said, standing up. "I don't care if you're doing anything in that attic or not. It's infidelity enough, just being there."

She walked to the mirror above the dresser and stared at herself. She tried to tame a curl by sliding it behind her ear, but it just popped out again.

"I don't mean to hurt you," Graham said.

"I know that. You're a good man, Graham. Why do you think I married you?"

Her civility stung; in truth, he wanted her to rant at him. He wanted her to give him an easy out. But Ginny was no fool. She got undressed and went into the bathroom to brush her teeth. Then she got into bed beside him and turned out the light.

Graham closed his eyes. He'd begun wishing again. Just today, he had wished Ginny would come to her senses and leave him, to save him from having to be the villain. He had wished himself someone different. Someone capable of violence and complete and utter hopelessness, so he would stop all this pointless wishing.

"You're a good man," Ginny said. In the darkness, he could not make out her face. "But that doesn't mean I'm an idiot. Don't push me, Graham."

He held back his question, *What if I do?*

The next day, after laying out the floor insulation in the attic during his lunch break, Graham hopped in his car and rushed back to the office for his afternoon appointments. He slowed on Main Street, looking for a place to park, then saw Devon Zeke standing on the sidewalk, blood pouring down his right arm. Marjorie Dumas and Sandy Aberdeen were clucking over him, not even caring if they got blood on their hands, as long as it was Devon's blood.

Graham actually stepped on the accelerator for a moment, and the burst of speed felt like a shot of adrenaline. Then Sandy spotted him and waved, and though his foot was heavy on the gas, though he could have kept on driving forever, the doctor in him moved his foot to the brake. He pulled into a spot in front of his office.

He got slowly out of the car. Devon leaned against the office door, smiling, as if the blood were painted on.

"Well," Graham said, when he walked up beside him.

"It's nothing," Devon said.

"Don't be silly," Marjorie said, tightening her fingers around his good arm. "It looks like a serious laceration."

"You were riding?" Graham asked Devon.

"Out near Hagerman's Woods. There's an

awesome hill. I went over the handlebars. It's nothing but a little scratch."

Graham nodded. He picked up Devon's arm and studied it. It calmed him to take in the amount of blood, the set of the bone, to use his trained fingers to figure nothing was broken.

"Let's go inside," Graham said. "Ladies, if you don't mind."

Sandy and Marjorie stepped back reluctantly. "We could assist," Marjorie said.

"It's not necessary."

"Thanks for the concern." Devon flashed them his smile. Sandy started giggling and couldn't stop. Graham led Devon into his office, where Beth jumped to her feet to help, and a sixteen-year-old girl stared wide-eyed at Devon's long hair.

Graham ignored them. He walked to the back examining room without saying a word, leaving Devon to follow. He found antiseptic and bandages and tossed them on the counter. Devon sauntered in a few seconds later.

"A doctor," he said, shaking his head. "See, that's something I could never be."

No kidding, Graham thought, taking in Devon's mangy hair, the way he could not hold his hands steady even when he was standing still.

"I could never work in an office," Devon went on, hopping up on the table and holding out his arm. Disappointingly, he did not gasp when Graham soaked his skin with antiseptic.

160

The cut was, actually, quite deep, and Graham decided it needed stitches. It gave him an unprofessional delight to open the drawer with the needle and thread. "I'm just not cut out for it," Devon went on.

"What are you cut out for?" Graham held the needle up to Devon's eye. "Besides Jane?"

Devon grit his teeth as Graham injected the area with mepivacaine, minus the sodium bicarbonate that would have reduced the burning. The two of them stared at each other as they waited for the anesthetic to take effect.

"You're married, right?" Devon asked.

Graham felt a momentary flutter, but his hands remained steady. "Yes."

"Right. Well, that means you're cut out for mortgages and babies and nine to five. Me, I'm cut out for biking. And music. For a life without any strings attached. I'm gonna make it big. There's no way around it. Once you're in the top ten on the pro circuit, it's nothing but riding and women and more money than you could ever spend."

Graham inserted the needle into Devon's arm without asking him if the anesthetic had numbed the area. Devon did not flinch, however, and Graham quickly stitched up the wound. He found it amazing that he could concentrate with so much blood rushing to his head. He kept thinking, *I will not do this again. I will not.* But no matter how many times he thought it, Devon's arm remained fixed in his grasp, the man did not go away.

Finally, he finished the stitches and put a bandage over the wound. "I'll take them out in ten days or so."

Devon hopped off the table, but instead of walking to the door, he stared at Graham's diplomas on the wall.

"It's something to be proud of," he said. "Being a doctor."

Graham threw away the needle. He busied himself cleaning up the counter and sink. He noticed a spot of Devon's blood on the floor and found the ammonia and began to scrub.

"You look like you're in good shape," Devon said. "You ride?"

"A little."

"You up for a race up Pendleton Hill?"

Graham stood up slowly. "I don't think so," he said, though what he was thinking was, *Don't you see? We're enemies.* He looked in Devon's eyes and realized he didn't see, just as Ned hadn't seen. People like that, so used to being adored, could not recognize hatred when it was right in front of them, staring them down. If Graham was another kind of man, he could punch Devon in the nose. The man would never see it coming.

"Your choice," Devon said, turning to go. Graham started to take a deep breath, but then Devon turned back. "You and Jane," he said. "What's the story?"

Graham reached back and found the counter.

"There's no story. We're childhood friends. She was engaged to my brother."

The man leaned against the doorway and smiled cockily. "So she's got no ties."

"None that are still alive."

Devon studied him. "Well, that leaves her to me then."

And though Graham wanted to argue, he had no case. He had to stand there and listen to Devon whistle as he walked out of the office.

The morning after Graham helped her rip up the floor, Jane took a cup of strong coffee up to the attic. Through the skylight, she could make out a deep purple sky and maple leaves the color of fire. The hard frosts of the last week had killed off most of the lawns on Sycamore Lane, except for hers, which had shot up another four inches.

She stood directly beneath one of the skylights when the last star winked out, and a purple stamp of light touched the attic floor for the first time. The whole room turned smoky; she could see floating dust and spider webs and a handprint so high up on the wall, she had no idea how it had gotten there.

She set down her coffee and picked up the box of finishing nails. Bob Wylie had left her a ladder, and she climbed it to nail in the first strip of molding. But before she could hammer in a nail, her eye caught something blue in the old cubbyhole in the corner. She climbed back down and walked over. The blue was a post-card pinned to the wall, a photo of Fiji, with a white sand beach and two sets of footprints leading to the water. She untacked it and turned it over. Written in Graham's hand was a single line, *Wish you were here.*

She leaned against the wall, the postcard tucked over her chest. It wasn't hurting anyone but herself for her to just think about it, but that was pain enough. She slipped the postcard in her back pocket and took a deep breath. She wasn't about to start wanting a good man who would never leave his wife. She wasn't about to start wanting another Payton.

So that afternoon, when she rushed back to the attic after Graham left to see if he'd left her something new, she knew she was in trouble. Especially when she spotted the postcard of Jamaica, and the room suddenly got hot. She was walking a tight line on Wednesday, when she found the one from the Galapagos Islands, with the words *So happy we may never come home* on the back.

Thursday morning she woke at dawn, feeling desperate, so she drank a straight shot of chokecherry sap, which could make a colicky baby coo. But the syrup did not soothe her a bit. When she turned quickly, she caught an extra shadow behind her, six feet tall, with rock-star hair. She was anything but calm, because she knew if she even thought about falling in love again, Ned was going to stop her.

She stepped out on the porch to get some air. A boy in a neon blue jacket that looked exactly like the one she'd bought on sale at the Gap whizzed past on his bike. For a moment, Jane did not do a thing; she knew for a fact Alex was asleep in his bed beneath a down comforter. Then she recognized his helmet, shiny black with purple stripes down the sides. When Alex disappeared around the corner, she stood with her hands on her hips, the late October air slicing through her cotton pajamas.

Alex came around the block a moment later, his face a mask of concentration. He hunched over the handlebars of his Schwinn, his tiny legs worked the pedals. She called his name as he passed, but he didn't even look up. He took the turn at a forty-five-degree angle and she rushed down the porch steps, but by then he was upright again and flying away.

Jane looked across the street and saw Devon standing on his own porch, watching Alex ride. He was smiling, and when he saw Jane watching him, he gave her a thumbs-up.

She marched across the street. "This is your doing."

Devon cocked his head. "You mean turning him into an athlete? Sure, I'll take the credit for that."

By that time, Alex was coming around again. Devon stared at her son intently, as if willing him faster, and she stepped between them. A woman went to pieces over a look like that;

what kind of spell would it weave on a little boy? Alex whizzed around the corner, not even seeing them.

"It's five o'clock in the morning," she said. "He should be in bed sleeping."

"Look, I didn't tell him to ride. When I came out to get the paper, he was already out here."

Jane searched his eyes, but she'd never been good at spotting insincerity. All she saw in them was recklessness, and desire so strong she stepped back.

"I made reservations at the Renaissance for tomorrow night," he said. "Booked us the table in the corner."

"I'm not going."

"Come on, Jane. Stop playing doctor and have some fun with someone who's free and clear."

Jane wrapped her arms around herself. Alex came around the corner yet again, like a racer in a criterium. This time, he looked up as he neared the corner and his feet flew off the pedals. For a moment she thought he might fall, but he merely came to a stop beneath the fiery maple.

Jane started across the street. She couldn't get to Alex fast enough, though she didn't know why, though he'd only been out riding. The helmet fit him perfectly; it brought out the gray in his eyes. He leaned away when she reached him, but she managed to touch his cold, red cheek.

"It's awfully early for riding," she said.

Devon's footsteps came up behind her and Alex pulled away from her touch.

"Excellent," Devon said. "Perfect technique around the turns."

Alex smiled and Jane wished he would stop. He didn't know it yet, but that smile would cost him something. One day, when Devon was long gone, he would remember how he'd felt when he'd stood on this street corner. He would remember the exact color of the sky and how good it felt to adore someone. One day, when he smiled, it would fill him with a sense of loss.

Alex lifted his bike over the curb and dropped it on the mottled grass. Devon touched Jane's arm. He did it so confidently, she forgot to pull away. He did it so softly, the rest of her skin grew jealous and achy. He was right about Graham. She was only playing at loving him; only Ginny knew how to do it right. Devon, on the other hand, just gave her something to do. He was so lacking in tenderness, Jane couldn't help wondering what a little time and effort would do. He was so irresponsible, so flawed, she just assumed she could make him better.

"Now about tomorrow," he said.

He brushed the back of his fingers across her cheek and Jane figured there must be times when a woman simply wanted to lose her mind, because she was losing hers. She was cold as ice, but she just kept standing there.

167

"What time will you pick me up?" she asked.

That night, Esther's medicine jars broke in half and her aloe and ribwort salves all turned to powder. There had been no tremors or strong winds, yet when she opened her apothecary chest, hoping to relieve the sting of a minor sunburn, shattered glass and worthless brown dust flew at her. She stepped on a two-foot-high mound of debris, and left an imprint of size ten-and-a-half army boots.

She closed the door and clutched her robe to her neck. She shivered, not only because she was losing her magic, but because she didn't like the looks of things. Glass only shattered on its own for a reason, usually in protest of an icy winter or when someone was about to get hurt. Every bulb in the back bedrooms had blown in the last two days — always a sign of turmoil. And she'd been dreaming again, not of Robert O'Brien, who had taken her to the garden show and out to lunch every day for two weeks, but of Walt — except he wasn't the Walt she'd known. The Walt in her dreams wrote her love poems and kissed her like he meant it. The Walt in her dreams was both wonderful and a fake, and she woke up every morning with her hands still clutching her pillow and the smell of sulfur in the air.

She walked through the dark house to the front door. She stepped out onto the front porch, into smoky October midnight. All the lights were on in Devon's house. Music seeped through the cracks of his doors and windows, something from a decade back, something bassy and shrill.

Jane had agreed to go out with him Friday night and Esther didn't even want to think about everything that could go wrong. At dinner, Jane had said, "I'm entitled to feel something again."

"Of course you are, Janie," Esther had told her. "But not the same things all over again. Don't do that to yourself."

"I'm not doing anything. I'm going out with a man, that's all. Alex likes him. I like him. It's better than sitting here afraid of wishing."

"Honey," Esther had said, "I've told you a thousand times, wishes are just wishes, they have no magic in them. We've all wished our men dead at one time or another. If wishes worked, there wouldn't be a man left standing."

Jane had set down a spoonful of peas and walked out of the room.

Now, Esther walked across the street. Aside from her creaking bones, she made no noise when she walked, not even when she stepped on an empty Marlboro soft pack. She stepped right up to Devon's front window, where a red candle burned. She peered in, expecting to find the usual disarray of bachelor furniture — concrete blocks for tables, a torn brown velour couch, a metal dining table with two wobbly chairs. Instead, she saw nothing, or close to it.

Just an old radio blaring, a guitar leaning against the wall beside Devon's mountain bike. An expanse of hardwood flooring that looked naked and strange without a coating of furniture.

"*That's* interesting," she said.

She turned to find Devon standing on the porch, watching her.

"Hello," he said, smiling. He was wearing his usual attire of jeans and a white T-shirt, despite the ice that coated the grass. He leaned against the rickety porch railing, which showed no sign of straining beneath his weight.

Esther said nothing. She walked right up to him, beneath the yellow porch light, and stared into his face. She studied the line of his chin — more flat than Ned's had been — and the bridge of his nose, oversized but less hooked than the Payton boy's. His cheeks were too high, the top of his head a good two inches too tall, but there in his eyes was everything she needed to know. There was Ned.

"I know," she said.

"Good thing," Devon said, "because I sure as hell don't."

He still smiled. Ned had smiled a lot, too. What was there not to smile about when you were twenty-six, handsome, and everyone was in love with you?

"You can't fool me," Esther said.

"Esther" — Devon held up his hands — "you've got me at a loss here."

Esther moved even closer and sniffed him. She had a nose for evil, but she did not smell it on him. The problem was, she couldn't sniff out anything clear. One minute he smelled of mint leaf, almost bitter, then the wind changed and she caught a whiff of something noxiously sweet, like bad milk.

She looked through the open door to his living room. It made her heart race, all that emptiness, just a vast expanse of scratched hardwood floor. It made her ache to be young again, to take off her shoes and slide over it in a pair of cotton socks.

"You're not even living here," she said.

"I just don't need a couch. It's not a crime."

"How do you survive? Where does your money come from? How do you eat?"

Devon still smiled, but he didn't meet her gaze. He looked over her shoulder at her house. She imagined he looked straight through walls, to where Jane and Alex slept, that he sent a message that infected their dreams.

"I get by," he said. "You want to come in? I think I've got some coffee."

Esther just stared at him. She'd seen a lot of things in her lifetime, and she had rarely been surprised. But Devon surprised her, if only because she didn't know what to make of him. He made her doubt her judgment, and wonder if she was just getting old and carried away.

"I want you to know I'm on to you," she said firmly, though doubt lifted the hair on her forearms. "I know who you are."

"Who am I, Esther?" Devon asked.

She didn't like the hint of curiosity in his voice. She didn't like anything about this. She turned and walked toward home.

"Esther!" Devon called after her, but she kept on walking. She walked faster than either of them had thought she could.

Jane wasn't lying when she called in sick Friday morning. She woke with a pounding headache and a mouth so dry her voice was a whisper. The moment she had said yes to Devon, a strange thing had happened: She had remembered what it had felt like to be touched by Ned. No one would believe this, but Ned had the ability to stop thinking of himself and concentrate solely on making someone else happy. He used to spend half an hour just stroking her legs, tickling the undersides of her knees with his tongue. When he finally did make love to her, he never came before she did, and he never let her come fast. He brought her to the brink and back half a dozen times before letting her fall. And when she finally exploded, he held her against him so tightly, pieces of her melted into him, so there was never any chance that she would leave him.

She drank three cups of coffee before Alex even left for school, but still couldn't produce more than a faint hum. After the bus drove away, she took a fourth cup of coffee to the couch by the window.

It wasn't long before Josie Aberdeen and her visiting sister stealthily made their way to the rosebush, scissors in hand. They each cut off a perfect pink rose, then held the blossoms to their noses. They tucked the roses down into the clefts of their bosoms, close to their hearts.

For a moment, Jane felt a jolt of electricity surge through her. She'd seen the green footprints on the lawn. She'd smelled the scent of rain on her. The homemade potions might not be working, but when women walked into the gift shop, she found herself picturing the faces of the men they'd left behind twenty years ago. With absolutely no facts at all, she knew if they met up again, they'd find their hearts' desire.

She knew, though she didn't dare admit this, that magic wasn't a choice. Like love, it came in its own way, from out of the blue.

She finished her coffee and walked into the bedroom. She closed her eyes and reached into her closet. A woman on the verge of bad love made all kinds of bets with herself. *If I pick out the black dress,* she told herself, *then it's all right to want him. If I grab the sweater Alex bought me for Christmas, then I'll call the whole thing off. I'll never look him straight in the eye again.*

Jane plunged her hand into her clothes and came out with a white blouse she hadn't worn for years. She clutched it to her chest and sat down on the bed.

If he calls now, it means he'll be faithful. If the

sun strikes the top branch of the maple tree, I'll let him kiss me, but if it blinds me, I'll know to turn and run. If my grandmother comes in to warn me away again, I'll swear off love forever, and this time I'll mean it.

Her grandmother had gone out for a walk an hour ago, so Jane just sat with the blouse clutched in her hand. Finally, she put it on, along with an old pair of blue jeans, and let herself out of the house.

She had no intention of doing anything special for her date, but once she got in the car, she headed straight to Rutland. When she reached downtown, she took a pass down Kendall Street and saw a dress in a boutique window that stopped her cold. It was six cascading layers of green chiffon and silk, so airy Jane knew it would slip right through a man's fingers. She parked and went into the shop.

The salesgirl found her size and when Jane slipped the silk over her head, she knew it was the softest thing she'd come into contact with in years. She stepped out of the dressing room, and the salesgirl, no more than nineteen, clapped her hands.

"That is so gorgeous," she said. "If I could afford it, I'd steal it off your back."

Jane looked down at the price tag and gasped. It was four hundred and fifty dollars.

"I know," the girl said, "but just look at yourself. No man will be able to resist you."

Jane looked at herself in the full-length

mirror. The color made her eyes seem a richer blue. The truth was, she had not noticed they were blue for years. She had not worn bright color for years. Her closet was full of grays and khakis and browns.

"Four hundred and fifty," Jane said, but already she was imagining Devon coming to the door and seeing her in this. She imagined them going somewhere to dance, and him slipping his arms around her waist. She imagined feeling the press of his hands through silk, the tickle of his fingers as he traced the scoop neckline, the warmth that spread deep beneath her skin when he ran a hand down the curve of her hip.

"Jane Gregory?" a woman said. Jane turned from the mirror and saw a vaguely familiar woman walking into the store. "Jane, is that you? My God, it is. I can't believe it."

The woman hugged her, and Jane wracked her memory for a name. The woman's hair was bleached blond and she was about Jane's age, with large brown eyes and rings on every finger of her right hand.

The woman drew back. "You look beautiful. But then you always did. I used to be so jealous of you." She looked her over. "I take that back. I still am."

Her laugh was high-pitched and quivery, and her name finally came to Jane. Lenore Renfrow. Lenore had transferred to Pendleton High as a sophomore and was never happy again. She had been chubby then, and had not gotten her braces off until she was a senior, which was too late to do any good. Lenore had sat alone every day during lunch, pretending to read. If Jane recalled right, Lenore had had a serious crush on Hank Valerio, who had gotten a snake tattoo at sixteen and spent most of his time in shop class.

"How are you, Lenore?" Jane said, brushing the silk down her arms. She was down to her last two thousand dollars in savings, and she still had a ton of work to do on the house. Blowing five hundred dollars on a dress should not have been an option, but suddenly it felt like exactly what she needed to do. She wanted to buy a dress she would wear only once. She wanted to not feel like a mother for five seconds, to look so good a man couldn't take his hands off her.

"I'm fine," Lenore said, though her hands fluttered around her face, saying something else. "Married Jim Canter. We lived in Pendleton awhile, then moved here. Divorced after five years. No kids, so thankfully we didn't ruin anyone's lives but our own. Know any eligible men?"

Her laugh got even more unsteady, and Jane had an urge to wrap her up in her arms. She remembered once, in their senior year, urging Lenore to say something to Hank, but Lenore had not had the nerve. Her braces had been like gates on her mouth.

"Whatever happened to Hank Valerio?" Jane asked.

Lenore went still. "God, I haven't thought of him in years."

"You adored him."

Lenore looked at her. "I did, didn't I?"

"You never gave him the chance to adore you back."

"Oh Jane, that kind of thing happened to you, not me. Hank would have laughed in my face."

Jane put her arm around Lenore's shoulders. She felt another spark of electricity, probably from the swish of silk against Lenore's cashmere sweater.

"Call him," she said suddenly.

"Don't be silly." Lenore stepped out of Jane's embrace. "It's been twelve years."

"So? Lenore, I'm telling you, call him. I'm absolutely sure of this."

Lenore stared at her, as stunned by Jane's certainty as Jane was. But all of a sudden Jane knew that if Lenore called Hank, he would remember her. She knew he would not be married and in fact lived just twenty minutes away, in Ludlow. He worked as a welder, stayed home most Friday nights, and would like nothing more than to buy Lenore a good steak dinner. This all stood before Jane like a picture.

"Well," Lenore said.

Jane twirled left and right. The fabric was so luxurious, it brought tears to her eyes.

"Maybe I will," Lenore said. "And you . . . you should buy that dress. Who are you trying to impress? After Ned died, I figured . . . Well, I went to the funeral. I was hoping to see you, but everyone understood it was too much for you. Everyone agreed you'd never fall in love again."

Jane dropped her hands to her sides.

"Everybody felt for you back then," Lenore went on, "when Ned and Carol . . . on the night Ned died, of all things. What you must have gone through, knowing she was the last woman he touched."

Jane went very still. She looked at herself in the mirror. Actually, the sleeves were puffed too high and the waistline was snug; she suddenly realized this dress had been cut for a much younger girl, for someone like the salesgirl who was on the phone now, repeating everything they said to someone on the other end.

"I didn't realize that was common knowledge," she said.

"Oh, you know Carol. Blabbermouth if there ever was one. At the funeral, she was sobbing like a widow. She told anyone who would listen that Ned had told her he was leaving you for her, that he loved only her. But we all knew she was just blowing smoke. Ned might have been a bastard, but he was a bastard who loved you. Anyone could have seen that."

Jane had not realized before how heavy the dress was, as if each of those layers was another thing to carry. She walked back to the dressing room and closed the door. When she took off the dress, her skin was pink and puckered where the elastic had bitten into her.

"I hope I didn't upset you," Lenore said over the half-sized door.

"No," Jane said. "Of course not."

"I think I'm going to call Hank," Lenore said. "I really think I am. What harm can it do?"

Jane got back into her jeans and white blouse. She flung the dress up on the hook and opened the dressing room door.

"Aren't you going to buy it?" Lenore asked.

"No."

"But you looked so pretty in it."

Jane shrugged and walked out of the store. The wind had picked up and tasted of apple smoke, of somebody else's cozy morning. She raised her chin and walked to her car.

Lenore ran up beside her and took her arm. "I shouldn't have said anything about Ned."

"No, it's all right." Jane realized the headache she'd had all morning had finally disappeared. It had been a long time since she'd known anything as clearly as she knew this: She was not going to do this again, not with Devon or with Graham. She didn't care how many postcards Graham left for her to find, or how much Devon looked like Ned. She didn't even care if Alex adored them both. She would never again feel hysterical over a man.

"It was a long time ago," she went on. "You can say whatever you want." She opened her car door and slid in.

"I'll call you," Lenore shouted as Jane started up the engine, "if anything works out with Hank."

Jane nodded, then drove off quickly. When she glanced in her rearview mirror, Lenore Renfrow was already making her way to a phone.

Six

The night Jane would have gone to the Renaissance with Devon, she and Esther and Alex went to the Eat 'Em Up for dinner instead. Jane ordered chicken-fried steak, but even after she'd eaten everything on her plate, she still felt hungry. Alex had pointed to a hamburger on the menu, but when it came he only poked at it. Jane noticed he had a bruise just beneath his left cheek.

"What happened here?" she said, reaching out to him.

He leaned away and shrugged. She would have said more, if he hadn't started smiling like crazy. He looked over her left shoulder and started laughing his silent laugh.

Jane turned and saw Devon standing in the parking lot outside the diner, leaning against his bike. His hair was pulled back in a ponytail, and he was making faces at Alex. When he saw her, he stuck out his tongue, then headed toward their window.

"Oh, shit," Jane said, but all Devon did was tap on the window, right beside her ear.

When she looked at him, he was smiling carelessly, as if he'd never lost a moment's sleep to panic. He put his hand up on the glass, right beside her cheek, the gesture of a man who eventually got everything he wanted. She jutted out her chin, but he just blew her a kiss. He walked back to his bike, did a few wheelies in the parking lot, then rode off.

"Well," Esther said, "that's that. Good job, Janie."

Jane was not so sure. She had not bought the expensive dress, she had stood up Devon, but those were just the things she'd done. It didn't mean she'd stopped feeling things.

She stared out at the parking lot, where Peter Aberdeen and his gang were passing around cigarettes and staring at a carload of girls who had driven in from Middletown Springs. Beyond them were skid marks in the parking lot Ned had left one summer night, and beyond that, at the mayor's office across the street, there was the headless statue of Thomas Pendleton, its head at the bottom of the Poultney River, where Ned had flung it.

Esther stared at her. "You all right, Janie?"

Jane looked up. "I've been taking your herbs. Trying to come up with some combination to stop all this wanting."

"You could have asked me. Or I suppose you think I'd just mess it up."

"I don't think that." Jane reached across the table to take Esther's hand. "It's just that it sounds ridiculous. I'm getting them all confused. All three of them."

Esther squinted at her. "I thought you didn't believe in ghosts. Or magic."

"I don't know what to believe."

"Well, I do," Esther said. "I'd tell you if you'd just ask."

Jane sat back. "All right, I'm asking."

"Good." Esther glanced at Alex, who was watching them both closely, then tapped the table with her thick, pasty fingers. "Love's contrary. You can yearn for a man most of your life and then, in a heartbeat, start despising him. Just when you think you're set, that you've got it all figured out, it'll start making you sick to your stomach. Love's just not a thing you control."

Jane blinked, then followed Alex's gaze. The girls had gotten out of their car and were pairing off with the chain-smoking boys. A few couples disappeared behind the huckleberry bushes, to make out in the thick, soft grass. "So I'm stuck then," she said.

"Oh no," Esther said. "That's not it at all. There are still plenty of things you can do."

When they got home, Esther showed Jane how to grind up a powder of rock salt and bone meal, and how to light a flame to vinegar and then splash the burning liquid onto the powder. "Ghosts won't cross it," Esther said. "Don't ask me why."

Jane took the powder across the street. She was trembling, but still she hunched over in the moonlight and sprinkled the mixture around the perimeter of Devon's house. She didn't look up while she worked; though she very likely did not believe in any of it, she still imagined she might see a handsome blond ghost standing on the lawn, furious with her for caging him.

She crept back to her house and waited in the shadows of her porch. Two hours later, when Devon rode up the street, Jane knew she could no longer feign disbelief in her grandmother's magic. Because when Devon did not fall down gagging, when he simply rode smoothly over the line of white, she was more than a little outraged.

It had gotten so Graham could fool even himself. When he stepped out his front door on the second of November, he believed, as Ginny did, that he was going to walk to his office. He had a number of files he wanted to review. He had to check his inventory and reorder supplies. Besides, Ginny had been studying him too closely over their respective bowls of Multi-Grain Cheerios, and he wanted to be alone.

The air was getting thicker every day, loaded down with apple smoke and the soot from the slash piles people left unattended. There had been a few snow flurries yesterday, causing a run on antifreeze and hot chocolate at Jim's Mercantile.

Graham jammed his hands in his pockets and

managed to kid himself all the way past Main Street, where he turned north instead of south toward his office. But once he reached Sycamore Lane and walked right over Jane's lawn and kept going, all pretenses stopped. He crossed the street to the corner where every woman in town had already informed him Devon Zeke lived, and stood on Devon's icy grass.

A few minutes later, Devon opened his front door. He wore only jeans, and his hair was wild. He crouched down to pick up the newspaper, then saw Graham.

"You're here," he said, as if this visit had been expected and, in truth, Graham was late.

Graham nodded. There were certain moments you walked toward your whole life. As he stepped forward, he knew where the cracks in Devon's sidewalk would be. By the time he reached the porch, he felt he'd already stood on it a hundred times.

"You want to ride some single-track?" Devon asked.

"I've only got a ten-speed."

Devon laughed, then threw the paper into the house. It slid across an empty hardwood floor and landed in a heap of newspapers, all still bound and unread, piled near the kitchen.

"That's no problem," Devon said.

Graham turned his back while Devon picked the lock on the back door of Michael's Bicycle

Shop. He had every intention of turning Devon in, of waiting until he had actually committed a felony, then running across the street to Nate's service station to call the police. Instead, when Devon broke the lock, Graham took one step, then stopped and leaned against the tree.

"Be back in two minutes," Devon said, then disappeared inside.

Graham checked the street for cars. He had no compassion for Devon; he just wanted to see how far he — the town doctor, the good husband — would go. He wanted to see how bad he could be.

Devon was back out in two minutes, a sparkling gray Manitou FS in hand. He smiled as he reset the lock in the back door. He wheeled the bike over to Graham.

"They're not going to notice their best bike is gone?" Graham asked.

Devon shrugged. "You're just breaking it in for some lucky customer. I'll get it back to them eventually."

Graham shook his head, but he also stepped on the bike. Devon's own bike rested against the back door, and he hopped on.

All morning, Graham had wanted to ask him about his date with Jane — the date every single one of his patients had informed him was last night. But now that he had the chance, he just kept quiet. After all this time, he knew what he could and could not stand. He didn't even look at Devon squarely, in case an image

186

of Jane kissing him had stained his eyes.

"Follow me," Devon said.

He was a blur within seconds. Graham rode after him, wishing the mountain bike's tires were not so bulky, and that he'd ridden for speed instead of exercise these last few years. He kept Devon just in sight as the man headed up Pendleton Hill.

A quarter of the way up, Graham's thighs burned, but he kept riding. He had ridden this hill dozens of times, but always at a slow pace, checking his heart rate every fifteen minutes. Now, he rode as fast as he could, which wasn't nearly fast enough because when he was only halfway up, Devon was already at the top, staring down at him. He pedaled harder, his heart thundering in his chest. He pedaled until his lungs were on fire, and his right leg cramped in agony. When he made it to the top of the hill, where Devon was leaning casually against the Franklins' white picket fence, he started right down the other side.

"Come on, then," he called over his shoulder, then spit out a mouthful of bitter saliva.

He flew down the hill, cold wind crystallizing the sweat on his face. His legs twitched from pain and overuse, and he stretched them out above the pedals. Devon took just that moment to whiz past him, pedaling hard. He took the quick turn into Hagerman's Woods.

Graham thought about just riding past. He could stay on the highway, set his own pace, make the loop through Middletown Springs and be back home in time for lunch with Ginny. But when he reached the woods, for reasons he would probably never understand, he hit the brakes and turned.

His wheels had just hit dirt when he heard the car behind him. He would not have paid any attention to it if he hadn't heard the sputtering that came when it hit thirty, just like Ginny's Volvo. It slowed, but he did not dare turn around. He rode so hard, he was sure even Ginny would not recognize him; she'd think him a daredevil, a man with nothing to lose.

He rode heedless of rocks and dips. He took hairpin turns at twenty miles an hour, and sometime in the next hour his hair began to fly out behind him. His hands conformed to the grip on the Manitou's handlebars. He didn't even think about braking. Sometime in the next hour, Devon was no longer a blur; he was a steady target just ahead and Graham was gaining on him.

Jane slept late Saturday, long past the time Alex turned off the latest post-apocalyptic cartoon and walked to the Common with Esther. Long past the roar of lawn mowers, making a final sweep over yellowed lawns. She slept and dreamt of the attic, which now had two finished skylights and R-30 insulation in the ceilings, walls, and floors. She dreamt the room was a boat, the clouds a sea, and she and Graham

188

and Alex were sailing to an island in the South Pacific, where Alex's voice had washed up on shore.

She woke to knocking. She stumbled to her feet and felt blindly around in her closet for her terry cloth robe. She put it on and walked out of the bedroom.

The knocking got louder, then suddenly stopped. Jane opened the front door and found Graham heading back down the steps.

"What time is it?" she asked, running her hand through her hair.

He stopped and turned around. His hair was disheveled, the tip of his nose bright pink. "One thirty. Were you taking a nap?"

Jane stared at the line of white across Devon's yard, then stepped back to let him in. She walked into the kitchen praying for coffee, but her grandmother had apparently thrown the remainder out that morning. She cursed and fumbled with the coffeepot. She stuck in a filter and made the coffee strong. She didn't wait for it to finish; when there was enough for half a cup, she poured it, regardless of spills.

"So," Graham said, leaning against the kitchen wall she'd repainted light tan, "did you have a good time? Ginny heard from Hannah who heard from Marjorie that he was taking you to some Italian place last night."

Jane looked at him for the first time and noticed he'd been sweating. There was a line of dirty perspiration down his neck. He put his hands in the front pockets of his jeans.

"We didn't go." She sat down at the table. Graham hesitated, then walked up behind her.

"Devon stood you up?"

She could sense him right behind her; she felt his breath on the back of her neck. "Amazingly enough, I stood him up."

His breath against her came long and slow, then he walked down the hall, studying the pictures of Alex she had put up. She finished her coffee, then went to stand beside him. He smelled of sweat and adrenaline and wood smoke. Over these last few weeks, his hair had not only gotten longer, his smell had changed too, gotten richer, tangier. Pretty soon, she wouldn't be able to make out a single familiar thing.

She looked up at his face and saw he wasn't staring at the pictures at all, but straight at her. He suddenly took her hand. "Jane," he said.

She yanked her hand away. If he was going to talk that softly, she just wouldn't listen, not when Ginny was half a mile away, not when Ned was turning up everywhere, even in his brother's eyes.

She stepped back and pulled the collar of her robe tighter around her. "Is that why you came? To grill me about Devon?"

He walked past her to the living room window, which had finally come clean, strangely enough, with carburetor fluid. He touched the sill she had scraped down to wood. She had bought five gallons of "Matte Sunflower" at the paint store yesterday. She was going to roll it on thickly, until there was no chance any of the old stains could leach through.

"Actually," he said, "I came to ask you all on a picnic. The weather's changing so fast, we need to enjoy it while we can. Will you come?"

He turned around, and though she was clear across the room, she knew to step back from a look like that.

"Only if you call Ginny and invite her along."

Graham looked away. "Of course."

Jane and Esther made tuna fish sandwiches while Graham stood by the phone. He twirled the cord around his finger when Ginny answered.

"Honey," he said, "I'm at Esther and Jane's. We're thinking of going to Lake St. Catherine for a picnic. Why don't we pick you up on the way?"

Ginny said nothing for a long time and Graham held his breath. He waited for her to ask him why he wasn't at the office. He waited for her to mention seeing him this morning on a stolen bicycle on the other side of Pendleton Hill, or perhaps even to toss him out.

"I've got to go into work," she said instead. "Hal called. There's some crisis on the Beverman account. I couldn't get to the park until at least three."

"Come then, at least." Graham suddenly

stopped twirling the cord. He thought of Ginny this morning, watching him over her Cheerios, trying to read his face. He thought of how easy it had been to tell her he was going to the office, when deep down he'd known he would never get there. He thought of the kind of man he was turning into, the kind to watch out for. He thought of how that made him smile.

"All right," Ginny said.

Graham hung up and leaned against the wall. He shouldn't be here. He shouldn't have asked Jane a thing about her date, and she sure as hell shouldn't have told him she'd canceled it. Now everything was up for grabs. He was letting himself feel things, imagining all sorts of improbable happy endings, even though he knew desire could turn a man inside out, it could eat him alive.

"Everything all right?" Jane asked.

"Yes," Graham said, though somehow he knew it wasn't. Sometime between this morning and now, he'd crossed over another dangerous line.

The cottages along the lake were packed with families and Labrador retrievers. Little girls begged their fathers to let them fly stunt kites, boys shot plastic arrows out in the woods. A silver sedan with California plates pulled into the lake parking lot just before Graham, and the family just sat there and stared. The eleven o'clock news had a fall-foliage report and for

192

all of October, the weathercasters had sounded panicked. The leaves had never taken this long to change before. They blamed it on the Gulf Stream current, on El Niño and global warming. But there was no denying that once the change came, it was the best show in decades. The leaves looked like drops of blood, the sky was blue enough to blind. It was the time of year when a woman couldn't walk out the front door without crying.

Jane helped Esther down to the grass near the lake, while Graham and Alex brought the food and blanket. The family from California now stood by their car, the two teenagers holding on to the hood, woozy and slow from so much fresh air.

Esther sat down on the blanket. "Beautiful," she said.

Graham made himself see it. Thirty years in Vermont had dulled his color vision. In the last few years, even during autumn, everything had just looked gray. The rich palette seemed a part of someone else's world, someone who'd gotten everything he'd wanted, someone who'd been happy.

Alex took only one bite of his sandwich before Graham felt him studying him again, surveying each hair and line.

"Your father was taller," he said, and felt Jane stiffen. "Blond, with eyes just about the same color as yours. He and I were nothing alike."

"You were more handsome," Esther said, opening a thermos and pouring out a cup of hot tea. Graham laughed, it was so ridiculous.

"You were," Esther went on. "That boy needed a haircut."

Graham looked at Jane. She was staring at the lake, watching a Labrador dive in again and again for sticks.

Alex picked up the football they'd brought. Graham followed him down to the shore, then played catch with the boy he had always assumed he'd hate. He called out patterns and led Alex away from the deep end. Somewhere along the way, everything had gotten confused. He had set up an appointment for his nephew with the specialist in Boston, he had ordered all the tests, but what he really wanted to do was cure Alex himself. He wanted to be the hero. He wanted to do this despite the fact that, from a distance, Alex was a dead ringer for Ned at the same age.

Half an hour later, Graham lay down on the blanket, while Alex ran around on the grass.

"He's got Ned's energy," Graham said. They were all silent, and though Graham knew he was an idiot for doing it, he looked at Jane for her reaction. She was staring at her son, her face unreadable.

"Why are you doing this?" she asked.

"Doing what?" he said innocently.

"You know what. Talking about him."

"Why can't I? You ought to have told Alex

all this years ago. He has the right to know about his father."

Jane finally looked at him. "Know what? That Ned couldn't hold a job for more than two months? That he stole from every merchant in town? That he slept with any girl who asked, even after we got engaged? That I wished him dead?"

The vehemence in her voice could just as well have been a knife in his chest. All these years and her passion was just as fierce. Devon wasn't the enemy; Ned was. If anything, Jane probably loved his brother more now, because he hadn't hurt her or cheated on her for years.

"You could just tell him why you loved him," Graham said. "Actually, that's something we'd all like to know."

Jane blinked a dozen times, but no tears fell. Alex had finally tired of running, and had headed off down to the lake.

"I'll leave you two to talk," Esther said, getting up slowly and going after Alex. Jane waited until Esther was out of earshot before she turned back to Graham.

"Don't," she said.

"Don't what?"

"Just don't bring him up."

"Why not? He's been dead seven years. He's dead as dust. He can't touch us."

But even as Graham said this, he knew it wasn't true. In the middle of Hagerman's Woods, at the moment he'd caught up to

Devon's back tire, the sunlight had turned Devon's hair blond. Before he could stop himself and think things through, he had called out, "Ned, slow down." And Devon, before he could think about it either, had turned around, nodded, and slowed.

"Why did you stand him up?" he asked at last. "I would have thought Devon would be just the kind of man you'd fall for."

Jane looked at him, her eyes swimming with tears, but furious. "Then you don't know a thing."

"I didn't mean —"

"Just forget it, Graham. Just leave it alone."

She stood up and started for the lake, but Graham caught up to her. He grabbed her arm, swung her around, then stared down where he'd made contact. Her skin was so pale he could see veins; he imagined he could see her blood, still tainted with love for Ned.

"I'm sorry," he said. "I wish I knew the right thing to say to you."

Jane shook her head. "Don't wish for anything."

"Come on. You don't still believe . . ."

He let the sentence drop when he saw her eyes. They were so black with guilt, everything she saw must be muddy and misconstrued.

"Make a wish right now," he said.

"No."

"Come on. Wish for a rainbow. Or a million dollars. Wish for three more wishes."

Jane shook her head. She tried to pull away, but for once Graham held on tightly. He wasn't about to let go now.

"I can't, Graham," she said. "Getting what you want usually messes up a perfectly good life."

"Wish for another sunny day. What harm can come of that?"

"I only wish for Alex's voice."

Graham took her chin in his hand. He lifted her head until she was staring into his eyes. He didn't care about the rumble of the car in the parking lot. He didn't hide anything. He stared at her the way he'd wanted to all his life, with so much intensity wind could not blow between them. Her chin began to tremble in his hand.

"Then wish for that," he said.

"I wish for Alex's voice."

Graham leaned his forehead against hers. "I'll get it for you."

Jane pulled away abruptly. She looked down to the lake, where Alex was braving the cold water up to his ankles. Esther sat on the small dock, watching him. "If you have that kind of power," Jane said quietly, "then you're capable of anything, especially heartache."

She walked toward her son. Graham took one step after her, but his legs suddenly ached from all the riding he'd done that morning. His chest was sore from his pounding heart. He knew he would hardly be able to get out of bed in the morning, though not because of the biking. He'd be exhausted from wanting the one thing he couldn't have, and that was just the way it was going to be. If he'd gotten Jane years ago, he probably would have grown vain and uncharitable. He would have started to depend on happiness rather than seek it. He would have had nothing to hope for in his wildest fantasies.

He heard footsteps in the grass behind him and stiffened. He knew one other thing: Ginny had arrived, and the sniffles he heard were hers.

Devon never brought up their missed date. He didn't call or come by or send Jane nasty letters. Jane sat on her porch swing every night, giving him ample opportunity to confront her, but she never saw more than his backside, as he rode past in a blur. This annoyed her to no end. She had hoped to be the first woman to look him in the eye and tell him she didn't want him.

On the first Saturday in November, a night when the asters in Thomas Ezra's garden shattered like glass and Lionel Davis, out at the senior center, decided on the spot to move to Miami Beach, Jane sat on her swing again. It was Lenore Renfrow, though, not Devon, who skidded into the driveway in her Honda, then ran up the steps.

"I called Hank," Lenore said. "I can't believe I had the nerve, but I called him."

Jane led her inside, where the walls were now sunflower yellow and the kitchen cabinets painted pure white. The old frosted light fixtures had been removed, replaced with wrought-iron chandeliers Jane had found at an antiques show. At the end of the hall, a pine staircase led to the attic that still needed wiring, wallboards and flooring.

They sat down at the dining table and Lenore squeezed her arm. "We talked for an hour," she said. "He was going out of town to visit his mother for a couple weeks, but he asked me to meet him for coffee when he came back. I didn't think he'd show, but he did. Oh Jane, when I saw him, it was like time had stood still, like I'd never loved anyone else. It was like finding my heart in his eyes."

"So you're happy then," Jane said.

"God, yes. I don't know how I can repay you."

She finally released her grip on Jane's arm, revealing a red handprint.

"You don't owe me anything," Jane said, and meant it. She was thinking about all the repercussions she hadn't thought through when she'd urged Lenore to call Hank. She was thinking that Hank might turn out to be an ax murderer, or that once they kissed, Lenore would wonder how she ever could have wanted him. She was wondering if she would be to blame if things went wrong, if her grandmother had ever been sued.

"I just can't believe it," Lenore went on. "It was all so perfect. I can't help thinking of all the wasted time."

"You need to be careful," Jane said.

"Careful of what? Of love? Are you crazy? Careful is for children in trees. Love is like almost drowning. Like feeling your lungs fill up with water and floating precariously between life and death."

Jane kicked back her chair and stood up. A woman could lose her mind in a second, if the right man smiled at her. In a heartbeat, she could start believing everything he told her.

"I hope you won't hold me responsible," she said, but Lenore only laughed. She got up and wrapped her arms around Jane's shoulders.

"I do. I do. You're wonderful. A million thank-yous. But I can't stay. I've got to go to him."

She was out of the house, flushed and certain, before Jane could say another word.

Esther came out of her bedroom after she heard the door slam. "It's a good thing, Janie," she said.

"I don't want to mess up anybody else's life."

"It sounds like her life was already messed up and now she considers it fixed."

"What if —"

Esther put her weathered hands on Jane's shoulders. "No what ifs. First the roses and now love. You have the power to make things bloom. What can be wrong with that?"

Jane looked her in the eye. "If they can bloom, they can die. And I don't even want to think about that."

Devon did not believe in ghosts. He believed in destiny and passion and getting what he wanted in this life, because he was sure there wouldn't be another one. Even if there was a heaven, it was a good bet he wasn't going there.

He believed there were no limits. Danger was all in the mind. Any woman could be won with the right attention to detail, so it was only a matter of time before he got to Jane. He knew how to play it; he'd ignore her until she found herself up late at night, wondering what he was thinking. He would hop on his bike without saying hello, flirt with every woman but her, and soon he would become all she thought about. When she finally ended up on his door-step, looking a little out of control, he would pretend he hadn't been waiting there. He would just smile and ask her in.

Or, if all that failed, he might tell her the truth, that something was happening to him he didn't understand. He should have given up on her weeks ago; there were a hundred other willing women. He would have walked right past her that first time she turned him down, if it weren't for Alex. But for the first time in Devon's life, he was a hero to somebody. He had to stop at signals, so the boy beside him would not get run over by traffic. He had to go

201

around cliffs rather than down them, but the reward was the look in Alex's eyes. It had gotten so Devon was living on that adoration; beyond that, he ate only coffee and PowerBars. The only trouble was, once he'd gotten a little devotion, all he could think about was getting more. He wanted Jane to look at him that way, with thirsty eyes. He even wanted old Esther to like him, as if that would matter in the slightest. He was not at all happy with the way things were going. He didn't understand how normal people stood it, all this yearning all the time. It was like living hungry.

In the meantime, until he got what he wanted and satisfied this craving, there were plenty of other women to keep him occupied. Cindy Davis bought him banana daiquiris whenever he played amateur night at Orion's Bar. Tammie Wren came right to his door in skimpy negligees. There were still cliffs to ride that could potentially break his neck and stereo equipment no one else dared to lift. Other people might expect to get caught or killed eventually, but Devon knew he was not cut for tragedy. His blood was oil, his bones stainless steel; he couldn't get stuck or bruised by anything. He'd lived twenty-six years and forgotten every second of it, that's how easy his life had been. Sometimes he recalled flashes of color and pretty faces, girls he'd seen naked, gigs he'd played, but it was hard to tell if these were true memories or flashbacks from a bad acid trip.

He didn't beat himself up about things, either. He didn't think of the things he took as stealing. He just used the CD player or cellular phone or bike until someone, with money, wanted it back. If he didn't digest what he borrowed, he eventually returned it, no harm done. What good was an aisle full of unpurchased merchandise anyway?

He'd borrowed the Manitou mountain bike for Graham and an Iron Horse for Jake Orofino, another struggling cyclist without enough money to get himself the right equipment. He had his eye on a Marin for Alex, though he'd have to be quick about it; the last time he'd gone into the bicycle shop, Mike Murray, the owner, had been installing a top-of-the-line security system and toying with the idea of loosing a trained attack dog in the store at night.

By November, Devon's house still had no furniture, but it did have a borrowed power saw, so he could make a tree house for Alex; a refrigerator full of cold cuts swiped out of the deli case at Jim's Mercantile; and Graham's Manitou. He ought to have taken that bike back days ago, but he'd known Graham would be back for more riding. He'd known it the day they'd ridden through Hagerman's Woods, when he'd looked back and seen something hot and mean glowing in Graham's eyes, something far beyond his own understanding.

Every morning for the last week, Devon had looked out his window and seen Graham standing on the other side of the street. As soon as he noticed Devon watching him, he walked away, but Devon knew there were some things a man couldn't stop himself from doing, no matter how hard he tried.

This morning, when Devon woke, he walked straight to the window. Outside, the sky was low and white. Two jet streams had collided over Vermont, producing late-season lightning and fog so thick it burnt the eyes. Ninety-six-year-old Thomas Ezra, who had nothing to lose, had hiked up to Mt. Carmel with a lightning rod. The rest of the town was on edge from the unrelenting fog. Hazel MacNamara had finally kicked her twenty-eight-year-old son out of the house; five hours later, she tossed his high school soccer trophies in the garbage and finished repainting his room sky blue. Soon teenagers would be jumping off high bridges and dogs would be running away for no reason at all. In a gap in the mist, Devon could make out two young mothers walking past his house, no baby carriages in sight. They were smoking cigarettes and giggling, and by the end of the week, if the fog didn't let up, one of them would probably leave her husband.

The fog swirled around the hair they'd brushed a hundred times that morning while their babies cried for formula. In their wake, Devon could make out Graham standing in his tan trench coat across the street. When he squinted, he could nearly see the fevered glint in Graham's eyes. He shivered, though he did not believe in fear, either.

He went to the kitchen and found the borrowed coffee and coffeepot and filters. He made a pot, poured two cups, then stepped barefoot into the fog.

Graham did not see him until the smell of coffee stung his nostrils. He jumped back, startled, as Devon held out a cup.

"Come on," Devon said. "It'll get cold."

Tentatively, as if the contents might be poisoned, Graham took the cup. His eyes were bloodshot; for all Devon knew, he had been standing on the street corner all night.

"Are you going to tell me what this is about?" Devon asked.

Graham drank the coffee and looked everywhere but at him. He looked straight into the fog and seemed to see something, because he shivered.

"You remind me of someone," Graham said.

Devon stepped forward. He always looked men in the eye, but that didn't mean he listened to what they said. Usually, he couldn't care less; he smiled and laughed, but he was really planning his next ride, he was figuring how to sleep with their girlfriends.

But now he found himself standing on tiptoes to listen to Graham. The veins on the sides of Graham's neck were pulsing and there was a hum of electricity coming from deep inside him.

"Who?" he asked.

Graham looked right at him then, and Devon felt a jolt. His right hand shook, spilling coffee all over the sidewalk. His head suddenly got heavy with the weight of a thousand unsaid words and misunderstandings.

"Never mind," Graham said. "It doesn't matter. Let's ride again."

He walked past Devon into Devon's house. Devon stood on the corner alone, wrapped in fog and memories of someone else's life. When he looked into the haze, he imagined two boys standing on the corner, one taller, more handsome, climbing up the lamppost as if he were a monkey. Once he reached the top, he had every intention of lending a hand and hoisting the shorter boy up, but the boy hated him for that, for going first, for knowing how. The shorter boy was planted to the ground and he knew it; he had feet made of lead. He had eyes full of envy and hatred.

Devon blinked and the image was gone. He looked down at his hand, dripping with coffee but unscarred. He turned and followed Graham into the house.

On a frigid November morning, when the sky was so blue and cold it shattered windshields, Ginny woke before Graham. She reached over, as she always did, to hold her husband, but this time drew back before touching him. The sheets wound around his legs smelled feral. She hurried into the shower, afraid some of what was poisoning him might be coming off on her.

When she came back out, dressed for work, Graham's breathing had turned so shallow, she knew he only pretended to sleep. She kissed his forehead and pretended he had her fooled.

She did not go directly to the office. Instead, she drove around the block, parked behind Warren Seznick's RV, and waited.

Graham showed within the hour. He wore cycling pants and a hooded shirt and never looked up while he walked. She had parked here twice before, and twice Graham had passed right by her Volvo without a glance. He took care not to step on any cracks in the sidewalk, as if he were a child again, playing some superstitious game.

Ginny waited until he reached the end of the block, then she started her car and followed him at a distance. The first time she had followed him, she'd been stunned at his destination; she had assumed, of course, that he was going to Jane's, using that damn remodeling project as an excuse to be alone with her. It was like following a stranger, following her husband to Devon Zeke's door.

She parked on the corner of Sycamore and Vine and watched Graham walk straight into Devon's house without knocking. Ten minutes later, the door was flung open and Devon came riding out. He bounced his treadless tires down the steps, then skidded to a halt on the icy pavement.

Graham rode out the door next, his face a picture of concentration. At some point in the last couple weeks, he had learned to do tricks. He, too, hopped down the stairs on his bike, then slid to a stop beside Devon. Even from across the street, Ginny could see the challenge in his eyes.

The two of them took off down Sycamore Lane, going from zero to thirty in seconds, turning the far corner before she could blink. Ginny sat back and closed her eyes. She was married to a man she did not understand. She'd had a good life, and a good life had not prepared her for marriage. She'd had no idea love could hurt so much, that some days she would wake up and flat-out despise Graham. Or that a man could be loved this much and not be changed by it. Graham ought to have grown four inches because of her devotion.

She was a good wife. She knew Graham thought this of her, that in his own way he loved her. She knew he would never leave her, not even if he wanted to, because he was a good man. What she hadn't known, until the sun struck her windshield and did not warm up a thing, was that it was finally time she left him.

Seven

At dusk that evening, the first snow of the season started falling and didn't stop for two hours. It coated the Perfume Delight rosebush, but the flowers went right on blooming. Jane stood beside the bush in her heavy jacket and boots and counted thirty-eight roses. She ran her hands down the stalks and could not find a single thorn, and the truth was she didn't know what to think of anything.

She walked along the dusted sidewalks toward the edge of town. The weathercaster had talked of two competing weather fronts, producing flaky snow and fog as thick and heavy as paint. It hung in patches, curling around the tail of Francis McGinnis's tabby cat and hugging the roots of the sycamore tree that stood sentry by the gate of the cemetery. Jane opened the wrought-iron gate and waded through, feeling a chill straight through to her toes.

She walked first to her mother's grave and laid a hand on the tombstone. She was having trouble hating her mother now that Sal was dead. She had seen Sal's chipped china, slept in the lumpy bed Sal had lain alone in for twenty years, seen her mother's misery manifested in cracked plaster and windows so grimy everything outside was blurry. Sal had not been a good mother, but she had not been a monster either. She had been a woman with a rotten life.

Jane headed toward the back of the cemetery, where the families with money dug their graves, as if the soil were richer, as if anything could make a difference at that point. Ned would have wanted something flashy, a headstone shaped like a skull and crossbones, so she was unprepared for the gray slate memorial set neatly in the ground. She thought she might even have the wrong grave, but then she saw the football placed where his right hand might rest, and the frozen carnations at his head.

Jane stepped right on top of his grave. She tapped a foot on the snow-covered grass. Though she'd already killed him once, she'd obviously botched the job. The fog would have to be three times as thick to cover up the blond ghost perched in the lowest branch of the sycamore tree, plucking off dead leaves and tossing them at her feet. She turned her back to the tree and knelt by the memorial. She traced the carving of his name, the year he died. She imagined the cause of death etched in also:

Killed by a wish from Jane Gregory

She sat back on her heels. She'd become a practical woman; she knew, if Ned had lived, he would have hurt her. She knew the kind of love she'd had for him could not have lasted; it would have burned like a volcano, then suffocated itself with its own ash. Still, all things considered, she would have chosen a life with him over any alternative. She doubted there was a woman alive who wouldn't choose, if she had the chance, to be eaten alive by passion.

That passion stirred her senses again, and she heard the breaking of a twig beneath the thin layer of snow. She stood up quickly to find him off the tree, standing knee-deep in the fog. He wore a tan trench coat, his hair, for once, was neat and swept back from his eyes. As soon as she saw him, she starting crying. She cried for all they might have been, for all she had imagined. She cried, at last, in grief, which still seemed a luxury, like something she didn't deserve.

She cried as he came forward, as he blew the fog away with a warm breath and she saw that his hair was not blond, but brown, that it was he, and not Ned, who had always come when she was crying, and that it was entirely possible she wasn't done with the Payton boys yet.

"I saw you walking," Graham said.

She cried harder and he wrapped his arms around her. He tucked his head over hers. Jane didn't even look around for Ginny. For a moment, she didn't care who saw — she just had to hold onto him. Long before she'd started conjuring ghosts, even before she'd fallen in love with Ned, he'd been the only real thing around.

"You shouldn't be out here," he said.

"You shouldn't either."

He only squeezed her tighter, and in the moment before sense returned, Jane ran her hand over his cheek. She made sure she concentrated hard, so she could call up the feel of him later.

"Let me go to Boston with you and Alex," he said. "I'll introduce you to Dr. Swirling myself, and then we can take Alex sledding. I hear they've already got a foot of snow at Wachusett Mountain."

Jane pulled her hand away and stared at it. The tips of her fingers were pink and warm, but the rest of her had gone stone cold. "And where will Ginny be?"

Graham stepped away. "Can we have one conversation without bringing her into it?"

"She's your wife."

"I don't love her, Jane."

They both breathed heavily, white smoke forming around their mouths. Jane wrapped her arms around herself. "You won't leave her, either," she said. "And even if you did, we'd still be all wrapped up in this."

She waved her hand around the graveyard. Graham just stared at her, then headed toward the wrought-iron fence at the back of the cemetery. He took care to walk around Ned's grave, to step only on solid ground. He leaned against the fence and stared out at the woods, which disappeared in fog one hundred yards away. Jane stared at his back and decided she was tired, because the longer she looked, the slimmer his shoulders became, the more youthful the cut of his chin. The longer she looked, the younger he got, until he could have passed for eighteen, and he had it all to do over again.

She shook her head and walked over to him. She grasped the wrought-iron spikes and leaned back. When she finally chanced a look at him, she saw freckles across the ridge of his nose.

"I'm sorry you haven't been happy," she said.

"I made my own choices. I thought I could make it work."

"Maybe it still will."

Graham stared at her hard, then finally looked back out to the woods. "What about you? Are you going to be all right?"

Jane shrugged. "I'm going to help Alex. That's all I can think of."

"And Devon?"

"I'm not going to fall in love with him, if that's what you're thinking. No way. Not again."

When he didn't contradict her, when he only looked over his shoulder to check the integrity of Ned's grave, she reached over and took his hand. She threaded her fingers through his and just held on.

When Graham got home from the cemetery, he nearly fell over the suitcases by the door. There were three of them, packed so tightly, they bulged. His stomach dropped, though that seemed a strange reaction, considering he'd secretly been hoping for this for weeks.

He looked around the room and finally spotted Ginny in the chair in the corner, her feet curled up beneath her. She had scrubbed off her makeup and looked no more than seventeen. She had tied a scarf around her head, but red frizzes still poked out.

He stepped over the suitcases and walked to the chair beside her. He sat down and waited. She didn't take long to speak, and the words came out smoothly, as if she'd been rehearsing them all day.

"Here's the deal," she said. "I have to leave here. You can either come with me or not. It's up to you."

Graham looked into the fire, then over to his wife. Her voice was strong, but her hands were clasped tightly in her lap. He reached over and laid his hand on top of hers. Her skin was ice-cold.

"I've got my practice here," he said. A perfectly reasonable response, though they both knew it was only smoke. He had Jane here. And Alex. And now, in some strange way, Devon. His feet had been glued down a long time ago by forces he never could control.

"So you're choosing your practice over me? Is that the excuse you'll tell yourself in the middle of the night?"

Graham let go of her hand. He stood up and walked to the fireplace, keeping his back to her.

"Ginny, what do you want me to say?"

"I don't know. Maybe, after all this time, I just want the truth."

He turned around. He had imagined his freedom a thousand times, but now that he might be granted it, he could not figure how it would work. This house would not function without Ginny. The clocks would all stop, the oven would burn the roasts, the sewer would back up. If he called Jane, when he called her, all the circuits would go down. Most likely, she would not even hear him when he told her he was free.

"Do you really?" he asked, his throat raw.

"Yes. I want to know what you're doing with Devon, why you're playing some game you can't possibly win. I want to know what you think is going to happen between you and Jane."

Those questions she'd kept locked inside her charged the room. The fire crackled and spit its embers three feet, onto the new chenille rug. Before it could spark a flame, Ginny reached out a tiny foot and ground out the smoke.

Graham felt a moment's panic; the hair rose up on his arms. Then he looked at his wife and merely sat down again in the chair beside her.

"I'm going crazy, Ginny," he said. "What other explanation can there be? It's like I was born to hate him. What do all the women see in him? He's nothing. He'll never be anything. All he does is smile nice and they all go to pieces. And you should see him when he rides. He moves like the wind. He doesn't even sweat."

Ginny reached over and squeezed his hand — he would remember that later — then she stood up. She tried to tuck her frizzes beneath her scarf, then gave up and merely stared down at him.

"You know what's funny?" she said. "You go on and on the same way, thinking it's all right. You even have a kind of happiness, if you don't shoot too high. And then, all of a sudden, you just can't stand it another minute."

She walked to the door and opened it. She took one suitcase out to her car. Graham heard the thump as she lowered it into her trunk. She came back twice more for the others.

He should have gotten up to help her, but he couldn't make himself move. He thought he was dreaming it. He had always thought he would be the one to do the leaving; Ginny deserting him had never been a possibility. Her not loving him anymore was not something he'd ever considered. And so, of course, when she stood in the doorway to say goodbye, the loss of her was worse than being burned.

"Ginny," he said, stumbling to his feet and

coming to her side. He grabbed her hands. "I'm sorry. I never meant for this to happen."

Ginny shook her head. "I'm done fighting her. You can have her, although the truth is, Jane is still in love with Ned. It's so obvious, it's silly."

Graham shook his head. "You don't understand."

"Oh yes I do," Ginny said softly. "You're being haunted. You and Jane both. You're reliving something I thought sad and, frankly, melodramatic the first time around. It just goes on and on and I'm sick of it."

She turned to go, but Graham touched her shoulder. "Ginny, come on." He tried to copy the smile Devon used, but succeeded only in making Ginny plant her feet firmly on the ground.

"I'm going," she said. "I should have gone a long time ago."

"You're the only one who's always been on my side."

Ginny hesitated, but only for a moment; then she walked out the door and down the path where the snow had already melted.

"At least let me leave," Graham called after her. "This is your house. Just let me pack."

Ginny shook her head again. When she got to her car, she turned around. "No," she said loudly enough that he and all their neighbors could hear. "I want to be absolutely clear about this. I'm the one doing the leaving."

The snow was only two inches thick and melting fast, but Jane still took Alex's snowsuit out of the back of his closet and helped him into it. She dressed in ski pants and a turtleneck, and the two of them went out onto the white lawn.

"Let's see if we remember how," she said. Alex usually leapt into the snow, but this time, he looked across the street before lying down beside her. Devon's house was a swarm of yellow light, rock music, and laughter. Jane had been hearing bass guitars and the popping of champagne corks all night. There was a mini-snowman by his front porch, its head already melted down to the size of a baseball.

"Come on." Jane slid her arms up and down through the snow. Alex turned his head away from Devon's house and did the same. They made snow angels while a warm wind came up out of the south, turning flat roofs into lakes and rain gutters into waterfalls. The warmth from their bodies turned the air to mist and melted all the snow beneath them. When they stood up, Alex's angel was colored in yellow grass while Jane's was green and lush as mint.

"Let's make another," Jane said. "We don't have a lot of time." Even as they walked across the lawn to a deeper spot, the snow beneath their feet melted. Alex yanked at the collar of his snowsuit. When a car sped around the corner and pulled up into their driveway, he looked up thankfully.

Ginny Payton left the engine idling and got out. She could not have weighed more than a hundred and twenty pounds, but every step she took shattered another icicle hanging from the eaves.

"I wanted you to know, I've left Graham," she said when she reached them.

Jane felt a surge of yearning so strong it had to be bad for her. She stepped back, so Ginny would not discover the type of heat she was giving off. The wind that struck her turned hot as summer.

"Oh, Ginny," she said.

"It was a long time coming. You know he's still in love with you. The truth is, Jane, you've never done a thing to stop that."

Jane had been about to touch her, but now she dropped her hand. Alex walked to the porch and sat down on the top step. He un-zipped the top half of his snowsuit. Across the street, the music got louder. Someone had put on a Metallica CD. Jane glanced at Devon's front window, where two figures occasionally passed by, slow-dancing despite the quick tempo.

Ginny stomped her foot in the snow. "Make up your mind, would you? You're not being fair to anybody."

Jane jerked up her head. "I never went after Graham. You know that."

"I don't know anything," Ginny said, "except

that I'm sick of all of you. This place is suffo-cating. I don't know how you stand it."

Jane tucked her hand up beneath her chin. "Maybe I don't have a choice."

Ginny shrugged. All of a sudden, her shoul-ders just slumped. She headed back around the car.

"I just wanted you to know about me and Graham," she said over her shoulder. Jane walked up behind her and reached her just as she opened the car door.

"Ginny, he loves you."

Ginny whirled around. She grabbed Jane's arm and squeezed until she touched bone. "I want to say one thing. I've loved Graham as long as you've been toying with him. I can state with absolute certainty that I know a little more about him than you do."

She shoved Jane's arm away and got into her car. She started to back out of the driveway, but Jane walked along beside her, tapping on the window. Jane watched her eyes dart to the ground, where she was probably thinking about hitting the accelerator, maybe even aiming for a foot. Instead, Ginny hit the brake and rolled down the window.

"What?"

"You don't have to leave. Believe me, this isn't going anywhere."

"Don't be stupid. It's already gone too far."

"You know what Ned was to me. How does a woman let go of something like that?"

"Jane, I'm not giving you pointers, all right? Do what you have to do. I'm going."

"You know what the problem is?" Jane said, holding tight to the car door. "It's way too easy to fall in love."

She saw Ginny watching her, even, despite everything, getting a little concerned.

"If that's true," she said, "then fall in love with someone else. Fall in love with Devon Zeke and leave Graham in peace."

"I never meant to hurt you," Jane said.

"I don't care what you meant. You did."

"I'm sorry."

Ginny shrugged, and at the end of it, she looked like someone totally different, as if she had shrugged off her head of frizzy hair. She left a skid mark on the driveway peeling out, then blasted the horn when she hit the corner of Sycamore Lane.

The next day, Jane expected Graham to call her. She even hid out in the attic for a while, thumbing through his postcards and then tacking them up on the wall insulation she'd put in herself. She tried to plan exactly what she would say, but when no call came, she knew what had happened: she had grown a little too sure of Graham's wanting her. It was always easier to love the one you couldn't have, and she figured Graham had just realized he couldn't live without Ginny.

Bob Wylie arrived to put up wallboards, and

he stomped through the attic in his hefty boots. "You gonna take that stuff down?" he asked, gesturing to the postcards.

"No. I want them up here. Just seal them in."

He nodded and got to work, and Jane left for Mementos. She had no intention of calling, but by three o'clock, she was on the phone to Graham's office.

"He canceled all his appointments," Beth said. "Can you believe this? I swear to you, I would have thought Ginny would be the last person on earth with the guts to leave a good man."

Jane tried Graham at home, but he was either out or not answering the phone, because it just rang and rang.

By five o'clock, she was standing at the shop window, on her fourth cup of gritty afternoon coffee. When the phone rang, she stared down the block, looking for Graham's car, wondering if he'd gone after Ginny.

"Dammit, Jane," Bill called from the back. "Answer the goddamn phone."

She walked back to the counter and picked it up. "Mementos."

"Jane?" Graham said. "Is that you?"

"Graham, where are you? I've been calling."

"So you heard."

"Yes. Ginny came by last night. Graham, what happened?"

She thought she heard the lighting of a match, his inhalation on a cigarette, though

Graham had never smoked.

"Will you come by tonight?" he asked.

When she'd been hiding in the attic this morning, she had decided to stay away from Graham, to stay away from all of them until she felt on stronger ground. But that was this morning, and now she was tempted by the catch in his voice, and by her own curiosity. She wasn't going to be able to sleep until she saw what he looked like now, exactly what Ginny's leaving had done to him.

His house lights were off when she arrived two hours later. She walked up to the dark porch and knocked. He answered immediately; he must have been waiting on the other side in darkness.

"Well," he said, running a hand through his hair. He opened the door and led her inside. She looked over the matching chintz sofa and chair, the gray wool rug, the floral wallpaper. Ginny was stitched into every seam. The house seemed unnaturally hushed, as if awaiting her return.

There was a small bed of dying coals in the fireplace. Graham sat on the couch and Jane hesitated, then sat beside him. He leaned away and she stiffened.

"Is this my fault?" she asked.

Graham laughed harshly and put his head in his hands. "You have no idea, do you?"

She shook her head. All she knew for certain was that she'd gotten in way over her head.

Every time she looked at Graham, she felt a little too giddy. Every moment was another chance for catastrophe, when she just might do something stupid, like say what she felt.

"Graham, I don't know what to say."

"Then I'll tell you," Graham said, leaning toward her. She could feel his sweet breath on her face. "Tell me I make you feel beautiful. The way Devon does. The way Ned did."

Jane blinked. She wanted to break down in tears and she wanted to wrap him up in her arms. Instead, she leaned forward and kissed him.

He didn't move for a moment, then his lips opened in surprise and need. He kissed her so intently, he took something from her, sucked it up through her marrow and her skin, and tucked it away inside himself. She wasn't sure exactly what he took, she only knew she would have given him more.

She heard a car drive by then, with a deep roar similar to Devon's Mustang. She was not sure if she pulled away, or if he did. Either way, the spell was broken. She walked to the window and peered through the blinds. She saw receding taillights and heard the echo of a thumping bass beat.

When she turned around, Graham had stood up and had his back to her. "Always the same," he said.

Suddenly, Jane was furious. She didn't want this wanting, and she certainly didn't deserve his scorn. Every time she looked at him, she risked remembering not only *that* night, but every other night she'd taken ten abuses just to get to that one *I love you.* Every time she looked at Graham, she saw a thousand things that could go wrong. She stomped across the room and grabbed his arm.

"You want my love because it's what Ned had," she said. "It isn't even about me. You just want everything Ned had."

Graham slowly raised his gaze to hers, and then Jane knew she was in trouble. She knew that when a man looked at a woman like that, it was all she could do just to remember he might be lying. If she didn't take a step back, she could very well hand him everything.

"You're wrong," he said softly. "It has always been about you. Just you."

Jane backed away slowly. She had learned a few things in seven years, mainly to walk out of a room when a man started talking softly, long before he started making promises. She had learned, no matter what her heart might be saying, she was still probably better off alone.

When she was out the door, she took a deep breath and made herself start walking. She was not about to go back.

The women arrived in the early mornings, before Alex left for school. They came armed with scissors and with hope. They were not deterred by the snows that fell and quickly melted, because the rosebush went right on blooming, even through heavy frosts. They snipped rosebuds and talked about the rumor that his mother could get them their heart's desire. Some were skittish; halfway up the path, the shadow of a crow sent them running. Others, though, stomped over the still lush grass and pounded on the door until Jane came out. Jane sat with these women on the front porch stoop, while they poured out sob stories about bad men and broken love affairs and lives that, to Alex's ear, sounded silly and already doomed.

His mother, it seemed, thought differently. She sighed while she did it, but she always gave these women something, a flower, a strip of lace, an old photo cut out of her yearbook. Then she told them to do something ridiculous, like pin the lace on the tallest alder in Hagerman's Woods or dip the flower in blackened honey. The women rushed away to do as she said, and Alex got to thinking his mother could have told them to jump off a cliff and they would have done it. They were as bad as kindergartners — they took the first thing someone told them as fact. They actually wanted to be told what to do.

On a morning when ice crystallized on his bedroom window and the last three leaves on Devon's maple tree fell, Alex heard his mother talking to a woman he recognized as one of the crossing guards at his school. A woman who had always smiled at him and laughed so easily, he hadn't given her a second thought.

"You should stay with Ryan," his mother said. "You know he loves you. Brad's a heart-breaker. He'll cut you in two."

"No, no, no," the crossing guard said. "What good is someone loving you if you don't care when they walk out the door?"

It had gotten so Alex could hear his mother's sighs over the roar of chain saws and rock music. She sighed loud enough to crack glass, but the women were oblivious. They just held out their hands until she gave them what they came for.

"Put this begonia on Brad's back porch then," Jane said. "It's not supposed to bloom this late, but it will. When it does, he'll call you. Just don't come running back here when he cheats or walks out. Don't come back when you realize it's not his love you wanted."

"Don't be silly, Jane," the woman said. "I know what I want."

An hour later, the crossing guard was on her post in front of Pendleton Elementary, smiling like crazy. Alex avoided her gaze as he got off the bus, then looked around for Billy Weinstock. Thankfully, the bully must have already gone inside. Most of the other kids were drifting into class, and Alex leaned against the flagpole until they were all gone. He turned to go, then a soft voice stopped him.

"You're not coming?"

He turned around to find Linda Carlton, the girl in braids, emerging from behind Mr. Hiawatha's classroom. Linda was the only girl in class brave enough to come out back when he and Billy were fighting. She always waited until they were through, then kicked Billy in the shin as he passed. He instantly reared up, spread his legs for another fight, but when he got a good look at her, he dropped his fists. Whatever was in her eyes gave him the shivers for an hour. He couldn't get away fast enough, though he made sure not to start running until he thought he was out of sight.

Alex looked down the street, then turned back to her. He shook his head.

"Billy's a jerk," she said. "But that doesn't mean the rest of us are."

Alex could feel his throat tightening. He wanted to get away before he did something stupid, like cry in front of a girl. He started backing up.

"So go then," Linda said. "See if I care."

But the thing was, just before he turned and ran, he could see that she did care. He could see it written all over her face. He hesitated, and in that pause his breath came in real smooth. He filled his lungs for the first time in years, not with dragon smoke, but with cool air that smelled strangely of peanut butter.

He turned and ran down the street fast as lightning, but when he got to the corner, he turned back to see if she was still there. She had not moved at all, and he sucked in another breath that went down his throat like clear, blue ice.

He ran to Oak Park Lane, two streets over from Sycamore, and stared at his watch until eight forty-five, when his mother left for work. Then he walked to the corner of Sycamore Lane. He glanced at his house and breathed a sigh of relief; he had drawn the blinds before he left, and his great-grandmother had not yet opened them.

He turned toward Devon's house, where Devon was standing on the porch beside his bike, staring right at him.

"Hey, sport," he said. "No school today?"

Devon spun the tire on the bike he was tuning. Alex had heard what the girls at the Eat 'Em Up said about Devon, that he was perfect, that he was too gorgeous for words, but all Alex knew was that no matter how much Devon had watered, he hadn't been able to get a single flower to bloom in his yard. When snow melted everywhere else, it stayed an inch thick on his lawn.

He walked up the porch steps to Devon's side.

"Cutting class already, huh?" Devon said. "I don't think I started until the second grade." He laughed, then stood up. "Hey, I'm glad you're here. I've got something for you."

He led Alex into the backyard, where a shiny new downsized Marin Nail Trail mountain bike stood in a patch of snow. It had an Easton aluminum frame and looked slick as oil. Alex stared at it in awe.

"You like it?" Devon asked. "I couldn't resist. You can't be riding that Schwinn anymore, not with your power and speed."

Alex stepped tentatively toward the bike, then stopped.

"Go on," Devon said, smiling. "It's a gift."

Even before he hopped on, Alex knew the bike would fit him perfectly, that Devon had already adjusted the pedals to his height and set the toe clips just the way he liked them. He rode the bike around the snowy grass while Devon looked on.

"See? You're a natural. You probably want to keep it here, though. Your mom . . . Moms always want to know where things come from."

Alex stopped the bike and stared at him, but Devon only smiled. Alex played with the brakes, he sunk into the cushioned seat. No one had ever given him a gift this nice in his whole life.

"Let me finish up my bike and we'll ride," Devon said.

Alex wheeled the new bike around the side of the house. Devon walked back up on the porch and adjusted his back tire.

"Your mom working?" he asked. Alex nodded.

"That's good for you. Back in my day, most moms didn't work. We got caught all the time."

He laughed again and spun the wheel. "Listen to that. I'm telling you, kid, I was made for this. Sponsors are gonna be crawling all over me. I'll make a million easy by the time I'm thirty."

Alex wanted to believe him, but he also knew the day of that big New York race Devon had been talking about had come and gone and Devon had not entered it. He knew adults worked, they didn't toss their dollar bills into the toaster oven and set them on fire the way Devon had one afternoon. "Just for the hell of it," he'd said. Adults didn't laugh as much as Devon did. They might chuckle now and then, but it was like it had to be pried out of them, like they'd forgotten how to do it right. They certainly didn't spend their afternoons riding with a kid.

Devon glanced across the street. "Better get going before somebody sees you," he said, flipping over his bike and hopping on.

Alex climbed on his new bike. Cutting class today had been a whim; he'd never done it before and he wasn't sure why he was doing it now. He wasn't sure of a lot of things these days, like why he was enamored with a biker, why his mother had cried herself to sleep these last few nights, why his great-grandmother went out with Robert O'Brien, then came back and stared at the picture of the sea as if she was trying to crawl inside it. He didn't understand anything except that every morning, when he

231

stepped out of bed, something tugged at him. Before the sleep had cleared from his eyes, he was marching in the direction of Devon's house with no idea why. He ought to have questioned this, but he didn't. As he rode down the street beside Devon, he knew better than most that some things, like silence and desire, were simply out of his control.

Robert O'Brien brought flowers every morning. First roses from his garden, then after the snows started, white carnations from Pendleton Floral, though it must have been obvious to him, every time he passed the gaudy Perfume Delight bush, that the last thing Esther needed was more flowers. When November turned frigid, freezing in place the ants on the huckleberry bush and turning the grass Jane hadn't stepped on brown as dust, the rosebush was just swinging into full bloom. It was covered with three dozen roses, all the color of rock candy.

Still, Robert left the flowers on the porch swing, alongside the newspaper he picked up from the curb. Tucked into the local section, he left love notes.

Esther had stopped reading them after the second day. She was seventy-five years old; she told Jane having a man write, "Your beauty runs deeper than the sea," was ridiculous, although the truth was the notes made her heart skip a beat, which at her age could be fatal.

Friday morning, Jane picked up the white carnation and newspaper and turned to the local section. She took out the note, read it, then smiled at Esther.

"Don't you have the slightest interest?" she asked.

Esther turned her back to her and went to make tea. At the flower show, Robert had assisted her over a gravel path, his hand on the small of her back. Over lunch two days later, he'd lowered his head, blushed a little, then put his hand over hers. Every day since, he'd made up some excuse to see her, and every day he'd gotten bolder, touching first her wrist, then her elbow, then the hollow beneath her ear.

His caresses shocked her. Walt's touch had been something else entirely, like being stroked by stone. After he had died, she'd only touched people in pain. She didn't know how to cope with tenderness, she didn't know what to make of gooseflesh. Up until this point, she hadn't thought her skin capable of it.

Jane came up beside her and shook the note beneath her nose. Esther sighed and looked at it.

Let me call you sweetheart.

Esther closed her eyes. She had loved only one man her whole life, and he had not been worth it. Walt had never courted her. He had never asked her to be his anything. He had thought tenderness was something that applied to meat.

For their honeymoon, Walt had flown her across the country in his vulture plane, a surprisingly tame Aeronca C-3 Air knocker he'd painted glossy black. He had tested her with freefalls and double loops, but aside from going pale, Esther had never even blinked.

"I told you," she'd said. "You can do whatever you want to me. I just don't scare."

He had looked at her admiringly, but also with a little bit of regret.

They touched down at a dozen back-country airstrips, dropping off mail and supplies to hermits and homesteaders. They flew until they came to the Bitterroot National Forest of Montana, where Walt had promised her a real honeymoon.

Ten years earlier, a man had given up investment banking, along with a wife and three daughters, in favor of a place where he could smoke a pipe without offending anyone and write poetry no one would ever read. He hoisted logs, one by one, up the side of a granite mountain until he'd built a tiny cabin. He lived on wild strawberries and the dried meat Walt flew in. When he died in an avalanche at the age of forty-seven, Walt took over custodianship of the cabin and sent the man's poetry back to his wife.

Esther and Walt landed in the dark and hiked two miles by starlight. Esther had never been west of Ohio; she'd never seen mountains like these. Sharp and slick as fangs, so huge they created their own wind and weather. Fifteen minutes after they set out through stands of ponderosa pines, the mountains breathed fog up their flanks. Once they passed the tree line, water bubbled up through slits in the granite.

Walt did not measure his pace to Esther's, and her boots slipped often on the slick rock as she tried to keep up with him. After an hour, they were so deep into the shadow of the mountain, Esther could not see a thing. She only knew they'd reached the top when she could no longer breathe right, when she took short, choppy breaths that hurt going down. Walt suddenly reached back and grabbed her hand. He swung her left and then she saw the door to the cabin. He did not take the time to light a candle. All Esther could make out before his mouth was on hers were wood walls and an old, lumpy bed.

He made love to her quickly and cheaply, with only enough effort to find his own release. And still she wanted more of him. When he fell asleep, she kissed his chest, she put his arms around her and imagined gentleness. She made love to him the right way, without him even noticing.

When she awoke the next morning, a dim, purple light stained the room. Esther sat up, her hair draped around her breasts. She tried to find the source of the light, but when she stepped up to the small window cut out of whole logs, she was surprised to find it still pitch-black outside.

The cabin was no more than ten by ten, with a tiny twin bed, an old woodstove for cooking, and a battered chest filled with pots, pans, and blankets. She stepped out the door and nearly fell off the cliff. There was only a three-foot-wide landing before the edge of the world. She looked down the granite crevasse, but could not see bottom, only a richer blackness, a colder cold. Though she was rarely afraid, she thought of how easy it would have been for Walt to misjudge the distance, or to regret their hasty marriage and send her over the edge.

Walt came up behind her and wrapped his arms around her waist. He cupped her breasts in his hands. Then he turned her around and kissed her gently.

He made love to her there, on the three-foot-wide front stoop, and this time he did it right. He rubbed his hands down the insides of her arms. He drew soft pink lines into her back with his fingernails and wound strands of her hair through his mouth. He leaned against the cabin and lifted her on top of him. When he came, he dug his fingers into the flesh of her hips; he seemed like a man who might never let go.

They made love seven times in three days, and later on, when things got bad, Esther both clung to and doubted her memory. Not counting the first time, he was always gentle. He made love to her from the bottom up, and by the time he reached her kneecaps, she was begging him to hurry. He took such care that later on she was baffled by his lack of concern and tenderness. It seemed he'd spent himself that long weekend, that when he woke up Monday morning, he figured he'd done all that could be asked of him.

During their short honeymoon, he showed her his maps. He unfolded them on the old chest and proudly pointed out how he'd mapped every mountain, stream, and meadow he'd ever flown over.

"I'm the only one in the world who knows about these places," he said.

"Now I do too," Esther said, and was surprised when he looked at her as if she'd just spoiled his appetite.

It was during their second night, when Walt was sound asleep with his warm, thin back to her, that Esther heard the hot July wind. It shrieked up the mountainside like an animal in a fury, like a mother bear hunting down the man who'd shot her cub. She got out of bed, naked, and opened the door. The wind was hot and dry as sand. She licked her lips and tasted sage.

She walked to the edge of the cliff and looked down. The screaming blasted her eardrums. The wind whipped up leaves and rocks the size of quarters that riddled her legs with cuts. She didn't move, though, because just out over the crevasse swirled something black and glistening. She stepped right to the edge and reached out. Stretching as far as she could, and not looking down, she plucked the vulture's feather out of the air. When she ran her finger down its spine, sparks flew.

In the morning, when she made tea, the backache Walt had had for seven years suddenly went away. When his plane wouldn't start, Esther laid a hand on it and the engine finally kicked over. She didn't consider what had happened to her. She certainly didn't call it magic. The truth was, with Walt's seed inside her, with the marks of his kisses still on her neck, she thought it was love that had made her powerful.

She had not cried when Walt flew out the day after their honeymoon and did not return for three weeks. She had not cried when he never offered to take her flying again or, even, after he died. Yet the ingenuousness of Robert O'Brien's note brought tears to her eyes. She blinked until she'd forced them back down.

She looked out the kitchen window and saw Robert O'Brien standing on her patchwork front lawn, waiting for her. She took a deep breath and walked outside. She stayed three feet away from him. She was not about to start acting the fool.

"You don't know what you're saying," she said.

Robert placed his hand over his heart. "Of

course I do, Esther. I'm asking you to be my girl."

Esther looked away, so she wouldn't start crying again. She wondered if Walt would have aged the same way as Robert. If he would have gotten liver spots on his hands, grown timid, and taken to gardening. Then she laughed out loud, because Walt would have killed himself before planting a single begonia, he would have shot himself through the heart before he put on polyester.

"Does that mean yes?" Robert asked.

Esther turned back to him. Such a good man. Such a sweet, honest man, and she wondered why she didn't feel a thing for him except friendship, why, after all these years, she wasn't clamoring for the feel of a man's hands on her. She wondered why on earth the memory of a mean, coarse man like Walt Gregory seemed better than the flesh and blood of Robert O'Brien, why her daughter had loved a wife beater, why Jane had fallen for Ned. Why women, when it came to love, went against all their better instincts.

"I'm not your type," she said.

Robert walked across the lawn, stepping only on the size-six green patches. He finally reached her and touched her arm. "Esther, please. I only want your company. We're both getting up there. Why won't you let me take care of you the rest of the way?"

Esther looked down at his hand on her skin.

"I don't know how to do that."

"I'll help you."

Esther didn't need help; she never had. But the feel of his hand on her arm was not unpleasant. In truth, her skin beneath his touch got a little warm. There was no harm in letting a man think he was protecting you.

She nodded, though she was losing faith in her instincts, and it might very well be that she was making a mistake.

Jane tiptoed into Alex's room at dawn and held a candle up to his face. She'd seen some telltale signs, the bruise beneath his cheek, the grimace on his face when he sat down too quickly. But she wanted to be sure. She lifted up his pajama top and bit her lip at the sight of cuts and scabs all over his stomach. He had refused to go to the pool for two weeks now, and her worst fear was not that whoever was doing this to him would not give up, but that Alex would. It was only a matter of time before he grew afraid not only of bullies, but of water, before he forgot how to swim.

She leaned over and kissed his cheek. Then she walked into the kitchen and called her boss, Bill Burgis, and told him she would be late.

After Alex went to school, she went into his room and got his blanket, the one he slept with every night, though he would have been horrified to realize she knew this. Then she drove to Pendleton Elementary.

She parked the car across the street and waited until lunch. Alex was the last student out of his class, and he went to a brick planter and ate his sandwich alone. Billy Weinstock, one of the boys who had come to their house, occasionally beamed the ball at the back of his head. At first, Alex leapt to his feet with each strike, but Principal Dreyfuss was talking to Mr. Hiawatha on the far side of the courtyard, so after a while he just glared at the boy. He even took a bite of apple as the ball hit him square on the head.

Some problems — like bullies — faded on their own with time, but as Esther had said, there were still things you could do. She had watched Esther enough to know that camphor stopped nightmares and a dusting of witches'-broom on the fabric that lay closest to a person's heart could often change his whole life. Esther had rarely dared it, but at this point Jane was willing to try anything. She grabbed the blanket and walked into the field beyond the school. The snows and then warming trends had turned the lot to mud, but she plodded through until she reached the willows, under which the witches'-broom had bloomed and then frozen solid two weeks ago. She snapped off a branch, then swiped the yellow petals across Alex's blanket, until the pollen soaked into the ragged fabric, until there was no chance it would ever come out.

She clutched the blanket to her chest and

walked back to her car. When she looked over at the school, Alex was still sitting there. Billy Weinstock aimed another soccer ball for his head. This time, the ball went long, and straight through Principal Dreyfuss's office window. Billy Weinstock turned and ran, though the principal had seen everything, and Billy was going to be suspended for a week, whether he hid out or not. Jane looked at Alex. He still ate his apple. He hadn't even looked up when the glass broke, but if nothing else, she prayed she had bought him some time.

Eight

Within two days, the whole town knew of Ginny's departure, and most of Graham's patients gave him pitying looks or, worse, advice. Ninety-six-year-old Thomas Ezra told him to forget her, to find a twenty-year-old with nice legs. Rachel Simpson thought he should keep sending flowers. "Those paperwhites that make you sick after a while," Rachel said, "and she'll come home just to get you to stop." His receptionist, Beth, shook her head and said, "Well, it's no wonder, the way you were always lusting after Jane."

After Ginny had been gone a week, Graham took to eating his lunch in his office, with the door closed. He had his groceries delivered by Randy Weaver, who was half blind and the only man Graham trusted not to peek through his house, looking for clues as to why Ginny had left him. He drove ten miles to buy gas, so he wouldn't have to face the mechanics at Nate's service station.

He didn't go home until well after dark each night, and then he didn't touch anything. Since Ginny had left, plaster in their house had

243

cracked for no reason. Top-of-the-line appliances had gone on the fritz — the washing machine shredded his good shirts and the coffeemaker that usually brewed eight perfect cups of Ginny's special European blend just gurgled and spit out smoke.

Yet at night, Graham fell asleep as soon as his head hit the pillow, and he did not have a single nightmare. He felt as if he was finally living cleanly — the day Ginny left was the last day he would ever hurt someone.

Two days before Thanksgiving, Beth Shultz tapped on his door during lunch. She let herself in and he looked up over his ham sandwich.

"It's some man from Rutland. Says he's a divorce lawyer."

Graham should not have been surprised, but he was. He had not thought Ginny capable of such quick, decisive action against him. He reached for a glass of water and gulped it down.

The lawyer came in and Graham was surprised again, this time by Ginny's taste in attorneys. The man was slick and polished, with large garnet rings on his pinkies. He had jet black hair and a mustache curled like a pipe cleaner. He did not offer his hand and spoke without sitting down.

"Virginia asked me to notify you of her petition for divorce. She hopes it will be an amicable parting, a simple fifty-fifty split of all material possessions."

Graham stood up. Did they call her Virginia in Rutland? "What if I contest it?" he asked, though he knew he wouldn't.

"On what grounds, might I ask? As I understand it, Virginia has been a devoted wife to you for three years, loyally in love with you for much longer than that. If need be, I can bring in a town full of witnesses who will testify that you are in love with another woman, that in fact you always have been. Virginia has already spoken to a Mrs. Karen Wright, who saw you and Jane Gregory kissing in your living room the night after Virginia left you. That doesn't leave you much room for argument."

Graham would not have guessed Ginny would arm this man with so much information, that she'd prepare for a nasty fight. The worst thing he'd done hadn't been dreaming of Jane, it had been not getting to know his own wife. The worst thing was never asking if she'd rather be called Ginny or Virginia.

He turned back to the lawyer and caught the man smiling. The attorney lifted a hand to his mustache.

"I'll agree to whatever she wants," Graham said.

The lawyer nodded and dropped a stack of papers on his desk. "I think that's wise. Look this over carefully and sign it. You can be free in less than six months."

After he left, Graham picked up the papers,

then let them fall. He picked up a pen and signed them without reading a single word. He knew full well that, from now on, he couldn't blame his life on anyone but himself.

The next morning, like every morning since Ginny had left, Graham awoke before dawn. He had thought things would change after Ginny left, that he would gain some perspective, but the truth was, whatever was eating at him had only gotten hungrier. He was dressed in cycling gear and at Devon's doorstep before nine-year-old Luke Grisel had delivered most people's papers into their hedges. He had not yet won a single race, but sometimes he was so close to Devon's back tire, he could smell the aroma of victory.

When he knocked on Devon's door today, no one answered. A light snow had fallen and, leading from the porch, he saw two sets of tracks, one large and one small. He glanced at Jane's house, but all the lights were off. He could walk right up to the front door and pound on it until she let him in. He could make a scene, if love were a thing he could demand. Since it was not, he would just have to go on mailing exotic postcards to her house, now that the attic was almost done. He would just have to bide his time.

The sky was just opening up, turning the color of ripe plums, when he followed the tracks down the street and toward the Common. By the time he reached the park, a slice of sun broke over the bottom of Sandler Road, and he ran smack into his nephew. As he scooped Alex up in his arms, Devon came out from behind Ethan Allen's right arm.

Alex had been running full speed and now steam streamed out of his mouth. Devon leaned against the statue. "Hey, doc," he said.

Graham thought about setting his nephew down and turning around. He considered having nothing to do with this. Tomorrow morning, he could meet Devon for their ride as usual and perhaps the snow would work to his advantage. Perhaps this time he would beat Devon up Pendleton Hill and he could go home and sleep off whatever was happening to him.

But instead he hoisted Alex up so he could look in his eyes. "Hey there," he said. "You're up early. Does your mom know where you are?"

Alex was hot to the touch and instantly panicked. He shimmied out of Graham's arms. Devon walked up to him and put a hand on his shoulder.

"We're just having some fun," he said. "Losing a little sleep won't kill him."

Graham slowly raised his gaze to Devon's. All the exercise these last few weeks had made him not only strong, but quick. He was fairly certain he could close the gap between them and punch Devon in the nose before the man even saw him coming.

Instead, he looked at Alex. The boy was wearing only a thin turtleneck and jeans. He'd put on tennis shoes with no socks instead of snow boots. "Did frostbite ever occur to you?" he asked.

When he looked in Alex's eyes, he saw it hadn't. The boy had woken up this morning and darted straight to Devon's. There was no mistaking the worship in his eyes. Pure, unadulterated devotion, the kind that blinded him from seeing that the object of his affection was just not worth it.

Graham stepped forward and knocked Devon's arm off Alex's shoulder. Devon straightened himself up slowly, then his shoulders went slack and he only smiled. "Relax," he said. "It's not that cold. The kid just needs a friend, that's all. I don't see you hanging around."

"I am hanging around. I'm not going anywhere." He didn't have to say the rest; the words hung in the air between them, clear as ice. *I'm not going anywhere without Jane.*

"Ah," Devon said. "So."

Graham crouched down by Alex. "I'll bet a million dollars your mom thinks you're lying in bed right now, snug as a bug."

Alex reached out and clutched his sleeve. Some men found their courage on the battlefield; others on the day their child was born. Graham found the first traces of his when his nephew touched him. Devon might be an ace at stealing girls and mountain bikes, but Graham drew the line right here, at a boy's innocence. For the first time in his life, Graham wondered what it would be like to get into a fight. He wondered how much it would hurt to be beaten and if it might just be worth it anyway.

He brushed the hair out of Alex's eyes and stood up. "Leave him alone," he said to Devon.

"I told you —"

"You won't get to Jane this way, so don't even try. Leave Alex alone. He's just a kid. He can't even speak."

"Maybe none of you are listening hard enough. Maybe he talks to me all the time."

Graham felt the cold for the first time that morning. He noticed ice had formed on the ends of Alex's hair.

"Go home now," he said to his nephew. "Go on and slip into bed. I won't tell your mom this time. But I don't want to see you out here this early again."

Alex took off running. Graham waited until he'd disappeared around the corner before he turned back to Devon.

"What's your game?"

Devon shrugged. He had on a light jacket too, but it was unzipped and he wasn't shivering. "No game. He needs me."

"I don't like the way he looks at you."

"Jesus, Graham, lighten up. I'm not some monster. I'm just the guy across the street. I'm the guy who's got the time to be with him."

"That's just it," Graham said. "You've got too much time."

"It's not a crime."

"Maybe it is."

"Look —"

Graham shook his head and started back across the Common. He had a full schedule of patients this morning, though he hardly felt like doctoring anyone. If Josie Aberdeen came in with one more cold, he had no idea what he would do. He might start prescribing acupuncture or a warmer climate. He looked down at his hands and could hardly hold them steady.

"See you tomorrow, doc," Devon called after him.

Graham walked faster. He would have done anything to defy him, but he knew that when he woke at four in the morning, his legs would be itching to ride. He wouldn't be able to resist the idea that it might be the day he rode faster. Tomorrow might be the day he finally won.

Jane was in way over her head. She stood in the bathroom, the old speckled linoleum in a heap at her feet. She had watched a video on how to lay tile and ripped out the mildewy floor with confidence, but now that she was faced with forty glazed yellow tiles and a tub of dark blue grout, she knew she should have hired a professional. She could start in the center, snap a chalk line, even use a straightedge, but somewhere along the line she'd get nervous or lazy and set a tile in crookedly. Even if she did the best job she could, the floor wouldn't be perfect, and that was what she was after. She wanted to do just one thing without messing it up. She wanted to walk in this room and see lines of grout as straight as rulers. She wanted to step on tiles as solid as stone.

But all she could do was mix the adhesive and take her chances. She smoothed it out on the floor and carefully laid the tiles in place. She started in the center, set the tiles against a straightedge, then smoothed in the grout.

Her grandmother came in three hours later, as she was rinsing the excess grout off the tiles. "Nice," Esther said.

Jane sat back on her heels. "They're crooked."

"Sometimes it's best not to look at things too closely, Jane. The overall effect is sunny and warm. Be happy with that."

Jane stood up, woozy from the smell of epoxy. She took a shower and dressed in jeans and her thickest white cable sweater. She stepped out onto the front porch and was met by an assault of icy wind and spoiled leaves. She breathed in the smell of a fast-approaching winter, a mix of wood smoke and steaming exhaust pipes and air so crisp and cold it bites.

On the porch railing was the dried yarrow she'd harvested yesterday. Against the laws of nature, all the petals had rebloomed and were the color of vanilla pudding. While everyone else's grass had turned brown and icy, hers had stayed green and continued to grow through snow and hard frosts. She loved flowers as much as the next person, but all this growth was unnerving. She was getting used to it. When a killer frost killed off everything, she'd have no idea what to do.

She was still dizzy, so she walked toward Main Street. As soon as she turned the corner, she almost went back. Sandy Aberdeen had come out of Jim's Mercantile, her face blotchy red, the color of desire. Marilyn Ludlow rushed out the door of the real estate office, her high heels slipping on the icy pavement, but her skin so warm from wanting she gave off a shimmery mirage of heat.

Devon was whizzing down the street on his bike, dressed all in black Lycra, looking so good he made married women weep. Though Jane had sworn off him, though it annoyed her to no end that a good rain had washed away all that rock salt, there was no denying he made her feel every inch of her skin. Just the sight of him made the hair on her arms rise up in pleasure. He rode toward her, smiling, as Sandy Aberdeen reluctantly went back in the store and Marilyn Ludlow sighed when she saw he was not coming for her.

"Hey stranger," he said, pulling up beside Jane. He took off his helmet and all his shaggy hair spilt out. Josie Aberdeen had spotted him riding clear over in Fair Haven, when she'd been visiting a cousin. Rachel Simpson had sworn she'd seen a flash of his gold hair and sport glasses on the top of Tinmouth Mountain. Roy Carter had seen him as far away as Woodstock, riding just for the hell of it, to see how much distance he could cover. Today, though, he must not have gone very far at all, because he didn't have even the smallest gleam of sweat on him.

"I'm on my way to Graham's," he said. "He wants to make sure I healed up all right." He held up his arm, smiling at the impressive purple scar.

"I shudder to think how fast you ride with Alex," she said.

"You'll be glad to know I go well below the speed limit. It's Graham you've got to worry about. He's the wild man. Hey, come on in with me. I'm sure the doc would love to see you."

He didn't even look before riding out into the street, but it didn't matter because the moment Karen Wright saw him, she stalled her Subaru in the middle lane. He smiled at her, then parked his bike outside Graham's office. Beth Shultz was waving at him from inside.

"Come on," Devon called to her from across the street. Jane hesitated, then stepped off the curb.

As soon as they opened the door, Beth sprung to her feet. She smoothed her plump hands down the front of her skirt. "Devon," she said, "what can I do for you?"

"The cover is that I need to get these stitches out. But what I really wanted was to see your pretty face."

Beth blushed and Jane would have left then, if Graham hadn't come out of one of the examining rooms with Brenda Carlton. "Sometimes these things just turn themselves around," he was saying. "I'm happy for you and Dan. You've still got all the baby stuff in storage, right? Well, start taking it down."

Brenda squeezed Jane's arm going past, then rushed outside. Graham looked from Devon to Jane, then finally at Beth.

"He's here for the stitches," Beth said, as if things needed explaining.

"All right then," Graham said. "That should only take a few minutes. Are you here for support?"

He didn't look right at her, but still Jane could feel the heat of his stare. "No. I was a little dizzy. All those tiles, and then . . ." She realized they were staring at her. She could see the choice set out in front of her as clearly as if they were both holding out oranges, expecting her to pick the best one. Suddenly, the room was cloying with the smell of fruit, and she couldn't have taken a deep breath if she tried.

She turned and walked out. By the time she hit the sidewalk, she was running. She got clear to the statue in the Common before

Devon caught up to her.

"Wait a minute," he said, grabbing her wrist. "Just wait."

Jane was still unsteady, and she grabbed hold of Ethan Allen's bronze knee. She was in no state of mind to be looking at heartbreakers, but nevertheless she looked up, and there was Devon. He had a look in his eyes she hadn't seen in seven years. Purely passionate, probably disloyal, and totally compelling. She leaned against the statue and it all came back to her.

Her grandmother had given her the recipe for love when she was a child, and she had written it down in indelible ink. *Stand due north, clutch a piece of his clothing, and whisper the truest thing you know.*

She had taken the recipe out often those first years after she met Ned, but she had not used it. She had hoped he would fall in love with her naturally. She had hoped she would be magic enough on her own.

Then, on her sixteenth birthday, when she spotted Ned coming out of the Pendleton High girls' locker room with six different colors of lipstick on his cheeks, she stood in front of Ethan Allen's statue. The day before, she had taken a pair of scissors to Orion's Bar and, while Ned was singing, cut out a piece of his jacket. On the day she gave up all hope, she stood facing north, clutched that piece in her right hand and whispered, "I will

255

always love Ned Payton."

The robin that had been roosting atop Ethan Allen's head started singing like crazy. And before she could take a deep breath, or wonder if her wish would come true, Ned turned a corner and ran across the park.

"Jane," he said when he reached her, then suddenly stopped. He cocked his head, as if he suddenly realized who she was, and who she was surprised him. He started to walk past, then turned around.

"What are you doing here?" he asked. He looked down at her clutched hand, from which protruded a piece of royal blue polyester. He opened the jacket he was wearing and stared at the hole in the lining.

"I guess I'm waiting for you," she said.

She held her breath. The rumor was he was falling for Sue Jarvis, who was known to go all the way any time anyone asked, and to like it. Ned cocked his head again, then he stepped toward her.

He touched her arm above the elbow, then slowly massaged his thumb over her skin. He looked into her eyes and his mouth fell open a little. For the first time, she saw what no one believed was possible to see in Ned. She saw hesitation, a moment's uncertainty of himself and what he wanted. Need of her.

"Jane," he said, "what have you done?"

He closed the gap between them and kissed her. His lips were so much sweeter than all her fantasies, the pleasure spread clear down to her toes. She heard the rushing of blood between her ears. She heard the sound of her loving him forever — it was both shrill and familiar, like the constant hum of traffic. He slipped his arm around her waist and pulled her close to him. She could feel the rap-a-tap-tap of his heart against her chest.

He pulled back just long enough to whisper her name, then kissed her again. The robin trilled on above them, and Jane blessed her grandmother and magic for making a man who had vowed never to fall in love fall in love with her.

Now, Devon squeezed her wrist. "So?" he asked.

"So Graham's my friend," she said. "He's always been my friend. I'm not asking for anything more."

He nodded, and his fingers worked their way up her arm to her shoulder. Before she knew what he was doing, he'd run one across her bottom lip. He was kissing her long before she came to her senses and pulled away.

"That doesn't mean I'm interested in you," she said.

Devon laughed and let her go. He hopped up into the crook of Ethan Allen's arm and shouted, "I'm in love with Jane Gregory!"

"Devon, stop," Jane said, but deep down she didn't want him to. Deep down, she thought his devotion was just what she deserved.

The morning of Alex's appointment with the Boston specialist it was near freezing, and Jane picked up her coat. Alex was already waiting in the car, Esther was up in the newly walled-in attic, painting stars on the ceiling. Jane locked the front door, then turned to find Graham standing on her porch.

"My slate is clean today," he said. "I'm coming with you."

She hesitated, then walked past him to the car. Alex had turned on the radio and was flipping stations, but when he saw Graham, he smiled and climbed into the backseat.

"No," Jane said. "I don't think so."

She tried to get into the car, but Graham grabbed her arm. "I'm coming. Don't even try to stop me."

Beneath the threat, she heard the plea. She took a deep breath and glanced at Alex. She ought to resist, but she was already clinging to the hope in Graham's eyes. If she went to Boston alone, she would spend the entire drive preparing to be disappointed again, and trying to figure a way to soften the blow for Alex. Without Graham, there would be no hope at all.

"You think Doctor Swirling is good?" she asked.

"The best. Come on. I'll drive."

She walked around the car and got in. "How about country?" Graham was asking Alex, and

Alex stuck his finger in his mouth.

Graham laughed. "KLZX? A little pop?"

Alex nodded and sat back after Graham had adjusted the station. Jane could feel Alex's foot tapping the back of her seat. The bruise beneath his left cheek had almost vanished. Billy Weinstock, she'd heard, had been shouted down by his father in the middle of the frozen-food aisle of Jim's Mercantile. He'd been told if he ever got suspended again, he'd get a whipping he'd never recover from.

"All right, then," Graham said. "We're off."

The appointment lasted an hour and a half. By the time they came out, there was a light dusting of fresh snow over the parking lot. Alex walked backward, to see the tracks they left. They all got in the car, then Graham squeezed the steering wheel.

"All right," he said. "No go. But I know a neurosurgeon at Cornell. The best, Jane. I'll call him first thing tomorrow."

Jane shook her head. She did not dare turn around, where she knew Alex sat looking out the window, his face pressed up to the glass. "No more. They're not going to find anything. You know they're not."

"Let's not talk about this now. I'm still hopeful. I think —"

Jane reached over and took his hand. She squeezed so tightly he went quiet. By the time she let go, he just started up the car.

259

When they got to Westminster, he didn't even ask, just took the exit toward Wachusett Mountain.

"I don't think —"

"Hey," he said, "I promised Alex some fun. You up for some sledding, big guy? Wait till you see this hill. Half a mile of cool, clear ice. You can't help but crash."

"You don't have to do this," Jane said.

Graham glanced at her. "Oh yes I do."

They rented a four-man toboggan and Graham lugged it up the hill, maneuvering around small bodies plastered all over the snow. What seemed a delicate rise in summer turned treacherously irresistible as soon as the first snow fell. There were a pair of Eastern redbuds halfway down, their trunks dented and leaning from novice sledders. At the bottom, a snowbank had been built up six feet high, to keep people from flying onto the highway.

Graham steadied the toboggan on the crest of the hill. Alex took the front spot, his small hands holding tight to the wooden curl. Jane wrapped her legs around him, then Graham got in behind her and slipped his arms around her hips, resting his hands just above her knees.

"You ready?" he said, and before waiting for an answer, he pushed off.

It was a directionless ride; they skidded right and left, just barely missing toddlers and their terrified parents. Jane would have cried out, if she hadn't heard something like a whistle coming from Alex's mouth. When they hit their fastest speed, it burst through like magic, a sound like *whish, whish.*

With that melody in her ears, she leaned back, and Graham wrapped his arms around her waist. She tucked her face into the curl of his neck; she was still there when they finally crashed into the snowbank. Alex jumped up delightedly, snow-covered and ready to go again.

They sledded until the sun dipped below the mountain, the temperature slipped to the teens, and the teenager in the rental booth shouted at them to come in. Back in the car, with the heat on full, Graham shook the snow out of his hair. "Have you ever gone that fast in your life?" he asked, his voice hoarse from screaming.

Alex smiled. He curled up on the backseat and Jane reached back to put a blanket over him.

"It's too far to go all the way home tonight," Graham said. "What do you say we find a place to stay?"

She could feel him watching her, but she just smoothed out the blanket, then stared straight ahead. She was so cold her fingers had trouble working. She kicked off her shoes and looked down at blue toenails.

"I'm not sure that's such a good idea."

"Why not?"

There were a thousand reasons — because it had felt too good to lean against him, because she was leaving Pendleton after the house was done, because she'd spent all these years trying to climb up out of the past and he was stuck knee-deep in it. But all she said was "Because things just might get out of control."

"And that's a bad thing?"

"Absolutely."

"Look at him," he said, and Jane turned around to find Alex already asleep. "Two rooms in a dingy hotel. Trust me, no one's going to be thinking about anything but sleep."

She nodded reluctantly, but of course by the time she got Alex tucked in beneath a stained orange comforter, in a small room of the Fitchburg Motor Inn, all she could think about was Graham, two doors down. She tried to watch the local news, but after fifteen minutes of traffic accidents and miraculous rescues, she gave up. She took a hot bath and finally purged the blue from her toes. She put back on her jeans and sweater, which she'd have to sleep in, kissed Alex's cheek, then grabbed the room key off the dresser.

She only had to knock on Graham's door once. He'd taken a shower — his hair curled around his ears, a dark brown clump clung to his forehead. She reached out and brushed it off and before she could pull back, he grasped her hand.

"It would be unfair," she said.

"Then give me unfair."

She shook her head; she was already crying and knew she wouldn't be able to stop for a long time. "Can't you feel him? He's right here between us."

Graham looked down, but if he saw the third shadow he gave no notice. He just squeezed her hand harder.

"I can't keep asking you," he said. "You can't keep breaking my heart."

"Look at me, Graham," she said. "He's ruined me."

He stepped back, and it was probably that retreat that made her step forward, and wrap her arms around him, and kiss him for all she was worth. He was made up of nothing but yearning, but she knew, no matter how hard they kissed, he still wasn't getting what he was after. He wanted that deepest part of her, the part where blood formed, where her most fervent desire swelled into a tight ball in her chest. He didn't want to steal her soul, he wanted her to give it to him, and he was just now realizing how impossible that was, unless he could somehow talk Ned into giving it back.

So in the end, it was Graham who pulled away, who stopped in the middle of a kiss they couldn't start up again. It was Graham who stepped back without saying a word, and just turned his back on her.

"Don't hate me," she whispered. "I couldn't bear it."

He flinched, but did not turn around. Not even when she closed the door. Not for a long time after.

When a man finally gets his heart's desire, he sometimes doesn't know what to do with it. True love and a million dollars are like someone else's clothes; they hang on him strangely, in lines he had not anticipated. For weeks, sometimes months, they reek of the unfamiliar.

Even Devon Zeke, who'd gotten most everything he asked for, felt momentarily flustered when Al Miguel, owner of Techline Bicycles of Moab, Utah, called him early one morning. He had expected success — in fact he'd never doubted it — yet when the man asked him if he was interested in coming to Moab to join the Techline cycling team, Devon put his head in his hands. With a path set ahead of him, he felt like he no longer had anywhere to turn.

"You'd be based here," Miguel went on. "It's prime mountain bike country. We were very impressed with the résumé you sent in, your placings in the East Coast races. We think you could be a valuable asset to the team."

Devon looked at the palms of his hands. He had a short lifeline, or so Cindy Davis had told him after she'd read a book on palm reading. He knew he had to take advantage of every opportunity because he was the kind of man found beneath avalanches or among the crash wreckage of experimental planes. He knew this, yet he hesitated. His whole life seemed a fluke. He wondered why he kept getting all these chances and when his luck would finally give out.

Then he shook his head. A man grabbed his opportunities, he went crazy thinking too much. "When do you want me?" he asked.

"How about right after the holidays?"

"I'll be there."

After Devon hung up, he walked out on the back porch. He stood in jeans and a T-shirt, despite the thirty-degree temperature. He had never been west of the Mississippi; he knew about Moab only from pictures he'd seen, things he'd heard from more traveled racers. He knew only that he belonged there, that this was destiny, and it didn't matter one bit that he was going only because he'd lied.

The résumé, of course, was faked. He'd run a couple of the races listed, but he'd never come in anywhere close to the top ten. He'd forged the numbers because he knew he could have come in higher, if he'd wanted to, if he hadn't noticed the girls along the route, wearing short-shorts and bikini tops, whistling each time he passed. He could have come in number one, he was sure, if he'd trained more — which he would, once he had the guarantee it would net him something.

He felt only a flicker of conscience, then brushed it aside. Everybody fudged their credentials. If Techline didn't check their applicants' stats, that was their problem. The truth was, he was a hell of a racer. They should feel grateful to be getting him. He should feel grateful, but strangely he did not. His head was dizzy and his hands tingled, as if all his blood had flowed to his brain, leaving the rest of him empty and weak.

He went back inside and threw on a sweater he'd lifted off the shelf at Patrini's. It was dark blue, with thin strands of white. When women saw him in it, they touched him in full view of their husbands, they rubbed the fabric between their fingers and licked their lips. When Jane saw him wearing it, she would imagine herself standing with him beneath a pastel desert sky. Jane was part of his destiny, too. He could feel it as if electricity streaked the air when she was around him. He didn't know where they would end up. He didn't know how long he could love a single woman; he only knew he did love her, and that was unexpected enough to warrant further action. When he asked her to come with him to Moab, it would all seem inevitable. She'd have no choice but to say yes.

The first real snow came at the end of November and didn't stop for six days. It piled so high, so fast, the winter songbirds nesting on the Simpsons' windowsill were buried in the middle of their songs. Richard George, of George's Plow, could not believe his good fortune. He hired two men just out on parole, but even with incentives like minimum wage and all the whiskey they could drink, they could not keep up with the storms. Within twenty minutes, the roads they'd plowed were covered again. The drifts they piled along the sidewalks grew fifteen feet tall and hard as granite.

Jane went out in it every morning before work. Today, she walked the perimeter of town, her head down, not seeing the snowmen in the Aberdeens' front yard, or the bright red berry wreaths Hazel MacNamara hung on her picket fence every winter. She liked it best during snowstorms, when she didn't meet anyone, when all she saw was white. Pendleton was picturesque, but she'd like to know how many people here had died of heartbreak. She'd like to test the water for traces of despair, because she was close to the breaking point and Alex, if this was possible, might even be getting worse.

Last night, Devon had shown up on their doorstep, holding out two white lilies he'd gotten from God knows where. Alex had run out of his bedroom and straight into his arms, and Devon had swung him around as if he weighed no more than an empty sack. He threw him straight up in the air and Alex squealed, a deep, throaty croak that did not sound like a little boy's voice at all.

"Want to hear that again?" Devon had asked, staring at Jane. He had not been smiling. Then he threw Alex up again, and her son squealed once more, giving her the shivers.

It was not the voice she had expected; it was short-lived and shrill, nearly dead on arrival.

Still, Devon had pried it out of him. What was a mother compared to a strong, reckless man? Devon was not bound by love, so he could induce fear, the kind that brought a scream from an otherwise silent boy.

Finally, he had lowered Alex to the ground. He had looked at her as if she should thank him, and that made her straighten her back. It made her, the moment he left, take out Ned's picture and stare at it. He wasn't an average ghost, obviously, because rock salt didn't bother him at all. A woman telling him to shoo after all these years just made him show up in a stranger's hairstyle, or his brother's eyes. So Jane did the only thing she could think of. She took the photograph to the kitchen stove, turned on the front gas burner, and dropped the photo into the flame.

The picture curled in on itself; Ned's white teeth were the last to go. Jane stood with her hands on either side of the stove, she stood until he was ashes. Then she turned off the burner, took a deep breath, and blew what was left of him as far as she could — which turned out to be only to the edge of the kitchen sink.

Now, she walked toward the Common. She put her head down and started across the deep snow, sinking three inches with each step. She didn't see the men until she was nearly upon them; their race made no noise at all. Devon and Graham were buckled into snowshoes, flying across the soft snow around Ethan Allen's statue.

They were both fast, but it was easy to see who was winning. In the softest powder, Graham sunk a good inch, but Devon just flew by. He was light as air and his laugh shattered the icicles on the highest branches of the leafless maple trees.

Finally, when Devon raced toward the end of the park, uncatchable, Graham just stopped and leaned against the statue. He was breathing so hard, his breath melted the snow on Ethan Allen's knee. Jane thought he might have hurt himself, but by the time she reached him, she saw he was just staring up at the sky, furious. He kicked off his snowshoes, and one went flying past her face.

"Graham," she said, "what's wrong with you?"

The fury in his eyes did not abate when he looked at her; it was simply coupled with something else, something very close to despair. She reached out and touched his cold cheek. He lifted his hand up over hers.

A shadow crossed them and Jane looked up to find Devon standing directly in the path of the sun.

"Maybe next time," he said to Graham.

Jane was aware of many things at once. The chill of Graham's cheek beneath her fingers, the fact that all the snow had melted beneath Devon's feet, and that it was impossible to have a decent conversation with three people. Someone was always left out.

Graham stepped back. Very deliberately, he uncurled his fingers from hers. Jane tucked her hand up beneath her chin. She felt cold to the bone. She felt like breaking down and crying. It wasn't just that she'd used her spell on the wrong man all those years ago. It was that sometime in the last few months, she had lost her best friend.

Graham picked up his snowshoes and strapped them on.

"You can't be wearing those old wooden shoes," Devon said. "I'll score you some aluminum ones. Then you might have a chance."

Graham left without saying goodbye. Jane started after him, but Devon grabbed her arm.

"Let him go," he said quietly. "You'd only be hurting him more."

Jane turned on him. "What are you doing to him?"

"Surprisingly, nothing. I wouldn't even be here if he didn't get me out of bed every morning. This is all coming from him, Jane."

Jane watched Graham turn the corner, still pounding his snowshoes into the packed snow, and knew Devon told the truth.

"Anyway," he went on. "I'm glad you're here. I've got a proposition you can't refuse."

Jane stepped back. She even thought of running, which would have been something, which she would later think would have been the smart thing to do.

"I got an offer from a huge sponsor in Moab," he went on. "It's what I've been waiting for."

Jane felt relief and panic in equal portions; she felt what she had always felt, that she could love him or hate him, it made no difference. He worked only the extremes of her heart; everything in the middle was just left to rot.

"You're leaving?" she said.

"Not just me." He took her hand. "You, me, and Alex. Hell, your grandma if she wants to come. Let's get the hell out of here, Jane."

Jane looked down at their hands. His fingers were looped through hers, he stroked his thumb across her knuckles. She felt heat straight down to her toes, which wasn't a sign of anything, except that she should have bolted the moment she saw him coming.

"Devon . . ."

"I know. This is where you grew up. But I'm telling you, Utah's the place. Techline's going to put me up, pay all my expenses. This time next year, I'll be a household name. You'll have money and houses and cars like you wouldn't believe."

"You don't understand," she said, stepping away. "I can't go anywhere with you."

"What's here for you?" Devon reached out and plucked at the strings of her hair. "A bunch of bad memories? A crappy job in a gift shop? Look, I just don't do this sort of thing. I don't

271

know why I'm doing it now. I only know we're meant to be together. I'm telling you, I can feel it."

He stared at her and didn't smile. He looked straight into her soul and jumbled what was there. He made her weak. He made her remember. He made her believe everything he said was true.

"Devon . . ."

"Talk to Alex," he said. "The kid will love the idea. He was made for a life of adventure."

"You still don't understand about Alex."

"That's just it. I do. He needs a dad, and he's the only person in the world who's ever thought I could actually be a good one. You think I'm gonna mess that up? Come on, Jane, run away with me. Take a chance. I'm honest enough to say I'm not perfect. Can you be with a guy who will probably end up hurting you?"

Jane closed her eyes. The past felt like a presence, a sultry mass of air that would always cling to her unless she took her deepest breath and blew it away. Jane, though, could hardly breathe at all. She had trouble just removing her hand from his.

"I'm not going," she said, but they both heard the quiver in her voice. They both knew she could very easily be saying something else.

She backed away from him. He just smiled and watched her go. Once she was across the Common, she turned and ran toward home. Halfway there, she realized she'd just lost more

than her will. The scent of rain on her had vanished and, by the time she reached her house,
the Perfume Delight rosebush had split in two.

Nine

Ivy Blake had always known what she wanted, and it wasn't much. She wanted what every person was entitled to, what teenagers scorned and their parents didn't appreciate: a middle-class life. A peach tract house with a television in every room, a dozen maxed-out Visas, and Sundays at the zoo.

No one would ever know this by looking at her; she wore miniskirts and black lipstick and could drink the men in Orion's Bar under the table. She had a fake ID that she altered annually to keep her twenty-six and a natural redhead forever. In truth, she would be thirty in December, she bought a box of Number 361 Crimson Tide hair dye once a month, and she was no fool. She dressed like a hooker and never cried when a man sneaked out in the middle of the night because she knew the second she admitted she wanted anything, she'd be doomed. But Ivy had not given up hope. She knew if she held out long enough, one man, just one good man, would finally look her way.

One good man, not someone like Brady

Gardner, who had almost killed her with a baseball bat one summer night after he'd downed seventeen shots of tequila and suddenly didn't like the look of her hair. Not someone like Zach Leyland, who followed her night after night into Orion's Bar and Jim's Alibi, but had never, in five years, said a single word to her.

The kind of man Ivy Blake wanted was sitting ten feet away, beneath the purple-tinted light bulbs in Orion's Bar. A man like Jake Orofino, Adam Gottlieb, or Devon Zeke, the racers who congregated nightly at Orion's. She wasn't picky, she would have taken any of them. They all had that look she loved — long hair pushed casually behind their ears, lean, sinewy lines, and eyes so disinterested, they were irresistible.

Ivy had been coming to Orion's for five years now, since she moved into the deserted shack on the edge of town that had once housed Bill Whitaker's pet rabbits. Mr. Whitaker had thought them all females, until fuzzy little bunnies started popping up everywhere — in drainpipes and soup pots and, most remarkably, in his locked gun cabinet beneath a classic Remington revolver. He'd shot them all dead one afternoon, but he must have taken care to clean up after himself, because when Ivy moved in, there wasn't a speck of blood on the concrete floor. There was also no electricity or running water, but Ivy had paid Brady a blow job to put in an old woodstove for heat. She took showers at her friend Hannah's house, and worked three nights a week as a cocktail waitress in Rutland to make enough money to buy beer and hair coloring. She had an unpolished life, and she knew it, so she came to Orion's and Lenny's Bar and Jim's Alibi every night, in search of the man who would shine it for her.

The first week of December, Ivy stared at the three racers, then down into her drink, where she saw her own reflection in ice cubes. She had blue eyes lined with kohl — eyes that had been pretty in high school but now were garish everywhere except under dim bar lights. There were lines around her mouth that would not have come for another twenty years, if she'd gotten her middle-class life.

She turned back to the men and stared so hard, Jake Orofino turned around in his chair. They'd grown up together in Pendleton, she and Jake, but he had never said a single word to her. He had ditched most of his senior year and, later, failed the GED. Despite having the blackest hair and bluest eyes, he had never had a girlfriend — he'd been more into getting stoned and looking bad enough to rip someone's heart out.

Now he stared at her, and Ivy knew enough not to smile back, just to stare over the rim of her drink and pretend he didn't raise her pulse. When his gaze skipped off her to eighteen-year-old Tammie Wren, who everyone knew threw up after every meal to stay that thin, she did not let herself be disappointed. Self-pity on a thirty-year-old was more pathetic than desire; it looked like ten extra pounds and the wrong color of eye shadow. It looked like everything Jake would never want.

She ordered another vodka and looked up to find Zach Leyland at his usual spot at the bar, watching her. He was only five feet two; his feet dangled off the stool like a child's. He worked at the liquor store and would not sell beer to pregnant women. Last Christmas, Ivy had come home from Orion's early to find him stringing battery-operated white lights around her shack. He'd sent her unsigned love poems and sometimes, late at night, she thought she heard his asthmatic breathing through her thin walls.

As soon as she caught him looking, he turned away. He gave her the creeps, but that didn't mean she had ruled him out entirely. She was not getting any younger and would only be bone-thin so long. She knew plenty of women who had married thieves and psychos, just so they could have a decent roof over their heads and steak once a week.

But for now, she believed she still had a shot at something better, so she sat in Orion's for one hour, then two, then three, waiting for one of the racers to approach her. At midnight, Jake Orofino finally got to his feet. He took a wad of bills out of his pocket and tossed them on the table. He slapped his friends' hands, then walked toward the door.

When he passed Ivy's table, he slowed. From the way the hair rose on her arms, she knew he was watching her, but she didn't look up. She studied his boots — dark brown, leather, nice. She stared at the cut of his jeans — tight and tapered, just the way she liked them. Then he marched past and was gone.

Adam Gottlieb left next. He had sunny blond hair and a nice smile, and Ivy knew he wouldn't be worth a dime in bed. Still, she smiled when he passed, because sex was cheap and if she didn't find it with her husband, she could easily get it somewhere else. But Adam had a girl-friend in Middlebury and didn't even look her way.

Only Devon Zeke was left, and Ivy finished her drink. The rumor was he had fallen for Jane Gregory, and every girl in town knew there was no competing with her. Jane had her grand-mother's magic; she concocted potions and had men eating out of the palm of her hand. Ned Payton had been wild and horny, and look how she had tamed him. Devon Zeke was the kind of man who should be forgetting women's names the moment he whispered them in their ears, but instead he was getting serious about Jane. Ivy had dreams, but she also knew when a man was out of her league, when it would only hurt to dream about him.

So she was speechless when Devon walked to

her table and sat down, when he looked right in her eyes. He smiled, and she covered up her blush with long pink fingernails.

"You're looking good tonight, Ivy," he said.

She had watched him drinking — half a dozen beers, two tequila shooters, one brandy — but he did not seem the slightest bit drunk. She was the one who wavered when he reached over and took her hand.

"What do you say we go for a walk?"

Ivy could not say anything. She barely felt his hand when he helped her to her feet and guided her to the door. Her skin prickled from all the stunned gazes on them.

When they got outside, the cold wind stung her bare legs below her miniskirt. "I thought you were taken," she said, shivering.

Devon let go of her hand. For a moment, she was so certain he would leave, she reached into her purse for her keys.

"What if I am?" he said.

Ivy shrugged and followed him to his car. She pounded her feet hard enough to leave heel marks in the snow, just to make sure she wasn't dreaming. Despite all her hoping, she had never actually believed that wishes came true.

Graham was up and dressed in his cycling gear at three in the morning. The roads were icy; the lawns covered with another inch of new snow. He thought about telling Devon these were unfavorable conditions for riding, but knew he'd get only a laugh. Devon would ride through snowdrifts. As soon as Pendleton Pond froze over, he would no doubt ride over that too.

Graham walked with his head down, his hands jammed in his pockets, and got to Sycamore Lane by a quarter to four. He didn't look up until he was halfway down the street, and then he saw the woman on Devon's porch. She had long red hair, snow stuck to her bare knees, and she was clutching Devon's sleeve. Graham stepped behind Marjorie Dumas's holly bush.

When the woman's scratchy voice drifted up over the bush, he recognized it as Ivy Blake's. He had treated her for bronchitis half a dozen times in two years, always for free because everyone knew she lived in a rabbit barn.

"I thought you wanted me to . . ." she said, and then the wind took her voice the other way.

Graham stared across the street to Jane's. After that night at the Fitchburg motel, he had gathered up the rest of his postcards and dumped them, unaddressed, into the mailbox. He was done with it, or so he told himself. He was through, but already he could tell it was like giving up smoking. Long after the habit was broken, he was going to go on wanting it. His dreams were nothing but taunts; night after night, he dreamed her beside him, he made her love him, he made Ned powerless as dust.

He waited for Devon's reply, but it was garbled in the breeze. He did, however, hear Ivy crying. He heard those four-inch heels she always wore punching cracks through the snow as she ran. He didn't dare peek out behind the bush until all was silent and, by then, Ivy was long gone.

He walked to Devon's house and didn't knock. He opened the door and found Devon leaning against the bare wall, his hands slung under his armpits, his face dark.

"All right," Devon said. "Let's ride."

Graham and Devon rode around Tinmouth Mountain, down to Danby Four Corners, and back around by Lake St. Catherine, so they did not hear the sirens, nor did they pass by Pendleton Common, where two dozen Pendleton residents stood in their flannel pajamas, wondering aloud how so much blood could have come from just one person.

By the time they reached Devon's house, at six in the morning, the coroner had already arrived from Rutland to photograph and wrap up Ivy Blake's body. Tyler Ludlow, who had been walking back across the Common after staying at a friend's house all night, and who had found the body stabbed in forty-eight places, was already in the backseat of his mother's banana-scented Saab, on the way to the coast, where Marilyn Ludlow was certain the rough sea air would make him stop shaking. Mark Sharkey, Pendleton's sheriff, had dried his eyes, soothed his stomach with half a roll of Tums, and was standing on Devon's front porch.

Graham knew the look on Mark Sharkey's face — he'd seen it often enough on his father's — the mixture of dread and perverse excitement. He drew away from it, but Devon dropped his bike on the snowy lawn and walked right up the steps.

"What can I do for you, Sheriff?" he said, smiling.

Mark Sharkey was fat and silly; he played golf every summer afternoon and answered the phone at the police station with "Howdy." He had been a pool man before becoming sheriff when Graham's father, William, moved to Florida. He couldn't stand the sight of blood and had blamed William personally for the four murders during the older man's tenure.

Now, though, a woman he had repeatedly hauled in for drunk driving had had her chest split open. Mark Sharkey took one look at Devon and started crying.

"Hey," Devon said, reaching out to the sheriff, then dropping his hand. "Whatever it is, I didn't do it."

He laughed, but the sheriff only turned away to dry the tears that had already turned to ice on his cheeks.

"It's Ivy," he said at last. "Ivy Blake. Murdered last night. You were the last one seen with her, Devon."

Devon's smile did not falter as he stepped back. Graham finally took off his helmet and walked up the steps.

"I left Orion's with her," Devon said. "We walked a while. Talked. She left here at, I don't know, four."

Graham was sweating, though the morning had gotten steadily colder and just a moment ago he'd been chilled. He was thinking of Ivy Blake and that red hair that looked like it had been dyed with food coloring. He was thinking of the way she had stared at the wedding ring on his finger when she came in for exams, like something inside her was burning.

Mark Sharkey asked questions from a manual he'd brought along. He wrote down Devon's answers painstakingly, crying all the while, soaking his pad.

"Well," he said at last, "I probably should bring you in, do this officially. You got a lawyer?"

"Am I under arrest?"

"Nope."

"Then I don't need a lawyer."

Mark Sharkey seemed to notice Graham for the first time. "Hey Doc, you with Mr. Zeke last night? You his alibi?"

Graham looked at Devon and his mouth got dry. Graham could already see relief in Devon's eyes, a slick confidence that made Graham tense, then take a step back. Ned had made the same false assumptions, that everyone was for him, that in a pinch there wasn't a man alive who wouldn't defend him.

There was a man, though, and Graham was him. "No," he said. "We just ran into each other riding."

Mark Sharkey nodded, then started down the steps. "All right then. Come on, Devon. Let's take you in."

Graham expected Devon to contradict him, maybe even to throw a punch as he walked by, but all he did was stare. Graham expected rage, but he had looked in the mirror enough to know it was only disappointment that stained Devon's eyes black. Graham turned into the wind, until he was cold enough to know exactly what he was doing. He waited until Devon got into the police car with the sheriff before starting down the steps. He didn't look at Jane's house as he walked home.

The news of the murder, and Devon's possible involvement, was all over town within two hours. Mark Sharkey kept Devon at the small station for an hour and a half, read him every question in the manual William Payton had written for murder investigations, then released him for lack of evidence and because he — the sheriff — had a splitting headache. As soon as Devon left, Sharkey took four aspirins and called Roy Carter, his best friend and, fortuitously, the owner of Orion's Bar. Roy Carter filled a blender with triple kamikazes and took the drinks to the station.

By the time Mark Sharkey was passed out in

one of the open cells, Roy Carter was beside Ethan Allen's statue, staring at blood splayed fifty feet in all directions. Roy Carter had gotten into fistfights with bad tippers, he'd left long-term girlfriends when they put on a little weight, but when he thought of a girl struggling for her life, with blood dripping from every inch of her, he sat down on the strawberry-colored snow and cried.

Marjorie Dumas found him there. She'd heard the sirens; she had only been waiting for daylight to find out for herself what was going on and why no one had called her. Once Roy told her the news, she headed straight for Jane's.

Jane listened without letting Marjorie inside the house. With every word, she held herself tighter, until there were white handprints on her arms.

"So I guess Devon left the bar with her," Marjorie said. "He might have even taken her home. He's their only suspect at this point. Can you believe that?"

Jane looked past her to Devon's house. "No," she said quietly. "I can't."

After Marjorie left, Jane walked to the kitchen and picked up the map of Utah and the sego lily Devon had left on her doorstep two nights earlier. She had not opened the map or put the flower in water, but nevertheless, since then, she had been overwhelmed by the scent of desert flowers and sage. Her dreams had been drowned out by the hum of air conditioners that ran all night long, and in the mornings, her throat was parched, her lips cracked in a dozen places.

Ivy had been in the class behind hers, but Jane had not known her well. She hadn't paid much attention, to tell the truth. She'd been too involved in her own life, in winning Ned, to worry about a girl who wore too much makeup and tried to look like she cared about nothing. These last three months, she'd heard about Ivy living in an unwired shack on the edge of town, but she hadn't gone to see her. She hadn't brought her extra blankets.

Jane was still standing at the kitchen counter, clutching the lily, when her grandmother walked into the room. She told Esther the news without turning around.

"Let's hope that makes up your mind about him," Esther said.

Jane turned around suddenly. "I'm not going to Utah. Give me some credit."

Esther looked at the lily in her hand. "It's funny the things you'll consider when it's late at night and you haven't slept well for weeks."

"I can be friends with the man. I can manage that."

"Come here, Janie."

Esther walked out the front door and down the drive. Jane closed her eyes a moment, then followed. Something bad was happening; not only had the scent of rain left her, but yesterday, after a ferocious windstorm, she hadn't been able to generate the slightest shock. Worse than that; she had lost control of her thinking. When she ought to have been concentrating on sanding the floors down to a smooth, even finish, she was instead dreaming about balmy winters in Moab and the kind of sun that bakes out trouble.

"Look for yourself," Esther said, as Jane came up behind her. Esther stepped aside to reveal the withered, blackened roses. The bush had split and then curled over on itself, dropping most of its flowers. Those remaining were stiff and black, and when Jane reached out to touch one, the petals crumbled as if made of sand.

"The snow killed it," Jane said, but she shoved her trembling hands into her pockets.

"If you say so," Esther said.

"What do you think?"

Esther looked at her. "I think things are up for grabs now. If you can't mold things with magic, fate can take you anywhere."

Jane stared at the dead rosebush as Esther walked back in the house. She reached for one of the black petals clinging precariously to its stem, but the wind got to it first. It lifted it into the air over her head, then pulverized it. What was left fell to the ground like ashes.

Even though Richard George plowed away the bloody snow the day after Ivy's murder, for a week no one in Pendleton went out of their house after dark. Mothers kept their children home from school, fathers slept with shotguns beneath their pillows. Girls wore turtlenecks and mittens, as if the police were looking for a vampire instead of a man.

Mark Sharkey got help from the police force in Rutland, and Devon was brought in twice more for questioning. Graham was asked to verify the time he met Devon out riding, which he said to be somewhere around dawn. For a while, the young mothers stopped pushing their baby carriages past Devon's house. No one over sixty stepped foot on Sycamore Lane unless they lived there, and those people all wondered what they'd done to deserve such a fate. Teenage girls, though, who believed death was something that happened to the weak and frightened, called Devon nightly and hung up as soon as they heard his silky voice. The most daring peeked into his windows after midnight. The idea that he might be a murderer made their blood tingle. They got insomnia confusing violence for passion; at three in the morning, they swore they alone had the key to tame a beast.

Ivy had no family or close friends, but everyone in town turned out for her funeral. The Presbyterian church was stuffed with orchids Pendleton's best families had flown in from South America, the pews were jam-packed with neighbors trying to convince one another that this had only happened because she was trash. If Ivy had dressed nicer, gotten a decent job, and taken off that horrid lipstick, she'd be alive today. They left blood-red roses on her coffin and wrapped their children up in blankets for the ride home.

After two weeks, Mark Sharkey announced there was not enough evidence to arrest Devon or anyone else. There were no fingerprints, no traces of hair or foreign blood on the victim. There was no motive or murder weapon. Marjorie Dumas began spreading rumors of another murderer, a lowlife from New York City who was terrorizing small towns.

When the pond by the cemetery froze over, Randy Weaver strung up the lights and most parents once more let their teenagers come out at night to skate. Though senior citizens remained skittish when Devon passed by, most of his neighbors invited him to their Christmas parties and wondered how they ever could have doubted someone with such a charming smile.

Teenagers began making love again over the hole on Pendleton Bridge, but when twigs snapped nearby, they went running, leaving their clothes behind. When a van slowed on a street filled with children, someone invariably screamed. Eventually, the young mothers took to pushing their carriages in front of Devon's house again, but only long enough to prove it was a safe world for their children.

Jane had never considered it an especially

safe world, and after Ivy's death, she could no longer sleep through the night. She put her grandmother's .38 beneath her pillow and lay on the side of the bed closest to the door, in case she should have to run. She jumped at shadows and checked on Alex twice an hour. Two weeks after the murder, she got up at three in the morning and stood by her living room window.

She wondered what Devon was doing with all the lights on. Every other house on Sycamore Lane was dark except for the security lights that had sold out three hours after Ivy's body was discovered. Jane put her jacket and boots on over her pajamas, then walked across a smooth coating of new snow to Devon's front door.

She lifted her hand to knock, then lowered it. She'd been surprised, these last two weeks, when Devon had not called to declare his innocence, when he had left her to her imagination. He expected her to run away with him, but more than that, he expected her to believe in him. He had no idea his silence had a thousand holes in it, that people, if given enough time, considered everything a possibility.

She stepped away from the door. When it came right down to it, she didn't know a thing about him and she wanted to keep it that way. She could take almost anything, except being disappointed by another man. She turned around and started walking.

Because she was looking for it, she spotted the exact moment she fell in love. It happened when she turned the corner onto Welton Place, when she realized there was only one place to go, after all. But when she reached Graham's driveway, she didn't run to him; she only bowed her head. She did not know how to walk the fine line between loving someone and losing herself. She knew love cooled, that after ten years and two kids and a hundred-thousand-dollar mortgage, passion got a little more refined. But she couldn't get there, she couldn't take one step past the point where love just ate her up.

She heard a coyote howl, followed by a crash of aluminum garbage cans. She turned away, tears in her eyes. She'd meant what she'd said to Graham; Ned had ruined her. Ruined her for everyone but drifters and rock stars, men she didn't trust anyway and so was not taken in by their sweetness and lines. Men who offered her so little, she could not possibly hope for more. Men she would be careful never to love back.

Alex knew the school policy. Two absences in a row and the secretary called your parents. So he ditched only sporadically, and then brought in typed excuses, signed in the best forgery of his mother's hand he could master.

He hadn't ditched since last Monday, so this afternoon, while he ate lunch, he eyed the front gate. Billy Weinstock sometimes loitered there, tripping the kids who had to leave early for dentist appointments, but today Billy was eating lunch in Mrs. Hazelton's room, catching up on the work he'd missed while suspended. Billy had not said a word to him since he got back, which was some kind of miracle. Fred Weinstock, a former heavyweight boxer and Billy's father, had started picking him up after school, so there was no time to fight. The strangest thing was, every time Mrs. Hazelton called on him in class, Billy's voice got a little higher. Yesterday he gave the answer to a math question in a squeaky girl voice, and every single kid in class, even the nice ones, fell over in their chairs, laughing.

Alex finished his tuna sandwich, then tossed the brown bag in the garbage. He picked up his notebook and was headed for the gate when Linda Carlton blocked his path.

"You're gonna get caught," she said.

By an act of God, obviously, Mrs. Hazelton had moved Billy's seat to the front of the class, and Linda had taken the one beside Alex. During reading time, she tilted her head so far to the right, one of her braids dangled against his arm. It got so bad he had to read the same paragraph five times, just to take in what it said.

Now she reached out and touched his arm, just like that. He could feel the dragon hissing in his throat, but he swallowed hard and flushed him down. He could feel the monster battling, his legs and tail swatting the smooth cavity of his chest, but this was one chance Alex wasn't going to miss.

He reached into his back pocket and took out his spelling quiz, on which he'd scored an 85. He slid a pen out of his notebook.

Linda turned her back and Alex turned the paper over and pressed it against her pretty red jacket. He wrote softly, so the pen wouldn't break through and poke her.

He finished just as the bell rang. She turned around and he handed her the paper and ran. He got through the gates and around the building, then crept back to see what she'd done. She was still standing there, staring down at the paper, then she clutched it to her chest. Someone called her name, and she walked back to class.

Alex could have flattened Billy Weinstock on the spot, that was how high he was. It hadn't been much of a note, actually. If he'd had more time, he would have thought of something smarter. But since he'd been pressed, he'd only had the truth and indelible ink to work with. He'd only had the time to write *Yor butifel, Linda.*

He turned and ran all the way to Devon's house. Devon was sitting on the floor, playing his guitar. He smiled when Alex came in, then thumped the floor beside him.

Alex sat down and watched him play. He couldn't stop himself from coming here, not during school hours, or late at night, when he woke from dreams of speed and daredevil tricks and started walking toward Devon's before he'd even thought to put on snow boots.

He couldn't stop himself because, the second he walked in Devon's door, he knew he was in the one place on the planet where no one cared if he ever talked. He was free to throw a football, or play one of the pinball games Devon had picked up in Rutland, or watch the pay-per-view wrestling matches Devon had gotten off a neighbor's satellite dish without someone watching for his reaction, or doing all they could do to make him laugh out loud.

He couldn't stop himself because Devon seemed his one shot at happiness. Devon wanted them all to go to Utah, to breathe some clean desert air. Alex had seen enough Westerns to know the desert was where men found their souls, or gained forgiveness, or finally got their revenge. He figured that was where he'd find his voice, if it was a thing to be found.

Devon finished playing, then walked into the kitchen and found them Cokes and Hershey bars and Pringles. They ate everything, heedless of what the combination might do to their stomachs, then Devon led him into the backyard, where two shiny skis were waiting.

"Telemark skis," he said. "The best. You want to give them a try?"

Alex smiled so wide, Devon put his arm around him. "You know what, Alex?" he said.

"Keep smiling like that, and I'll give you the world."

He held on tight, and that was the other reason Alex kept coming here, because he knew, in some way, that Devon needed him too. Despite his looks, and the girls who hung on him, and obviously plenty of money to buy anything he wanted, he was still waiting whenever Alex arrived, and there was no resisting that. Alex knew he was a difficult boy — no one had ever turned to him for anything.

He sat down to put on the new boots, then Devon helped him into the skis.

"We'll just slide around back here," he said. "After a little practice, we'll head out to the woods. By then, we might even be able to talk your mom into coming along."

Alex nodded. He knew who his mom loved, but he didn't mention that. Yesterday, Shelley Riverdale, their mail carrier, had dumped a bag of unaddressed postcards onto their dining room table. "They were in Graham's mailbox," she said. "So I knew they had to be for you."

Jane had waited until Shelley left, then she curled over in her chair and cried. She cried until Alex couldn't stand it, until every shrill intake of breath seemed to slice another layer of skin off his back. He ran out on the porch, and his great-grandmother followed and put her arm around him.

"Now don't you worry," Esther had said. "Believe it or not, that's a good thing. Your mother hasn't cried like that for seven years."

So Alex knew who she loved, but if all she was going to do was cry about it, he wasn't about to start rooting for his uncle Graham. The one thing he knew for certain was that Devon Zeke wouldn't sit still for tears like that. He'd either make Jane laugh or be gone in a heartbeat. Either way, all that sobbing would stop.

"Yep," Devon said, slowing pulling Alex forward, so that he slid effortlessly across the snow, "it's only a matter of time before your mom comes to her senses. Just the three of us, Alex. Won't that be something?"

One week before Christmas, Devon left yet another sego lily, the state flower of Utah, on Jane's doorstep. He'd left one every night for weeks, which she had to be grateful for, considering the state of that rosebush. It hadn't just died of frostbite; it had putrefied and was giving off some kind of stink. Those black petals were turning up everywhere — on his windowsill, on the bottom of his boots, frozen solid on the hoods of cars where they'd leave a blood-like stain in spring.

He kept leaving lilies and did not call once, leaving Jane to her imagination. Pretty soon, all these freezing temperatures would get to her. She'd look through those new skylights of hers and wish for pastel skies and a sun that rose above the rooftops, even in the dead of winter.

Once she got cold enough, she'd start yearning for hot desert winds and the feel of a man's hands on her.

He turned from the house and walked through the snowy streets to Orion's Bar. Main Street was all done up in twinkling white lights and wreaths hung on every lamppost. They'd had caroling three nights in a row, and free cider at the mayor's office, into which Devon had poured a flask of Jack Daniel's, then tipped off the teenagers, who kept coming back for more.

The bar was two streets over, where no one had decorated except for the owner of the pawn shop, who'd strung up a few ghoulish green lights. He pushed open the door to Orion's, then let out a breath it seemed he'd been holding for days. He looked in the mirror over the bar, smiled at himself, then the smile faded. All this murder suspect stuff and waiting for Jane had put him on edge. He had slept with twelve different girls in fourteen nights and now did not like what he saw in mirrors. He was made up of fake smiles and good looks and inherited athletic ability. He was made up of air. He didn't even know what he cared about, except Jane and Alex. He didn't have an opinion on abortion or capital punishment, and though this had never bothered him before, it suddenly made him feel weightless. It made him look in every mirror he passed, checking to see who he was. It made him come to Orion's night after night and play his music, re-inventing himself in each girl's eyes.

He spotted Jake and Adam at a table in the center of the bar. They'd just gotten back from a race in Florida, the fifth race in two months Devon had passed on. He was only interested in the big Western races. He wouldn't have settled for anything less than Techline. Adam was smiling, but Jake was staring into his drink. Devon smiled a smile of air and walked over to them.

"You win?" he asked Adam.

"Nah. Eighteenth. Jake came in second, though."

Devon sat down and slapped Jake on the back. "That's great."

"I was five seconds behind," Jake said. "Could have made it up if that bastard hadn't cut outside the track. Total violation, and of course no one saw it but me."

Devon patted his back and ordered him another drink. "Still, second. That's something."

Jake looked up suddenly and glared into Devon's eyes. "As if you've got any idea."

Devon shrugged. "I'll enter the big one in Moab."

"Sure," Jake said. "And even if you don't, it won't matter. The women here will still think you're some kind of celebrity. They'll still get hot for you. Maybe even dead for you, like Ivy did."

They all fell silent, then Adam laughed.

"Come on, Jake. Lighten up."

Jake stared into his beer. Zach Leyland came into the bar and headed right for Ivy's chair, which he'd been crying over for weeks. Roy Carter beat him to it.

"Not today, Leyland," Roy said.

"I just wanted —"

"I know what you wanted."

"I wanted to tell her I'm sorry."

"Then go to the cemetery. Tell her there. This ain't no seance parlor."

Zach looked around the bar and, for a moment, his gaze met Devon's. The agony there was plain, even to a man like a Devon, who usually saw only his own reflection in another man's eyes. Zach walked out of the bar.

"Guy gives me the creeps," Adam said.

"He was always watching Ivy," Devon said. "You think . . . ?"

"He wouldn't have had the balls," Jake said, and gulped down the rest of his drink.

Jane was glad for the snow; it covered up the fact that, during the month of December, her lawn turned as brown as everyone else's. She stomped all over it, but nothing grew. She was fairly certain the grass was not only dormant, but dead to the root.

Graham left only one message after the disaster at the motel, but Jane did not listen to it through. While rewinding it, a usually indestructible ivy on the kitchen counter folded over and died. The Christmas tree she bought fresh from Harry Blankenship's tree farm lost half its needles in three days, despite the gallons of water she fed it.

Four days before Christmas, when the temperature rose to a balmy thirty-four degrees and the holly wreath on her front door dropped all its berries and started to rot, she walked out to get the paper. Instead, she found Rachel Simpson standing on one of the bare patches on her dead front lawn. The woman had thrown on her coat inside out and failed to button it.

"Jane," Rachel said, clutching her sleeve, "you've got to help me. Carl left last night. Packed all his things while I was at the market and left a note that said, 'That's it. I'm going.' Like I'm supposed to know what that means. The kids are going to be up in a couple hours. It's almost Christmas, Jane."

Jane looked over at the Simpson house, its roof lined elaborately with flickering red and green lights. Carl Simpson had strung up those lights two weeks ago. He'd been humming "Rudolph the Red-Nosed Reindeer." When his two teenage children had come outside to look at his work, they had given him high fives.

Jane looked back at Rachel. She squeezed her hand and tried with all her might to think of some remedy, to summon up some kind of magic to bring Carl back, but even before she started, she knew she wouldn't be able to save

Rachel or anyone. She no longer had a clue about love. She felt cold to the bone and magicless, the way her mother must have felt her whole life.

She bowed her head. "I'm sorry, Rachel."

"Jane, come on. I know you helped Lenore. And Pat and Hannah, and god knows how many others. Help me. I *need* you."

Jane tried again. She closed her eyes and tried to force a vision of Rachel and Carl together again, but all she imagined was Rachel's children waking up to abandonment. All she could figure was that, with love, everyone was just taking their chances.

She opened her eyes and looked across the street to Devon's house. He had not decorated his house for the holidays. Marjorie Dumas had offered him one of her plywood reindeer to plant on his lawn, but he had refused. Though Jane was not a fan of tinsel and flocking, Devon's dark house bothered her. It bothered her that he was not pushing her to come to Utah with him, that he just assumed she would.

She turned back to her neighbor. "Believe me, if I had some magic I'd use it. Just look where you're standing, Rachel. Look at my lawn."

Rachel stared at the dead grass then shrugged. "Look, Jane. I don't care. I just want you to help me. I can't let my family disintegrate on Christmas."

"I don't know what to tell you."

"Tell me anything. I've got two children who are going to wake up Christmas morning without a father."

"Rachel, I'm sorry. I'd help if I could."

"Great," Rachel said. "Just great."

She stomped back to her house, pausing for a moment to stare at the twinkling lights Carl had strung. When she went inside, she turned them off first thing.

Jane stared once more at Devon's. She shivered, not because of the cold, but because she felt he was toying with her. His silence was a ruse, and she'd had just about enough.

Graham only went that morning because of the call from the neurosurgeon at Cornell — the man had had all kinds of theories on what might be causing Alex's muteness. He didn't bother putting on aftershave, and he wore an old pair of shoes that pinched his toes, just to remind himself what pain was.

Esther let him in. "Well," she said, "it's about time."

She led him into the living room, where a scotch pine nearly devoid of needles stood in the corner. He heard thumping in the attic, then Alex raced down the new stairs and into his arms.

"Hey, sport," he said. "Looks like you need a new tree."

Alex shrugged, then ran to the corner where

he'd scattered the pieces to a new motorized erector set.

"I could never wait until Christmas," Esther said.

"It's only a few more days."

"That's a long time, Graham. Who knows what could happen?"

Jane came out of the back bedroom, then stopped when she saw him. She was wearing jeans and a sweatshirt and she looked tired. Her bangs had grown down over her eyes.

He tried to curl his toes, but couldn't. Two of them had already gone numb. "I got a call from Doctor Arlene," he said. "He's the neurosurgeon at Cornell I was telling you about. I think we ought to talk about it."

"No, Graham."

"Jane, I really think —"

"The French toast is ready," Esther said. "Come on in and join us, Graham."

He tried to catch Jane's eye, but she wouldn't look at him. She sat down on the far side of the table, and he took the chair opposite her. Alex grabbed the syrup and started pouring.

"You want some toast to go with that?" Graham asked.

Alex smiled and stuck his finger in the puddle he'd made at the center of his plate. Graham reached over and tousled his hair.

They ate in silence awhile. Graham got sidetracked by the sweet maple syrup, and forgot all about pain. He heaped powdered sugar on his French toast and slid his leg beneath the table until it bumped Jane's. She looked up, startled, then he watched her reposition herself, legs tucked beneath her.

"Pass the butter please, Jane," he said, though Esther was closer to it. Jane pushed it across the table. "And the syrup, if you don't mind."

She handed him the syrup and he brushed a finger over her knuckles before taking it. She drew back quickly — anyone would have thought he'd struck her — and Graham whistled while pouring all the syrup he wanted, because he had never in his life had this much effect on anyone.

"So Doctor Arlene said he can get Alex in right after the holidays."

Jane set down her fork and looked at him, as he'd known she would. He smiled right into the face of her fury.

"I told you no. I told you we were done with that."

"It was all I could do."

"Graham," she said, "I appreciate your concern —"

"No, I don't think you do."

"Don't you think I would take him if I thought it would cure him? Don't you think this is killing me, that I'd do anything?"

She stood up and walked to the window. She pretended to look at the sky, but he knew very well that Devon's house was directly in her line of sight, that there was more than one obstacle here.

"He's gone, you know," he said, and when she whirled around, he planted his feet flat on the floor.

"Gone?"

"Not forever, Jane. He'll be back tomorrow. He just went skiing. Cannon Mountain, I think."

He pushed his plate away and stood up. He wasn't about to be bested, not today, not when he was the only man in this room. He reached into his pocket and took out the four front-row tickets he'd gotten to the opening day Red Sox game. He tossed them on the table.

"Merry Christmas," he said. "I'll pick you up in April." He touched the top of Alex's head on his way out.

Ten

Marjorie Dumas just happened to be in line at the gift shop when Jane got the call from Mrs. Hazelton. She pretended to study the birthday card she'd picked out for her nephew, but actually she was taking it all in, inferring exactly what Mrs. Hazelton must be saying to produce so many incredulous rebuttals and then, at last, that slack-mouthed look on Jane's face.

When Marjorie got home, she called Marilyn Ludlow first thing. Marilyn hung up and called her youngest boy's second-grade teacher, Mr. Duvall, to make sure Scott had been going to class. Scott was a notorious copycat; he'd pierced his ear after his older brother Tyler came home with a diamond stud and had once tried to match his father ounce for ounce in vodka, resulting in a trip to the emergency room and a visit from Social Services.

Mr. Duvall said Scott had been in class every day except last Friday, when he and Ryan Flint slipped out during the holiday parade to light the wastebaskets in the gymnasium on fire. He also told Marilyn what he'd been telling her for years, that he was hopelessly in love with her, despite her husband, and his wife, and the six kids they had between them.

Marilyn allowed herself a moment's longing, then hung up on him. She went next door to Josie's Hair Styling and told Josie Aberdeen — who had three eerily well-behaved teenagers — what Alex Payton had been up to. Josie didn't say another word about it until three o'clock, when she called Sally Weaver and admitted how nervous all her good luck made her. Something terrible, she said, must be in store for her.

Sally Weaver was best friends with Karen Wright, who was jogging carefully down the icy sidewalks of Sycamore Lane when Jane pulled up. Karen jogged right up the driveway as Jane got out of her car.

"Now here's the thing," Karen said. "I've got two kids, both older than your Alex. Every time I've told them they can't do something, they've done it all over the place. You tell Alex he can't cut class and he'll never go to school again. You've got to tread carefully, Jane."

"Good God," Jane said. She didn't even want to consider how this tidbit had gotten around. Mrs. Hazelton had said she'd even hesitated before calling, because it was the last day before Christmas break and all of Alex's excuses had seemed so legitimate — appointments with more specialists, sore throats, the death of a cousin. Jane hadn't even had time to figure out what she was going to say to Alex.

She'd just gotten off work early so she could be home when he pretended to come in from school.

She walked into her house and slammed the door. Esther was sitting on the couch, knitting, though she'd never been any good at handiwork, and this scarf or blanket or whatever it was had taken on gargantuan proportions. She never used the same color twice, causing everyone but babies to turn away.

"So you know," Esther said.

"Are you telling me you did, and you didn't tell me?"

Esther shrugged.

"Grandma," Jane said, sitting down beside her, "you can't withhold information from me. I'm his mother. I have a right to know."

"You don't listen. You don't want to hear certain things. Alex is over at Devon's, I'd wager. He goes there every day. That man's got a hold on him. That man just might be a murderer."

She looked past Esther to the table beside the couch, and the cyclamen on top of it. Yesterday, when she'd bought the plant, it had been in full bloom. Today, the leaves had wilted to the color of a bruise and curled over.

She stood up and tucked her hair behind her ears. "You're telling me you've actually seen him going to Devon's when he should be at school?"

"I'm telling you I've seen a lot of things,

Jane. You'd see them too if you'd open your eyes."

Jane was out the door in a flash and across the street before she could take a deep breath. She pounded on Devon's door and the stereo suddenly stopped. Devon opened the door in blue jeans and a T-shirt.

"Oh," he said, "looks like the cat's out of the bag."

Jane looked past him to Alex, who sat against the wall, his legs curled beneath him, an opened bag of potato chips beside him. She pushed past Devon into the house.

Alex stood up and wiped his hands on his jeans. He looked like a boy who'd been ready to go for a long time, but his parents had wanted to linger. He looked like this was all her fault.

"Alex," she said. "God, Alex, you can't do this."

He hung his head and she walked to his side and grabbed his arm. "You have the potential to be such a good student. You can't mess it up. It's your whole future."

"He's not missing much," Devon said, closing the door. "It's only first grade, Jane."

Jane abruptly let go of Alex and marched over to Devon. She held her finger up to his face.

"Don't you dare," she said. "How could you have done this?"

"I didn't do anything. The kid cut class a few times. Big deal. We all did it. I just didn't play the law-abiding adult with him. I was his friend. I think that's what he needs."

Jane lowered her hand and jabbed her finger against his chest. "What he needs is to get the hell away from you. He needs to not be friends with someone accused of murder."

Devon turned away, obviously stunned that she could doubt him. And she knew he would always be like that. It wouldn't even pay to get mad at him when he imagined himself everything but a villain.

She grabbed Alex's hand and turned to go, then noticed two shiny bikes resting against the wall. One was Devon's, but the other had once been prominently displayed in the window of Michael's Bicycle Shop.

"You stole it," she said.

"Jane, I'm crushed."

She put her hands on her hips, then dropped them. What could she say? Ned had stolen too, and she had loved his daring; she'd gotten faint over the devilish glint in his eyes. Beer, music, occasionally cars — cars he always brought back and parked in a different location, just to shake people up.

She looked around the rest of the room, but it was nearly empty; only a guitar, a different stereo than the one he'd had before, a stack of rock CDs, and a black beanbag chair adorned the room. There was a single photograph on the wall, and she stared at it.

It had been taken at some club, while Devon

was on stage. The sign on the wall behind him said Graineys. He'd been in the middle of a song, a high note she surmised from the way his chin was tilted up and his face strained. He held an acoustic guitar in his hands, his fingers curled delicately around the strings. Smoke blurred his features, but not enough to stop her from thinking he was the most beautiful man she'd ever seen, besides Ned.

She marched Alex out of the house. She was down the path and halfway across the street before Devon came out on the porch.

"You think I did it?" he called after her. "You think I killed a woman?"

Jane stumbled in the street. "Don't ask me now."

"I don't believe this."

Jane stopped and turned around. "Why not? Why can't I come to my senses now?"

"That isn't sense. It's rumor. There's not a scrap of fact to back it up."

"Maybe you were careful."

"Maybe I took a girl home, then decided not to sleep with her because I'm in love with someone else. Maybe I'm worth more than you think. It's entirely possible, you know, that I've just been sitting here waiting for you."

Jane trembled and Alex slipped his hand into hers. "I can't talk about this now."

Devon started down the path after them, his hands held out in truce. "Look, I'm sorry about Alex. I wasn't trying to hurt anybody. I just wanted to be his friend. I thought he needed that more than an enforcer."

Jane's head had begun to throb. "Don't come any closer," she said, and Devon stopped at the curb. He looked as heartbroken as a handsome man could look, but she just turned around. She marched Alex back to their house.

That night, Jane and Esther sat up late. Alex had gone to sleep at six o'clock, as if the thrill of getting caught had worn him out.

"I should have known," Jane said.

"Known what? That that man would try to get to you through your son?"

"No, I don't think that's it. Devon already assumes he'll get me." She got up and walked to the window. "I should have known, before Devon, that Alex never got to be a kid."

Jane turned back to her grandmother. She had not paid enough attention to Alex or to Esther. The skin on her grandmother's arms had turned yellow and slack. She had been spending time with Robert O'Brien, but that had not inspired her to put on makeup or fix her hair. When she stood, which was rare, she now came only to Jane's chin.

"Maybe we ought to sell the house right now," Jane said.

"Maybe. But then what about Graham?"

Jane swept her foot over the floor. She had manhandled that monstrous sander and managed to smooth most of the gouges out of the floor. Sometime during Christmas break, the Ludlow boys would come by to help her move all the furniture, then she'd put down three coats of water-based urethane.

The attic was finished, the pedestal sink for the bathroom on order, and all she had left to do was touch-up work, so it was entirely possible she would be out of here in less than a month, that she never had to set foot in this town again.

She looked back out the window, but lately even this view had been ruined. Every time she glanced in Devon's direction, she felt unfaithful to Graham. Every time she remembered the things she'd done with Ned, she felt she'd done Graham some terrible wrong.

She and Esther were quiet a long time, so Alex must have thought they were asleep when he tiptoed into the living room. He was so quiet, neither Jane nor Esther heard him until he opened the front door.

"I beg your pardon?" Jane said, whirling around. "Where do you think you're going?"

Alex looked out the door, then back at Jane. He blinked a few times, then simply walked over to her and laid his head against her stomach.

Jane looked over his head to her grand-mother. Esther leaned back and stared at her portrait of the sea. Jane put her arm around Alex's shoulders and walked him back to his bedroom. Beneath his clothes, he still had on his pajamas. She put him back into bed.

"You were going to him, weren't you?" she said. They both listened to the haunting melody she knew Devon played for them. She knew a lot of things deep down. She brushed Alex's hair away from his eyes and leaned in to kiss him. When she looked right at her son, everything was clear: He came before everything.

"Has he ever hurt you?" she asked quietly.

Alex shook his head and Jane uncoiled her fists. "Do you think he's your father?"

Alex started crying. She got into bed beside him and rocked him in her arms.

"Don't cry," she said softly, as he fell asleep right on top of a sob. "What we need is some solid information, something to go on. Tomorrow you and I are going to New York. We're going to find out who Devon Zeke is."

It took only two hours to reach the town of Paradox, New York, along Highway 74, then another fifteen minutes to locate the small town of Laughlin north of it. Alex had stared out the window the entire drive; he had not even turned his head when Jane put on a country station, music he usually hated.

It was Christmas break; the highway was jam-packed. Alex breathed so short and quick, he fogged up the windows. Just looking at him made her bones ache straight down to her fingertips.

She turned onto Laughlin's main street,

Cambria Avenue. The town was small by New York standards, only twenty-five thousand residents. It had a K-Mart, 7-Eleven, and Chevron. Where Cambria met Katella Street, there was a fancy new strip mall, complete with the Gap and Ho-Ho's Do-Nuts.

Jane pulled into the parking lot and cut the engine. She turned to Alex. "I'm going in to ask a few questions. Want to come?"

He shook his head, but did not look at her. Jane touched his hair, then got out of the car. Her boot disappeared beneath two inches of gray slush littered with Pepsi cans and scrunched-up Marlboro boxes. She went into the Gap.

The cashier was no more than seventeen and thin as angel hair. She had a piece of black licorice protruding from her lips.

"I'm looking for someone," Jane said. "A man, about twenty-six, with long, light brown hair, gray eyes, very handsome."

The girl giggled, revealing a black-stained tongue. "I'm looking for him too. Or his brother, if he's got one."

Another employee, also in her teens and stick-thin, laughed hysterically while refolding sweatshirts. Jane ran a finger along the counter.

"Is there a bar in town? Graineys?"

The girl shrugged. "Not that I know of. Katie, you know a bar named Graineys?"

"Uh-uh," she said.

315

Jane dug her hands back into her pockets. "Thanks."

She went into the doughnut shop and got the same results. She ran across the street to the Chevron, but the man behind the counter had begun work there only the week before.

She walked back to the car and got inside. Alex was now slumped in his seat. She put the key in the ignition, but did not turn it.

"Tell me this," she said. "Did he make you cut class to be with him?"

Alex finally turned to her. His eyes were filled with tears.

"Don't let anyone make you do anything, Alex. It doesn't matter whether you talk or not. You're as strong as anybody."

She touched his arm — so thin she could close her thumb and forefinger around his elbow. She tried not to be frightened of his whole life, of all the things that could possibly go wrong. She tried to imagine him growing into a man, but there was no image to sustain it. She felt both trapped and joyous at the thought of keeping him with her forever.

"Come on," she said, taking the keys back out of the ignition. "I'll buy you a jelly roll."

Jane spent the day going in and out of stores along Laughlin's commercial strip, asking questions no one could answer, producing giggles whenever she gave Devon's description. No one had seen him and, by three o'clock, she had a pounding headache. She began to think how easy it would have been for Devon to pick up a map of New York, choose a city, and pretend he'd had a life there. She began to wonder what it took to drive a man to murder.

By five, she was famished, and she slowed along the strip to allow Alex to point to where he wanted to eat. As always, he picked a fast-food restaurant, Burger King this time. She ordered him a Whopper with fries and a Coke, and a chicken sandwich for herself. They sat in the corner and ate in silence, while the rest of the customers talked and laughed and shouted with no idea that words were luxuries not everyone had.

Jane massaged her head, the pain forming tight spirals around her temples. She was beginning to wonder if she would ever know anything for sure. Was it so much to ask to look in a man's eyes and believe everything he said?

After dinner, they checked into the Motel 6 on Cambria, and climbed into the king-size bed. *Toy Story* was showing on the pay-per-view channel, and Alex curled up in her arms to watch it.

He fell asleep before the credits. He sighed and pulled away, while her body stayed wishfully indented. Though this wasn't a thing she would admit out loud, the truth was, her whole life was in his little body. She could fall in love all she wanted, but only after she'd made sure Alex was breathing, only after she'd done everything she could to make his life right.

She twined her fingers through his hair and didn't sleep for a long time. She listened, instead, to his gentle snoring. It had a rumble to it, like a living being trapped in his throat. She wondered, for the thousandth time, what he made of his own silence and if, somewhere deep down, he blamed her.

In the morning, after a very bad breakfast of runny eggs and dry toast in the hotel restaurant, Jane made one more tour through the town of Laughlin. She didn't expect to find anything new, and she didn't, but instead of heading back toward Vermont, she went west, to Interstate 87, then south toward Albany.

Once on the interstate, Alex quickly fell asleep. She drove south, past Schroon Lake and Pottersville and Chestertown. She turned on a soft-rock station and, long before she spotted the exit to Lake George, she knew that was where she would get off.

The week after she and Ned had gotten engaged, he had promised to take her somewhere special to celebrate. Instead, he had taken her to Lake George, an uninspired resort town, and invited a dozen of his friends to their hotel room. Jane had sat on the bed, an untouched beer beside her, and glared at Ned for hours, though he only smiled back, as if anger were invisible to him. When the beer ran out at midnight, and they all decided to go to a bar, Jane folded her arms over her chest.

"I thought this was supposed to be our celebration," she whispered to Ned while he put on his shoes.

"It is," he said. "The guys just want to help us celebrate. They came all the way out here. The least we can do is show them a good time."

"I'm not going."

Ned stood up and tried to pull her to her feet.

"I'm not going," she said again, yanking her arm away.

Ned stepped back. His friends were shouting at him from the hallway, and Jane would always remember the way he looked from her to them and back again. The way he considered his alternatives with a cock of his head, then chose his friends.

He didn't come back until five in the morning, when he was so drunk he tripped on the shag carpeting and passed out trying to kiss her. She watched game shows while he slept until noon, and then they drove home. He cranked the radio the entire way, so, she imagined, he could not hear her crying. The next day, he brought her eight long-stemmed white roses. He told her she was beautiful and he couldn't wait to marry her and, without much fight at all, she went back to loving him.

Eight years later, Jane drove through Lake George again. The motel Ned had taken her to was still there: the Traveler's Inn, two dingy stories, with ripped carpeting in the exterior hallways and cableless TVs in every room. She slowed as she passed it, to pinpoint that second-floor room they'd stayed in, to see if another woman was standing at the window now, her face pressed up to the glass.

She would like to see Ned one more time, if only to tell him what she thought of him. She would like the chance to walk out on him, just once. She understood that she'd loved him, but she did not understand why she'd let him walk all over her. The problem with growing up was that she remembered the facts, but forgot all her motivations. What seemed like passion before was only melodrama now. She'd aged past the point of understanding how she could have been so stupid.

She was being stupid again, she decided, driving through her past. She looked for a place to turn around to get back on the highway. A souped-up truck, loaded with teenagers, came up fast behind her. The kids flashed their lights. Jane hit the brakes and slowed to fifteen, and the purple-haired driver gave her the finger and tapped her bumper.

She was not too old to pick a fight, to stand on a street corner and shout down a gang of seventeen-year-old truants. But Alex was curled up on the seat beside her, so all she did was pull into another strip mall parking lot and let the teenagers by.

They sped past victorious, saluting her with

contraband beer. She turned the car around and put on her left blinker. As she was waiting for an opening in traffic, she looked across the street and spotted the bar.

It was an old brick building, with two flashing neon Budweiser signs in the window. The parking lot was empty except for one old Pontiac parked near the door. Smoke spewed from the bar's crumbling chimney, and a small black sign hung on the brick said *Graineys*.

Jane did not move. The street opened up and she could have turned, but she merely sat and stared at the bar. She didn't do anything until a car came up behind her and the driver honked her horn. This awakened Alex, who looked at her.

She eased out into the street. She almost drove past it. She almost didn't want to know. At the last minute, though, she pulled into the parking lot.

This time, Alex got out with her. She tried the door to the bar and found it locked. She could have knocked, but instead breathed a sigh of relief. She even started back to the car, but the door to the bar opened behind her.

"You need something?" a man asked.

Jane stiffened her shoulders and turned around. The man was middle-aged, potbellied, his hair shaved down to almost nothing. Jane reached for Alex's hand and found he had met her halfway. She smiled at this small thing. Sometimes the small things were all you got.

"I was wondering if you might know a friend of mine," she said. "Devon Zeke. He might have played here awhile back."

"Devon, sure. He was here about six months ago. The girls all went crazy for him. Why don't you come on in? I'm just cleaning up. Rough night last night."

Jane squeezed Alex's hand as they walked into the bar. The man had not lied. Chairs had been overturned and the place reeked of spilt beer and probably vomit. The man picked up chairs as he went.

"I was wondering where he went," the man said. "Did a set Saturday night, promised to be here Monday, then never showed his face again."

"Did he live around here?" Jane asked.

"Couldn't tell you. Never knew a thing about him, except that he could make the women cry with his singing."

"Was there, you know, any trouble when he was around?"

"Like what?"

"I don't know. People getting hurt. Girls getting killed."

The man stopped his cleanup and stared at her. "You a cop?"

"No. Really, no. I just need information."

The man stared at her a moment longer, then bent down and picked up broken glass with his bare hand. "There was no trouble. Devon was a lover, not a fighter. The girls might have killed

322

to be with him, but I don't think he ever killed any of them once they got their wish."

He laughed and Jane squeezed Alex's hand. "He was here," she said.

"Of course. Played for a couple weeks. Said he was getting ready for a big gig near here and was honing his talents. Said he used to have fantasies of being a rock star."

Jane began steering Alex toward the door. She would leave before any more was said. She would leave with her feet planted on solid ground. She reached the door just as the man continued.

"Said there was a girl somewhere who'd been waiting for him a long time. I never bought that. He could have had anyone, and he knew it and took advantage of it, let me tell you."

Jane pushed open the door and hurried to the car. When she did not start the engine right away, when she just sat there, Alex looked at her.

He must have seen something in her face then, because he opened his mouth and tried to speak. When she imagined that bits of steam came out instead of words, she pulled him tightly to her and held on for dear life.

Graham no longer knocked on Devon's door; he pounded. "You said you'd get me some new snowshoes," he said, two days after Christmas.

Devon laughed and walked to the kitchen. He picked a box off the counter, with the price tag still on the top. Inside were lightweight aluminum snowshoes, thirty inches long.

He handed them to Graham, who sat down on the bare hardwood floor to strap them on. Every morning for nearly a month now, he had expected Devon to punch him in the nose, to beat him to a pulp for trying to ruin his life, but all Devon ever did was smile. He had never asked why Graham had not come forward as his alibi. That silence was so full of self-confidence, it drove Graham crazy. How could he assume that he would get off anyway? What if things hadn't gone his way? What if his hair had been found on Ivy's body? Would he have finally begged for something then, and what would that look like, Devon down on his knees?

It had gotten to the point where Graham prayed Devon would just slug him, or drag him into the police station and force him to confess, but all Devon ever did was laugh, or talk about sponsors, or beat him at yet another race. He acted like nothing Graham did — not even the worst things — mattered. And Graham wondered how much longer he could stand it, if one of these days he was just going to pop.

"Those shoes will take you anywhere," Devon said, "except past me."

He laughed again, then went into his bedroom. When he came back out, he was wearing his own stolen snowshoes.

"To Hagerman's Woods?" he said.

Graham nodded. His throat was already dry.

He'd spent the last six nights snowshoeing in his old wooden shoes. Every day, he'd gone a little faster, until last night he was running full speed through Hagerman's Woods, scaring woodchucks out of the trees.

They stepped out onto the porch, where the snow fell so fast, their jackets were coated within seconds.

Devon looked at him. "I'll even give you a head start."

Graham pushed him off the porch. "I don't need it."

He let Devon lead. He wasn't about to give away anything. Then at the top of Pendleton Hill, when Devon paused for breath, he took off running down the other side.

He picked up speeds he couldn't believe; he sliced a hole right through the wind. He glanced over his shoulder and nearly stumbled; the distance he'd opened up between himself and Devon seemed miraculous. He heard Devon shout, but then the blood rushed between his ears and drowned out everything. He turned around and ran harder. Somehow, he pulled farther away.

He turned into Hagerman's Woods and flew across the snow. He was so fast he imagined he didn't even leave tracks. He ran all the way to Baker's Clearing, where one year Harold Baker had cut down all the birches for a house that caught fire from his first cigarette, then bent over to catch his breath. He listened for Devon, but could hear nothing. Then he pumped his fist in victory, though what he felt was not joy or exaltation, but only relief that, for once, he'd been better.

Devon arrived a few minutes later, breathing hard. His face looked surprisingly pale, as if this was the last thing he'd expected, as if this changed all the rules.

"You cheated," he said.

"It's not my fault you had to stop to catch your breath."

The exaltation was creeping in now, turning the sweat on his arms to steam. Devon shifted his weight and the gray of his eyes got a little darker. He stepped forward and pushed up the sleeves of his jacket. The muscles in his forearms were hard as brick. Graham had once seen him break a four-inch-thick piece of firewood with his bare hands.

"So are we done now?" Devon asked.

The exaltation faded quickly, replaced by a flash of panic. Graham did not feel done, that was the trouble. All he felt was that he wanted to beat Devon again.

He sat down in the snow against the prickly trunk of a pine tree. He turned his head up to the sky and took the snow in his face.

"I don't know," he said.

Devon stepped forward until he was standing right over him. "I don't get you."

Graham shrugged. He didn't get himself either. He was stuck knee-deep in something he didn't understand.

The snow came sideways now, on a hard wind that snapped branches in two. Devon's hair flew out behind him and the smile that was usually glued to his face faded. Graham felt a prickle of fear. Though he knew Devon was no murderer, he didn't know what else he might be. He was out in the woods with a man he didn't know the slightest thing about, except that he could break a piece of firewood with his bare hands.

But all Devon did was hold out his hand. Graham just stared at it.

"Come on," Devon said. "The storm's getting worse. Take my hand. Don't be an idiot."

Graham hesitated, then took Devon's hand. The man hoisted him up, then turned his back on him.

"I'll beat you back," he said, taking off running.

Graham just watched him go. The wind sliced through his jacket and turned the sweat on his back to ice, but he made himself stay there. For once, he was not going to rise to the bait.

But he had to start walking; he was chilled to the bone. From there, it was an easy jump to running, to slamming his feet into each of Devon's tracks. By the time he was gaining on Devon halfway up Pendleton Hill, he knew the truth: Jane had been right. He could be defined with one simple truth: He wanted everything Ned had had.

Once his mother discovered him at Devon's, Alex felt strangely relieved. Something he hadn't understood in the first place was over. He'd been caught red-handed and now he'd have to toe the line.

He might even have been happy if his uncle Graham hadn't gotten it into his head that he had to cure him. He'd come by three times already, pleading with Jane to let the three of them go to Cornell University, where he knew another specialist. The first time, Jane had turned her back on him; the second time she sat down and listened. Yesterday, when she'd asked Graham for the doctor's credentials, Alex had shaken his head in disgust; unless his uncle knew a specialist in dragons, no one was going to cure anything.

It was all just a cover anyway. It was plain as day why his uncle was really there; every time he sat on the couch by Jane, his fingers crept toward her. It was like he couldn't help himself; he leaned away, but his hands circumvented his commands and landed within inches of the curve of her hip.

Today, Graham sat on the couch beside Jane, his fingers a hairsbreadth from her thigh, while Alex sat on the floor beside his great-grandmother's rocking chair. She could hardly get up from it anymore, though she said she was just comfortable, that she had suddenly become obsessed with knitting. Her scent over-powered everything, even all the rotting plants in the house. She smelled of memory — dense and moist, like soil deep down. She talked crazy — not of what was right in front of her, but of the pearl necklace her mother had always worn, the kisses her father had given her only after he thought her asleep. At night, Alex found himself dreaming her dreams, as if she was fading and all that would be left was what he could remember of her.

She creaked back and forth steadily, while Graham pleaded once more with Jane. "Just one more time," he said. "If it really is a psychological problem, he'll ferret it out."

"I told you, I'm done with it." Jane's voice was scratchy, like it was wearing out.

"And I told you I'd help Alex find his voice. You've got to give me a chance."

His hands were nearly on Jane's knees by now and Alex watched his fingers dance. They played with the air around his mother; they were like dogs on a leash, snapped back when they moved into forbidden territory.

His mother, for her part, didn't even seem to notice how she sat on a slant whenever Graham was around, so that their heads were almost touching. She couldn't have noticed, because she never made eye contact, she kept her hands behind her back.

When Jane looked out the window, Graham opened his mouth, then closed it. He must have had some kind of dragon in his throat, too, because whatever it was, he just couldn't say it. He drew his hands back to his sides.

Finally, Jane sighed and said, "I'll think about it."

Alex tapped his knees, but neither his mother nor his uncle looked over. He tapped them harder, then realized he made no sound. And that's when he realized the dragon had grown too strong for any psychiatrist or little boy to fight. That's when he realized he was just getting worse.

So he decided to run. One night, when everyone was asleep, he would slip out with a bag over his shoulder. Since his mother had found him at Devon's, he hadn't held out much hope for the three of them moving to Utah, so he'd have to head west — always the direction of freedom — on his own. He was tired of people making decisions for him, anyway. He was tired of waiting for his mother or uncle or a specialist to fix him. He would find his own voice. He would fix himself.

Since they couldn't hear him, he got up and walked outside unnoticed. He ran smack into Linda Carlton, who'd been about to knock on his door. She had woven red ribbons through her braids.

"I came to invite you over. My mom's making Rice Krispies treats."

Alex had never believed in monsters or miracles, and he did not believe in this. In the prettiest girl in the first grade standing on his doorstep. In love at first sight.

He looked back in the house. His mother had heard Linda's voice, and she was sitting on the edge of the couch, watching them.

"Go on," she said. There were tears in her eyes from God knows what. He was tired of tears, too. He was going to live in the desert, where it was too hot to cry.

Linda took his hand and led him home. They sat in her kitchen and ate Rice Krispies treats and cold milk. Her mother came in and out, chattering constantly about the new baby brother or sister Linda would have next year, but Linda never said a word. Her mother checked her head for fever, then muttered something about putting a stop to this right now.

He and Linda went out to the insulated barn, where Linda had a stash of coloring books and crayons. They lay in the loft and never went out of the lines of Barbie dolls and Barney. They wrote notes back and forth, *Pass the magenta* and *I got a Spin-Art for Christmas* and once, when he was really brave, *Would you be my girl?*, to which she answered *Alex, where have you been?*

After an hour, Alex began to think he might not leave right away. Actually, he thought he'd be an idiot to leave right away, especially when Linda began drawing big red hearts in her coloring books and putting *L.C. + A.P. 4-ever* inside each one. He could stand it another week or two, at least until Christmas break was over, when Linda would undoubtedly come to her senses and wonder what she'd been doing with him.

It was just before midnight when Jane heard the rumble of Devon's Mustang. It woke her with a start, with a sting against her cheek. She sat up and smelled the lingering scent of sweat and woods, she caught the shadow darting across the wall, and she angrily tossed back the covers. She realized she'd been hanging on by a thread and that thread was snapping. There was nothing else to do but yank free and throw herself into the air.

She got dressed and put on her boots, but by the time she stepped out her front door, the Mustang was gone again, a fresh puddle of oil near the curb. Down the street, Rachel Simpson's teenagers were sitting on the curb, their arms around each other's waists. Most of her neighbors would leave up their Christmas lights until New Year's Day, but Rachel Simpson had yanked hers down yesterday and left them in a heap by the front door.

Jane walked across the street to Devon's. The windows were flooded with empty light. She tried the door and found it unlocked. Who would steal from Devon Zeke, aside from fools and heartbroken women who wanted to lay their hands on something he'd touched?

She walked inside. A black stereo sat alone on the vast expanse of hardwood floor. When Devon was there, the white walls turned purple, rock music took up as much space as furniture, but without him the room just felt cold. She walked across the naked floor, but her footsteps echoed so loudly she stopped. She looked into the kitchen, where a stack of unread newspapers had piled up near the stove. She turned around and walked out.

She knew where to find him. She shoved her hands in her jacket pockets and headed toward Orion's. The night was so pure and quiet, her neighbors woke to the sound of her breathing. Woolly owls, nesting miles away in the woods, went flying when her boot heel cracked through the brittle snow.

She crossed the Common, then turned off Main Street to Second. Orion's was halfway down and, as she neared it, the quiet gave way to bass beats and laughter. A group of teen-agers loitered by the parking lot, drinking beers one of them must have bought with a fake ID. A young man and woman came out of the bar, her stumbling right into him, him holding her breast to keep her steady.

Jane opened the door to the bar and went inside. She stood for a moment just inside the threshold, letting her eyes adjust to the smoky haze. It all came back to her instantly — which floorboards would creak beneath her feet, the hole in the roof above the second stall in the women's bathroom, how much deeper a woman could fall in love just by listening to a man sing into a slick microphone.

In front of her were twenty small, round tables, each lit by a glassed candle encased by red netting. The overhead lights were tinted purple, which made everything in the room seem a little fishy. A few couples had already paired up, but most of the tables were occupied by women sipping strawberry daiquiris, looking hopefully toward the men drinking straight shots at the bar. Jane took a seat in the back.

She ordered a glass of water. The waitress, Lynn Fallon, who had been in the grade below her and voted Most Likely to Succeed, slammed down a cocktail napkin.

Joe Brandt was on the small stage, singing "Stairway to Heaven" a cappella, which everyone was trying to drown out with talk. Lynn brought the water, spilling a quarter of it on the table as she set it down.

Jane leaned back into the shadows. The place had been wallpapered long ago, but what was left was so tattered, it was hard to tell the print. There was a hole the size of a fist beside the door.

Joe Brandt finally finished, drawing grateful applause from the audience. Roy pushed him off the stage before he could begin another song.

"You all know who's next," Roy said, then looked backstage as Devon came out.

Jane held her breath. All the women in the place did the same. How could they not? Beneath unnatural light, with his hair pulled back, his smile like a caress, they got to thinking they'd lived their whole lives just to be in the same room with him. They got to thinking they were crazy for wanting more, that it was just too much to ask.

He picked up his guitar and Jane braced herself for a rock song. Instead, he stroked the strings slowly, and sang a song that took a voice range she hadn't known he had.

When Lynn stomped by again, Jane ordered a double Scotch. Devon's voice was deep and rich; it stilled all conversation.

> *When I look at you,*
> *I tremble*
> *When I touch you,*
> *you cry*
> *It is too much,*
> *this love of ours,*
> *sometimes it feels so good I want to die.*

Jane grabbed the Scotch when it came. She gulped it down and tears came to her eyes. She leaned her head back against the wall.

> *Leave me,*
> *Don't leave me.*
> *Love me,*
> *God, stop.*

It hurts,
the way we love and hate.
It's heaven, it's hell, it's a curse.

Jane stared right at him. She knew the song was for her. She dared herself to feel what she would, and was stunned when all she felt was yearning for Graham. She wanted him there beside her, holding her hand. She wanted him to tell her it was time to leave, to walk with him through the snowy streets and hear nothing but his breathing. When they reached home, she wanted to lay down beside him, their heads on the same soft pillow. She wanted to sleep with him a whole night through.

Devon played his last chord and there was first a hush, then a cheer from the crowd. He stood up, smiled, then stepped off the stage.

Jane looked down at her drink and tried to think what she would say to him. By the time she looked up again, he was ensconced at the front table, holding hands with Wendy Wainright.

Jane just stared. For a moment, she didn't believe it. Wendy was eighteen, a cashier at the Stop-N-Go convenience store heading out of town. She lived with her parents and spent all her earnings on French tips and conditioner. She giggled whenever she counted out change.

Devon sat forward and whispered something in Wendy's ear that made her lower her head, then raise it slowly. They looked at each other without speaking.

Jane couldn't have stopped the wish if she tried, just like before. Sometimes a woman just felt things; sometimes, whether she wanted a man or not, she at least wanted what he offered to be pure. From the back of the bar, she whispered, "I wish him faithful. Please God, make him faithful."

Devon and Wendy stood up together. He held her hand and led her to the door that led backstage. A few of the men up front whistled, and Devon gave them a thumb's up. The couple disappeared backstage.

Lynn came by once more and pointed to Jane's drink. Jane simply stared at the door Devon and Wendy had gone through. She stared until her eyes burned, then she blinked.

When she could no longer remember what had made her want him, when all she felt was sorrow, she knew it was time to let go. Ned slipped through her right hand, and Devon through her left. Numbness was all that was left after she squeezed them out of her heart.

A hand fell on her shoulder and Jane jumped.

"You all right, Janie?" Roy Carter asked.

Jane nodded. She looked once more at the backstage door, then walked out of the bar.

Outside, the cold stung more than before, as if she'd lost a protective coating. She looked up at a sky full of wood smoke and stars. She wished for everything she could think of, for

Alex's voice, for a million dollars and a warm wind and the certainty of a happy future. She wished the right wishes worked, but she knew none of these would come true.

It didn't matter that the magic had vanished, because magic was only point of view. Either you believed good things would happen, or you believed they wouldn't. Either you believed a man lost his life to fate, to drunk driving, or you believed you killed him with a hasty wish. Both were true, depending on your point of view.

The seven-year chill exited slowly through her toes. It killed the grass beneath the snow, so that in the spring there would be two brown spots, no matter how much fertilizer was used. The seven-year chill left the way it came, with point of view. Seven years ago, she believed a wish had power, and now she believed it did not.

She walked toward the woods, then back again. She walked up and down Main Street three times. And with every step, she let her wildest fantasies run rampant; she imagined her life if Ned had lived. She imagined him a rock star, and their house on the beach in Malibu, and him loving her every day of his life. She thought this whole vision through; she caressed it, then let it fly. It splintered into a thousand pieces; it lit up the sky with white light late-night drivers mistook for comets. She felt little stabs of pain all over, and then she felt something else too, a jolt of electricity through her veins, as if somewhere deep inside her, a long-forgotten switch had been turned on again.

She got back to Sycamore Lane at three in the morning, and Devon's Mustang was parked on the street again. Jane looked at her house, then turned around. She walked up the steps to Devon's. Somehow she knew he'd be alone, that despite the show he put on, he had always been waiting for her.

He opened the door before she got there. "Jane," he said.

There were a million things to say, but none of them would ever get said. It was too brutal to tell someone they were no longer the love of your life. So instead, Jane just reached for him and before she could get there, he turned out the lights.

Every touch was another way to say goodbye. Her fingers across his back were love letters left on his pillow, her leg curled around his was her sneaking out in the middle of the night to save them the agony of words. The last kiss she gave him was her leaving a white rose on his grave the way she should have, so that no other girls would have bothered, so that everyone would have known he was hers.

Sometime during the night, it started to snow, then the snow turned to rain. Crocuses beneath the grass got confused and started sending up shoots of green. The rain battered the roof, and every now and then lightning ripped through the sky, just to remind her that anything can happen.

Toward morning, she realized they were his tears, not hers, that sealed their skin. She put her hands on either side of his face. Her hands trembled from knowing she'd gotten what she wanted, and was going to let it go.

"I'm sorry," she said, but he just took her hands from his face and kissed her fingers.

"I'll send you photos from the desert every winter," he said. "I'll make you wish you came."

She slipped out of bed and opened the blinds so there would be no more confusion. The sunrise was like a fresh wound. It stained the room red; it made her wonder how she'd ever mistaken his brown hair for gold.

She let herself out. The rain had turned the streets to ice, and she slipped twice walking home. Finally, she reached her driveway and crouched down beside the dead Perfume Delight rosebush. Her tears were so hot, they melted through the icy cracks in the sidewalk, and in the spring would bring up tufts of green. She wrapped her arms around her waist, then stood up and raised her chin. The loss was like a hollow in her stomach, but around that empty space she felt something else — new blood, clean and clear of anything to do with Ned Payton. She felt like Jane Gregory, who she hadn't come into contact with for a long, long time.

A stem of brittle aster had gotten tangled in the rosebush and died as if poisoned. She pulled it out and tucked it into the crook of her arm. She turned toward her house and did not look back. By the time she walked in her front door, she was another woman.

Eleven

Esther hardly slept at all anymore. Three hours a night, tops. She didn't need it, and even if she did she was running out of time and wasn't about to waste what she had left lying in bed, useless.

She walked into the living room and, instead of turning on a light, lit a candle. She'd spent a lifetime giving people fair warning, but she no longer knew what was going to happen. It was so up for grabs, Jane could end up with anybody, Alex might start talking tomorrow and never stop; he might grow into a man neither of them expected. As for herself, she could look Robert O'Brien in the eye when he proposed marriage and say just about anything.

She had not read her own future; she'd just seen Robert standing on his porch with his head in his hands. At the beginning, love is often mistaken for food poisoning — it twists your insides out and makes you oblivious to everything but your own suffering. Robert hadn't looked good for weeks, which meant he was about to ask her to marry him.

In addition to not knowing what would

happen, Esther didn't even know her own mind. She didn't know if she was capable of living with a good man.

She lifted the flame to her oil painting, where Walt's face had once been. She tried to make out her dead husband's eyes through the waves, but everything was lost in a sea of blue. She massaged her chest. It was such a mass of pain now, she felt a ripple of fear. It wasn't death that frightened her; in truth she thought a good, long sleep was exactly what she needed. What scared her was all the things she would leave undone: the Christmas stocking she'd been knitting for Alex for three years, his name still only half stitched, and the letters from old friends she would never answer. It was a bad omen to leave things behind; it could turn you into a ghost. Just look what had happened to Walt. He'd been so unprepared for death, he hadn't even spent all his money; when she'd gone through his things, she'd found four hundred dollars cash in his jacket pocket and two front-row tickets to a Boston Celtics game. Obviously, he hadn't had time to work out a game plan for getting into heaven because, instead, he was lurking behind her oil painting, never letting her forget just how rotten he had been.

A marriage can sour for many reasons, but she and Walt had taken the surest route — neglect. He let a day, then a week, then months go by without saying 'I love you.' She assumed, in the beginning, that he would never cheat, so she never bothered to look beautiful for him. He figured she would always be waiting when he got back from doing what he had to do, so he was stunned to find the airstrip empty and her planting lavender in the garden when he drove up, as if it were any other day.

Esther knew her marriage was over six months after it began, but she didn't admit that out loud for another twenty years. She and Walt settled in Pendleton, Vermont, a small, clean town with an unmaintained dirt airstrip no one but Walt had the guts to use. Actually, only Esther settled; Walt flew out most every week, taking routes that led him to Alaska and Idaho, ferocious, spread-out places that sung to him. Sometimes, when he drove up after a long trip, Esther caught him standing in front of their house, staring at the black shutters as if he'd come to the wrong location. The first words out of his mouth were often, "Good God, Esther, what am I doing here?"

Esther never answered him. She had made a life and vowed to stick to it, and there was nothing else to do but forget how awful it made her feel. Better just to love Walt the best she could when he was around, and make the most of his extended absences. When he was away, she could stretch out diagonally in bed and eat nothing but peanut butter and crackers. She could practice her newfound magic without the door closed, since the smell of her herb mixtures made him nauseous.

Within weeks of their return from their honeymoon, Esther knew that hot wind had given her more than a feather. Suddenly she could see her neighbors' futures in storm clouds. She instinctively knew to use white willow bark for headaches and fennel seed and vinegar to stop a girl crying over some boy who wasn't worth it. Spells came to her in her dreams, and pretty soon she was weaving away women's ulcers and panic attacks. She was handing out talismans to make men fall in love.

Esther might have spun a love spell on Walt, if she hadn't figured her pregnancy would do the trick just as well. A child would be their salvation. Even a man like him, with wanderlust where his blood ought to have been, would have to feel something for his own flesh and blood, and for the woman who'd given birth to her.

But Walt insisted on flying to Alaska two days before Esther's due date, and he didn't get back until their daughter, who Esther unabashedly named Salvation, was a week old. He held Salvation for five minutes, until her urine seeped through her diaper onto his hands, then literally tossed her back to Esther and washed his hands with scalding water.

"Salvation," he said. "Good God, what kind of name is that?"

He never sang Salvation to sleep. After their honeymoon, he never touched Esther below the waist or called her darling again. He flew his routes, drew his maps, and went out drinking on the few nights he was home.

People might have pitied her, if Esther hadn't made it clear that her life was a series of choices within her own power. Walt did not slowly desert her; she chose to live with less of him. She could have tried to change him, but she knew the chances of that, so she just concentrated on other things, on Salvation and her magic.

Then he started in with the women.

It was just like men, Esther thought, to be so unoriginal. When they were unhappy, none of them ever tried to change the world; they simply found a new woman who made them feel young and handsome again. Esther knew about Walt's affairs years before she let on that she did. He was adventurous, but not particularly careful. He brought home receipts from hotels in Billings, flower shops in Spokane. He came home reeking of cheap perfume.

The surprising thing to Esther was her own lack of feeling. It only stung the first time, and not because he'd cheated, but because he'd become so common. She spotted lipstick not on his collar, but on the fly of his pants. She had thought, if nothing else, she had married an individualist. If he had to cheat, he could have picked a rugged Eskimo woman who wouldn't know the first thing about lipstick or kissing a man's fly. He could have picked someone worth having.

She confronted him only when he took up with Salvation's geometry teacher. Esther spotted them one afternoon in the field behind the high school, his hands cupped around her buttocks, hers tucked in the back pockets of his jeans. Esther took her car up to thirty and hopped the curb; she chased them until they both dove headfirst into the willow grove, then she blared the horn all the way home. That night, Walt did not say a word when he found the fly cut out of every pair of pants he owned. He even looked a little frightened when she leaned over his shoulder in the bathroom and plucked the razor out of his hands.

"You've become a whore, Walt," she said.

Half his face was still covered in cream. "I was wondering when you'd find out."

"Years ago. Don't think me a fool. But let me tell you something. You will not carry on with Salvation's teacher. Your daughter's no fool either. Can't you see the things you're teaching her?"

"Salvation's nearly an adult. Nothing I do now makes any difference."

"Everything you do makes a difference, and it always has. You've already taught her that men don't stay. What else do you want her to know? That you've sold yourself out? You used to be an extraordinary man, Walt. Now you're just ordinary. You're like every other adulterous man in the world, just lazy and stupid and so common I couldn't have imagined it."

"What would you have me do?" Walt asked. "Pretend to be happy with a life like this?"

He waved his hand around the room, as if everything — her and Salvation and this house — was the absolute bottom of the barrel, as if a man couldn't sink any lower than chaining himself to a wife and family.

"I never made you marry me," she said.

"Oh yes you did. You and your magic."

Esther tossed the razor in the sink. She didn't point out that she hadn't had any magic until after they were married. All she'd had that day he flew into her life was hope and courage, and the naive belief that love could never steer her wrong.

"Just don't do it in front of Salvation," she said.

"That's all you're asking?"

Esther squared her shoulders. "That's all."

Now, Esther held the flame once more to the painting and this time saw Walt clearly, as handsome as he'd been on the day she met him. She squinted until his eyes were just waves again. Her chest practically quivered with pain, and she knew there would not be time for Alex's stocking. Decisions had to be made on the spot, so she made one. She was ready when Robert O'Brien came to her door the next morning, a basket of forced spring bulbs in his hands.

The crocuses had already bloomed, and thick stalks of daffodils poked through the dirt. In a few weeks, he told Esther, she'd have enough color to make her forget it was winter. He held out the basket eagerly, not because of the flowers, but because in the middle was a box wrapped in red paper, just large enough to hold a ring.

Esther did not take the basket. She walked past him onto the porch. She sat on the swing and, a moment later, Robert came and sat beside her, the basket on his lap. They both shivered in the cold.

"I won't be alive to see those flowers grow," she said.

Robert put a trembling hand to his heart. She wanted to soothe him, but what was the point of comfort now, if she was only going to hurt him later?

"Esther, don't say that," he said. "Don't even think it."

"I can't help but think it. A person just knows these things. Your wife must have known."

Robert said nothing, but the basket slid off his lap. It hit the ground, scattering dirt and swollen bulbs everywhere. The ring box was flung through the railing and lost in a juniper bush.

Robert reached out for the box, but Esther grabbed his hand. She had loved the feel of his hands from the beginning, soft except for the calluses he'd gotten on his palms from gardening. Strong, but not too strong. Hands for touching things.

She let herself imagine what it might have been like if she'd met Robert O'Brien in her youth. If she'd married him instead of Walt, and had his children, along with a nice white house and a garden people envied. She let herself dream up the whole fantasy, then forced herself to forget every minute of it, because she knew it was ridiculous. She wouldn't have fallen in love with Robert in her youth. She wouldn't have even seen him. He would have blended into the background along with everything else she found too common or nice to note, like tract houses and boys who kept their promises. She wouldn't have seen the point in loving him if there was nothing in him to change, if he already loved her.

Now, she held his hand. "I'm not going to marry you, Robert. Don't even ask."

"But Esther, I love you."

"That's a silly thing, at our age. It can't last long."

"It will last as long as it lasts."

Esther shook her head, but she was not angry. She thought he was wonderful. She didn't care if the temperature dipped below zero, she wanted to sit on that swing with him forever. She wanted to hold his hand until the moment she died.

"I've got plans," she said. "There are things I have to do, and you can't come with me."

Robert looked into her eyes. He was dull, but

not stupid. He could read intensity and purpose as well as anyone.

"Will you be all right?" he asked at last.

"I'll be fine. You're a good man, Robert. Too good for me."

He leaned forward and kissed her. Not the kisses he'd given her in his garden — those kisses had been for public consumption, quick and dry, acceptable for old people. This kiss was long and deep; it was a kiss of youth. He reached up to let the pins out of her hair. The white strands tumbled around their faces, veiling them in privacy as his tongue searched out hers. He kissed her until her heart hurt from pleasure, until he proved good men were just as hard to leave.

Ever since Devon Zeke first stepped foot in Jim's Mercantile, Sandy Aberdeen had been thinking about love. It was like he'd cast a spell on her when he counted out his own change. One minute, she was thinking about whether or not she could make it out of the house wearing mascara, and the next she was way past that; she was envisioning what it would be like to kiss a boy or to maybe even go all the way. Even when her boss, Randy Weaver, swore up and down that Devon was a murderer, Sandy didn't blink. When Devon Zeke looked her in the eye, murderer or not, she felt beautiful.

She'd been thinking about love, but she hadn't felt the real thing until two weeks ago, when she fell in love with Tyler Ludlow right in the middle of a sip of Cherry Coke. She was in the Eat 'Em Up diner with her friend Bridget when Tyler walked in with half the varsity football team. She'd seen Tyler in school a hundred times and never given him a second thought. He was a jock, she was in A.P. Science; it was like they lived on two different planets. But that day, Tyler was dressed in jeans and a black sweater, his blond hair fell over his eyes, and all of a sudden Sandy just knew. Her Cherry Coke went down real smooth and put a hum in her throat. When Tyler turned around, when she saw the blue of his eyes, she bit a hole clear through her straw.

Tyler barely glanced at her. Since he'd found Ivy's body a month earlier, he had hardly looked at anyone, as if he might spot an abrasion and start shaking all over again. Sandy thought that was wonderful. She thought he was the kind of boy who would want to hold you after making love, who would cry just saying your name.

He hardly glanced at her, but by the way his shoulders suddenly slumped, she knew she'd done something to him, too. His heart must have gotten heavy, as if everything she might be to him weighed him down. One morning, he would simply arrive on her doorstep with flowers; there would be nothing left to do but bow his head beneath his love for her.

For two weeks, she had waited for him to

352

gather up his nerve, but waiting was agony — it sent pulses of pain clear down her legs. So tonight she had decided to take matters into her own hands. She had always gotten straight A's and never broken a single curfew, so when she told her parents she was too tired to go to the New Year's celebration on Main Street, they didn't question her. She went to bed at eight and feigned sleep. When her mother came in to check on her half an hour later, Sandy didn't even twitch. As soon as the door closed, she leapt out of bed, fully clothed. She ran to the window and flung it open.

She was out and free in seconds. She wore a black miniskirt and thin angora sweater, despite the icy night. She ran across the crusty grass, so young and rapturous that moonlight clung to her even when she slipped behind the shadows of trees. She wondered how people in love kept their hands off each other, why her parents weren't kissing every second of their lives.

She ran past Main Street, where her neighbors were already drunk on champagne and optimism. She flew beneath the red flares of cherry bombs and through the flickering trails of sparklers. Horns and screamers pierced the air, but they were not as loud as the sound of her wanting something for the first time in her life.

At the Common, there wasn't a soul in sight. The Main Street party was a dull rumble in the distance. The Ludlows lived in one of the fancy homes facing the park; Sandy could already imagine her wedding in their house, walking down that long, curving staircase, with all the boys who had teased her about her braces staring up at her with longing.

She wrapped her arms around herself as she ran across the park. She'd paid Bridget ten dollars to ask Tyler's brother, Scott, which bedroom was Tyler's, so she could know where to send her thoughts. She imagined if she concentrated hard enough, he would come to the window, but nothing moved behind the curtain.

With moonlight tickling the hair on her knees, she suddenly stopped. She wondered if she'd gotten it all wrong. Maybe Tyler really hadn't noticed her when she'd seen him at the Eat 'Em Up. Maybe love was not the bright future she imagined but something more down-to-earth, like the grass in the Common, covered in a sheet of ice. Maybe it was stuck there, dormant, and when it came back in the spring it would not be as green and true as she'd thought.

Sandy bit her red fingernail, which she'd polished yesterday, sure Tyler would like it. She was so uncertain what to do, she did not hear the footsteps behind her until the man was on her.

When the hand came around her throat, she went absolutely still. The arm was thick and hard, covered in a black jacket. The scent of the man was overpowering — the stink of sweat and fury. He lifted his gloved hand to her mouth and yanked her back against his chest.

"Don't scream," he said.

Sandy had read enough romance novels to know she'd just lost her one chance. If she hadn't hesitated, she would be safe at Tyler's door right now, she would be that one in a million who finds true love.

Instead, the man yanked her back and she noticed what she hadn't before; the hum of an idle engine, the car he would kill her in. Then something went cold in her. With Tyler's house still in sight, she decided right then she was not going to go easily. Tyler was not going to find *her* blood splattered all over the snow. She was going to wait for her opportunity, then fight like crazy. She was going to get to Tyler Ludlow's doorstep. You could bet on it.

As the man pulled her back to the car, she didn't resist. His hand — she noticed dark hairs just above the wrist line of his glove — slackened a bit on her mouth, allowing her to take a deep breath. When he pulled her up beside the car and loosened his grip to open the door, she wrenched herself away and ran.

She ran like the girl she'd been before love made her slow, the one who had won every two-hundred-meter race she'd ever run. Because she had everything to lose, she turned light as a feather, she never slipped on the ice. She could have run straight across the ocean if she had to.

"Fuck," the man said, and started after her.

Sandy ran toward Main Street, toward people. Behind her, she heard the man's ragged breathing, his steadily gaining footsteps. Then she turned onto Main and was momentarily stunned by the brightness and the crowd. Every year on New Year's Eve, Randy Weaver changed all the bulbs on the Main Street Christmas tree to silver stars and set off gold fireworks at the stroke of midnight. Every year, boys slipped away from their parents just before the countdown, so they could be beside the girls of their dreams when they looked for someone to kiss.

The footsteps behind her stopped abruptly and Sandy burst out crying. Relief made her believe in God for the first time in her life. She ran straight for her neighbors, and when she was certain they could hear her, she started screaming.

Esther had been too tired to go to the New Year's Eve ceremony, so Jane and Alex went alone. They didn't arrive until eleven-thirty, and by then the square around the Christmas tree was jam-packed, so they stood at the back, shivering, watching the pink tails of cherry bombs someone shot off into the air.

"This will take the chill off."

Jane turned around to find Graham holding out a thermos. "Hot chocolate," he said.

"Straight from a can."

His face was momentarily lit up in red light, then thrust back into darkness. He wore a denim jacket and corduroy pants, and Jane thought not even Ned had ever looked as good. The one thing she hadn't counted on was that good love would be a sneak. It had come up from behind and ensnared her in netting. It offered no explanation for why it had not come before. It just came, and infiltrated her blood so completely, all she could think about was getting more.

She reached out, then dropped her hand. How did she explain that the moment she kissed Devon, she stopped feeling unfaithful to Graham? The moment Devon touched her, her heart closed just enough to allow only one man into her heart. These were not things a man would understand, and that was the other thing about good love — it harbored no secrets, except the ones that might hurt him.

Graham still held out the thermos, but Jane didn't take it. She lifted her hand again and enclosed it around the warm spot of his wrist.

"What?" he said.

"I'm glad you came."

He smiled and looked down at her hand. He looked back up slowly, then Sandy screamed.

It took a good twenty minutes for everyone to calm down enough to pass the word that Sandy Aberdeen had nearly been abducted. Someone, in the panic, pulled the switch on the dazzling tree lights, and in the darkness everyone bolted for home.

Jane pulled Alex to her. She watched her neighbors scatter, while her own legs felt glued to the ground.

"Come on," Graham said. "I'll walk you home."

"It's not home anymore."

He looked at her, then started walking anyway, checking in the backs of cars, kicking the frozen branches of hedges. She was still putting the house up for sale as soon as the semester was over. She was going to move to Los Angeles or Dallas, a place where crime was not so personal, and for better or worse, girls learned early not to go out alone at night. She had the whole thing worked out; she would start a new career renovating houses, enroll Alex in one of those magnet schools for electronics or math, and find a place with a ground-floor bedroom for Esther. She had thought it all through, except the part where Graham fit in, because though he'd said a lot of things these last few months, he had never said a word about coming with her.

Jane walked stiffly and carefully. When Marjorie Dumas raced past her, pale as cotton, Jane opened her jacket and wrapped it around Alex's shoulders.

When they got to Devon's, where all the lights were off, she started shivering and couldn't stop. She didn't believe it, but that

358

didn't stop her from imagining shadows passing inside his dark windows. It didn't stop her from pushing Alex across the street and into their house. Graham followed them inside, then she bolted the door behind them.

"Don't worry," she said, but she was the one rushing Alex into his bedroom and into his pajamas, as if cotton were bulletproof. She put him into bed and pulled the covers up to his chin.

"It's all right," she said. He looked out the window, where fireworks from someone's backyard party stained the moon red. She got up and checked the lock on the window, then pulled the shade all the way down.

"Go to sleep, honey," she said, and turned around to find he already had. She left the light on when she walked out.

She walked past Graham into the kitchen. She yanked open drawers and tossed out masking tape and corkscrews and rusted salad tongs.

Graham came up behind her. "What are you looking for?"

"This." She held up her old pocketknife. She tried out the blade on the masking tape, and was happy to see it cut through the outer layers easily. She put it in her back pocket.

She glanced once more out the window, but Devon's house was still dark. "You don't think —"

She let the sentence hang, and Graham did not say anything. When she turned, he was standing by the front door, breathing hard. "Lock this behind me," he said.

Three hours after Sandy Aberdeen was attacked, Alex was packing. Two shirts, his favorite pair of sneakers, the old blanket he didn't let anyone know he still slept with. He jumped every time the wind rattled his window, and he didn't even want to think about the long, dark walk to the bus station. Still, anything was better than staying here where people were dropping like flies. Sandy Aberdeen had always given him free bubble gum when he went into Jim's Mercantile. She slipped it to him while his mother had her back turned, and it was always the good stuff, thick and cherry-flavored, the kind that made bubbles the size of softballs.

Now she'd almost gotten murdered, and he figured that was as good a sign as any that it was time to leave town.

He waited until his mother and grandmother finally went to sleep, then he left a note on his pillow and slipped out the window.

He headed west, as he'd intended, but when he reached Olive Street, he turned and ran up the road. He'd had one friend his whole life and he wasn't about to leave without telling her goodbye. He tiptoed up to Linda Carlton's window and tapped lightly against the glass.

She awoke immediately, as if she'd been waiting for him. Her hair, for once, was not in braids; it twisted in the most amazing blond coils down her back. She lifted up her window.

"Are you running away?" she asked.

He nodded and she glanced back at her room. It was done all in pink, with a wallpaper border of hats and bunnies. She had at least thirty stuffed animals piled on a chest in the corner, and a jewelry box with a ballerina that went round and round when opened.

She had parents who put her to bed by seven o'clock, after reading her as many stories as she wanted, but she still squared her shoulders and smiled at him. "Just let me change. I'm coming with you."

He wouldn't have argued even if he could speak. Someone like her choosing to be with someone like him went beyond all reason. It was the stuff of dreams.

She was out her window within ten minutes, a pillowcase stuffed with clothes and her Barney piggy bank slung over her shoulder. They headed west. She didn't take his hand until they neared the woods, and then he tried not to squeeze it when he heard twigs snapping. For once he was glad he couldn't speak; otherwise he would have blurted out how much he wanted to go home, or that Sandy Aberdeen's attacker could be hiding behind any number of trees.

Linda's step never faltered. Even when they walked out of the reach of the searchlights Mark Sharkey and a posse of fathers were aiming into backyards and cul-de-sacs, she whistled while she walked. She never asked where they were headed. Her trust should have thrilled him, but instead it thinned his skin. The first brush of wind made him jump. He couldn't look up at the stars without crying.

It must have been his fear that drew the wolf. He'd read somewhere that wolves can smell blood from fifty yards, uncertainty from farther than that. Alex stopped suddenly when he heard the splitting of crusty snow.

For a long time, he saw nothing. Finally, the snow split again, then a sleek, gray wolf emerged from the trees.

Alex would have run, if he hadn't been holding Linda's hand, if he hadn't felt this was when he proved he was capable of doing something right. All he could think to do was step in front of her. He prayed shaking was not visible in the dark.

For what seemed like hours, they stood there, boy to wolf, and the silence was piercing; it would have had any other boy in tears. But Alex heard silence like that every day of his life; silence like that was nothing.

The wind slammed into his back, and the wolf flared his nostrils. The hair rose on the back of the animal's neck as he pawed at the ground. And then Alex understood; the wolf had picked up the scent of dragon.

Alex stepped back slowly. Linda was rigid as ice behind him, and he had to push her to get her to move. She stumbled every other step as he pushed her back toward home.

The wolf followed them for half a mile, coming in and out of the trees. The steam that rose off his gray coat stank of barely checked violence. He followed them until the security lights and hum of panic in the streets turned him back. Until Linda let loose her tight grip on Alex's hand.

"I thought we were running away," she said. "I'm not scared anymore. Really I'm not."

Alex nodded, but still led her toward home. The dragon burned so hot in his throat he wondered why flames didn't shoot out. She might not be scared, but he was. He was scared because he had not been attacked, because a wolf had let him go, because this meant the dragon was real.

He led her back to her house and opened up her bedroom window. When she wouldn't go inside, he turned around and started walking.

"Alex," she said, but he only shook his head. So far, he'd managed not to cry, but if she said another thing, he'd be done for. He ran across the snowy lawn. He tried to make his feet go west again, but once he hit the corner, he was running as fast as he could toward home.

Twelve

Graham's New Year's resolution was to get control of himself. To stay away from Devon and learn how to ride for pleasure again. To look Jane in the eye and tell her everything. That he'd loved her forever and it was not going to stop.

On the third of January, when his last two appointments canceled, he stepped out the door onto the salted walk and wondered what he was waiting for. Jane was either going to love him back or not, and his other resolution was to live with it either way.

He drove home to put on his best suit, but when he tried to pull into his driveway, Ginny's Volvo was already there. For a moment, he just sat behind the wheel and stared at the new license plates she'd gotten — SLOCUM, her maiden name, in block letters. He was surprised, since she had been the one to insist on taking his name when they married. She had not even wanted to hyphenate.

He backed up and parked along the curb. When he walked in, Ginny was filling a box with their good crystal. Though he must have surprised her, she didn't jump. "I thought you'd still be at work," she said.

She had lost weight. A good ten pounds, leaving her thinner than he or the government charts recommended, but probably not as thin as she wanted to be. She had on more makeup than he remembered her wearing, but then maybe he had just never looked at her this closely before.

"My appointments canceled," he said.

She nodded and took a pair of Waterford candlesticks out of the cupboard. "I figured you wouldn't care. We never used these."

"I don't care."

She wrapped the candlesticks in newspaper, then tucked them into the box. She pulled a chair to the counter and stood on it to get to the champagne glasses in the back.

Graham walked upstairs to change. The house seemed to breathe easier with her in it. The stairs did not creak beneath his weight, the crack he'd noticed in the bedroom wall was not nearly as bad as he'd first thought. He put on his dark blue suit, the black shoes that needed to be polished, and stared down at the chintz comforter Ginny had picked out. Above the bed was a Monet print she'd had specially framed. In the bathroom, of course, were her little hearts around the sink.

He realized he hated every room, every single stick of furniture. He wanted a modern house, to tell the truth, with hard angles and steel joists. He never wanted to look at chintz again.

He walked back downstairs, where Ginny was ferreting away silverware.

"I'll just use plastic," he said.

She emptied the silverware tray into the box and turned on him. She took in his suit and narrowed her green eyes that had never looked clearer.

"Look," she said, "these are my things. You know they are. I haven't bothered you about this house. I haven't pressed you to sell it."

And that's when he knew he would. He would call Marilyn Ludlow and ask her to list it low, so it would sell fast. He didn't know where he would go; he only knew he wouldn't take a thing with him, except Jane and Alex.

"You look good," he said.

Ginny turned away, but she wasn't blushing. She was hard as nails, and he figured he was to blame for that, along with everything else.

"I'm almost done," she said.

He poured himself a glass of wine and sat on the chintz sofa he would take pleasure in donating to charity. Ginny rummaged through the plates and glasses. He knew she would leave behind the everyday stuff and take the china they had used only on holidays. She would use it every day. She would not deny herself anything ever again.

Finally, she finished packing and came into the living room. "I've got a couple boxes upstairs, too. I'm sending a mover over tomorrow."

Graham nodded. He really had no idea what to say to her.

"Look," she said, grabbing her keys off the entry table. "I'm sorry, okay?"

He set down his wine and stood up. "Ginny, you don't have to be sorry for anything."

She turned away. She started for the door, then turned around. "You're not going to her, are you?"

He looked right at her. He wasn't going to hide it anymore, not from anyone.

"Graham," she said softly, "you might be able to beat Devon up Pendleton Hill someday, but you're not going to win this one. I was in Jim's today. It's all over town that they're an item. Marjorie saw Jane going to his house the other night. She didn't leave until morning."

Graham stepped back. He ran his hand through his hair. He could have done a lot of things, but all he did was sit down. He'd run out of gas; he couldn't go any farther even if he wanted to.

Ginny came up behind him. "You didn't know." She put her hand on his shoulder briefly, then walked to the fireplace. She ran a finger along the mantel that had been breeding dust since she'd been gone. "It could very well be just a rumor. You know Marjorie."

It was not a rumor. It had been happening his whole life. He stood up and loosened his tie, then yanked it off. He picked up his wine-glass and threw it at the fireplace. Ginny jumped back as glass exploded around her feet.

Graham looked at her. Ironically, she was the only one who understood that his heart had been straining all these years and now it had ruptured; she was the only one even slightly sympathetic.

"Well," she said.

"I'm selling the house," he said. "I'll ask whatever you want, but I'd like to sell it fast. I'd like to get the hell out of here."

Ginny stepped right on the glass; she ground shards into the wood floor. "You can't just forget someone," she said, and he realized he hadn't hardened her at all. Whether she knew it or not, she was going to fall in love again. She was going to set out the candlesticks and use the good china every day of her life.

"I can try," he said.

After Ginny left, he grabbed his keys and went outside. He walked to his car, opened the door, then shut it without getting in. He wanted to see this town he was leaving. He wanted to figure out why he had stayed so long.

He didn't even stumble on the ice, that's how clear-headed he felt. He was going to set up practice in a large, faceless city. It would be a luxury to have patients whose names he couldn't remember, to eat out without running into anyone. From this moment on, he decided to give up house calls, so he would never again have to look in a dying patient's eyes and recall the indentations in his dusty couch or the rows and rows of family pictures on his living room wall.

He walked past Francis McGinnis's colonial, where the three-foot-high weeds were covered in snow. He walked to the place where Ned had died and then right past it. And, of course, he ended up on Sycamore Lane.

He stood in front of Jane's house and heard the clanking of dishes as she made dinner. He had figured a man overwhelmed by heartache would snap in two or fall to pieces, but instead, he just got mad. She ought to have loved him, but if she couldn't, then he could no longer be her friend. That was just too much to ask.

January is the worst month. It starts off with promises and ends with regret. The holiday shopping sprees show up on the MasterCard, the water damage from the Christmas tree attracts termites, and a week after New Year's, people bite your head off if you even mention diets and the ease of quitting smoking with the help of the patch.

So when Graham stopped coming by, Jane blamed it on January. She blamed it on the weather — so far the coldest on record. On black ice that sent six cars to the junkyard in a single afternoon, and the sniping that was going on around town now that the sun had not shined in nine days. Randy Weaver had accused Scott Ludlow of stealing a can of chewing tobacco. Josie Aberdeen had cut the bangs off one of her clients, after the woman asked what Josie's daughter had been doing out in the first place on the night she was almost killed.

When Jane started getting headaches again, she blamed them on her neighbors' panic. All the fear in the air had turned the Red Delicious apples in Jim's Mercantile sour and green; there was no telling what it would do to a woman's psyche. She curled around her pillow at night for the same reason there were no more twenty-two-caliber bullets to be found within a fifty-mile radius — because Sandy Aberdeen's face got paler every day, and people were preparing for the worst.

She sent Alex off for his last few days of school, while she worked like crazy on the house. She installed the pedestal sink, put the finish on the floors with the help of the Ludlow boys, and painted the back bedrooms lemon yellow. She left the attic empty of furniture, and every time she walked up the stairs and looked over the glossy pine floors, she saw the future. An old man would set up his electric train in the attic and boys from the neighborhood would come to watch, boys who cussed like crazy but also mowed the man's grass while he slept. Someone would put a crib right beneath one of the skylights, and a baby girl would wake up every morning at dawn but not cry out, because she'd want to see the sunrise. That baby girl, when she was grown, would sneak in her lover; they would make love beneath the maple leaves and he would swear on the rising moon that he would never leave her.

The house was not perfect, but Jane decided it was done. She invited over Marilyn Ludlow, and the real estate agent said nothing until she saw the attic, and then she told Jane it would sell like that.

"I'll be leaving as soon as Alex's school semester is over," Jane said to her, as Marilyn took off her high heels and skated across the floor in nylons. "I've already given notice at the store."

Marilyn slid to a stop in the corner. "God, this is lovely."

"I want out fast," Jane went on.

Marilyn looked up. She walked back and put on her shoes. "I don't blame you. All these maniacs running around. Poor Tyler was just calming down over the Ivy thing. Now he spends every day at Sandy Aberdeen's, trying to comfort her."

Jane had seen the two of them huddled close together at the Eat 'Em Up, both sipping Cherry Cokes and gazing into each other's eyes. The scare had sapped the color from their cheeks; it had put a fevered sheen in their eyes. When they held hands across the table, they seemed to be holding on for dear life.

"You're not the only one, you know," Marilyn went on. "Graham called me yesterday. He's listing his at two seventy-five, though I've got to tell you I could get a lot more than that. He's trying to find a doctor to take over the business. I thought he was going after Ginny, but Beth told me he just wants out."

Jane looked up at the roof, unable to say a single word. The thing was, despite the ominousness of January, she had already planned what she would say when she told Graham she was leaving. She had planned to tell him the truth, to just open her mouth and say *Graham, I need you with me.*

"So like I said," Marilyn said, "we'll try yours at one thirty-five. That's the high end, but then we don't want to give it away."

Her high heels sunk into the snow when she left, and Jane sat down on the couch. She stared across the street at Devon's. Two days after Sandy's attack, on a night when half the town saw Devon performing at amateur night at Orion's Bar, a young girl in Rutland was killed under strikingly similar circumstances. Otherwise, things might have gone very differently. Otherwise, Mark Sharkey might have asked Devon a few more questions instead of just sitting on his porch and drinking a beer with him.

She stood up and grabbed her keys off the table. She walked out the door and down the drive. Marilyn had already put up a small For Sale sign — she sent her boys around town in the evenings to pound the large ones a foot deep in her clients' yards. Devon was just stepping out his front door and reaching for his snowshoes when she opened her car door.

"Hi," she said.

He leaned back against the porch railing. He might hate her, that might just be the price she had to pay. He snapped on his snowshoes. Then, just like that, he smiled.

"Hi, Janie," he said.

"Why didn't you tell me you were selling your house?"

Jane had walked into an office oddly hushed at midday. No patients sat reading *Ladies' Home Journal* in the waiting room. Beth was not at her usual chair and most of the pictures had been cleared off her desk. Jane sat in Graham's office beside three boxes packed with books and diplomas and the pictures of him and Ginny that used to cover the walls.

"I'm selling my house," Graham said, throwing a few more things in a box, sealing it with masking tape, then sitting down in his chair.

"Would you have left without saying goodbye?"

He stared right at her, he stared as if there had never been a moment in his life when he'd cared about her. "What would be the point? Haven't we already said it enough?"

"I thought you loved it here. I thought you'd stay forever."

Graham shrugged and leaned back in his chair. "You thought wrong."

Jane stood up and stepped over the boxes to

get to his side. "Are you going to tell me what's going on?"

He looked up at her. "Why don't you tell me?" Each word was slow and deliberate, each syllable mean.

She stepped back and reached for the wall. It seemed entirely possible that she had waited too long to come here.

"Graham?"

He stood up and turned his back on her. He walked to the window. She had planned what to say, but it was not going to get said, not when she was having trouble just breathing, not when her little gasps of air did not even make him turn around.

"I don't understand."

Graham whirled around. "What's to understand? I'm done, okay?"

"No. That's not okay."

He stared at her, then walked back to his desk. He yanked out his top drawer and dumped pens and pencils and paper clips in another box. His shoulders rose and fell quickly, but when he turned around, his eyes were stones. He wasn't going to take another step toward her. She could see that clear as day.

She stepped toward him and reached out her hand. "Graham, I want you to know —"

"Tell me this. Did you sleep with Devon?"

She dropped her hand into her coat pocket. She felt a bad chill coming on.

"God, this town."

"Thank God for this town," he said. "It's kept me from playing the fool again."

"Graham, please."

"Please what? Please play second fiddle all over again? Please live off another man's leftovers?"

"It's not like that. I only went to Devon to say goodbye."

"That's an interesting way to do it."

"It wasn't what you think. We just —"

"Spare me the details. Just spare me, all right?"

He turned away. She watched his shoulders rise and fall. She stepped up behind him, but he just slammed the last box shut and carried it to the door.

"I'm leaving. Turn off the light on your way out."

She heard his footsteps down the hall, then the slam of the front door. And then, into the space where he'd been, she whispered *Graham, I need you with me.* The words came right back at her, as ineffective as rock salt on ghosts. She walked to the door and turned out the light.

Graham dropped the box on the sidewalk. Pens and paper clips scattered all over the snow. He walked to his car and grabbed the jacket out of the trunk. He put it on, didn't bother to zip it up, and set off down the street.

He ignored his bundled-up neighbors who tried to stop him to ask what he thought of this

Arctic blast or the latest echinacea rage. He put his head down and walked through the slush piles on Main Street, out to where the new subdivisions were going in, and through Cobby's Field, where the snow was unplowed and two feet deep. He walked until his leather shoes were ruined, and there was ice all down his socks, and he could not feel his toes.

He walked up Pendleton Hill, past the wreaths strung on lampposts, up to the crest where the residents left up their elaborate Christmas lights all through January. There was a Santa Claus on a Ferris wheel that went round and round day and night, and Rudolph doing flips on the roof next door, and down the street a tropical nativity scene complete with a smiling baby Jesus on a surfboard, dressed in Hawaiian baby shorts and a tank top.

When he started down the other side of the hill, his stomach was a hard knot of pain. He picked up his pace and tried to make it worse. He tried to make it bad enough so he wouldn't feel anything else.

At the bottom of the hill, he headed east, over an unplowed road through Hagerman's Woods. With every step, he sank to his thighs in the snow. He figured he might have to walk forever to keep himself sane. He had thought he could shut himself down, stop feeling anything, but when Jane had walked into his office, he'd known he was fooling himself. He was just going to love her for the rest of his life, and it would not quite kill him. He would work and eat and function like a normal person, but all the while wanting would ravage his body like cancer.

The clouds thickened as he walked farther into the woods. It got so dark, he lost his shadow, raccoons thought it was night and came out of their dens looking for food. The snow began to fall again, thick, velvety flakes that caked on his eyebrows and lashes.

He came upon the snowshoe tracks after half a mile. They seemed to start out of nowhere, their entry probably covered by the newly fallen snow. He followed them, for lack of any better plan. He took two steps for every one of the man's.

The tracks ended in the clearing. Graham stopped, and the sudden inactivity made his legs throb. He looked to his right and saw him.

Devon sat in the snow beneath a tree, his snowshoes stuck out in front of him, a joint between his fingers. He smiled at Graham and waved him over.

"Come on, Doc," he said. "Have a seat. It's a long way home."

He'd known Devon would be there long before he'd spotted the tracks. He'd known it when he'd decided to search out pain, and every step had led him in Devon's direction.

Graham stumbled over to him, falling through the deep snow with each step. Devon was sheltered beneath the leafless tree and not a single flake stuck to him. He held out the joint.

"Go ahead," he said.

Graham stood in snow to his knees and just stared at him. The cramp in his left side intensified. The longer he stared at Devon, the harder it got, until he imagined his organs were all pushed to the sides to make way for it, this hard lump of envy and hate.

Devon, oblivious to this, took back the joint. "Your loss. It's straight from Colombia. Best you can buy, or bargain for."

He laughed and the lump spread out from Graham's stomach, through his arms and legs. In a few more seconds, he would be rooted to the spot by envy. He would be a gnarled tree people hurried by, scared off by talk of hauntings and something rotten in the air. It all came down to this: He was jealous of what he hated. Devon had a worthless life, and still Graham envied him. He envied all the things he himself lacked: Devon's athletic ability, his confidence, his simple joy. And of course, of course, Jane's love for him.

Because of that envy, he'd kept a secret that would have quickly cleared Devon of any crime beyond being perfect. Because of that envy, he'd become a man who had to risk frostbite just to get away from feeling.

"Get up," he said.

"I'm comfortable."

"Get up," Graham said again, then did something that surprised both of them. He lifted his foot out of the heavy snow and kicked Devon's boot out of the binding.

Devon looked at his snowshoe lying on the ground beside his foot, then up at Graham. He put the joint out in the snow and got slowly to his feet. He rose a good four inches above Graham's head, but Graham's memory pared him down two inches. Away from the shelter of the tree, the snow quickly coated Devon's hair, so it might have been blond. The eyes, at least, were exactly the same as Graham remembered them, and he hated them.

"You got a problem?" Devon asked.

The envy funneled hot blood to the tips of Graham's fingers and toes. It made his muscles rock-hard. "I want you out of here."

He knew, even before Devon opened his mouth, that he would laugh. And this time he was ready. When Devon started to smile, Graham clenched his fist and landed the hardest blow he could on Devon's perfect mouth.

The unexpected punch stunned the man. In fact, to both Devon's and Graham's astonishment, it sent him stumbling into the tree. He hit his head against the trunk and when Graham saw the blood oozing through his hair, the doctor in him nearly won out. But then Devon turned, this time with fire in his eyes, and came straight for him.

Graham took the first blow on his stomach,

the next on his shoulder, then he was suddenly on his back in the snow, struggling to crawl out. He battled with everything he had, with envy and hatred and fists used to the delicate job of stitching wounds. He heard the smacks of Devon's blows landing on him, and an ominous pop, but for the moment he felt no pain. He was too frustrated at his own ineptitude. Devon was so much stronger, much more skilled at fighting; all his blows landed right where he'd intended them. The snow and Devon's weight held him down; he couldn't do anything but take it.

Devon went on pummeling him, and Graham feigned unconsciousness. When Devon paused, Graham flipped him over.

In one quick round — all he'd ever get — Graham fought as hard as he could. He punched out envy with his right hand and hatred with his left. When he kicked, he kicked for Jane. He jabbed and punched and it was a long time before he realized Devon was not fighting back. He lay in the snow and took it and, all at once, the fury just went out of Graham.

He sat back in the snow. They were both sights, their knuckles cracked open and blood spilling from their noses. Graham suddenly became aware of the pain in his ribs, excessive, he thought, for a mere bruise. When he tried to stand, his legs buckled. His pants were torn and blood had already stained the fabric black.

Blood dripped from Devon's scalp, nose, and hands, but he still got to his feet easily. He wiped the blood off his mouth with the back of his hand, then stepped up to Graham. He lifted his boot over Graham's right hand.

"I could ruin your life," he said, lowering the boot over the fingers Graham made his living with.

Graham thought about moving his hand to safety, but for the first time in his life he dared to risk something. He ought to have asked for pity, but the words would not come. He held his breath as Devon brought down his foot, but it wasn't until his enemy placed it down harmlessly, a quarter inch from his hand, that Graham realized just how much he loved being a doctor. It wasn't until Devon spoke again that he realized the lump had gone out of him, and the only person worth envying all these years was himself.

"You're a damn fool," Devon said, and Graham nodded. He even smiled, though he would not remember this later when the pain really set in. "I could have killed you, if I'd wanted to. Why do you want to mess with me?"

Graham ran his fingers down his throbbing ribs. When Devon had been on top of him, that popping sound was probably one of them cracking. For some reason, the idea of broken bones excited him. Ned had always been the one with injuries, the one to crash his bike into campers and get himself electrocuted playing with live wires.

"I just . . ." Graham did not finish. He had no idea what the point had been. He only knew he was done here.

"You're crazy," Devon said. "Who'd have thought the doc would be crazy?"

Graham laughed at that, from way down deep in his stomach. He could be crazy and a doctor at the same time. Safe lives were stuffed with small heroics and tragedies; it was a risk just to walk out the door.

"You may have to call someone," Graham said. "I don't think I can walk."

Devon put back on the snowshoe Graham had kicked off. He knelt down in front of Graham and looked him over.

"Why should I help you? I've offered you friendship and you come after me with your fists."

"You're everything I'm not," Graham said.

Up close, Graham could make out the large pores on Devon's nose, the brown whiskers along his ear he'd missed shaving. He could smell sweat.

"You don't want to be like me," Devon said finally.

"No," Graham said. "I guess I don't."

"It all comes down to Jane, right?" Devon asked. "This is all about Jane."

A month ago, a week ago, Graham would have said yes. But now he knew it was more than that. It was about Ned. It had always been about Ned.

Devon stood up. "I don't need to tell you this, but she's not in love with me."

Graham breathed in deeply. He held the air in his lungs as long as he could, it was that clean and clear.

"I'll call someone," Devon said. "Pick your fights more carefully next time, Doc."

He walked away and Graham lay back in the snow. He had not realized that the snow had finally stopped falling. Above him, a crystal-clear blue sky had opened up.

The Pendleton police had invested in a snow-mobile back when Graham's father was the sheriff, imagining they'd have to chase down felons through the snowy woods. The only one who had used the thing regularly, though, was Ned; he'd stolen it weekly on winter nights to take Jane and his friends out for joy rides.

When Graham heard it whizzing through the woods, he felt an unexplainable joy. He still sat in the snow, bloody and bruised, but when Mark Sharkey came into view, he laughed out loud. As soon as he was seated behind the sheriff, he urged the man to take the machine as fast as it would go. He wanted to leave the woods in a blaze of white.

Mark Sharkey, though, never went over five miles an hour. When they hit the slick road and slowed even further, Graham shook his head in disgust. Luckily, when they turned onto Graham's street, the noise brought out his neighbors. Karen Wright held her toy poodle and gawked at him; the Francos' three teenage boys, who on New Year's Eve had sideswiped all the mailboxes, stood on their snowy lawn and cheered all the blood.

Graham drove himself to the emergency room in Rutland. Every time he stepped on the gas, the pain shot through his limbs and rib cage and, frankly, he was stunned he could take it without crying. Every jolt of the car was nearly his undoing, and he marveled at this strength he hadn't known he had. He marveled at how alive pain made him feel.

The doctor stitched up the gash in his leg and diagnosed a cracked rib and badly sprained right hand. When Graham told him he was a doctor too, the man shook his head. "You were risking your profession. What got into you?"

Graham didn't say it, because it would have sounded crazy. But he believed what had gotten into him was Ned.

Devon's face was still bruised when he stepped into Orion's Bar, but it was so dark and smoky no one noticed. He breathed deeply. This kind of air suited him; his lungs seemed to feed on carbon monoxide instead of oxygen. He had not minded the nearly constant cloud cover of the last two weeks. He couldn't explain it, but since Jane had left him, he'd gotten fairer. The slightest bit of sunlight now stung his eyes. While out skiing, he'd gotten sun-burnt for the first time in his life.

He'd been appearing on amateur night for four months now. Roy Carter usually asked him to close the set, because he made the women cry long enough to order one more Long Island Iced Tea, for which Roy charged eight dollars apiece.

Amateur night wasn't until Sunday, though, so Devon ordered a beer and sat at a table in the back. For two weeks, he'd lived on saltines and beer. He telemarked forty miles a day, until he brought on rare stomach cramps, because he couldn't figure what else to do. It was time for him to pack up and move to Moab, but instead he snowshoed all night beneath a billion stars.

It wasn't long before Cindy Davis walked over to his table. She had poured black leather pants over her plump thighs, and shimmied into a red-sequined Western shirt. She'd gotten a perm since the last time he'd seen her — last night — and her brown hair coiled like minia-ture Slinkies around her head.

She was garishly attractive, the kind of girl who wouldn't question anything a man did, so Devon asked her to sit down. He bought her another rum and Coke.

"What's a pretty girl like you doing here?"

She laughed and bumped against him, and the pain behind Devon's eyes began to ebb. At least nothing had changed here. Cindy would go home with him in a second. No one would question him about Sandy Aberdeen.

Cindy reached across the table and took his hands. "I was hoping —" she began, but Devon cut her off.

"Don't hope."

"Last night, though —"

"Was fun and games. I'm in love with someone else."

And as he said it, he knew it was true. Love might not run pure in him — he might cheat even as he was declaring it — but still it ran. It ran for the one girl who didn't want him, and he didn't think it would ever change.

Cindy got up huffily and stomped away. Once her perfume had dissipated, Devon took a deep breath. Roy brought him another beer, on the house.

Ten minutes later, the door behind Devon opened and a blast of bad January air blew in. There was the stomp of boots, then a man in a black leather jacket walked past Devon. The man ordered a beer, then looked around.

When he spotted Devon, he walked over to his table. "Happy fucking January," Jake Orofino said.

Devon nodded as Jake sat down beside him. He did not need Jake tonight. He did not need to hear how many breaks Jake had missed, or how much better Devon's life was than his, when right now it did not feel better than anyone's.

"Jesus H. Christ," Jake said. "It's not like it

would hurt to have a little sunshine now and then. This goddamn month."

He gulped his beer. He checked out the women at the bar, then turned away in disgust, as if he could write off a person by the color of her hair.

"How's your little Janie?" Jake asked.

"She's not my anything."

"She set you out? The bitch dump you?"

For the first time, Devon looked into Jake's eyes. They were small and bloodshot. They were like rats' eyes, mean rats, and they suddenly set Devon's stomach on edge.

"She did," he said carefully.

Jake slammed his hand on the table, then looked around. He leaned in toward Devon. "I could've told you. She's too high and mighty. Always has been. At least until that night. I tell you I was there? At the bachelor party? Ned and Carol were at it all night. No wonder he couldn't drive straight."

Jake laughed and sat back. He gulped down the rest of his beer and signaled to Roy for another. He thumped his hands on the table, then curled them into fists. "God, I fucking hate this place."

His gaze settled on Cindy Davis, who'd sat down two tables over. "You fuck her, Devon?"

Devon was not in love with Cindy Davis, but he understood this was his chance to protect her, to do something right. "No."

"Hmmm. So it's just Jane then? And now

she's dumped you. There ought to be some price for that, don't you think?"

Devon slowly sat forward. "Yeah. What price do you think?"

Jake studied his face a long time, then slowly smiled. "You know it was me," he said, not at all with caution, but with a touch of pride.

Devon hadn't known until then. He'd just felt a little cold, a little sick to his stomach, as if he'd brushed against something evil. Now the cold went deeper, into his bones.

"Yeah," he said. "They thought it was me."

Jake laughed. "I know it. You're the new guy. You drew suspicion right away. I've been here forever. Never caused any trouble they know about, and they don't know shit."

"How'd you get away with it?"

Jake looked right and left, then sat forward. "Easy. Drive to Jersey and toss the knife in the ocean. And this guy? Vern Cash? He owes me big time for paying his way out of the slammer. He's my alibi. Airtight, my man. The cops questioned me right after Ivy went down, but not even smoke can get through. Vern's solid as a rock."

"You've got a lot of guts," Devon said. He was just bad enough to know what to say, what a man like Jake wanted to hear. He was just criminal enough to know that a man could sour for many reasons — because he's bored, or stupid, or he'd never fallen in love. He just woke up one morning and punched the first thing he saw. He dropped his conscience off in a bad dream and never went back to pick it up.

"Hell, yes," Jake said, sitting so far forward his rank breath was in Devon's face. "All these years, I've been dog meat, you know? A nobody. Could never get ahead racing. The girls never wanted a damn thing to do with me, and they're all trash anyway. Then Ivy started toying with me. Giving me the eye, then pretending she wasn't interested. She was messing with my head, you know? That night she left with you, I followed you home. When she left, I set the bitch straight."

"And Sandy?" Devon asked.

"Sandy," Jake spat out. "Teenage bitch never gave me the time of day when I went into the Merc. Always looking down her nose at me. I don't know what I would have done with her. She was out wearing a goddamn miniskirt, all dressed up to meet some boy, I figure. I was maybe gonna show her what a man was. Show her and then break her goddamn neck."

Devon revealed nothing. The worst part was knowing that, if he hadn't fallen in love with Jane, he might be sitting on the other side of this table. Lack of love didn't kill a man; it just made him mean. Devon hadn't thought it would make all that much difference, whether he loved a woman or just fucked her, but the truth was that loving Jane had saved him, it had stopped the badness in him where it was, at petty theft.

"There were others," Jake went on, smiling. "Others they don't even know about yet. You shouldn't take that crap from Jane. No man should take it. She's just trash. Always has been. In high school, I used to watch them, her and Ned. She couldn't keep her hands off him. Pulled off her pants first chance she got. She's trash, Devon. I know what to do with trash."

Devon lowered his head just enough to see how close his fists were to Jake's face. He could take him down, he might even be able to kill him if someone didn't stop him first. But he thought of Jane hearing of it, of her thinking the worst of him. He thought of the kind of man he wanted to be in her eyes. He uncoiled his fists.

The police, he knew, would not believe him. Jake had his alibi and the cops would think he was just trying to deflect attention from himself. But that didn't mean Devon was going to let him get off. That didn't mean there was nothing he could do.

"I'll take care of Jane," he said, looking straight into Jake's eyes. "I've got something better in mind for you."

He reached into his pocket and took out the card Al Miguel had sent him, with the address of what ought to have been his new home in Moab written on the back. He slid it across the table.

"This is your future, buddy," he said. "Setup in Moab. Techline racing team. You can even take my bike. Best money can buy. All you've got to do is say you're me. It's all made up anyway."

Jake slowly reached for the card, then drew back, and Devon realized the man had never been given anything his whole life. Devon shoved the card beneath his fingers.

He couldn't think of any other alternative. He had to get the man out of town. The most the police would do was slowly, cautiously question Jake, and in the meantime a man like that might just snap. In the meantime, there were Jane and Alex to protect.

That woman had blinded him to everything but her. He didn't have a chance in hell of having her, but for the first time in his life, getting what he wanted didn't matter much. If something happened to her, he'd die right along with her. He was sure of it. He wasn't filled with air at all; he was filled with her.

So he sat in Orion's and told Jake about the forged résumé. He told him everything he needed to know to take on the already strained identity of Devon Zeke. He told him to take the bike and failed to mention the ounce of marijuana stuffed beneath the seat, the ounce that could net him ten years to life, if a tip came in to the Utah police that he was dealing across state lines. He failed to mention that, once a man was in custody, he invariably talked. He tried to one-up his cellmates, and if enough information was phoned in through anonymous sources, a man like Jake, stupid and mean, would eventually confess; he'd flaunt his crimes like gold badges.

He told Jake to leave tonight and never look back. Jake sat for a long time just staring at the name and number. Then he finally slipped the card in his pocket.

"Why?" he asked.

"Because I'm through," Devon said. "There was never much behind the name anyway." He stared straight ahead, until Jake stood up and put his hand on his shoulder. Devon did not jump, but beneath the table he pressed his feet into the floor. Jake squeezed harder, then walked out of the bar.

Devon stood up wearily. Jane might not know this, but her soul had attached itself to him for protection. Somewhere deep down, she must have considered him a hero, and the strange thing was, her opinion carried more weight than his own.

Cindy Davis came up to him again. "You look like you could use some company."

Devon looked in her eyes. She was expecting more than he could give, and he would surely disappoint her. He ought to just walk away, he ought to be a hero through and through, but that was just asking for too much.

"You're right," he said. "I could."

Thirteen

Graham had never been inside Orion's Bar, not once, which was why, one week after his fight with Devon, he went in and bought himself a gin and tonic. Since the moment he'd lain in the snow, with blood all over him, he'd known quite clearly that things were going to be different from then on.

Roy Carter brought him the drink. He smiled around an unfiltered Camel.

"Heard about the fight," Roy said, gesturing toward Graham's bandaged hand. "Didn't know you had it in you, Doc."

Graham downed half the drink and held his hand up to the light. Vince Ludlow walked into the bar then and took the seat beside him. Vince didn't even say anything; Roy just mixed him a vodka martini. Vince, Graham knew from taking tests of his liver, had to be Roy's best customer. He was miserable and so uncreative, all he could think to do about the wretched state of his life was fill his blood with vodka. He came in faithfully every night after work and downed at least six drinks.

"You see that?" Vince said, gesturing to the

front table, where Devon Zeke and Angela Goldman, the mayor's daughter, were laughing over drinks. "That guy can get anyone he wants. She's half undressed already. I swear to you, Marilyn has never looked at me like that in her life."

Angela Goldman was a straight-A law student, a born-again Christian, but in Devon's company she had already undone the top two buttons of her sweater and said things she would later not believe. She had gulped down two Long Island Iced Teas, though she knew they made her sick and silly. When Devon stood up and offered his hand, she didn't even hesitate.

They walked toward the back room, and though a week ago Graham would have prayed for winter lightning to strike them on the spot, today he only wondered why Devon wasn't smiling. Why it seemed that, right before he walked through the back door, he looked around for some other option.

"He's screwed a different girl every night for a week," Roy Carter said when Devon disappeared, "and they're all still in love with him. But I'll tell you something. They're overlooking one thing. Devon Zeke is fading right before their eyes."

Vince scoffed. He'd already drained one drink and Roy poured him another.

"You think I'm kidding?" Roy said. "I know it sounds crazy, but just look at him closely sometime. You can see spiders crawling up the wall behind his back. In broad daylight, he doesn't cast a shadow. And I'm telling you, under starlight, that boy just disappears."

Graham laughed, but Vince just stared into his drink. Vince was fifty-five years old, but Graham had seen his blood count, he'd tested the amount of alcohol still present in his urine. He wasn't going to make it to sixty, yet he worked from six to six, hating every second of it. He brought in one hundred forty thousand dollars a year, had made partner in his firm four years ago, and still acted as if everything he really wanted was just out of his price range.

He downed his second drink, then asked Roy for the phone. He did not slur his words a bit, while Graham was already a little drunk off half a glass of gin.

"How many can you drink?" Graham asked him.

Vince punched in his home number, then stared at him. "As many as I want. It's a curse. I am destined to live the rest of my life in utter clarity."

Graham could hear the phone ringing, then Vince's son Scott picking up the phone.

"Get your mother," Vince said, without a greeting. A few years back, Graham had spotted Scott sitting on his father's lap in the Common, playing itsy-bitsy spider. Then came that scene a year ago, when Scott invited every neighbor on the block to come over and watch him smash twenty-six bottles of his parents' best liquor against the curb. When Vince had gotten home from work, he hadn't shouted or slapped his son; he'd just put his head in his hands and cried. He got back in his car and drove twenty miles to the nearest liquor store, where he maxed out his Visa. As far as Graham could tell, Vince had not had a thing to say to his son since.

Vince looked back at Graham. "On the other hand," he went on, "my wife gets drunk on a single glass of cheap Chablis."

Graham heard Marilyn's voice over the phone.

"Your boyfriend just left," Vince said to her. "With Angela Goldman. It looks like he's screwing everyone but you."

Graham pushed away his drink and stood up. He grabbed his jacket off the back of the stool, but by the time he'd gotten it on, Vince had hung up the phone.

"I can't make her cry," he said, to no one in particular. "Not anymore."

Graham walked out of the bar. He gulped at the fresh air, but even without it his head was clear. His ribs had ached all week, his right hand was swollen and sprained, but he hadn't taken a single pain pill. He'd gotten by these last few nights on a couple hours sleep and pure adrenaline. He'd taken every chintz blanket in the house to the homeless shelter; he wrote a long letter to his parents telling them he was moving, and the best part was, he didn't know where.

He'd come to some conclusions, and the most important one was this: He'd been headed in one direction all his life, and he figured it was about time he got there.

So he walked toward Sycamore Lane, but halfway across the Common, he realized someone was sitting in the crook of Ethan Allen's arm. Marilyn Ludlow was indeed drunk on cheap Chablis; the glass was still in her hand, and she'd put her snow boots on over her pajamas. He wasn't going to say a thing about being in the bar, but then Marilyn just started crying.

Graham helped her down and put his good arm around her. He walked her back to her house and helped her off with her boots. Her boys, Scott and Tyler, were up in their rooms, their radios blasting. Yesterday, Tyler had come into Graham's office with Sandy Aberdeen and held her hand when she asked Graham to prescribe the Pill. Graham wasn't sure why, but the sight of the two of them clinging to each other while he slid a sample pack of Ovulen across the desk had made his chest hurt.

"Don't let him hurt you," Graham said, holding Marilyn's hands.

Marilyn looked up, surprised, then she sunk into the couch. "Oh, *he* can't," she said. "I'm just old, Graham. And I don't know how it happened. I know you won't believe this, but I used to be the kind of woman men beat down doors to get to. I used to be the kind of woman men want."

He laid a blanket over her feet and held her hand. "I believe that," he said, then he let himself out.

From then on, it was easy. It was the clearest night in weeks, the sky saturated with stardust. When he turned around fast, he caught only his own shadow, stretched as tall as three men. Above him, winking planets would never be this close to Earth again, and he took that as a sign. From now on, he was going to take everything as a sign. Falling stars would mean it was time to act; four-leaf clovers proved he didn't have to anguish over loving her anymore, because Jane was about to become his.

Alex answered the door in his pajamas. Yesterday, Graham had set up the appointment at Cornell, and he would get Alex there if he had to kidnap the boy himself.

"Hey sport," he said. Alex slipped a small hand in his. When he stepped back into the light, Graham saw his brother's son smiling at him. He saw all that had been good about Ned, his innocence and enthusiasm for life. The way he had never felt shy about touching someone he loved. The way he had loved everyone.

With his free hand, he touched Alex's head. "I've come to see your mom."

Alex led him to the kitchen table, where he

and Esther were doing a thousand-piece puzzle of the sea. Graham heard the shower running, so he sat down beside them and worked on the bottom border of sand.

Graham could feel Esther watching him. He looked up and caught her smiling.

"What?" he asked.

Esther shook her head, but instead of reaching for another piece of the puzzle, she grasped his hand. When the shower stopped running, she squeezed it.

"Come on, Alex," she said. "Let's go for a walk."

Alex looked at her like she was crazy. It was thirty degrees out and falling fast. But he got up and followed her. They loaded themselves into jackets and scarves and opened the door just as Jane came out of her bedroom in a calf-length white robe.

"Grandma?" she said, then she turned and saw Graham. Her hair was still wet and clung to her cheeks. She jumped when the door slammed behind Esther and Alex.

She walked past him and sat on the couch. Graham was not afraid, that was the amazing thing. He got out of his chair and walked into the living room. He sat right beside her. He slowly slid his leg over until it was touching hers.

He had it all planned out, but for the moment he didn't say a thing. He just savored the illusion that everything might turn out the way he hoped. He paused in the moment where anything was possible.

Then she turned to him. The fire flushed her cheeks. She reached down and picked up his injured hand.

"You didn't have to fight him," she said.

"Actually, I did."

She stood up and walked to the window. Graham had had two offers for his house in five days, and this morning he'd accepted the highest bid. Yesterday, a doctor from Manhattan, who wanted fewer hours and less stress, had contacted him about his practice. Graham could go at any moment, but of course he couldn't really. He'd just been fooling himself with all these attempts at change. He couldn't go anywhere without Jane.

"There's something you should know," he said. "Devon didn't kill Ivy. I was with him that night. We were out riding and he never left my sight for a minute."

Jane did not turn around. Her chest rose and fell quickly, then tapered off into long, slow breaths. Finally, she looked down at her hands.

"You didn't tell the police."

"No."

"You didn't tell me."

"No again."

Jane turned around. She reached over and turned on the overhead light.

He blinked at the brightness. He wondered if this was when she left him for Devon, and she wanted to make sure he saw clearly that she wasn't coming back. But all she did was wrap her arms around herself. All she did was look at him.

"Do you want to explain why?" she asked.

Graham stood up slowly. It was funny because, after all these years of being mute as Alex, the words now rose up easily. They were sweet as honey, the best things he'd tasted in years.

"Because I love you," he said. "I always have. Devon's no good. He'll never be a world-class racer. He can't give you the kind of life you deserve. But I can. *I* can."

And then he waited. For a moment, it didn't even matter what she did, if she laughed or walked out on him, because he'd said it. At least, that was what he told himself. But when she crossed the living room and he saw the tears on her cheeks, when she slipped her hands up beneath his shirt and held on so tightly she might never let go, he discovered the real truth about love — it's the worst thing in the world until the moment she loves you back.

Jane drove the long way around to Wassal Trail, where Graham had asked to meet her at first light, instead of the more direct route across Pendleton Bridge. She parked at the trailhead, which was closed for the winter. Graham was already there, leaning beside his car. He opened the door to her Toyota and climbed in.

She sat with her hands in her lap. His breathing sounded different now that she wanted him. All of a sudden she heard the hoarseness in his throat, she noticed he breathed mostly through his nose except when he turned to look at her, and then he just went still.

Graham sat beside her and didn't move an inch. From now on, she knew, it was all up to her.

She looked over at him. He was still Graham, but everything about him had changed. There was a hollow beneath his cheek she hadn't noticed before. He smelled of something wild. There was no spell at work here, which meant there was no antidote. In truth, she was a little nervous; she had no idea how to go about loving someone for the rest of her life.

She lifted a hand to his cheek. "I was always in love with the wrong Payton."

He lifted her hand to his mouth and kissed the tips of each of her fingers. When he ran his tongue along the palm of her hand, Jane leaned back and closed her eyes. It was hard to remember what she'd been thinking all those years, loving Ned. Except that she'd been young, when the only boy worth having was the one with a police record, and he squeezed her heart so tight she had to sit down until the dizziness passed.

"I want to show you something," Graham said.

Reluctantly, Jane opened her eyes. She didn't want to see anything. She just wanted him to keep kissing her.

They got out of the car and walked an eighth of a mile through deep snow. Graham moved slowly, still sore from his fight, and Jane stepped right in his tracks. They followed Wassal Creek, which was still frozen along the edges, snagging twigs and unlucky fish. Buds had swollen on the birch branches, though, and here and there in a bare patch beneath a tree, the soil steamed with promise.

Graham led her off the path, to a grove of birch trees. He stepped back and slipped his hands in his pockets.

Jane wrapped her arms around her waist. In the heart of every tree, carved so deeply the trees had wept to fill the gouges, were the words *Graham loves Jane*.

She walked to the closest tree and ran her fingers over the carving. It was years old, scarred over, and it warmed her to the bone. She didn't feel the snow in her boots or the sudden wind. She only knew that a man had loved her without any hope of having her and suddenly she felt beautiful.

She could hear Graham breathing behind her. She could feel him waiting. She reached into her jacket and took out the pocketknife she'd been carrying since Sandy Aberdeen was attacked. She carved her own words just as deeply, and before she'd started on the second letter, the sap had wept over the first. Graham came up behind her, but didn't touch her, as if he still doubted where all this would lead.

Finally, when she was through, he reached past her and touched the carving. He traced every letter, sap sticking to his fingers. Then he rested his chin on her shoulder. She lifted her hand and stroked his cheek. He took off his jacket and laid it down in the snow.

They lay on top of it and never felt the cold. When he slid his hand inside her shirt and cupped her breast, it could have been the heart of summer. By the time she kissed the bruise along his ribs, their skin was golden brown and glistening. When they took off their clothes and Graham kissed her the whole time he was inside her, weather made no difference. Nothing could touch them.

The other thing Jane remembered about young love was that it had hurt. It was half ecstasy, half panic; by the end, most boys had taken to drinking and girls had torn out their hair. Now, as she watched her breath rise with Graham's in a single cloud that tied the bare branches in knots, all she felt was certainty. She was thirty years old, a mother and a cynic, but she figured if she was going to love him, she might as well go all the way.

Graham loves Jane. Jane loves Graham. Forever.

When your oldest, most fervent wish comes true, you can only wonder, why now? Does a wish, if wished enough, really come true? Does a man in love have that much power?

Graham didn't care whether he did or not. He was not about to quibble over timing or reasons why. After coming home from the woods with Jane's scent on him, he started walking. He stepped on every crack in the sidewalk and took his first deep breath.

He reached the statue in the Common just in time to see Bess Arnold's porch give out beneath the cold, the six-inch-wide timber posts shattering into sprays of sawdust. It had gotten down to three degrees last night, though Graham would not have believed this if he hadn't touched Ethan Allen's hand and snapped off two bronze fingers. He'd slept without blankets last night. He'd dreamed of summer, of sun so hot, it boiled blood.

He looked across the street at the house he had grown up in. On the left was his old bedroom window, and next to it Ned's. He waited for something to happen, the sky to change color or Ned's ghost to dance on the rooftop. Instead, a cloud passed in front of the sun and all he felt was that Ned was dead. There was not a trace of him anywhere, not a single scent of aftershave or sex appeal. A few weeks ago, this would have made Graham smile, but now he merely turned from the house and looked over the sparkling white Common.

Esther and Alex were at the other end, walking slowly toward him. Esther was shrinking, there was no doubt about it. She stood only a head above Alex now, and she held his arm tightly as she took small steps across the snow.

Graham met them halfway. He ruffled Alex's hair and took Esther's arm. Love had not made him walk on air; it had made him heavy. It had loaded him down with yearning to get Jane all of her heart's desires. There was no choice now; he had to make everything right. He had to cure Alex's muteness and stop Esther from dying. He had to make Jane happy for the rest of her life.

"Everything all right?" Esther asked.

Graham nodded. He put an arm around both of them and walked them across the Common, taking care to avoid the deepest snow. When they reached the other side, Alex took off running toward Sycamore Lane.

"I love Jane," Graham said. He was going to keep saying it to whoever would listen.

Old age comes and goes; it vanishes entirely when you're thinking about love. When Esther smiled, she was a young woman again; she was breathtaking.

"I know, dear," she said, watching Alex turn the corner at full speed.

"I'm going to convince her to let me take Alex to Cornell."

"Do you think that will help?" she asked.

"I've got to do something."

She nodded and patted his hand. "We all do, Graham." Then she set out slowly after Alex.

Alex and Linda had been building a snow fort in the afternoons. In her backyard, between two towering, bare hickory trees, they patted ice into bricks and stacked them. At first, a few days of forty-degree weather had turned their walls to slush. But the last few days had seen the temperature dive to the teens again. Their ice bricks were hard enough to shatter windows, and in no time at all they had a fort three feet high.

After the last day of school, they sat behind their wall, drinking hot chocolate in the Santa Claus mugs Linda's family used all year. Alex had been happy right up to the moment when Linda's mother came out to ask her what she wanted for dinner. Linda took a pad out of her pocket and wrote down *macaroni and cheese.* Linda's mother crumpled the paper and tossed it in the snow. She went inside and slammed the door.

Alex looked at Linda. His silence was a curse and she was catching it. One morning, she would wake up and not be able to tell her parents she loved them except by writing it down. One night, she would open her mouth to breathe and see smoke instead.

He set down his hot chocolate and took her hand. He wanted to build that snow fort until it was thirty feet tall. He wanted to live there permanently and never come out. Instead, he squeezed Linda's hand for the last time. There was nothing more beautiful than her voice, and as soon as he was long gone, he figured she would realize that.

He leaned against the ice block and closed his eyes. The tears might have started at any point, when Linda leaned her head against his shoulder, or yesterday when every student but Linda and him got up and said what they were going to do during the two-week break between semesters, or maybe even years ago when he realized he was a freak. Probably, the tears had been there forever, and it was only now, when no one but his best friend could see, that he finally let them all out.

Linda held him tightly, her braids pressed against his mouth. He was glad he couldn't speak, because he might be tempted to tell her he was afraid of everything. Of losing her and his mother and Esther, of the dark and running away. Of growing up and still not being able to speak. Of being a freak forever.

Then he realized Linda knew all this anyway. She'd known everything from the very beginning, which was why she'd given him every lucky penny she'd found. She had known he was the one who would need them, if he was going to get anywhere. He was the one who had to go out and slay a dragon.

He held her hand tightly. An icy wind swept

over the top of their wall and made their hair stand on end. Quickly, before the dragon could stop him, he pushed what he thought were words up his throat.

Linda pulled back and stared at him. He wasn't sure if he'd actually said anything, because the dragon was steaming again and his throat was a hard ball of pain. But Linda smiled.

"I love you, too, Alex," she said. "Don't forget me."

As if he ever could.

That night, there was no moon, and the storm that had passed through a week ago circled back in from the east. It had dumped all its rain in the Atlantic; by the time it hit Vermont again, it was just cold smoke and blackness. Bats lost all sense of direction and flew straight into houses. Porch lights couldn't be seen from the street and, after six o'clock, no one but Esther Gregory had the guts to go outside.

No one but the coyotes, who were picking through the Simpsons' trash can. Strangely enough, Esther didn't have any trouble seeing them; she could also see clear into Robert O'Brien's living room, where he was sitting in his chair, reading the local news. She turned away and hissed at the animals. They went scurrying as she carried her suitcase to Jane's car.

When her marriage had soured, Esther could have done a lot of things. Slipped gypsum into Walt's morning coffee to give him hives, put a rat's tail under his pillow to plague him with nightmares. But over the years, withstanding Walt became inexorably intertwined with her honor. The crueler he became, the more she ignored him, until he turned away in disgust, unable to ruffle her. Besides, he paid the mortgage and left her alone with her magic and Salvation. Very early on, she realized she would never fall in love again, so what was the point of divorce?

Then Salvation met Dan Carey, a man who professed to be an auto mechanic but really specialized in beating up women. When Sal ran away to get married, just as Esther had, when she, too, did not think things through, Esther started painting over Walt's portrait. She knew in her heart that if Walt had been different, gentler, less selfish, Salvation would have fallen in love with someone better. She would have taken one look at Dan Carey and spit in his eye.

By the time Esther painted the last stroke over Walt Gregory's eyes, he was on a flight over the Rocky Mountains on a crystal clear day. His fuel gauge would read nearly full when he crashed, and he would never radio that he was having engine trouble. Esther calmly put away her oils, then went to stand by the phone in the kitchen. Her heart raced until it rang, then it slowed to a trickle. When the man from the FAA told her Walt was presumed dead, she took it in calmly. When she hung up the phone, she began humming show tunes and didn't stop for three weeks. Then she never sang again.

It took Salvation four years to evict Dan Carey from her life, but evict him she did. Esther believed she had won the battle — until Jane fell in love with Ned. When Jane announced she was planning to marry him, Esther nearly cooked up a potion to stop tragedy, but then Ned did her a favor and died all on his own.

Seven years later, Esther was not all that surprised to meet Devon Zeke, or to watch her great-grandson write out his requests for supper. She didn't need any more proof. There was a curse of bad love over the Gregory women, and there was no telling what it would do next. She had to go back to the beginning, to the place where she had found her magic — magic that had obviously been laced with something toxic. The only way to break the curse was to give the magic back.

She dumped the suitcase in the trunk and walked faster than she had in years. She figured her legs would stay strong, her weak heart would go on pumping, as long as she had somewhere to go. That was why she had never gone to Europe — too many people she'd known had died the day after they'd finally seen the Louvre. She'd never built her dream house either, because once that last shingle was nailed, she would have sat down in her easy chair and had a heart attack looking over her handiwork.

She returned to the house, her bones not creaking for once, her feet as light as a child's. Jane had gone to Graham's hours ago. She'd gone every night for a week, usually forgetting to take a jacket and running the quarter-mile in two minutes flat. Tonight, she'd left in such a hurry, her hair had not yet dried from the shower, and the moment she stepped outside, the ends froze in a single sheet of ice.

She'd been in such a hurry, she had not seen the green shoot that had poked out of the Perfume Delight's withered stalk. She had not seen the sparks that flew from her hair, or that the dried bunch of asters she'd brought in weeks ago had grown fresh petals the color of a blush.

Esther had waited as long as she could. Jane deserved that much, a few days of bliss and the belief, however naive, that happiness, once found, went on and on. But when Graham, and even Jane, had started talking about taking Alex to yet another doctor, Esther knew she had to act. This was where she drew the line. She would not let them medicate the soul out of that boy.

"Magic is the only thing that will cure him," she'd told Jane this morning.

"It runs deeper than that," Jane had said.

"Can't you see that?"

Esther saw nothing of the kind. If heartache ran deep, magic ran deeper. And if she had to teach Jane that the hard way, she would.

She went into her bedroom and looked, without regret, at all the things she would leave behind. Her hat collection, all her jewelry, a closet full of sweaters and blouses she'd gotten as gifts but never worn. She hadn't packed much, just one small suitcase with her good jacket and army boots, a pair of long johns, and one of Walt's old work shirts.

There was only one other thing she needed. She went to the closet and took down a dusty box from the shelf. It was just six inches square; she hadn't saved much from those early days with Walt, and hadn't once looked inside this box of mementos since he died. She blew off the dust and opened the box. Right on top, where she'd left it over fifty years ago, was the feather that had floated up to her on that warm Montana wind. She ran her finger along it, expecting sparks to fly again, but this time got nothing but static. She slipped it into her shirt pocket.

Beneath the feather was a stack of Walt's old maps. She had saved them because they'd been the only things he'd ever touched lovingly. She had been more jealous of those maps than of his women. She remembered the sensual strokes of his pen as he'd drawn in that lonely cabin in the Bitterroots, the way he'd caressed the page as if he were fondling a breast.

She looked through the maps and found the clearest one of the Bitterroot area — with scaled drawings of the old cabin and landing strip. She tucked that into her pocket too.

At the bottom of the box, she knew, was the single love note Walt had sent her during his first trip away, and the silver wedding ring he'd bought from a Navaho woman outside Santa Fe. She had taken it off one year before he died, but Walt had never noticed.

She closed the box and put it back on the shelf. Then she walked down the hall to Alex's room.

The handle turned but the door would not budge. She turned on the hall light and pressed all her weight, which was no longer much, against the door. It moved a mere two inches. She looked through the slit and saw the backpack stuffed with everything a six-year-old boy would consider necessary for running away. She pushed the door a little further and saw that he had fallen asleep in his clothes, wearing his best track shoes.

She smiled at that. At last, here was a child who would take matters into his own hands. She pushed her hand through the opening and slid the backpack to the side. She opened the door and stepped into the room.

She kissed Alex's forehead. In his backpack, she found nothing but shorts and T-shirts. She added his heavy jacket and snow boots, two pairs of pants and turtlenecks, and took every-thing to the car.

Her muscles didn't ache as she lifted the backpack into the trunk. If she looked in the mirror, she knew she would see a vision of her former self. She heard rock music coming from Devon's house, and her heartbeat picked up the steady rhythm.

She walked into the house and down the hall to Jane's bedroom. Her sheets were tangled, half a dozen discarded clothes littered the floor. The longing in the air was overpowering, like way too much perfume. Esther opened a window, to let it all fly.

Whatever heartache Jane had learned from Ned would be nothing compared to what she'd feel when she came home from Graham's to find her child gone. Her panic would be flammable. Suddenly everything she thought important would cease to matter. There would be only loss and pure fear, the kind that made a heart rise up to the base of the throat and beat so hard bruises showed on the skin. The kind that would bring her to her senses, and make her believe in things she couldn't see.

Esther had tears in her eyes, but that did not stop her from doing what she had to do. She was seventy-five years old; she'd lived long enough to know when it was time to hurt someone for their own good.

She took the note she'd already written out of her pocket and laid it on Jane's pillow, then she walked back to Alex's room. Desperation gave her strength and, as she gathered up blankets and carried her sleeping great-grandson to the car, her arms didn't even quiver. She laid him down in the backseat and covered him with half a dozen blankets. His eyes fluttered open for a moment, but when she laid a warm hand on his forehead, he went back to sleep.

She had no choice but to take Jane's car. She hadn't driven or had her own automobile for over a decade. She imagined using a stick shift was like riding a bicycle — as soon as she took off it would all come back to her.

She got into the car and stalled only once trying to ease out of first. Then, with only Walt's handmade map and her love to guide her, she headed west.

Fourteen

On the way to Graham's bed, Jane prayed for snow thick enough to clear her senses. Sometimes she prayed for an ice storm bad enough to turn her back. Because once she walked in Graham's door, she was done for. There wasn't a chance in hell she was leaving before morning.

At dawn, she never let him walk her home. She didn't kiss him goodbye. She wrapped herself up in his jacket and stared straight into the rising sun. She stared until she was half blind, until she could no longer see the visions of the things she'd done in his bed. She stared until she was once again a mother who could talk in whispers and brush the sleep from her son's eyes.

On the night when everything would change, she tucked Alex into bed, kissed her grandmother goodbye, and ran all the way to Graham's. She ran through night so thick and black, it would send half a dozen motorists to the emergency room in one night. She couldn't see a thing, but she ran on instinct anyway. She turned left when she started anticipating the things he would do to her with his fingers; she cut through the McDermotts' pasture when her skin turned red-hot.

She found Graham in his kitchen, packing up his everyday dishes. He had stripped the walls of all the Monet prints. She moved close but didn't touch him. In his bed, she couldn't keep her hands off him, but beneath the track lighting Ginny had picked out, she often just felt ashamed of herself. She felt like the woman who had spoiled everything.

"Doctor Worrell's receptionist called today," Graham said. "Alex's appointment is at twelve on Monday. It's nice he'll be out of school. We can even spend a couple days there."

And then what? she wanted to ask. But all she did was wrap her arms around herself and say, "I got an offer on the house. A low one, but I'm going to take it."

Graham packed up the last of his dishes and looked at her. Though she knew he loved her, she still did not know where all this would lead. That he could up and leave her at any moment unsettled her. She thought she had him spellbound, but she really had no idea what he would do.

They had spent their entire childhood talking, but once Jane had carved her name into that birch tree, there seemed little else to say. This last week, Graham had kissed her until she'd curled up her toes in pleasure, he'd made love to her like a man on fire, but he had not told her what was going to happen next.

There were no weddings or sunrises in January. When Jane left Graham's at dawn, there was only blackness, then a brittle band of ice on the eastern horizon, then a shocking sheet of blue.

By the time she passed Devon's house, the sun hung low and cool behind the Simpsons' naked maple. A pile of newspapers clogged up Devon's front porch. She had not seen him in days. Rumor had it, he had not gone into Jim's Mercantile once in the last week, and both Beth Shultz and Marilyn Ludlow had taken up smoking, to satisfy their craving for something wicked.

Twice in the last week, Jane had thought she smelled the tail end of Devon's woody scent, as if he'd passed by a few minutes earlier, but she never caught his shadow. Once, after leaving Graham's, she saw Devon's neon jacket flying around the far corner, but after she followed the tracks of his skis for two blocks, he slid beneath moonlight and disappeared.

Already, their night together seemed like an illusion. His kiss was a memory, and it was fading fast.

She turned and walked home. The Perfume Delight had sprouted a leaf. It was nine degrees out, but snow had melted in a three-foot circle around the bush. That's where Carl Simpson stood, his sneakers lost in soggy, gray grass, while trying to figure out how to go home. Jane put a hand on his arm and he jumped.

His clothes were rumpled, as if he'd worn the same thing every day he'd been gone. He'd grown a beard that he now scratched at. In no time at all, he'd get so sick of it he'd start shaving. He wouldn't stop until things were back to the way they used to be.

"She'll take you back," Jane said. "She's never even looked at another man. She probably never will."

Carl bowed his head. He'd gotten a bad burn on his bald spot that was already peeling. He shoved his hands in his pockets, then started for home.

Jane looked down at the leaf. She had to believe in it now, because she could already see the beginnings of a pink bud on the stalk. It was only a matter of time before the plant sprouted a rose in winter, before she and all her neighbors started believing that anything could happen.

As she made her way to the front door, she heard Rachel's sobs. She turned the knob, then suddenly whirled around. Her car, usually parked in the driveway, was gone.

She might have suspected a teenage prank, if her blood had not gone cold at that moment, if Rachel hadn't slammed the door in Carl's face. She ran straight to Alex's room, but the bed was empty. No one had turned on the heater all night, and ice had formed on the insides of the windows. Long before she reached her grandmother's room, she knew Esther's sheets would be cold to the touch. She opened the closet and the blood rushed from her head. Her grandmother's shirts and army boots were gone.

She ran to the kitchen and looked for a note, but all she discovered was that her grandmother had taken all the tuna fish; the cookie jar had been swiped clean. She searched the living room, but there was no note beneath the sofa cushions. Panic singed the hair on her arms; it melted the new finish on the hardwood floor. Finally, she ran back to her own bedroom.

On her pillow, she saw the note. She snatched it up, though for a moment her eyes would not focus enough to read. The house was gobbled up by silence; the only life came from outside the walls, where she could hear the footsteps of the Simpson teenagers running after their father. Jane's hand trembled as she read the note.

> *Janie,*
> *I'm taking Alex to where the magic is. Trust that I'll do what's best for him. I love you.*
> *Grandma*

Jane could not get enough air. She gulped twice and bent forward. She had no idea how long she stood like that, hunched over and broken, except that when she finally stood up, every last trace of Alex's smell — part dirt, part sweet boy-sweat — was gone. When she tried to visualize him, she could not do it, as if memory only lasted so long.

She stumbled down the hall to Alex's room and sat on his bed. She crumpled the note in her hand. At any moment, he would walk in the door and wonder why she was so upset. She would be furious with him and Esther, but that night she would still be able to sneak into his room and kiss his warm forehead. She would be able to think, *Another day safely gotten through.*

But Alex did not come, and the sweat from her hand smeared her grandmother's shaky handwriting. The house grew quieter and quieter, until the quiet was nearly a scream, until it was so much worse than anything Alex had ever produced that Jane put her head in her hands and cried.

Jane was still crying an hour later when she tried to call Graham. She dialed his home number half a dozen times, but he never answered and his machine did not pick up. His office number was automatically forwarded to his answering service, but the woman told her Graham was not wearing his pager and could not be reached until he phoned in.

She slammed down the phone and walked into the living room. Her gaze fell on the reborn aster, blooming like it was summer. She grabbed the plant out of the vase and flung it against the wall. Pink petals flew everywhere; they got stuck in her hair, they stained the new coat of yellow paint going down.

She sat at the dining table, her grandmother's note still clutched in her hand. Without Alex, the silence was so intense, she berated herself for not having realized he'd been making noise all along. His footsteps and breathing, the crinkle of his pajamas, the way he crunched Cheerios on one side of his mouth and then the other.

Finally, she wiped away her tears and got to her feet. She had to find him, there was no other option. She couldn't trust his welfare to anyone else, not even her own grandmother. Esther meant well, but she was fading fast.

She walked into the living room and stared at the portrait of the sea Esther had painted over Walt Gregory. Esther had claimed she'd found her magic on her honeymoon, on some remote mountain. There was no more to go on than that.

She walked into Esther's bedroom and began flinging open her grandmother's drawers. She looked for old love letters, ancient receipts, souvenirs, anything that led to Esther's mountain. But she found nothing. Esther had never been sentimental when it came to Walt. She could not even tell Jane which dress she'd worn for her wedding. Sometimes she had trouble recalling the color of Walt's hair.

Jane kicked the bottom drawer, then walked

to the closet. She rummaged through pockets and took down all the boxes from the top shelf. She found old shoes, useless herbs, scarves given to Esther by women she'd cured, scarves she'd never taken out of the boxes. She was crying by the time she reached the last box. She lifted off the top, and then her heart quickened.

She found a mound of homemade maps, printed on fine parchment. She carefully opened each one; in the creases, the paper had already begun to disintegrate. The curled ends came off in her hands. There were charts of the San Juan Mountains in Colorado, the Bitter-roots in Montana, Wyoming's Absaroka Range. Walt had drawn in mines, old landing strips, cabins he'd stayed in, but there was no way of knowing which was the cabin he and Esther had spent their honeymoon in.

There were twenty-one maps in the box and Jane studied each one. They detailed back-country from Alaska to Florida, and the more Jane looked, the harder it was to breathe. By the time she laid down the last map on the bed, she was light-headed and blue. She bent over and sucked in air until her teeth hurt.

She had no idea which mountain was Es-ther's mountain. Esther had never given her specifics, and Jane had never asked. She had thought of Esther as a grandmother and a ma-gician. If she'd had passion, it was in another life, one Jane could not even imagine. She had never thought to ask Esther if she'd used her love spells herself, if she'd ever slipped Walt a potion of crushed honeysuckle and milkweed, which stopped a man from thinking he could ever have anything better.

She walked to the window. The day was going to be crystal clear. Her neighbors would bundle up their children and take them to the Common. Little boys would eat snow so perfect, they would swear it went down like ice cream. Jane turned from the window. She felt an ache for Alex so strong her vision blurred. For just a moment, she contemplated a life without him and the image was so horrifying, her knees buckled. She slid down to the floor.

She rocked back and forth as Luke Grisel hung out the backseat of his Dad's Acura, tossing newspapers that invariably landed in the branches of trees. She finally got up and went back to the kitchen. She tried Graham once more, but when he didn't answer, she realized he couldn't have helped her anyway. Love was love; it was not insulation. It was her job to save Alex, and it always would be.

She had nothing left to do but trust her intuition. She walked back into Esther's room and ran her hands over the maps. They crinkled in protest and, for a long time, she did not feel a thing. Then, at last, her skin began to warm. Electricity streaked through her veins. When it shot to her heart and added an extra beat, she looked down at the map beneath her fingers. It was the chart of the Bitterroot Mountains in

Montana. She didn't know whether or not to believe in it; she only knew she had no choice. She picked up the map and tucked it in her pocket.

She walked into her room and packed her suitcase with warm pants and sweaters. Then she went into Alex's room and grabbed his favorite blanket off the bed.

She was halfway down the porch with her suitcase when she remembered her grandmother had taken her car. She dropped the suitcase and leaned against the porch railing. When she looked up, Devon was standing on the curb, the snow around his feet all melted, as if he'd been waiting there for days.

"I thought I heard crying," he said, looking at her suitcase.

Jane didn't answer him. She turned and walked back inside the house. She tried Graham once more and, when he still didn't answer, slammed down the phone and opened the phone book. She started searching for car rental companies, even though she knew there were none in Pendleton, that she'd have to take a bus to Rutland, that the waiting was going to kill her.

Devon came in behind her. "What's up?" he asked.

"Alex is gone," she hissed, as if this were all his fault, as she somehow thought it was. "Grandma took him. I don't know where."

He didn't move until she was through crying,

then he ran his hand through his shaggy hair. "God, Jane, I'm sorry."

His voice was soft as breathing. It was a voice made for melting women, but at the moment all she was was a mother, and it didn't soothe her a bit.

"That doesn't help me," she said. "I've got to go after them. My grandmother . . . I just don't know if she's up to taking care of him. If something were to happen to her, with him not speaking, I just —"

"Take my car," he said, reaching into his pocket and handing her his keys.

Jane looked at him. She waited for him to laugh, to tell her he was joking, but he simply picked up her hand and put the keys in it.

"Why?" she asked.

Devon's face fell. He shoved his hands back in his pockets. "Jesus, Jane," he said. "You know I love that boy."

He walked out of the house. Jane stood in the doorway and watched him cross the street. He stopped on the sidewalk in front of his house, where Carl Simpson now stood alone, staring helplessly at Blackbird Peak. Devon said something to him that made him snap his head up. By the time Devon reached his porch, Carl was walking back toward his house.

Graham turned on every light in his office. He had already packed up the things from his desk and cleaned out all four of his examining rooms. Soon this place would belong to Doctor Fred Silverstein, who had told Graham, without a hint of sarcasm, that he planned to simplify his life in a small town. The man had no idea that where the crime rate went down, hauntings went up. If there were no gangs to join, teenagers learned to drink tequila. They made love outdoors without condoms. Wives slept with out-of-towners, so talk wouldn't get around, and grown men, without a pro football team to root for, sometimes turned over the idea of faking their own deaths and running away to an island in the Bahamas.

Graham walked into his waiting room, where he would leave behind year-old magazines and vinyl chairs that had been vomited on more times than he could count. Beth was going to be kept on by Doctor Silverstein, and the picture of her dog Scrubb still sat on her desk. A few of Graham's patients had called in a panic, asking how they were supposed to let a strange man look at them with their clothes off. Graham had told them Doctor Silverstein was the best, though all he really knew about him was that he had treated more than his share of AIDS cases and gunshot wounds, and that he'd admitted he was sick of the sight of blood.

Graham's patients had also asked where he was going, and he'd told them the truth: he had no idea. The house would close escrow in a week and his half of the profits would grant him a few months' indecision. He only knew one thing for certain; he was not going any-where without Jane.

He walked out of the office into another freak January morning. The temperature had dipped to the single digits last night, but now it was soaring. The newscasters were saying it would reach twenty-five by eleven, forty by this afternoon. The milk Francis McGinnis left out for his cat would no doubt curdle, and everyone on the block would start complaining about that pitiful meowing. Bill Wendall, who had always been a mean son of a bitch and itching to prove it, would no doubt get out his BB gun and climb the Presbyterian church steeple, where he'd have a clear shot.

Graham stepped over a river of runoff in the gutter coming from somewhere warmer up-state. He jerked when a car sped around the corner, leaving black tracks in its wake. He stood up straight when he recognized the Mustang.

But it was not Devon who pulled up beside him in a skid. Jane jumped out of the car, and right away he knew the worst had happened. He could make out blood on her bottom lip where she'd bitten through.

She grabbed his arm. "Thank God. I've been calling you all morning. Alex is gone. Grandma took him."

"Took him where?"

"I don't know. The mountains, I think, but I'm just going on instinct."

Her eyes filled with tears that didn't fall. He tried to hold her, but she was a moving target. She paced up and down the street, heedless of the slush that soaked through her boots. She walked back to the car and looked at him over the hood.

"I can't live without him," she said.

"I'm coming with you."

He walked around the car and got in behind the wheel. It smelled of a mixture of Devon and Jane, and it made him a little sick. The steering wheel was wrapped in leather, indented from Devon's fingers, coated with Jane's sweat.

She got in beside him. "He just gave me the car," she said. "Just like that."

Graham looked out the window. "Where to?"

Jane took a homemade map out of her jacket pocket. "Montana."

Graham drove for six hours, Jane for another six, then Graham again. When Jane drove, she stopped only for gas and coffee, and every mile made her someone different. By the time she passed Toledo, she was a woman who would never see snow again without feeling sorrow; by Rockford, Illinois, she was a mother who would never find a good enough reason to raise her voice to her son.

She had cried over the first few state crossings, but by the time they passed into Minnesota, where the snow turned to freezing rain, her eyes were dry as sand. The panic was like a passenger beside her, talking constantly of disaster. Every time she passed a car with a child in it, another part of her was swallowed whole.

When the highway broke into frost heaves, Jane didn't think she was going to make it to Montana without getting hysterical. She felt she was made of glass. Every time they hit a bump, something shattered.

"We've got to stop for food," Graham said. "We're not going to make it otherwise."

Jane could make it on adrenaline alone, but she agreed to pull into a truck stop. She took Alex's blanket into the smoky dining room. While Graham ordered them steaks and salads, she held it up to her face. At some point during the last eighteen hundred miles, she'd inhaled so hard his scent had faded.

Outside it was dark, but not dark enough to cover up the flat land. Montana lay one hundred miles ahead, but instead of the snowy peak Esther had described, there were only a few mountains in the distance, all small and treeless.

Graham went to the counter and bought a map of Montana. He brought it back to the table and spread it out. "Let's try to match up this map to Walt's," he said, and all of a sudden, Jane realized they were crazy. They were trusting fifty-year-old drawings and a hunch. Alex and Esther could be anywhere by now. They could be back in Vermont, wondering where they were. They could be out there freezing to death.

Graham took her hand. "Hold on, Jane. We've come this far."

She took out her grandfather's map. Walt had drawn in two peaks between the Sapphire and Bitterroot mountain ranges in western Montana — one rising over ten thousand feet, the other in its shadow. The trouble was, that part of Montana was crowded with peaks, and now there were roads leading to nearly all of them. She looked over Graham's new map of Montana. Copper Mountain sat right where Walt had drawn the largest mountain, but that smaller peak where the cabin supposedly sat was not on the state map at all. Instead, there was a symbol of a skier.

Abruptly, Graham gathered them up. "We'll just keep heading west. I'm sure it will be clearer when we get there."

When the food came, Jane felt queasy and pushed it aside. She looked out the window, where it was dark and bleak as poverty.

"Without that blanket," she said, "he won't ever go to sleep again."

Graham set down his fork and stared out the window too. Two semis pulled in, blocking their view of the plains, and Jane leaned back her head.

"He has never admitted he needs it," she said. "He keeps that blanket stuffed beneath the sheets. He only takes it out after I've tucked him in."

The other diners stared when she started crying, but she didn't care. She hated them for their easy conversation, their cars loaded down with cross-country skis and toboggans, their kids running back from the arcade, begging for more quarters.

None of them could imagine that a boy would try to sleep tonight and have to find a way to do it with his eyes open. None of them could imagine what it was like to be not quite seven years old, without words at your disposal. To be unable to even cry out for help.

"I imagine he thinks he's on an adventure," Graham said softly. "Adventurers forget about blankets, at least for a night or two."

Jane wiped her eyes, though more tears just fell. She had made a hundred deals with God already, but she silently made another one. Please, please, please let him be all right and she'd take any kind of life He wanted to give her. She could take anything, she could take a hundred Neds, but she could not lose Alex.

"Eat," Graham said. "We've still got a long way to go."

He pushed her plate back toward her and she ate a few bites of steak, which hurt going down. Her head throbbed from lack of sleep and too much caffeine. Her head throbbed from caring too much. She remembered every single day of Alex's life. She had told him this once and he had looked at her as if she were a bug he couldn't shake off. And she realized that Alex suffered most not because he was silent, but because she held him too tightly.

She put down her fork and drank another cup of coffee despite her pounding head. She was to blame after all; she'd simply loved Alex too much. When she had poured her heart into Alex, she unwittingly poured out everything, her love and fears and passion and guilt. And then she had gone one better. She had poured Ned into him, poured in a love as empty as this landscape, pure and white, stretching out forever. She had filled her son with a ghost.

She closed her eyes. For a brief moment, she let herself dream. She saw herself and Alex on a long, sandy beach. He stooped to pick up a seashell. He turned it over in his tiny palm and then he simply asked her where it had come from. His voice drifted up above the roar of the surf, up past the hovering seagulls. It became a star that lovers gazed at.

But even as she dreamed, she was aware that they lived far from the beach, that she might have unwittingly taught Alex to step right over the little things, like seashells, in search of buried treasure or shipwrecks, storybook things he was sure to never find. Even as she dreamed, she realized she was Alex's mother, not his best friend, and when he finally spoke, it would probably not be to her.

"Tell me what you're thinking," Graham said. "Don't shut me out."

She opened her eyes. At points along the

drive, she had been surprised to find Graham beside her. At the Pennsylvania border, she had figured he would simply stop the car and tell her he'd had enough. Instead, he just kept driving. When she was behind the wheel, he reached over and massaged her neck.

She was better at being alone. She didn't like the radio stations he chose or his penchant for changing lanes. She was taking her chances even looking at him, but she raised her gaze anyway, and then, of course, she was just a fool for love.

"You can still leave," she said. "I'll drop you off in Billings and you can book the first flight back home."

She almost wanted him to go, before he discovered she was made of glass and cracking fast. But all Graham did was come around to her side of the booth and slip a hand behind her neck.

"Don't be an idiot," he said. "And don't worry. Everything's going to be all right."

Fifteen

When sunlight stained his dreams red, Alex thought he'd made it to California. He was lying on a white sand beach, watching the sun burn a hole in the center of the sky. The waves blasted against the shore, but they were not louder than his own voice, which rose above the dunes. Men stopped barbecuing and women put down their cocktails to listen to him sing his favorite song, "My Corona." Each word was as clear as glass.

Then he was jolted, and his hand slammed not against sand, but against something suspiciously man-made. The dragon let loose a stream of fire and he opened his eyes. Sunlight nearly blinded him, but he could still make out the car's familiar vinyl ceiling, which over the years had faded from gray to dusty brown, and the back of the fake-leather seat that he grasped. He heard his great-grandmother's voice.

"Good God," Esther said. "I've stalled again."

Alex sat up. He was in the backseat of his mother's Toyota on a flat white highway. A truck honked and swerved around them to the right; Esther had forgotten to pull out of the fast lane.

"I'll get it," Esther said, glancing back at him. "Don't worry."

Alex looked out the window, but there was nothing to see but white. The land was flat as paper and coated with white ice. He had no idea where he was, he only knew a boy could not live here. Without hills, there was little, if any, chance of death from head injuries. He could never get going fast enough to squeeze the *whish, whish* through his teeth. He could ride forever here and not even break out in a sweat.

He sat forward between the seats. His great-grandmother had managed to ease slowly out of first and only chugged a little going from second to third. Another truck blew by, blaring its horn.

"I kidnapped you," Esther said. "You could ask me where we're going. It wouldn't kill you."

Alex looked around. This changed everything, which might not be the worst thing. Last night, he'd been all set to run away. He'd packed his things and tried to outlast Esther, but he fell asleep listening to the creak of her rocking chair. If he'd actually sneaked to the bus station as he'd planned, he might not have had enough money to get out of state, let alone to the West Coast. This way, he'd at least get something good to eat along the way. And he liked the sound of the word *kidnapped.* He liked that Esther couldn't drive worth beans, that there was a chance a semi might steamroll them.

They were headed west, that much was certain — the sun glared through the rear window and already the air that came through the vents smelled cleaner. There wasn't a cow in sight, which meant they were already far from Vermont.

"Fine," Esther said. "Don't ask. I couldn't tell you anyway. I've got one of Walt's old maps, but this is a place you find with your heart, not a compass."

Alex leaned back. When he swallowed really hard, his throat was not quite so hot. He imagined if he stood out on those snowy plains and managed to speak, his voice would carry forever. One word would last a lifetime.

He blew air through his lips. The dragon must have been asleep, because not a puff of smoke came out. He did not whistle, but he thought he heard something, a sigh he'd been wanting to get out for years. Even his great-grandmother, who was riding the bumper of the semi that had passed them a while back, glanced over her shoulder.

"What's that?" she said.

Alex stopped trying to whistle. He was going to talk, louder than anyone could believe, but not on cue. He wanted to know what he sounded like, but more than that, he wanted to do just one thing his own way, on his own time.

Nothing in this world was his alone — except what he chose to say first.

Esther tried to pass the truck. A minivan coming the other way blared its horn and she swerved back into her lane. A coil of her hair had come loose and draped over her shoulder. She laughed when the driver of the minivan gave her the finger.

Alex would have thought that was wonderful if he hadn't smelled something faintly foul coming from the front seat. When he looked at his great-grandmother closely, he saw she was strung tight as wire; the bones in her neck looked ready to pop through her skin.

He sat forward again and put a hand on her shoulder. Esther jumped, then relaxed back into his hand.

"It'll be all right," she said. "You'll see."

Esther stopped only for food, gas, elimination, and an hour of sleep here and there. She'd been tired for the last six years, so a couple days of insomnia went practically unnoticed.

She had cashed her last social security check and had the money in her pocket — seven hundred dollars she looked forward to spending down to the last cent.

By the time she reached Illinois, she had mastered the art of the shift. Jane's old Toyota did not go above seventy, which was frustrating because she had never passed a big rig in her life and wanted to know what it felt like to leave a grizzled trucker in her dust. She had never sky-dived or ridden a roller coaster either, and suddenly she longed for speed and danger. She rolled down her window and stuck out her head; the least she could do was feel the smack of icy air against her face.

Thirty-six hours after setting out, she crossed the Montana state line and pulled to the side of the highway. She stared at Walt's map while Alex sat in the seat beside her and chewed on a powdered doughnut. His mouth kept moving up and down even when he was not eating. Curses — the kind that brought on bad love and silence — might be incurable, but from what she could figure they had only a limited range. Once she had Alex out of New England, the boy had the urge to whistle. All the way through Minnesota, he'd stared at the flatlands and pantomimed speech.

"You see?" she said, showing him the map. "This is where we're going."

He stared at the map, though it did not tell much. Walt had drawn in the Bitterroot and Sapphire mountain ranges, and between them, two peaks that stood alone, one tucked in the embrace of the other. That smaller mountain was her mountain; Walt had sketched in the old landing strip and the nearby mining town of Lindemar. But Esther knew very well that fifty-eight years was a long time for things to go unchanged. It was enough time for freeways to be paved and condominiums put in. Enough time for magic to go stale from disuse.

She massaged her chest, which had begun to ache in earnest ninety miles back. The pain now shot down her left arm, making it difficult to steer. Alex had finished his doughnut and now stared at her, so she removed her hand from her chest and tucked the map back into the glove compartment.

"Let me tell you something," she said. "We're going to find it. Magic would have cloaked itself in sky. When developers and backpackers looked into the heart of that mountain, they would have seen only blue."

She started up the car again, but a few hours later, as she neared Billings, the left side of her chest and left arm throbbed so badly she could not hold the wheel. Her arm slumped to her side and she swerved across the center lane. For a split second, even as she saw the jacked-up truck coming the other way, and heard the driver blaring his horn, she could do nothing. She had a strong desire to just let go, to be done with it. She saw the same thing with her eyes opened or closed, just a vast expanse of white so pure, she wanted to lie down right in the middle of it.

Then Alex reached over and grabbed the wheel. He yanked them back into their lane and beyond it. Esther blinked, but still saw only white. The ruts of the dirt shoulder jerked her clear up to the ceiling.

She thought she heard screaming, but it

sounded far away and strangled. Then she felt Alex's hand on her leg, trying to pull her foot off the accelerator.

Through waves of pain, the road came back into focus, and Esther saw they were heading for a small embankment that led down to the Yellowstone River. She took her foot off the accelerator and grabbed the steering wheel with her good hand. She managed to find the brake and bring them to a stop three feet from the edge.

She leaned her head back. She hadn't realized how dangerous she'd become, even to the boy she was trying to save. She had so little to lose. She might jump in front of a car or throw herself out of an airplane just to see what it felt like.

Her heart burned and she closed her eyes. She wished she'd thought to bring a salve of echinacea and tea-tree oil, though probably nothing would help at this point. She searched her brain for one more spell, one that would keep her cautious and alive until she'd done what she'd set out to do, but her mind was blank. The pain muddied her thinking anyway; she might have magicked herself a million dollars or a promising love affair, when all she really needed was a few more days.

Alex tugged at her right sleeve and she opened her eyes. His face was coated in tears, his mouth open, stuck in the middle of a scream that would not escape him. Esther forced herself to sit up straight, to reach out her good hand and touch his wet cheeks.

"Don't be afraid," she said. "This is nothing. Just an old woman dying."

Alex laid his head against her chest. She could have moved but didn't, because while he cried, Alex's voice grew stronger. The air through his lips was first a sigh, then a dull whistle, then a raspy whisper. With her good arm, Esther squeezed him tightly.

He spoke so quietly, it could have been mistaken for a breath, or the wind. But Esther had waited a long time for this, and she made out the words clearly.

"Come on," Alex whispered. *Live.*

Esther closed her eyes once more and smiled. For the moment at least, the rush of oxygen soothed her burning heart. She put her mouth on top of Alex's head and kissed him.

Alex slept the whole way to Butte. He slept with his head against the cold glass, so that the tears he cried in his dreams turned to ice on his cheeks. Esther occasionally reached out and picked them off, and they melted quickly in the palm of her hand.

She had a choice of highways outside Butte, and she went on instinct, onto Highway 1, heading west. Past Georgetown Lake, where the landscape turned from bare sage to pines wrapped in snow so deep a man sunk to his chin with his first step, her heartrate accelerated. Highway 33 came up suddenly, and she took the turn south. As she drove around the flank of a mountain scarred by last season's wildfires, and came into a high, grassy valley, every part of her went still. She neared the place where loving Walt had come easily, and she remembered all the things she'd once tried to forget about him. That he'd known the lines to every Broadway show tune, and when he sang his voice crackled from too many cigarettes. That he'd shuddered in his sleep and sometimes woke with tears in his eyes. That before he left on his trips, he always chopped enough firewood to last her until he came back.

For years after he'd died, she'd completely forgotten she'd ever loved him. Now, when what appeared to be a lone peak rose off the valley floor, she felt it all over again. She saw Walt the way he had looked that first day on the airstrip, dressed all in black, standing cockily beside his plane. She saw him irresistible. And, for a moment, she wished to go back again. To feel hungry for his touch, to feel every inch of her skin. Suddenly it no longer seemed foolish, the way she'd just assumed, that day she married him, that everything would work out fine. It just seemed sad.

Highway 33 abruptly ended at the intersection of 168, and Esther stalled once more. A line of Jeeps sat in front of her, beneath a sign that read Copper Mountain, Greatest Skiing on Earth, 26 miles. Esther stared at the peak, recognizing it instantly, though it had not had bald spots for skiers fifty-eight years ago, and she had only seen it from the air. Walt had flown so close to it, if Esther had put her hand outside the plane, she would have come away with a chunk of granite. He had swung around the north side and there, nearly invisible in shadow, was a smaller, snow-crusted peak.

Walt had landed on a rough airstrip between the two mountains. He had led her on that solitary trail, stopping only to let an unpredictable moose cross the path. Today, solitude had been blasted away by helicopter rides to the summit of the greatest skiing on earth. Rock music blared out of car stereos and scared all the wildlife clear to Idaho.

Esther had no choice but to follow the pack of cars. She turned toward the ski resort and, two miles later, the stores began. A line of ski chalets, doughnut shops, minimarkets and coffee houses. She pulled into a gas station and took out Walt's map again. Alex woke up slowly, picking the last of the ice off his cheeks.

"Despite this, I'm not giving up hope," Esther said, though not convincingly. There was not an undeveloped lot in sight. Alex stared out at Copper Mountain, which had sacrificed most of its trees to a dozen lanes of skiable highways.

Esther could have quit then. She was certain Alex had spoken on the side of the interstate, so it seemed only a matter of time before he said more. But she could take no chances, not when the magic was so close, her spells might start working at any moment.

"We need to find Lindemar," she said. "It's a little mining town between Copper Mountain and my mountain. We'll just have to follow this road till we get there, then we'll find a way up to the cabin."

She started up the engine again and eased into the line of cars heading toward the ski resort. After a while, the traffic thinned out and she began to hope. The road began to curl around the base of Copper Mountain. The highway divided fifteen miles in, with a sign pointing west to Copper Mountain Ski Resort and north to Lindemar.

"You see?" Esther said. "Everything's going to be fine."

It was another thirteen miles on a snow-covered road to Lindemar. The pines lining the highway were so thick, no amount of salt could tame the ice on the asphalt. There were turn-outs every few miles for drivers to put on chains, but Esther did not own a pair and just drove past them. Lindemar was at an altitude of four thousand feet and, by the time they reached the last rise to the town, she could hardly keep the bald tires on the road. She glanced over at Alex and caught him gripping the edges of his seat.

"Don't worry," she said, but when she drove down the main street of the exclusive mountain community, she knew they probably should. Phony Bavarian facades housed espresso bars and delis. Million-dollar homes with security gates and seasonal residents clung to the sides of the mountain.

"Oh dear," Esther said as she pulled into another gas station. She looked down the street, where she could make out at least five stop-lights, guiding bumper-to-bumper traffic. She started to unfold Walt's map, then simply threw it into the backseat and unlocked her door.

"Wait here," she said. "I'm going to talk to someone."

She walked into the Gas and Eat, with its deli case and a whole wall of plastic-wrapped burritos and sandwiches. For ten minutes, she stood behind teenagers buying Doritos and Mountain Dews, then she finally reached the longhaired man behind the counter.

"I'm looking for a small mountain," she said. "It's behind Copper Mountain, not very well known. It's —"

"You must mean Breakers," the young man said. "The new ski resort. It's awesome."

"I passed the signs for the ski resort coming in."

"Nah. That's old Copper. That's for wusses. Breakers is the new one. On Whitecap Peak. They opened last winter. Half their runs are just for boarders. It's like all black-diamond runs."

Esther shook her head. She wished people

447

would talk English. "That can't be. You wouldn't be able to build a road up to this place. It's a single peak, snow-covered all year round. There used to be an abandoned cabin there."

"Breakers is so incredible," the man went on obliviously. "The snowboarding tournament's tomorrow. Two thousand shredders are shacking up in the Motel Six."

Esther turned and walked out. Halfway to the car, she could see Alex was not in it. She spotted him standing beside the store, staring up as a cloud lifted on what at first appeared to be a shadow of Copper Mountain. Once the sun hit it directly, though, she recognized it as her mountain. Only now it was just as mutilated as Copper Mountain, its trees plucked out for ski runs, its slopes filled with shredders, whatever those were.

Esther walked over to Alex and put a hand on his shoulder. The pain in her heart and left side was back now, dull and familiar. She could turn around right now, she realized, and everything might still work out fine. Or she could head up that mountain and steel herself for whatever she might find there.

Her hand trembled as she stroked her grandson's neck. She would never know which direction was fate and which was a mistake. Like everyone else, she just had to take a step and hope for the best.

"It's not much farther," she said. "I can feel

it now. I don't care what they say. The magic's still here, and I'm going to give it back. I'm going to give you a normal life if it kills me."

Alex turned around and stared at her. Jane had once seen Ned in him, but Esther saw everyone. Herself and Walt, her daughter, Salvation, Jane and Ned and Graham. When Alex breathed, she felt air stir in her own lungs. And that's why she wasn't at all afraid of dying, because she lived on in him. After she was gone, when he least expected it, he would get a chill up his spine that was her.

She saw something else now, too. A look in his eye that hadn't been there before. A steadiness to his hand when he reached out to touch her. Somewhere along the long stretch of highway they'd driven, he'd taken control of something, and she figured it was himself.

"Come on," she said, and led him back to the car. "And watch out for shredders. I hear they're all over the place."

The old silver mine had been turned into the Silver Casino, run by the Flathead Indians. A K-Mart and Subway sandwich shop had been built on top of the landing strip. Just beyond the strip mall, where the once nearly invisible trail had begun its twisted rise up Whitecap Peak, was a brand new four-lane highway.

"Oh, Walt," Esther said. If he had lived to see this, he would have blown .38-caliber holes into every developer within a twenty-mile radius, he would have crashed his plane dead center into that casino.

Esther followed the highway. There was nothing else to do. She could still feel the magic. It made her burning heart quicken, and her skin temperature rise five degrees. But a mile up the road, just when sweat broke out on her neck, she had to stop dead in her tracks behind a traffic jam of idling cars. Jeeps and Land Rovers loaded down with skis and impatient children sat in a three-mile parking lot that led to the Breakers Ski Resort, *the awesomest place on Earth,* the sign said.

Alex curled up in the seat beside her. On one side was the huge granite flank of Copper Mountain, on the other, a skimpy metal barricade that was supposed to keep them from tumbling down a nine-hundred-foot crevasse. Esther could not see to the bottom — at least that much was the same. Alex looked across the crevasse, then up at the mountain beyond.

Esther was not about to look, not through a haze of diesel smoke. She wanted her first gaze in nearly sixty years to be crystal clear. She stared straight ahead and inched forward. It took them two hours to go three miles, and she lived in the past the whole time. She didn't see where they'd scraped off trees and rich top-soil to make way for a highway; she remembered forests so dense you couldn't squeeze through sideways. The sky might look watered down and distant now, but she knew for a fact that at night it came down so close, you sucked in stars with every breath.

When the driver of the diesel truck ahead of them suddenly pulled over, Esther could no longer resist. She looked to the top of Whitecap Peak.

For a moment, she couldn't breathe. The sight was so painful, she hunched over the steering wheel, her elbow pressing on the horn. Alex pulled her back, then left his hand on her arm. Right on the edge of the crevasse, where fifty years ago a lone cabin had sat alone and impenetrable, stood two neon-lit golden arches beside a 7-Eleven sign.

Her tears slid down her wrinkled cheeks. She cried for men like Walt, who would rather have died than live in a place that covered up paradise with plastic playgrounds and parking lots. And she cried for herself. She understood now why her magic had been misfiring. All magic was misfiring. It was being plowed over and lined with asphalt. It was not meant for a world like this.

Alex did not let go of her. She looked over at him and stared into his eyes until she could breathe right. Magic was misfiring, but it was not dead yet. There was magic in loving someone, if you did it right, if you gave it all you had.

She rolled down her window. She ignored the exhaust smoke and faint odor of charbroiled hamburgers, and picked out the single remnant

451

of sage-scented air. She shut out the sounds of horns and blaring stereos and instead heard the creak of that old bed when she'd slipped in beside her husband.

"Let me tell you about your great-grandfather," she said.

She started from the beginning and imprinted her memories in her great-grandson. By the time they reached the top of the mountain, Alex no longer saw the old woman she was but the girl Walt Gregory had married. He saw her with long black hair and a figure that had stopped men dead in their tracks. He saw his great-grandfather, too, his vulture eyes and once tender hands. When it looked like he was swiping at air, Alex was really stroking the stubble on his great-grandfather's chin.

Esther drove along the commercial strip at the base of the ski resort, but when she passed the McDonald's where she was certain the cabin had once stood, she looked the other way. She squeezed Alex's hand, then let go and wiped away her tears.

"Well," she said, "I'll tell you the truth. I have no idea what to do."

So she just kept driving, out past the strip, past the condominiums and motels, through forest that had been logged five years ago and replanted with seedlings that didn't appear capable of growing over ten feet tall. When hers was the only car left on the road, she pulled over and cut the engine.

The two of them sat in silence until the cold seeped through the windows, until Alex shivered. Esther was so tired, she nearly fell asleep with her eyes open. Then she felt Alex's hand slip into hers. She turned to him.

"I've got seven hundred dollars to my name," she said finally. "What do you say we find some place to sleep for the night, then tomorrow we blow it all skiing?"

For the first time since they started out, Alex smiled.

Esther had seen all the No Vacancy signs on the hotels on the strip, so she just went looking for a nice house, a place where it looked like people would put up a stranger. She found a well-maintained cedar cabin on a dirt road off the main highway and pulled into the driveway.

The old man living there stopped chopping wood, but didn't let go of the ax. The woman came out of the kitchen and put her hands on her hips.

"I was hoping —" Esther began, but the woman cut her off.

"We don't take in boarders," she said, then turned to go back inside.

"I was wondering if you knew about a cabin that used to be on the peak," Esther said.

The woman whirled around. She looked at her husband, who set down his ax and came to stand beside her. "They tore it down five years ago," the woman said. "Right after they came

453

up here with their bulldozers."

"It was my honeymoon suite," Esther said. She took Alex's hand and started back for the car.

"Did you ever hear the wind?" the woman called after her.

Esther turned around. "Sounded like a bear on fire."

The woman took a deep breath, then slowly smiled. "You can stay. Anyone who remembers can stay. We were beginning to think we dreamed the whole thing up."

Forty years earlier, the couple had been rock climbers; they'd made it their goal to scale every ten-thousand-foot peak in Montana. They had slept in the same bed Esther and Walt had slept in and decided that first night that they could never leave. They had built this house farther down the mountain, long before the Rocketeer Development Corporation, which specialized in ski resort construction, had come in and gobbled up all the land around them.

"How did they get up here?" Esther asked. They sat in the couple's small, wood-paneled kitchen. The woman had already given Alex a steaming cup of homemade hot chocolate, which had put him right to sleep.

"Dynamite and money. Way too much money."

"Did you sense anything about the cabin when you were there?" Esther asked. "Any kind of magic?"

The woman turned to her husband with tears in her eyes. "You see? I'm not crazy."

Esther and Alex slept in down sleeping bags laid out beside the woodstove. Alex slept without twitches or sighs, and Esther kept her hand on his heart all night, to make sure he was still breathing.

In the morning, she drove him to the Breakers ski resort, which sported five quad lifts, ten black-diamond runs, and a liability release form one had to sign in order to take the helicopter lifts to the avalanche-prone north slope. Alex took an hour's worth of skiing lessons, then quickly tired of the bunny slope. He took a lift to a long, slender, blue run and skied it without falling once.

Esther sat in the crowded chalet at the base, the only woman over fifty, the only one not wearing neon. She sipped gourmet coffee, which she didn't like in the slightest, and watched Alex master the snowplow, then parallel down in long, wide arcs. The snowboarders' tournament was over on Shredder's Hill, as they called it, so the ski runs were nearly deserted. Esther dozed beside a huge stone fireplace, where a young man's only job was to toss thirty-inch logs stripped from Esther's beloved mountain onto the flames.

By late afternoon, Alex had skied the mountain twenty-three times and, when he came into the lodge, he could not stop smiling.

"We'll come back tomorrow," Esther said.

"And the day after that. You can ski until my money runs out."

They returned his rented skis and boots, then walked out to the car. Alex held her arm and matched her smaller and smaller steps. He looked ready to burst with happiness and Esther wished he would just do it, just blurt out how pleased and proud he was, so she could take him home. She wished she hadn't grown so old grand adventures were tiring.

The wind tugged at the coils in her hair, setting another one free. The mountain was still creating its own weather, hatching a storm out of a clear blue sky. She looked at the swirling clouds, sure she would not see anything. So it came as quite a shock when she saw hers and Alex's future as clear as a picture in the western sky.

She tousled Alex's hair, then looked at the sky again, just to be sure. "Well," she said, "won't that be something?"

Sixteen

Jane gassed up the Mustang before taking the new highway to Copper Mountain. Graham sat with the maps on his lap, studying them for her benefit, pretending this was all going to work out fine. At the base of Copper Mountain, they saw the billboards for Breakers on Whitecap Peak.

"I'll bet that's it," Graham said.

Jane might have believed him, if she hadn't slipped off the slick road at just that moment. She plowed into a snow berm, which saved them from sliding down an embankment, but which also splintered the windshield and tossed them toward the dash.

Jane hit her head on the steering wheel, and even though she got nothing more than a bad jarring, she just left it there. She was not going to get hysterical after all. She was just going to crack.

"Are you all right?" Graham asked, taking off his seat belt and reaching out for her.

She looked up at the windshield and saw her own heart, a spiderweb of cracks, totally unfit for use. Graham took her in his arms. "Hold on, sweetheart. Just hold on."

The thing was, she couldn't even wrap her arms around him, that's how powerless she felt. A mother's will was a force to be reckoned with, but it could not change fate, it could not pluck a lost boy out of the air.

"Let me drive," he said. "I think I can get us out of here."

He dug out the snow beneath the tires, then backed them out of the berm. He drove five miles an hour, his head cocked far to the left, where there were fewer cracks in the glass. At the town of Lindemar, they got caught in a traffic jam heading up the road to the Breakers ski resort.

Jane leaned her head back against the seat. She hadn't spoken for hours, and now there was only one thing left to say. "I'm going to lose him."

In the late afternoon, a day and a half after leaving Pendleton, they pulled into the jam-packed Breakers parking lot. Jane had doubted every step they'd taken, but she still ran across the icy parking lot. She pushed past a slow-moving family of four into the contemporary-styled lodge.

She nearly slipped on the slick black-and-white marble floor, but caught herself on the doorman. It seemed he'd had practice; after he steadied her, he kept his arms out, waiting for the next casualty. A man played the piano half-heartedly, not bothering with the hardest chords, because he knew full well the rock music they blared from up the mountain drowned him out.

Jane rushed to the main counter, where the desk clerk, a young woman, was giggling at everything a blond skier said. "Have you seen a boy and an older woman?" Jane asked. "She's a little shorter than me, with white hair coiled on the top of her head." The girl merely glanced at Jane, then went back to her conversation.

"So you went down Deathdrop," she said, with awe so feigned Jane could smell it. "That is so amazing."

"It was nothing," the man said. "You should have seen me on the north slope. I was just inches in front of an avalanche."

"Excuse me," Jane said. "I'm looking for my son." Graham came up behind her just as Jane grabbed the young woman's arm. She heard her own voice, the panic laced through the middle of it that could have stopped a mugger in his tracks, but the young woman just rolled her eyes.

"He's probably out skiing," she said, turning back to the man.

"Hey," Graham said, and though his voice was quiet, it was the one he used with patients who wanted to ignore lumps in their breasts, the one that got them in for mammograms that afternoon. The woman turned to him. "This lady needs your help. Her son and his great-grandmother might have come through here in the last day or two. You need to look them up in your computer right now."

"Okay," the woman said. "Jeez. They'll only be in here if they stayed in the lodge or used a credit card, though. What are their names?"

Graham gave her the information while Jane searched faces. She stared through the glass doors to the slopes, but all she saw was swooshing neon.

"Nope," the girl said. "No Gregory."

"How about Payton?" Graham asked. "An Alex Payton?"

The woman seemed about to make a flip remark, but the look in Graham's eyes silenced her. She typed in Payton.

"I'm sorry. They're not here. But there are a dozen new hotels on the strip. Maybe . . ."

Jane was already gone. She walked out onto the back patio, where huge halogen heaters blasted noisily. Families sat together sipping hot chocolate, while shredders drank just enough beer to rise to the challenge of the north slope.

She tried to move, but instead slipped to her knees. Someone asked her to move, a child ran straight into her, but she didn't budge. Finally, Graham came out from the lodge and put his hand under her arm. He lifted her back to her feet and took her face in his hands.

"Listen to me," he said. "I'm not going home without Alex. All right? Got it?"

She stared in his eyes. She had two choices; she could either dissolve right there or calm her breathing to his pace. She could trust him or not.

"What are we supposed to do now?" she said.

"We search every hotel on the strip until we find them."

Three hours later, when Graham pulled up to the last motel on Breakers Road, the Trinity Cabins, Jane didn't even bother to get out of the car. No one had had a listing for an Esther Gregory or Alex Payton. No one had seen them.

Graham put his hand on the door, then turned to her. "Look," he said, but when he saw her face, the red-hot rash coming up in the path of her tears, he stopped talking and got out.

She watched him walk into the lobby of a group of cabins that had managed to look dilapidated after less than a year of use. He'd left the radio on, and the weathercaster was saying there was always snow by midnight; Whitecap Peak set the record last year for freezing to death more stranded, unprepared motorists than any other mountain in Montana. Jane looked up through the cracked windshield; at least for now, the sky was still a cloudless sweep of deep purple. Yellow planets seemed close enough to leap to.

Graham came back out a moment later, and Jane could not look at him. He didn't even bother to tell her there was no news.

"They've got an unfinished room we can

sleep in tonight," he said quietly. "Tomorrow, we'll go out again first thing. I'm not through yet."

The clerk led them to a small room littered with sawdust and particleboard, but at least the sheets he put on the two twin rollaway beds were clean. After he left, Jane walked to a window she couldn't see out of. A thick sheeting of black ice coated the outside.

Graham walked up behind her. He wrapped his arms around her waist and she leaned back into him.

"You need to sleep," he said.

She shook her head vigorously. "Not on your life," she said. "Not until we find him."

She felt Graham stiffen, and she knew what he was thinking. He'd seen enough heart attacks to know a seventy-year-old woman could go just like that. He'd treated enough incidents of hypothermia, especially in children who didn't know enough to layer their clothing before going out, to know that every minute that passed lowered their chances of finding Alex alive.

They lay down together on the bed. Despite her pledge, she fell asleep almost instantly and dreamed of snow. Snow so thick it covered everything — buildings, trees, people. Snow so thick, even if she knew where to look, she couldn't wade through it to find her heart's desire.

Esther did not sleep all night — a night in

which the clouds materialized out of nowhere just after midnight, then dumped an impressive eight inches of powder. When Alex woke at dawn, she wasn't the slightest bit tired. She reached out and brushed the hair from his eyes.

"Today I'll buy you one of those surfboards," she said. "What do you think about becoming a shredder?"

He jumped out of his sleeping bag, smiling broadly, and Esther ignored the shooting pain down her side to get up after him. "We need to eat first. What do you say to McDonald's? Two Egg McMuffins and a double order of hash browns."

Alex was already stepping into his clothes.

As Esther drove to McDonald's, the snow stopped falling. The clouds in the eastern sky stretched out pink and thin as taffy. They walked into the bright yellow restaurant and Esther ordered the food. The shredders appeared to be sleeping off whatever they'd done last night, because they had the place to themselves. They found a table by the window where they could see out to the Ronald McDonald playland that had been kept snow-free with huge halogen heaters.

Esther watched Alex wolf down one Egg McMuffin, then stare longingly at hers. She pushed it across the table. She wasn't hungry, and she knew she wouldn't be again. She could feel the tingle in her feet and legs that signified things were shutting down. Everything was a little blurry and her heart skipped every other beat, so that she was always reaching up, for something to hold onto.

"I'm glad you like the skiing," she said. "At least I could give you that."

Alex put down his food and reached across the table for her hand. His skin was so young and smooth, it brought tears to her eyes.

"I wish . . ." she said. Alex looked out the window at the large, tubular slide, shaped like a snake.

"Alex," Esther said softly. Alex turned back to her, but then Esther did not know what to say. She had left his cure up to magic and there were no words that could perform the same trick.

"I'm dying," she said finally, and drew away her hand. Alex did not blink and Esther smiled. Words or not, he would be all right. He would be seven years old next week and he was already the kind of boy who faced things. He had seen this coming for a long time; perhaps he was the only one who had.

"It's not just the chest pains that tell me so," she went on. "I looked in the rearview mirror on the drive up here, and looked right through myself."

She shook her head. Alex stared down at the remainder of his muffin, then pushed it away.

"It's not a bad thing, dying," Esther said. "It's just that I still have things to do."

She stared at Alex until he wiggled. "I know

you spoke," she said. "I know you can. What-ever happened to keep you quiet, it's done now."

When she realized he wasn't going to speak, she stood up. The two of them walked outside to the Ronald McDonald playground. There was a generator just beyond it, filling the air with the hum of electricity. Alex walked to the swing while Esther approached the cliff. She could not see over. An ugly concrete-block wall had been built six feet high. She kicked at it futilely, then spotted a small metal garbage can a few feet away. She turned it upside down and dragged it to the wall. With rickety, tingly legs, she climbed on top.

The crevasse below was dark and dizzying. A few stunted trees had grown in cracks of granite, but mostly it was smooth stone and lifeless. She tried to imagine if this was where the cabin had stood, but she could not remember clearly. All of her memories seemed suspect now; her whole life seemed distant, like it had happened to someone else.

The concrete wall slithered past every store on the rim. Behind the Gap, where someone had evidently jumped to their death, a cross had been nailed to the wall. A cloud embraced her; it would be hours before the temperature rose above zero. Esther, though, had been cold a long time. She blew away the mist and, once more, looked down the crevasse. Even with the neon backlighting and headlights on the highway across the mountain, she could not see to the bottom.

And then she did the only thing she could think of. She reached into her pocket, pulled out the vulture feather, and tossed it over the edge.

Caught in the wind, it hung there for a moment, then gravity snared it. It flitted right and left while falling, no direction left of its own.

It all happened at once then, so that she could not be sure if it was her own doing or just plain coincidence. The feather disappeared into darkness and a warm gust of air rose up in its place. The wind uncoiled the last of Esther's hair as she stepped off the trash can. When a car sped into the parking lot and someone slammed a door, she felt the last, soft ticking of her heart.

Before Graham had even come to a stop in the McDonald's parking lot, Jane was out the door and flying. They had spent the morning going to every fast-food restaurant on the strip. The closer they had gotten to McDonald's, the tighter Jane had gripped the dashboard. When they'd gotten stuck behind a Subaru loaded down with a stony-eyed father and his crying children, she had begged Graham to go around.

Now, she didn't even think of going inside the restaurant. She ran to the Ronald Mc-

Donald playland, and her gaze landed instantly on the top of the tallest slide. Alex perched there, staring back at her, and though she could have said anything, she could have been furious, she was only amazed at the heat of the wind that brushed over both of them.

The wind smelled of a hundred scents, of pine and sage and clear water. When she took her first deep breath in two days, it went down like cool wine. All the heartache of getting there was worth that one moment of seeing her son alive and well, of smiling at him and not wishing for a single thing.

She walked to the slide and climbed the ladder. When she reached Alex and slipped her legs around him, he felt so good, she cried out. Graham ran into the playland. He stopped at the bottom of the slide and lowered his head. By the time he looked up, she knew he considered himself a father already.

She wrapped her arms around Alex and, for a moment, they hung there. Then Alex let go and down they went into the serpent slide, spinning, spinning. Jane clung to him and, somewhere along the way, she heard a distinctly boyish cry of "Wheeeeee!"

When they reached the bottom, they stared at each other. Jane brushed the hair out of Alex's eyes. She hoped he would say something more, but he did not. He merely looked past her, to the block wall along the cliff. Jane followed his gaze and found her grandmother.

She ran to Esther's side, but Graham had gotten there first. He crouched down beside her and checked for a pulse. Esther's eyes were closed, her hands tucked neatly on her lap, and she was smiling.

Jane picked up her cold hand. She tried to rub warmth back into it, but the only heat came from the strange wind that blew up the crevasse. Jane looked at Alex, who had turned his head away and started to cry.

"It's all right," she said, though she was crying too. "Look at her, Alex. It's all right."

Alex turned slowly back and, though he continued to cry, his shoulders stopped trembling. He crouched down and Graham put his arm around him. For a long time, the four of them sat there, encased in a warm silence that, for once, hurt no one.

Graham drove the Mustang home from Montana, while Jane and Alex took the Toyota. At first, the only sounds out of Alex's mouth were sobs. Passing drivers probably thought her cruel because she smiled at every wail. Each tear was a moment of silence he'd suffered, and they all landed in a puddle at his feet.

When they crossed the Pennsylvania border, his sobs turned to sighs. When they passed into New York, he turned off the radio and looked at her.

"Mom?" he said, and Jane clutched the wheel. She took a deep breath to keep herself from making too much of it, from pulling over and clutching him to her.

"Yes?" she said.

"Tell me about Dad."

At some point while he was gone, Alex's eyes had changed color, so that now they were a deep gray, almost blue, a color entirely his own. She realized, when he lost the silence, he lost the only part of his father he'd ever had.

"His name was Edward Payton," she said, "and the moment I saw him, I knew I'd love him forever."

Alex smiled and curled up on the seat, facing her. Jane pulled off the highway and into a gas station. She bought a cup of coffee, because she knew she would be talking for a long time.

They held the funeral three days later, on the day a high-pressure system floated up from the south, bringing bright sunshine and record-high temperatures to Vermont. In less than twenty-four hours, all the snow shoveled into high berms on the sidewalks melted and flooded low-lying basements. The runoff from Pendleton Hill turned into a torrent and plowed right through Henry Gingle's sliding-glass doors, leaving a living room full of mud and Pepsi cans and a dozen used condoms Henry could only stare at in amazement.

The snow coating the small Pendleton cemetery melted in an hour, and made the ground soggy and easy to dig. After Salvation had died, Esther had reserved the plot next to her daughter's, beneath the single sycamore tree. The crowd gathered around the unearthed plot, trying hard not to stare at the black coffin that seemed to vibrate whenever the wind brushed it.

Jane held Alex's hand tightly. She had not expected this many people to turn out. Even the men had come, their hats still pulled low over their eyes, though Esther was in a closed coffin, three days dead, and would have needed some pretty powerful magic to cast a spell on anyone.

Jane looked around the gathering for Graham. When they'd gotten home, he'd had a message from Marilyn Ludlow, informing him he had to be out of his house by this morning in order to close escrow. There hadn't even been time to hire movers. Last night, the young men on his block had gathered at his house, enticed by beer and heavy furniture.

Pastor Lovett looked to her to see if he could begin and she nodded. "Friends and neighbors," he said, "though we are all deeply saddened by the loss of Esther Gregory, this is not a day to mourn. Esther is on heaven's golf course now, where there's never a wait to tee off."

There was the distant sound of laughter. Jane looked over her shoulder as Graham and Devon emerged through the trees. They took her breath away, both of them, and she figured they always would. One made to thrill you, the other made to last. Devon was talking while he walked, making wild gestures with his hands, then Graham tossed back his head and laughed. Pastor Lovett stopped talking to glare at them. Jane, though, held out her hand and, when Graham reached her, he took it in his.

"I'm sorry," he whispered. "We went as fast as we could."

Jane looked over his shoulder to Devon, who was wearing blue jeans and a black jacket over his T-shirt. "He helped you?" she asked.

"The others left around midnight. Devon was the only one who stayed."

Jane stared at Devon. He listened to the eulogy, then while Pastor Lovett started on another prayer, he turned his gaze on Jane. He ignored the women who moved to be near him and smiled at her. He could no longer break her heart, but that didn't mean he had stopped making her feel beautiful.

He nodded slightly, then walked back toward the woods, stepping in his own tracks. Not even Ned's old retriever, who could have tracked anyone, would have been able to tell which way he was headed. He disappeared behind the trees.

Jane laid her head on Graham's shoulder. She knew from that moment on she was free.

"Esther Gregory," Pastor Lovett said, "was an incredible woman. Strong, caring, some might even say magical."

Alex leaned into her as the minister went on. Every once in a while, he sighed. He had not exploded with words, as she'd thought he might once he started speaking. In the last three days, he had simply exchanged silent for quiet. In his seven years, he had learned what most people never do, that words often just confuse things.

"May she rest in peace," the pastor said. "Amen."

The mourners gathered around Jane and Alex. They all meant well, as they gave her their condolences and hugs, but the truth was they had never known Esther. They had not known, for instance, that whenever a child or grand-child slept beneath her roof, she never slept through the night. She got up at least twice to check on their breathing, to adjust the thermostat, to tuck a blanket beneath their chins. They had never known that, no matter what she said about that mountain in Montana, the magic had come from inside her. She found what was good in a person and made that bloom.

The pallbearers, all men who had avoided Esther like the plague even though their wives swore by her remedies, lowered Esther's casket into the grave. The minister said one more prayer, and Jane heard a car door slam behind her. She looked over her shoulder and saw Ginny Payton, in a long black skirt and blouse, making her way across the soggy ground. She didn't even look at Graham, which Jane was certain stung in a place Graham would never tell her about.

She walked to Jane's side. "I'm sorry, Jane," she said, her voice simple and honest. "I remember the night I got chicken pox. Your grandmother came over with a salve, but better than that, she stayed up all night with me. We played gin rummy and I'm fairly certain she let me win."

She smiled, then finally turned to Graham, her face blank of emotions. "I hear we closed escrow today."

"You'll have a check on Monday."

Ginny nodded and looked across the cemetery. She rubbed her arms. "This place still gives me the creeps."

It probably wasn't ghosts that haunted her, but memories, an image of Jane and Graham and Ned playing football over the gravestones, with Ned beaming the ball into the heart of the sycamore tree.

She turned and stared at Graham's hand on Jane's waist. She stared until Jane's skin began to steam. Then, suddenly, hummingbirds flew in and coated the old sycamore tree like gray leaves. The wind shifted, bringing up a cold blast from the north.

"I'd better go," Ginny said. She looked Jane in the eye without flinching. She was the only one whose voice did not break.

"Thanks for coming," Jane said.

"Well, of course. I grew up here too."

She turned and walked away. As soon as she'd driven off, Graham ruffled Alex's hair.

"Well, sport, what do you say we head home?"

"Good," Alex said. "I'm starving."

They walked toward the car. When Jane looked back, she saw her grandmother's grave and her own trail of footprints. Where she'd stepped, the grass was green as jade and two inches high.

When they reached the car, the hummingbirds suddenly took flight. They swarmed up into a cloud of gray, then took off south, not considering how far they'd have to go to get warm again, not thinking one whit about the future.

When they got back to the house, Alex walked straight into the kitchen. "I'd like a grilled cheese sandwich, cut diagonally," he said.

If he never held Jane's hand again, it might not matter. Every time he opened his mouth would be as good as a kiss.

She got the cheese out of the refrigerator. After she'd made the sandwich, she found Alex and Graham in the living room, staring at Esther's portrait of the sea.

"Are we leaving here?" Alex asked.

Jane looked over his head to Graham. "We're leaving."

"Where will we go?"

Jane led Alex to the kitchen table, where he sat down in front of his grilled cheese sandwich, cut diagonally.

"You tell me," she said.

Alex squeezed his sandwich tightly, then looked up at her and smiled. His eyes opened wide, the possibilities endless.

About the Author

Christy Yorke was born and raised in the Los Angeles area, where she married and went to college, graduating magna cum laude with a degree in psychology. Craving quiet and a view of trees, she, her husband, and their two children moved to the mountains of southern Idaho.